J E Hall

Harry's Awakening

J E Hall

Ottery Books

Published in Great Britain by Ottery Books

First published 2020

Copyright © J E Hall 2020

ISBN 978 0 9955035 7 1

Typeset in Palatino

Cover picture by i-stock and Simon Cornish
Cover design by Short Run Press

website: jehallauthor.com

A full CIP record for this book is available from the British Library

Printed by Short Run Press, Exeter

To

Rosie with all my love

ALSO BY J E HALL

Flashbacks (2016)

IStanbul (2017)

Harry's England (2017)

Domain (2018)

Truth (2019)

"After nourishment, shelter and companionship, stories are the thing we need most in the world."

Philip Pullman

"I want this book to help others protect themselves from being radicalised, manipulated or intimidated by extremists."

Julia Ebner: 'Going Dark:
The Secret Social Lives of Extremists'
Bloomsbury 2020 p6

1

'Local pubs always sponsor the best parties,' said Harry cheerily. The cold night air hung still despite the warmth from the pressing hordes on every side. He pulled his dark green Barbour jacket closer, adjusted his Plymouth Rovers baseball cap and tugged on the shoulder strap of his small black rucksack, just to check it was still safely there. Harry realised it all felt vaguely familiar. Then he got it, it was like being at the football. He was on the street and this felt right. For the first time in ages his spirits lifted.

Taking advantage of his height, he swung his head round, looking left then right, to eye the rows of barrels, beer as well as cider, lying behind the temporary stalls and tables, some decorated with beer mats that had sprung up in every yard and alley like the one he was presently standing in. People pushed and shoved, jostling one another to get served.

Feeling himself to be at home, he rested his one elbow on a makeshift scaffolding plank bar to silently contemplate his second glass of dark Devon ale, only the glass was frosted plastic. 'Crap', he muttered, only to carry on drinking.

This particularly cheerful bar had been set up in a motor cycle shop backyard, 'Black's Cycles' shop front window was securely boarded and protected for the night ahead. Next to Harry was his mate, Stu Beamish, in an oversized purple Super Dry camouflage jacket, gazing skywards as if he was finding inspiration there. Seconds later he had an announcement to make.

'It's going to rain, Harry, feel the air. It'll be a wet night,' he offered flatly, holding out his upturned hand anticipating the first drops. 'Do you really want to stay for this, Harry?'

'Look here, this is Devon culture, our history, the chance to have some fun on the street like in the old days. Can't you feel the excitement, the anticipation. You just wait!' said Harry, sipping his beer noisily. 'This is raw theatre, our night out. This is where we belong, on the street.'

Harry saw a couple of policemen, bulked out in hi-vis yellow jackets, awkwardly tooled up as if expecting a riot. They ambled along in a protective twosome, looking in at the revellers apprehensively as they passed along the street. They were walking as only policemen do, in heavy oversize boots, planting their feet slowly, people parting to either side to let them pass unhindered. Harry ignored them. They were an unwelcome reminder that the law had cost him dear and he wasn't happy with that.

Even so, Harry felt a returning pride welling up in himself. Time had passed, tonight he was back on his feet; he could still hold his head up high. He chuckled out loud. Who'd have thought that an ordinary lad from Plymouth could rise to the top like bubbles in his beer, to end up a hero, an MP even? What a laugh, he thought. OK, he'd been out of his depth, then kicked out of politics for a fraudulent expenses claim after just a year in the House, but all that was behind him now. He'd made his mark, he'd stirred the political mire. It was time to forget politics, forget London and his lonely apartment there. Now he was back on home turf in Devon, here for the annual bonfire and barrels festivities in Ottery St Mary. This is where he liked to be, back with his mates, with people like Stu.

He considered how his had been the only authentic voice in the House, the lone voice of extreme right wing populist politics, and now that too had been removed from public life. Not that he really minded. Those bloody MPs would manage without him. After all, he surmised, the new government had stolen all his thunder with every right wing leaning MP switching allegiance as new members of the ruling Tory party. Personally, he would never have signed up as a Tory, not that they would have had him! He chuckled again at the thought, turning his attention once more to his pint.

Thinking back, it wasn't such a bad outcome to be back home, his voice, the voice of the people had been heard in the end, his job there done, his views mainstreamed, so sod the lot of them! His time had come in a different way, populist politics now ruled the roost and held the day, there was no going back. They could bloody well get on with it and do it without him.

He'd always felt he'd been set up to be the fall guy. Sending him off to the Middle East to look at some Omani sea port, just because he was a Plymouth man, well that was Parliament's way of sidelining him, getting him out of the way from the off. That he'd claimed extra "rations" for the trip was only what he'd been led to believe was normal practice. Too bad he'd been found out by that investigative journalist Adam Taylor who'd passed his evidence over to the House's bean counters.

The result – six months after entering Westminster he'd been expelled or rather suspended, booted out until they decide what to do with him. Technically still an MP, he was furloughed, probably so they could organise a timely dismissal. The papers had had a field day. Only thing to do now was to laugh it off. Anyway, it was all too much work and not enough play. Tonight was playtime! Time for all the national politics to be forgotten. He survived best at grassroots, in the mix, here with the people. This was where things mattered, with local beer loving people.

The dark and the surrounding crowd hung round him like a protective cloak of anonymity. He liked it that way and took another deep draught of his beer. How he hated plastic cups along with all those health and safety aficionados, small minded jobsworths with nothing better to do than poke their noses in where it wasn't warranted.

Turning his attention back to Stu, loyalty written all over his skinny mate's pale face, Harry asked enthusiastically, 'What time's it all due to start?' Stu knew how to be at Harry's beck and call. Stu had long ago mastered the dark art of serving Harry, keeping his diary in his own head, planning what was to be done next and reading Harry's explosive moods ahead of the action.

'Plenty of time yet for the main events. Still only 8 o'clock. Can get a few more drinks in,' Stu suggested shrugging, now realising Harry's mind was set and they were here for the duration. 'Same again?' He got up not needing to hear the answer, 'Yes.'

As he stood a volley of shots shattered and silenced the noise of the crowd. 'What the hell was that?' asked Stu in alarm looking around. Harry glanced up from his beer and stared at Stu in puzzlement. He'd no idea.

'Hand held cannons being fired,' said the young woman from behind the bar. 'First round was at five-thirty this morning. Happens at intervals throughout the day. You two not been to Tar Barrels before?' She reached across and a damp purple cloth swished around their beers, providing a token cleansing of the beer soaked scaffold plank which served as a table.

'We're visiting. Up from Plymouth. We do an annual firework festival, but without the gunfire,' offered Stu, swinging round to face his informant, wondering whether she was worth chatting up. She didn't look bad, fun written across her face, a specially printed lilac pinafore hugging her neat figure.

'You ain't seen nothing yet!' she said teasingly, laughing with her made up eyes, before moving away to serve a building line of waiting customers.

'Didn't know they played with guns,' said Harry, quietly impressed.

'Not guns, hand cannons,' she said.

'What do they do it for do you think?' asked Stu, who tended to think Harry knew all the answers.

'So we know who's in charge round here,' the girl chipped in. 'No-one tells Ottregians what to do! We do things our way in this town.' Then she'd gone again, on to the next customer, Stu's eyes following her, wondering what she meant. He began to feel she might be too high spirited for him, and told himself to forget it.

Harry felt a sudden flash of kinship with the people of Ottery. Somehow hand cannon fire sounded altogether more powerful and full of historical character than hand guns. He

5

raised his glass high and shouted, 'To anarchy, Ottery and England!'

'Cool it Harry,' Stu pleaded under his breath, tugging at Harry's raised arm, knowing as he did so he was wasting his time.

'I made the right decision to come here, to Ottery,' Harry said more quietly, raising his glass again. 'Find out where we see these barrels, will you Stu. Don't want to miss it,' he ordered, turning again to thirstily quaff the remainder of his beer.

Stu turned and leaned over the bar waiting for his chance to catch the eye of the young woman serving, who was trying to sort out the correct change after taking a big order. She soon returned and provided directions. 'Where do we see the barrels? Which way is it?' he asked.

'Best move up Mill St to The Square, that's turn right out of the yard and keep going. Follow the crowd...' she told him smiling. Then she'd gone again.

'C'mon Harry,' Stu said, seeing Harry had finished his drink and thrown the plastic cup on the floor in disdain. It looked a good time to leave for, all of a sudden, they seemed to be surrounded by a college outing or something. Someone had clearly bussed in a load of students, probably from Exeter, novice boozers, 'Overgrown posh kids', muttered Harry, loud enough to be overheard. He watched them, most rolling around quite unable to hold their drink. Harry had no time for them and led the way out, pushing a path through them as they strove to catch their sloshing beers. Once outside the bike shop's beery yard, the two headed up Mill Street as they'd been directed.

Several minutes later they entered The Square. Harry spotted an old pub, The Barrel Inn. It looked local, earthy, with a simple plain door opening directly onto the street. A black coated guy who looked like Harold Steptoe, blocked their path. He was checking for entry tickets and unsurprisingly wouldn't let them in. Harry reckoned that with one knock, he could have floored the guy, but checked his street instincts and stopped in his tracks.

'Only pre-booked entry mate,' the man explained straightforwardly, suspicion written in his watching eyes.

'What's happened to freedom?' asked Harry, the man not moving an inch. Harry had dealt with far tougher doormen in Plymouth a plenty, but once again Stu pulled his sleeve and Harry settled for another recyclable cup of beer from a street stall, the beer being thrust in his hand by Stu anxious they should avoid further trouble. Harry needed Stu. In fact they needed each other.

Soon the air in The Square reeked of paraffin and pressing bodies, then cries and shrieks of excitement went up, mobile phones flashed and there were flashes of orange followed by clouds of black, tarry, bituminous smoke swirling upward into the rain laden sky. The hellish fire and black smoke worked like a drug on the crowd who were baying for action, causing a frenzy of anticipation. The excitement spread out like ripples on a pond. Harry thought it was like being at Plymouth Rovers when a penalty was about to be taken, everyone pushing and shoving to get a view. Right now he wanted to be nearer the action and began elbowing forward into the melee, using his body weight to create a path, Stu following behind.

Then with a fiery, yellow-orange roar of fire and more screams from those watching, a flaming beer barrel was hoisted high in the air by a pair of heavily gloved hands, up and onto the shoulders of a waiting man it went, who promptly ran headlong into the masses in front of him. As if by magic the people parted as the flames approached them. It was like watching an orange surf wave building speed and hurtling forward, their cries, a heady mix of fear and delight. When the burning barrel became too heavy another took up the challenge, seizing the heavy item with manly vigour before once again making the charge full pelt through the crowd.

Harry looked on transfixed. 'Yes! Yes!' he yelled getting himself near enough to feel the burning heat. This was primitive and dangerous. How did anyone let it happen?

Then the barrel man turned with his posse and they were heading his way. He noticed the whole thing was being managed by a gang of strong men who piloted the man carrying the shooting flames. Then they were before him and he could smell the searing bituminous orange heat, feel his adrenaline surge as instinctive self-preservation urged him to move away. But Harry, being Harry, stood his ground with Stu once again vainly tugging at his sleeve to pull him clear. A sharp elbow from a minder catching him below his ribs settled it as Harry, much to his surprise found himself pitched sideways, the burning barrel passing him safely by. Forgetting the stabbing pain in his side, he pulled himself forward once again. He was just loving this.

Upright, and now on his toes, he watched as, in a moment of drunken madness one of the students he'd seen earlier, seeking to show off to his friends, tried to place his uplifted arm inside the flaming barrel. This time, there was no poke to the ribs, but a sharp fist to the side of the face throwing the youth back in an instant as the mesmerised crowd roared and cheered. A watching policeman turned his head away; he'd be arresting no-one. This was some crazy madness!

Harry felt the crowd surge first one way then another; he found himself being carried along like seaweed in a swell. Unable to move in any chosen direction, he yielded to the pressing throng tight against him.

Next moment a large man, staggering backwards, stood on Harry's toe, only to find himself floored as Harry's other foot automatically responded with a fierce kick into the back of the man's right knee. Entirely as Harry expected, the man went down heavily, or not as heavily as he might have done, had not the pressure of the crowd been propping him up. Cursing, the man looked vainly round for the cause of his fall as his neighbours pulled him upright, Stu innocently offered his own helping hand to this surprised and annoyed giant.

Harry's gaze shifted to see where the barrel had gone next and there it was on the opposite side of The Square in front of a boarded up chemist shop. Time and again as the barrelling group switched direction the crowd moved and swayed as best they could to avoid it. Harry was beginning to identify the strong men in charge. They made things happen their way. This was good, men on the street with years of training in their dark art, working the crowd how they wanted to. He was definitely in the right place. These guys knew the secret power of the flames thrust into people's faces on a dark night. It was enough to ward off both evil and good. They were ruling their streets and Harry felt envy of their visceral strength. He sensed this had deep history, English history.

Soon, as only the charred staves, metal hoops and glowing remains of the barrel were still burning, what was left was finally thrown down on the road, the minders gathering round to stamp on the embers with heavy, workman's boots. With the rain still falling in stair rods black puddles had formed in the gutters as the last of the glowing embers were extinguished and melted into dark water.

'Hell, that was something else!' exclaimed Harry. 'This is from the dark ages. Who gives permission for it? The health and safety officials must be wetting themselves!'

'Can't see any,' said Stu, pleased to see Harry so elated.

'I must be in paradise, where next?' he said, looking around him.

Stu reached down to the ground to retrieve a discarded programme and flipped through to discover they needed to move down by the Mill for the next event. 'Apparently the barrels get bigger as the night wears on… oh, and every barrel is sponsored by a local pub or family.'

'I already told you pubs sponsor the best parties,' said Harry, turning to leave The Square, the two shuffling their feet forward slowly, the crowd moving as one toward the next pulse of excitement. The sound of a fair could be heard somewhere ahead. Soon they could see its garish coloured lights flashing giving an orange glow coming from down by the river.

'There's a fair and a bonfire. We could check it out after we've seen the next barrel,' said Stu.

'Sure thing.'

Passing St Antony's Catholic Church, Harry directed Stu to patronise their stall, to get more beer and pick up burgers. Harry elbowed a way through for Stu and then, with their replenished supplies in their hands, the two headed down the hill. By now the rain was heavy and persistent, dark water rushing at speed down the gutters, but no one seemed to notice. Spirits were high.

Suddenly, in the shadow of the towering old Mill, out of nowhere another barrel was hoisted high just to their right, the red faced Herculean man, built like a prop-forward, clutching his prize and tearing into the crowd to fresh screams and cries. Soon he was a hundred yards or more away and from their slightly raised viewpoint Harry and Stu watched to see him eventually come to a halt where the ground rose at St Saviour's bridge.

'Some guy that one,' said Harry in admiration. His load was handed on to the next man and the bobbing orange flames could be seen returning, moving at running pace again. A shepherding group of men with asbestos gloves and protective hoods pushed back the pressing crowds to let the fiery barrel and its bearer pass through. Up and down the street they went, people diving and screaming in fear and delight.

As before it was soon over, the cries died down and smouldering embers were again safely extinguished in the wet gutter.

'Let's see the bonfire, dry ourselves off by it,' said Harry. 'It's on the way back to the car.' Stu nodded in agreement, pulling his jacket collar up to keep back the rain which was by now dripping from his hair and into the nape of his neck.

It took ten minutes or more to get over St Saviour's Bridge and onto the grassy expanse of the Millennium Field where, notwithstanding the pouring rain, a huge bonfire was beginning to get well alight. Here, Harry noticed an actual piece of health and safety was evident for a temporary restraining fence had been erected to prevent people getting too near the flames. As if people would throw themselves on it, he thought, idiots.

The intense heat could be felt many yards away and flames were licking up into the black night sky. To one side of the fire, some pallets and thicker logs had yet to catch and it was near them the two found themselves a space to stand and feel the drying smoky heat.

In seconds steam started to rise from their clothes as they faced the flames. The warmth was pleasantly soothing.

'This is better,' said Stu, immediately noticing that Harry wasn't really listening to him for something seemed to have caught his attention. Then Harry was moving away from him, over toward the remaining unburned pallets and logs, approaching ever nearer the fire. He watched as Harry lifted his arm and was using his hand to shield his eyes from the heat, peering through his fingers, looking ahead like an explorer in a hot desert, as if, as if he had discovered something.

'Stu, come here,' yelled Harry above the fire's roar, turning his back to it. 'What do you see there?' he ordered, turning again and pointing toward the nearest pile of twisted wooden pallets.

Stu slowly moved toward him, shielding his eyes from the heat and glare. He couldn't for the life of him see what had caught Harry's eye.

'Oi, You two, get back here, behind the fence. Come on, come back, back I say…' yelled a yellow vested steward, but Harry and Stu were not for turning and both stepped cautiously ever nearer the flames, so much steam rising as if smoke from both their jackets. Stu didn't know what to do, the official behind was yelling all the more, ordering them back, Harry in front getting ever nearer the flames, using one arm to beckon Stu forward and his other arm to protect his face. What was he doing? There had to be a good reason for this.

Then Harry turned, a startled look in his wide eyes.

'There's the body of man in those pallets. There's a man in the bonfire, Stu… Look! There!'

Stu's face fixed in horror. Twisted in pain, but unmistakably human in form, he found himself asking, is that a man in the base of the fire?

2

'You're an idiot, Harry. That's what's left of Guy Fawkes. Surely you can see that?' said Stu, trying to drag Harry to his senses, wondering whether he'd had just one too many of the local beers. The watching official was now talking into a walkie-talkie summoning help and Stu didn't want them both to be in trouble. Harry seemed to need to be taken care of more these days, right now he was really pushing his luck. Harry's father having died, his Mother gone to stay with her cousin and not on speaking terms with him, Harry had no one but a handful of mates to watch out for him, chief minder among whom, as he well knew, was Stu himself. No longer acting as a politician, he didn't seem to care, become reckless even. Harry shrugged him off.

'Stu, I'm not joking. That's no Guy, it's a real body, a sizzling dead bloke. They need to deal with it… Oi, you,' shouted Harry, beckoning the fearful official over as Harry now walked toward him. 'Get help, a 999 should do it, you've a body on your fire, right there and if you don't get hoses on it soon, it'll be incinerated and you'll have nothing. Come on! Come on!' Harry could be a formidable presence when he needed to be.

The man, duly intimidated, seemed to understand and after taking a look for himself, summoned a waiting fire tender into action. The firemen, just a few yards away, relaxing on stand by duty, had stood down with the rain. They'd retreated inside the shelter of their tender, drinking mugs of coffee from flasks, waiting for permission to leave. Thinking their's to be a quiet evening they were quickly disenchanted and summonsed into action.

In moments, two of the firemen approached, the leading one wearing a dark Dalek-like protective vizor. With no part of his body exposed to the searing heat he walked slowly and circumspectly toward where Harry pointed with the firm idea. To his mind he was dealing with a hoaxer. After a few more deliberate steps his pace slowed as if he didn't want to go further.

When he got to the point where Harry had been standing a moment ago, he suddenly turned and gave an urgent hand signal to his colleague who quickly called for back up from the engine. As he walked nearer still toward the flames the bonfire gave his entire body an orange halo. Meanwhile the team, watching from a distance were suddenly springing to life, and a hose was rapidly employed followed by great hissing clouds of steam rising into the rainy night sky. Step by step the crew got nearer to their objective. Within moments they had created a dark, blackened void, a saturated corner, exactly where Harry had directed them.

Someone had called 999. There were loads of police nearby for the tar barrels and almost immediately a siren could be heard.

'Idiots,' muttered Harry under his breath as he saw the police car approaching, its wheels losing traction, flicking mud and water across the grassy field as it came to a halt. The bloke's dead as a doornail, what the hell are they rushing for?

Two officers, a man and woman, pulled on yellow jackets and police caps and strode over toward the firemen, slowing their pace as they neared the fire. They'd called for more senior back up. A few moments later, someone said to be from CID arrived, photographs were taken. Anyone considered to be a witness, Harry and Stu included, were corralled to one side and told to wait whilst the team of firemen continued to play a cloud of misty water over the scene to keep the heart of the fire away from where their interest was focussed.

Fortunately the wind was blowing down the river valley into the bonfire, making their task easier, taking flames, steam and smoke away from them. Harry and Stu were standing still, silently observing the unfolding drama before being ushered further back. Also watching the action was a gathering crowd of curious onlookers who had detected there might be more of interest to see than a dying fire.

A police van arrived and a couple of burly officers erected temporary shielding. A two metre high barrier was hastily put in place to prevent people taking any more photos of the scene. Harry had to laugh as an ambulance, also with its blue lights and wailing siren announcing its imminent presence slowly entered the Millennium Field. They're not going to revive this one, he mused.

Two green uniform clad ambulance men dashed forward bearing a stretcher, bending low as thy moved toward the fire, then turning it sideways to shield their faces as they made a final, crouching approach.

A recovery operation was authorised and a shapeless bodily form was carried out under a cover on the stretcher toward the ambulance. Once they arrived there, the stretcher was lowered reverentially down to the ground. Harry could see smoke or steam or both curling up in wisps from under the plastic. The body was evidently still roasting hot. He looked on as an unseemly dispute seemed to be taking place to decide as to what they should do next, the CID man, whose arm was waving the most vigorously clearly winning the argument. To Harry's eye they were like vultures each trying to claim their piece of the corpse.

In the end a white van arrived and the body on the stretcher was carefully loaded into it. The ambulance men seemed resigned to the fact they no longer had a stretcher for their ambulance. Finally, they climbed back into their cab out of the rain and Harry watched as their heads went down as they began to assemble their report. Minutes later, slip-sliding their vehicle, they made their way gingerly back onto the road, and disappeared in the crowd.

With the ambulance's departure most of the curious began moving off, many to the nearby fair. Harry and Stu were beckoned over to one of the police cars and shown into the rear seats. The CID man, now with a colleague, sat in the front seats. A red faced man with flushed cheeks, he held his police notebook open and wore a fed up expression on his face.

'You were the man who first spotted the deceased and called the authorities. Isn't that right, Sir?' he asked looking straight at Harry. Harry with his coat collar pulled up. baseball cap pulled down, dripping water everywhere observed his breath steaming up the car's windows.

'Correct,' said Harry.

'You understand, I have to interview you as a significant witness. Name and address, please Sir,' he asked. Harry made a point of clearing his throat. This was going to be fun.

'Harry McNamara, The Yard Cottage, Ham Drive, Plymouth PL2 2NJ.'

'And you, Sir?' he asked, turning to Stu who duly provided his name and address.

'Here for the Bonfire and Barrels were we?' he followed up, looking first at Harry, then Stu.

'You're a bright one,' replied Harry, sounding bored, 'How long's this going to take officer, we've done our public duty bit?'

This was not a good move in the officer's eye and Harry saw the officer tense up, his cheeks going even more red.

'I realise this is a shock and an inconvenience for you both but we have a serious incident here, a deceased person in the bonfire and we need to establish the facts. Do you have any ID on you?' he asked officiously.

Harry showed his driving licence. The officer immediately passed it over to his colleague in a well practised routine, the man making a call before handing it back. A few moments later his phone bleeped in reply, upon which he suddenly nudged his colleague mid-sentence, indicating he wanted an urgent private word with him outside the car.

'We've been rumbled,' said Harry to Stu. 'The bright boys in blue have worked out who they're dealing with. My guess is they'll let us go now and arrange to ask us more questions later. If not, I'm going to insist on it. Can't have these guys spoiling our night out. Mark my words, these PC plods in the front line will want to talk to the office managers back at Police HQ before anyone talks any further with us,' he added, nodding in the direction of where an animated telephone conversation was going on outside the car.

Harry was right and after he'd obligingly said the two would rather make a full statement at the station next day they were both given a polite 'thank you, Sir' for their help and allowed to leave on the proviso they visited Exeter Police Station the following afternoon. Once the two agreed to this, they were turned out into the cold night rain and the next witness, the yellow clad steward, was next called into the police car. He would be spending rather longer helping with enquiries.

Harry and Stu slithered their way from the wet grassy field back to the pavement and over the river bridge. As they headed for the fair, the two were equally puzzled.

'Who do you reckon the dead geezer was, Harry? Did you get a good look?'

'Not really. It was his arm hanging out between the pallets I first noticed. When I got nearer I could see his head. All his hair, if he had any, had been burned off. I think, from the reach of his arm, he'd been trying to climb out of the fire, to pull himself out. Well that's my theory.'

They paused on the top of St Saviour's Bridge and gazed down on the dark waters of the river Otter swirling past far below.

'He could have been a homeless man or something, sheltering in the bonfire, then when it was lit he couldn't get out,' suggested Stu. 'I've heard hedgehogs go in to bonfires for shelter and then get burned to death.'

'He was no bloody hedgehog,' fired back Harry.

They could see people had started to leave town, passing by them over the bridge in the direction they'd come, heading for homes nearby or the temporary car parks in the fields up the hill. However, there were still lots of people at the fair to be seen and heard, waiting their turn to be scared on the Over The Falls ride or some other garishly lit contraption.

'No way was that a homeless man,' said Harry. 'Don't ask me how I know. I just know.'

'C'mon. If we want to try the fair we need to do it now before they start winding everything down for the night,' said Stu.

Five minutes later Harry paid his money and picked up a shot gun and fired at the passing ducks.

'Yes,' he cried triumphantly, before pressing a soft toy he'd won into Stu's arms.

As the Over The Falls ride lifted the two of them high into the night sky, they had a bird's eye view of Ottery. They saw the fair directly below, with the orange circle of the bonfire on the opposite bank of the river, circled by an even larger crowd of police and white clad forensics officers still busily doing their jobs. Firemen too in their yellow kit could be seen facing their fiery adversary, continuing to play a shower of water to damp down the one corner whilst the rest of the fire blazed cheerfully on.

It seemed an age that they were perched high in the night sky, but in reality only a few minutes, all so that another hapless two people could be belted into their seats at the other end of the connecting arm on the ground far beneath them.

Then they were spinning, slowly at first, then faster with a building centrifugal force pulling at them. Whereas most people screamed as they spun and turned, hurtling up and down, often upside down, Stu heard not a sound from Harry. But then he was always like this. His adrenaline might have kicked in, but when it did so it always seemed to heighten his senses and steel his will. Harry was clearly enjoying himself, his wet, white knuckles and glistening face smiling brightly in the night sky, flashing, reflecting the rainbow colours of the fairground lights as they whizzed round and round.

Then it was over and they stepped out on to the muddy ground. One by one the fairground lights were going out and the diesel generators were being turned off. The throbbing musical rhythm of the fair's sound system, gave a final crackle before it too fell silent and the night added quiet to its dark repertoire as it began to take back its control.

'Time to go,' announced Harry.

The two made their way back to the road passing the candy floss seller pulling his van shutters closed on his sweet smelling ware and the man selling luminous gadgets from a supermarket trolley yet determined to find that last illusive customer. They crossed again over the river bridge and headed in a dwindling line of others out of town in the direction of the car park.

It was only as they got up the hill and nearer to the field they realised a problem lay ahead.

'What's up?' asked Harry of a couple walking arm in arm away from the car park.

'It's impassable. It's a quagmire. All the rain… No one's going anywhere tonight. We've given up, going to the pub, we'll find a lock in.'

Undaunted, Harry and Stu finally got to the entrance to their field and Harry could see his red Audi Quattro sitting on the far side and between them a sea of cars, some with drivers trying hopelessly to move their vehicles. Even the other four wheel drives were struggling to go anywhere and if they could move they found their paths were blocked by abandoned motors. There was just one car park steward on the gate. He looked totally fed up and explained that a tractor would be coming to help people off the site in the morning.

Harry pushed past him.

'You won't get off this field, Harry,' said Stu. 'Even with your wide wheels, you won't be going anywhere.'

'We'll see,' said Harry, not being one to give up easily.

They walked around the abandoned vehicles, slip sliding on the slick grass and mud as they went. In places deep puddles had formed, the water hemmed in by the ridge furrows created by fresh tyre tracks. Both had saturated muddy feet, water oozing from their trainers but neither voiced the fact.

Before getting in his car, Harry looked around him and thought he saw a route out. If he swung immediately right and across the camber of the field staying above the abandoned cars he could then drop down and through the gate. He thought it was at least worth a try.

'I'm going to, "Fire up the Quattro", give it a go,' Harry yelled enthusiastically.

Stu was instructed to stay out in the rain and walk on ahead, ready to give the car a push whenever Harry shouted at him to do so through his open window. Turning on the ignition, Harry loved the surge of power the Audi's engine gave. At first the car jumped forward hopefully with Stu running alongside to keep pace. That was when things started to go badly wrong. Four wide wheels driving him forward notwithstanding, a sideways slide down the camber of the hill began which Harry for all his wheel spinning just couldn't control. He leaned across and yelled out the passenger side window.

'Stu, get the other side of the car you stupid bastard and push it up the hill,' knowing as he did so he was wasting his breath. By the time Stu's sticklike form had moved round, the Audi had already slid and hit sideways into a parked silver Toyota before coming to rest against a black Vauxhall, as if Harry had been trying to overtake on its inside. These two other cars were now locked as if by a magnet force to the side of the Audi and no matter how carefully Harry tried to prize them apart nothing gave, only the sound of grinding, complaining metal on metal signalling disaster.

'Hells bells and buckets of shit!' yelled Harry having come to a permanent stop and unable to get out of the driver's side door. He pulled himself across to the passenger seat and made an ungainly exit from his car through the front passenger door, the stylish leather bucket seat that had resisted his path now covered in mud from his trainers. 'What do you think you were doing?' called out the parking steward as he ran over. 'We really don't need boy racers. Can I have your name and contact details.' On seeing Harry's big form emerge he backed off and changed his tone. 'Sorry, but I need to do this.'

Harry was not a happy man. He duly gave his details, wanting to exit the scene as soon as he could. In recent months he'd had enough bad publicity for a lifetime and didn't want to see himself once again pilloried in the press and social media. Restraining his default instincts, he used his diplomatic skills to pour oil on the troubled waters of the parking steward's already over-stressed evening.

'Plan B,' said Harry to Stu once they were two again. 'We head back down into town. Spotted a place called The Coleridge Hotel, when we were standing near the Mill earlier. Failing that, we'll find a pub. They'll have a bed. C'mon Stu. The Audi's not going anywhere. It isn't the first time it's had to be patched up and I dare say it won't be the last.'

Stu gave his customary shrug of the shoulders. He knew, despite the show of stoicism, the prang would have hurt Harry. The car had been his pride and joy for years, going back to when Harry's father used to spoil him. The red Audi was Harry's trade mark, though when he started doing politics he'd kept it mostly locked up in a garage. Wet and cold they turned again toward the town centre and The Coleridge Hotel.

There were just small numbers of people still about, in ones, twos and occasional small groups. The incessant rain had either dampened the spirits of those people outside or driven everyone else to make for cover. Things were quiet. Harry was always taking stock of people on the street anywhere near him. Attention to such detail always paid dividends. A few paces ahead of them was a medium sized man with a limp, noticeably dragging his right leg as he walked. Next to him walking tall, was a wary, well built guy. They were an odd couple and for that reason he kept watching them. There was something vaguely military about the limping man and his initial judgement was the two were not to be messed with. But who were they?

The man with the limp seemed to be talking to his taller companion about the frustration he felt having to leave his van stuck in the muddy field until the following morning and that Ottery, as far as he could ascertain had no rail, bus or taxi services to offer them.

Then he was talking about the bonfire, complaining that the heavy rain had slowed the fire. Harry had very good hearing and what he heard next made him catch his breath.

'He nearly got out. You didn't deal with him. He nearly got out!' the limping man growled. His taller companion made a definite, 'Sh! Sh!' sound and swung round to see who might be listening. Harry responded instinctively, eyes down as if miles away and evaded suspicion.

But Harry knew what he'd heard. He had an animal like intuition for such things. This was undoubtedly about the body in the fire, of that he was certain and it was something he just couldn't ignore. They had to follow these guys, only they needed to do so most carefully.

He took hold of Stu's arm, gave him the knowing look he always used when the action was about to start on the football terraces and signalled they should drop off the pace to allow the two in front some distance. Picking up on Harry's meaning, Stu simply shrugged his shoulders as was his habit and followed on, slipping back a couple of paces to drop behind Harry, waiting to see what might happen next. Being with Harry, he knew it was as near as certain something would. Much as Harry could be insufferably demanding, there were moments when the excitement in being with him was such Stu wouldn't have wanted to be anywhere else.

3

It was well after midnight and Harry and Stu were once more approaching the town's Square. The two figures in front of them made their way directly to the Barrel Inn, a pub with an ideal central location. It had no doubt been supplying ale to the thirsty for many centuries. No longer was there a black coated man stationed on the door and the two, without taking a glance behind them, pushed open the door and disappeared inside. Harry and then Stu stopped on the garage forecourt next door.

'What do we do now?' asked Stu shuffling his wet feet impatiently. 'What are we doing this for Harry, what's so important here?'

'The body in the fire. These two had something to do with it. I overheard the shorter man saying "he nearly got out." He was talking about the guy in the fire. You saw the way his arm was, as if he were trying to get out and never made it. These two guys know what happened. Do they have to come this way out of the pub? Just go and check inside will you, that there's no rear way out. Don't want to lose them now. While you're in there, cast your eye around the place, check it out. I'll wait out here.'

Stu nodded, glad to be given the opportunity to get out of the rain. He pushed against the pub door, warm light inviting him inside and he disappeared. Harry remained standing in The Square with his back to the pub window. He could hear the noise of lively conversation inside. The high spirits from the evening's earlier festivities were continuing. There must be quite a crowd inside, in contrast to where he himself was, for looking around him there was hardly anyone about. All that remained in The Square was detritus, in the form of huge drifts of fast food litter, plastic beer mugs in the gutters and patches of black water where the remnants of barrels had been extinguished.

As he waited Harry knew he had to decide what they should do next. He had a good instinct for street situations and this was precisely where he functioned best. His instinct told him to stay calm and wait. Though the rain was falling more softly now, that wasn't a problem and indeed he hardly noticed it. The one thing he resolved was to wait and see what transpired. It wasn't as if they were in a position to rush off anywhere. Their choices were limited.

With a sudden crash, the front door of the pub swung open and Stu stepped out. He quickly spotted Harry and strode over to him, carefully caressing a beer in his hand.

'What you learn Stu?'

'There's no back door. They'll have to come out this way. At the moment they're in a corner talking quietly so as not to be overheard. But I'm sure you're right, those two have something to hide, but there's some bad news.'

'Spill the beans Stu, tell all.'

'They're not on their own, five others are with them. Here, it's yours, I had a pint inside,' he said, pushing yet another plastic beer mug into Harry's hand.

'I thought we were supposed to be environmentally friendly. Sod plastic, whatever happened to glass in this place?'

'Guess lots of people have had a few to many and can't take their drink. The town probably saw a trade-off between health and safety from glass and environment and plastic and the plastic argument won!'

'They got it wrong,' said Harry, 'it's against freedom of choice, it affects the taste and it's bloody patronising.'

Harry looked round trying to take in the layout of the street, what it offered them. Though the boarded shop fronts had changed many times over the centuries, the place itself felt ancient, the open Square once a meeting point of hidden tracks now buried under modern tarmac. What they'd seen earlier, anarchic fire barrel rolling, pumped up men charging into the darkness, thrilling the crowds, had been something very old, the custom's origins lost in time. But it seemed right for the place, Harry mused. A brilliant thing for boosting beer sales too.

He sipped his beer as rain dripped into it from his cap. Imagining he could be in any time in history, trapped in a place by the inclement weather, in a dark and boarded Square in the early hours, he considered his good fortune in having Stu Beamish at his side. They'd been together through thick and thin. Life had been a bumpy road of ups and downs, celebrity and notoriety, brimming confidence and crushing nemesis, but life had always been at its best on the street. They'd been through many scrapes and always emerged out on the other side.

'Shit!' he suddenly exclaimed, making Stu look at him in surprised alarm.

'What is it, Harry?'

'Should have phoned The Coleridge. We need beds. Do it Stu. I'll keep an eye.'

Stu strolled to the opposite side of The Square. He talked as he walked. Harry could see him in earnest conversation which was a promising sign. Then there was a thumbs up from Stu and he was strolling back to rejoin him. Stu was a good fixer, quick with social media, and could also turn on the charm when it was needed. It suited Harry he liked to be in the background. The two were like chalk and cheese.

The pub door banged open again. Harry and Stu pressed themselves against the window of a butcher's shop. A well-oiled young couple propping each other up fell into the street and then headed off up the hill opposite taking a faltering line. They hadn't even noticed being observed, their attention on the road home.

Harry and Stu had been waiting almost an hour and Stu was getting edgy and fidgety. Harry had read the familiar signs; Stu was all for leaving. When the pub door next swung open the pool of light in the rain showed a group of men heading into the night. There were three, then five, all strong barrellers by the look of them, still in their charred padded clothes, staggering more like ancient wrestlers, all pride and puffed out chests. Incongruously, the two men they'd followed earlier stepped out on their tail, nearly but not quite part of the same group. They swung right past them, just paces from Harry and Stu.

Beer and exhaustion dulled their senses and they passed the two, intently looking into the doorway of a boarded up butcher's shop, casting barely a glance at them. Once passed, Harry nudged Stu and they turned to follow at a distance. Moments later they were across the road, swinging left in front of Rosey's Fish and Chip shop. The group ahead paused to settle a point, and after a brief altercation of sorts, moved on again.

Harry began to wonder what the hell he was doing. Was he imagining himself to be some kind of Jack Reacher private investigator? Since being thrown out of Parliament in disgrace, life had been difficult enough. People whom he'd thought of as friends had taken off like rats from a sinking ship. Had he lost his sense of judgement? The sensible thing to do was to call it a night, turn round and head to the hotel with Stu, wasn't it? Sometimes Harry didn't understand why he did things. There was a dark and driven side to him he didn't comprehend.

Heads down in silence, their trainers so wet they squelched with every step, the two followed the limping man and his friends up the empty street, passed a few shops, an old chapel to the left, a Post Office and along a road that seemed to be lined with blocks of terraced cottages of several mixed historic styles. Then they'd gone.

'Did you see them?' asked Harry under his breath. 'Where did they go?'

'There must be an alleyway or something. Come on.'

The two walked a little more quickly not wanting to lose their quarry after so much time and effort invested. They could hear no sound apart from splattering rain in puddles and water from spouting and overflowing roof gutters. They soon spotted the alleyway, to the left, and turned into it. Darkness enveloped them, they could see nothing except a lit car park some fifty yards ahead.

They never made it to the car park. A trap had been set and was about to be sprung. At the point where the narrow alley between the high walls opened out into the car park, just where no one could see them, the two were hit hard from left and right, fists and boots crashing into heads and bodies. Harry saw Stu fall first, taking kicks to his ribs and groin. Then he too was down, curling to protect himself. Outnumbered and beaten they had to wait until it was over.

Stu groaned as Harry heard the unhurried footsteps of their assailants retreating into the distance. Slowly lifting his head from the ground Harry saw them making for two parked cars. Stu groaned in pain and twisted round beside him. Harry saw blood mixing with water. Was it his?

Harry thought that sometimes pain helped you see things more clearly. It was like that in the post football bundles with visiting fans. As his adrenaline coursed through his veins he watched their confident assailants casually departing the scene as if with HD vision.

The men confidently climbed into their cars, not bothering to cast even a backward glance in their direction. By now Harry was like a child in a sweet shop, freshly animated with eyes bright. He saw in the men a group with whom he felt a deep animal rapport. He owed them street respect and for that reason he was determined on one thing, to see and remember at least one registration number before they disappeared. He struggled, leaned on Stu and got to his feet to get a better view.

He hadn't finished with them though they undoubtedly thought they'd finished with him and Stu. In Harry's world scores had to be settled and he had outstanding business to settle in his pending tray. This was personal and Harry was nothing if not vengeful. He smiled as his eyes made out the important detail of a vehicle registration number.

4

Once the two cars had gone all was quiet and Harry leaned over to pull Stu upright into a sitting position. He had a few scrapes and a graze to his cheek. More serious was a bleeding cut where his forehead met his short cropped hair. It left a sticky mix of blood and wet trickling down past his eye, the side of his nose and into the corner of his mouth. Stu began to rub his side as he sat on the black tarmac. He wasn't worried about his head, just the sharp pain where a boot had done something nasty to his inside. He groaned loudly.

'You'll live,' pronounced Harry, ignoring the painful side and dismissing even the cut as a minor injury. 'C'mon, need you to get your phone out and write down this number.' Stu grunted and awkwardly dug his hand into an inside pocket to obediently pull out his mobile.

'What for?'

'Note this, PF58ODE, an old red Peugeot hatchback 107, I guess. Got it? PF58ODE, red Peugeot?'

Stu tapped and nodded and Harry began to laugh. It hurt him. Nonetheless he laughed more, deeply and loudly. A window on the opposite side of the car park opened, the sound of a sash swishing catching their attention.

'Can you please be quiet or I'm calling the police,' a woman's shrill voice yelled. Harry raised an apologetic hand in acknowledgment in her direction as they immediately cut their noise. The window crashed down shut, curtains swayed and finally stilled. All was quiet once again.

'You bloody get off on this Harry McNamara. You're mad! Mad, you hear me!' hissed Stu, wincing in pain, clutching his side.

'We're alive again, Stu. We're alive! We might be rusty, but we're alive! I can't remember when we were caught like this last. We asked for it! We weren't paying attention, fully deserved it. We walked into it like animals to the slaughter.' His fury began to subside as he added, 'We've been re-awakened. I like this town, Ottery St Mary. Nice people, English folks like us. They deal it out how it should be dealt. Let's go, but let's come back one day. Nice place.'

'We've just had the shit beaten out of us. What the F...' remonstrated Stu, wincing under his breath.

Harry, now upright, tried to pull the unsuspecting Stu up onto his feet, forcing him to take a sharp intake of breath. Stu was white as a sheet and bending forward with the pain. Harry could see Stu had also bitten his tongue and fresh blood was trickling from the corner of his mouth. He left Stu to come round in his own good time and felt around in the dark for his own black rucksack – it was there, a few paces away.

Slowly Stu was back on his feet, albeit unsteadily. They turned to head back into the alleyway and return to The Square, shuffling along the pavement slowly. From there they ambled into Mill Street, nursing their bruises, gently walking down to where they'd seen the turn off for The Coleridge Hotel.

As they walked they kept a careful eye around them, and as they approached their destination, and whilst briefly under a street light, Harry glanced at his watch. It was almost 1 a.m. He then caught sight of Stu's face.

'Hold it Stu. You got a tissue or something. You look like shit!' and began to chuckle again. His humour annoyed Stu, who pulled out a wad of tissues and obediently passed them to Harry who promptly spat into them.

'I hardly need to do this, enough wet on your face to look like you've just taken a shower! Come here. Let me wipe off the blood. It's that what's going to scare anyone we might meet. Believe me Stu, it's all superficial!' he said applying vigour to the task.

Ignoring Stu's protests and moans, Harry roughly wiped the worst of the line of blood down from Stu's forehead, but there was no disguising the red weals on his cheek. There was nothing Harry could do about the pain in Stu's side except tell him, 'Get a grip, c'mon be a man!'

'How come you got off so lightly?' wheezed Stu, looking Harry over for the first time.

'Skill, you need to learn to rock and roll with the flow,' came back the teasing response. 'Put it all down to you being a bit rusty. That's married life for you!' chided Harry, dipping his shoulders this way and that like a boxer limbering up. Stu took it all, he always did.

The Coleridge was a nice looking place, set back along a pathway from the road to the rear of the old mill. It had a thatched roof with water dripping from protruding straws and a nearby mill stream splashing past, tumbling into some sort of circular weir before disappearing into the river.

A ring of the bell got Harry nowhere so he banged heavily on the door, adding a kick from his foot for good measure. They waited.

'They should have heard that! It shouldn't be bloody well locked. Do they want customers or not? Make an effort Stu, stand up straight. Can't hurt that much,' he murmured.

A light went on down the corridor behind the hallway and a portly man in a dark suit stepped toward the door, slid the latch, stood facing them, viewing them with suspicion, his gaze eyeing then fixing on Stu's face.

'Yes?'

'We've booked a room. Two singles. The name's McNamara.'

'One moment, Sir,' he said, leaning across the doorway, reaching across to a table to grab a desk diary. He was not yet minded to let them inside.

'Were you the gentleman who rang around midnight?' he asked, now looking directly at Harry.

'Yes, that's right. Can you let us in?'

The man hesitated, before scrutinising them again. He looked again at Stu's face, his gaze lingering overlong upon it. He registered the injury, then how wet and bedraggled they both were and he sniffed the air, no doubt catching alcohol on their breath. Looking straight at them with one hand under the counter, he cleared his throat before speaking.

'I'm very sorry, Sir. There's been a problem this evening. The room is not free after all. We've taken a lot of last minute guests in, the weather, Sir, it's led to a rush for cover. I'm most terribly sorry we can't be of assistance. Every bed taken.'

Before Harry could respond the door was firmly shut and they were alone outside, the sound of the man's footsteps disappearing down the corridor from whence he'd come leaving the incessantly dripping rain falling from the thatch above making the only sound.

'That's not nice! What do we do now, Harry? I really need to lie down. Shall I call him again, try and persuade him…' Stu said without enthusiasm.

Harry paused before kicking over a plant pot. He looked for a minute as if he was about to punch in the glass window of the door, but managed to restrain himself. He'd made up his mind.

'Back to the car Stu, back to the car. We'll rest up in the car.'

Another twenty minutes and they were sliding into the car. Only the passenger side doors allowed access, the damaged driver's side remained scraped shut against the two battered cars in a field of abandoned cars. It was then Harry realised his retro leather bucket seats had no reclining mechanism. It grieved him to think that Stu's wet, muddy and bloody form would very likely soil one of them. Nonetheless he told Stu he was in the front whilst he himself took the only sensible option – to lie horizontal across the back seats. Stu knew better than to complain. Harry reached to grab a note someone had left on his windscreen, screwed it up and pushed it into his jacket pocket.

'Can't you run the engine for a bit to dry us off, warm us up…' pleaded Stu.

'Aw, shut it will yer. Time for a kip. You'll be fine.'

Harry never found it hard to sleep and woke to hear tractor engine noise outside as a pale and watery dawn was breaking. There was moisture, condensation, running down the inside of the car's windows. He rubbed the pane nearest his head with the back of his sleeve. Looking through the car pressed against his, he could just make out across the valley opposite a weak sun trying to climb above the hill.

Stu was already awake, shuffling himself in obvious discomfort and rocking the car with his movement. He leant forward to wipe the misty front windscreen with the back of his hand, also trying to see what was happening outside.

'There's a tractor and that steward fellow in his yellow jacket is back, the one that took your details,' reported Stu.

Harry ran his hand through his hair to smooth it, glancing at himself in the interior mirror. He looked rough, morning stubble on his chin, dark bags under his eyes. He didn't need to push the car door open to see there was a lot of mud out there. What had he been thinking to try and drive through it?

He stepped outside to try and inspect the damage in the daylight and didn't like what he saw. The Audi's rear wing and tyre had lodged themselves into the bodywork of the silver Toyota passenger door. Harry hoped the tractor would still be able to tow it. He decided he wasn't going to wait around to find out. Delegation, that was what was needed. Then he could go.

'Wait here in the car Stu while I go and sort it. You look like you're some kind of vagrant or hedgerow dweller. Stay out of sight will you while I try and get us out of here.' Stu duly sat back in the front seat again. He wasn't feeling comfortable and was only too glad of the respite.

Harry wasn't the first up. There was a small queue of people making their case for help with the hapless steward. The farmer had obviously seen a money spinner and was turning people's misfortune into cash at twenty quid a tractor tow. Harry returned to the car to get money from Stu.

Having paid his money to the steward he was handed a pink ticket telling him his car would be towed in about an hour and would be left in the nearby lane with the instruction that any question of roadworthiness arising from the previous evening's collision was his responsibility to assess. Towing, it was made clear, was entirely at the vehicle owner's, not the farmer's risk. Harry, having paid the man and told him to leave the keys in the ignition when he'd done, took it on the nose, slipping him another five pounds to spare himself any further possible grief.

A shout to Stu, the Audi keys left in the ignition, and they were walking back into Ottery, this time in search of breakfast. The roads were open once again to traffic and the two pedestrians were constantly having to step into the hedge to avoid being run down.

Soon however they were on a pavement, with a cafe near The Square in their sights. They saw its lights were on and it was open for business. Harry was surprised to see the streets cleared already, no detritus or plastic glasses to be seen, just black stains where the flaming barrels had come to their end. A street cleaner swished noisily by, its brushes hissing loudly on the tarmac.

The first coffee drunk, a blue and white plate of ham and eggs eaten and the day already seemed a whole lot better. Harry left a rather worse for wear Stu inside, nursing his aches and pains and drinking a second coffee, in order to make an urgent call to the family scrapyard or McNamara Metals as the business was formally called.

Since his father's death the business had, rather surprisingly, all been passed to him as an inheritance. He was sole beneficiary. To date he hadn't got involved. He wouldn't know how to anyway and he'd left the manager, Nick Grayson, to run things. His Dad's will specified his Mum got the family house, though since she went to live with her sister, only he was living there. She had all the money in the bank; he got the business and by default ended up sole occupant of the family home. To be sure it was a canny will.

Harry needed to call in to touch base with his manager Nick. Nick had been there for years, man and boy, never worked anywhere else, knew how everything worked and Harry had little option but to keep him on and try his best to work with him. It wasn't an easy relationship. Nick Grayson was one of those middle-aged managers, hard working, loyal, experienced in the trade and who had tirelessly committed himself to driving the business forward and keeping all their customers happy. Harry's father had no doubt employed him for his renowned ability to micro-manage everybody.

Unfortunately for Harry, since his father's death, Nick seemed to have had him in his sights too. There was a certain tension between them, but they both knew they ultimately needed one another's cooperation if things weren't to fall apart. The arrangement was Harry left Nick to it and both seemed to cope best with it left like that.

'Hi Nick, I've had a problem, my car's been damaged in an accident… Yes, I'm fine… but I've had to stay over at Ottery St Mary… yes, in East Devon. I won't be in today. Can you text me our breakdown man's number and then give him a call for me. It's the red Audi, you know the details, it's outside the first car park on the Exeter Road on the way into Ottery. Keys are in the ignition. Tell him he can't miss it. Get them to sort it will you. I'll make my own way back… ta Nick, you're my man. Bye.' Harry heard a resentful grunt at the other end just before he ended the call. The trouble was, Nick kept the business running and the money coming in. What could he do but keep him on? What did Harry himself know of running a business anyway?

Harry was about to turn and join Stu back inside the cafe when he spied in the line of cars one that looked very much like the one he'd taken the registration of last night. It was worth a second look and he stepped into the road. A young woman was driving and she had one, no two children, in the back – probably doing the school run, he thought. Typical family banger, fast food litter on the floor. The traffic was heavy and stationary. Seizing the moment he quickly strode right up to the car, and tapped her window gently. Then, as if out on the election campaign trail, Harry turned on the charm to speak to her. Her driver's window dropped down with a quiet hum, to return his beaming smile with one of her own.

'Hi there,' he said. 'I was just wondering... did the barrelling man get home alright last night?' A moment of puzzled hesitation as she tried to work things out, her smile slipped and then Harry's smile broke her down and she chirped back, 'Oh yes, they left the lock-in at The Barrel around midnight.'

'I was there too. Wondered if I could drop him some of the barreller's kit, a pair of heavy gloves... they got left behind... at the pub. Will he be in? Quick love, the traffic looks like it could be letting you go! Which house are you? I'll drop it by later.' He began walking alongside the car as it began to move. Next he was running whilst trying to keep his smile in place. He could tell she liked him, something in the smile she returned.

'40 Yonder Street, after 4 p.m. If no one's in, leave it by the front door...' and then she'd gone, leaving Harry with an even bigger smile, as he himself stood tall and stopped the following traffic to cross the road and make his way back to the waiting Stu.

'Got an address for you to add to the registration number. C'mon, get your phone out. 40 Yonder Street... Got it? 40 Yonder Street.'

Stu tapped in the address as instructed. 'What do you have in mind, Harry?'

'Another coffee. Something will come to me.'

'Look, who's doing all the work here? Car off the field, breakdown truck on its way, breakfast sorted. That address, my friend is the sweetest thing today!'

'What is it Harry?'

'It's where the life in this place is Stu boy. It's the way to reach the guys who bundled us last night. Not since I went into the House has a chance come by like this. It's time to taste sweet revenge.'

'There were seven of them, there's two of us and you saw them Harry, built like barn doors, rugby types, broad shoulders, barrel carriers. We need reinforcements Harry, seriously… Count me out.'

'Hmm… Maybe you have a point there Stu. Me being a bit rusty on the street. We're not on home turf which gives them an edge and we don't want to walk away with a nasty legacy. Yeh, I know, prudence is the word. No harm if we suss out 40 Yonder Street now is there? We'll walk past as we inspect the town. Just like tourists. Then Stu, we'll pop home, tool up, come back with a few of the lads and settle things Plymouth way.'

'That's it Harry, great thinking!' a much relieved Stu said, finally finishing the last corner of toast.

'Time to go. While we're out, can you note any cameras around, vehicle number plate recognition, CCTV and busy-body old ladies who peek out of curtains. This place looks full of them! Like you said, let's do this our way carefully and with reinforcements.'

They stepped out and crossed The Square, passing more cafes, a library and stood at the bottom of a flight of granite steps beyond which lay a church which looked far too imposing for such a small town.

'What the f...?' said Harry. 'Didn't expect this pile here. What are they doing with a mini cathedral in a place like this?'

'Not interested Harry. It's another church. Boring...' said Stu, turning away from the steps.

'We're looking inside,' said Harry bullishly, not really knowing why he'd suggested the idea. He began walking up the steps under a metal arch and along a path through ancient gravestones leading to a door. It all looked very well kept, the grass luxuriant and neatly clipped, even for early November. A pair of cawing, rasping crows dropped from the nearest tower and swooped in front of them before disappearing over the far stone wall. The extensive graveyard seemed to surround the ancient building, a tranquil raised platform of lawn and grey-white stone with occasional trees overlooking the town below them. Ancient stocks were a past reminder of how felons were humiliated by the townsfolk in days past. Harry gave one look and sneered contemptuously.

A man with a mower was tending to the immaculate graveyard. He stopped when he saw them.

'Tell me', asked Harry surveying the many gravestones, 'how many dead people are there buried here?'

'All of them I hope,' he laughed, before swinging his mower round and moving off.

They got to the church door, a modern contraption made of glass and metal no doubt intended to keep people out of the porch. It was closed but the electric door entry responded to Harry's touch and creaked slowly open as the electric motor took the load. Once inside the porch, a roughened wooden door, no doubt many centuries old, supported by rusted metal hinges and with two circular handle pulls had far more charm. It gave way to Harry's touch and as he leaned against the weight of it, it smoothly opened to reveal a warm and welcoming vast church interior.

Stu hadn't a clue what was on Harry's mind. Harry seemed to be in a world of his own, not saying anything. Perhaps he was serious about sightseeing. If so it was a first. He'd known Harry go to church very occasionally with his parents in times past and once during his election campaign. That had been a bit of an eye opener. People in the congregation he hadn't expected to see and a clue on the wall as to his grandfather's rejection of the Blackshirts, but church never crossed Harry's radar normally. Something must be on his mind, but what?

'What you doing Harry?' asked Stu in a hushed voice.

'Ah, I see it,' he said, as he started walking down the central aisle of the nave and down to the front. There was a small metal stand with a central candle on it. Harry went up to it and picked up a nightlight candle, then a second one. He lit each in turn and placed them on the stand and then just stood there quietly.

'What's this Harry?' asked Stu impatiently.

'A place to remember.'

'Remember what?'

'Those who've died. A candle for my father and grandfather. It's long overdue. I was let down by both of them, but that's life and family is family, right? It's about respect.'

'What you mean, let down?' asked Stu curiously.

'Take my grandfather. I was very fond of him as a lad. Then he became my political inspiration. He was committed to the cause, joined Sir Oswald Mosley's Blackshirts, played his part before losing his way because of a woman, a Jewish woman.'

'And your Dad. He gave you your red Audi, then left you the family business. What more do you want? He didn't let you down did he?'

'Sure did. He cut me off. Didn't speak to me hardly. Spent all his time building up his scrap metal business. We never saw eye to eye. He never got involved with my political campaigning, not once, kept his head down, stayed out of it. Then he died, bloody fool. What did he get out of life but grief? But, like I said, family is family. That's a candle for him.' Harry nodded to the right hand night light flickering in the stillness of the place.

'I've never known you to be sentimental before Harry. You alright?'

'Course I'm alright. Just doing the right thing, giving respect where it's due.'

'He left you a lot, Harry. I mean my dad buggered off when I was small, had no time for me. He left me and my little sister shit all. You Harry, had a real Dad, a man of standing in the community. A man with money in his pocket.'

'Have you heard from your Mum, Harry? You've not said anything about her.'

'She abandoned me.'

'You ain't no baby, Harry. She just didn't like your politics. It's a free country isn't it? And when all said and done, your Mum's your Mum. She's family too…'

Just then Harry's mobile rang sounding like a thunder clap, its musical tones echoing around under the vast roof space in the church. Harry answered it and began walking along the more enclosed, narrow side aisle for some privacy.

'Hi Nick, everything alright?…'

'Just to update you. The breakdown truck's on its way and will collect your Audi within the hour. You don't need to be there. Just saying… The other thing, why I rang really, well, I don't know how to put this, but Mrs McNamara has turned up at the factory. She's been sat down and given a cup of coffee. She's sitting in reception presently, but she's asking for you. When I told her you weren't in today, that you'd had an accident with your car, she insisted I ring you. I told her you weren't hurt, you're not are you…? What do I tell her?'

'Hell, Nick. Do you have an address for my Mum? What's she doing turning up out of the blue like this? Look, OK, it's my Mum, but we're an old fashioned business and you've always told me "we care for our own", so be a good chap, get her current address, ask her what she wants and tell her… tell her, I'll call round on her later. OK?'

'Alright. Get her address and you'll call her later… I'll look after her… Oh, Harry, one other thing. I took a call from Exeter Police just now, wanting to confirm who you were, who you told them you were last night and for me to tell you that they'd like you to come in to make a witness statement at Middlemoor Police Station any time between 2 and 4 this afternoon.'

'Was going there anyway, Nick,' said Harry.

'Trouble?' fished Nick.

'No trouble Nick… just doing my bit as a good citizen…' with that Nick had gone.

Still looking round in the church as if he needed to find something but didn't know what, Harry found himself in a little square room at the far end of the church. The light was streaming in through a stained glass window and above there was an ornately painted ceiling. He looked up to see a number of tiny gold strange looking faces peering down from the stone ceiling bosses. All seemed to be looking the same way, except one. Why was that? Suddenly he felt he was like that one strange face, the one person looking the other way to everyone else. It left him feeling frighteningly disconnected and unsettled him. It was if he knew from what he was seeing that church and all it stood for might mean something to others, but like the one green man face facing the other way, not himself. He turned to find Stu standing at his right shoulder.

'Time to go, leave… Let's find Yonder Street and then we'll pick up that bus, the number 4, from outside The Barrel Inn, the one for Exeter and home. Stu seemed happy with the decision and they both walked back, past the still flickering candles and out of the old door, through the modern one and into the crisp bright late autumnal sunshine to the sound of grass being cut.

'Inspirational that was,' said Harry, without explaining why, tugging on the straps of his black rucksack. Stu simply shrugged, wondering what Harry was carrying on his back and followed him out of the door.

5

The two strolled back down the hill to The Square, swung left past a couple of hardware shops and into Yonder Street. They didn't have far to walk before they were outside number 40. As they approached Harry's pace slowed and Stu's followed suit. They didn't want to look like they were casing a joint, but they were, and anyone paying attention would have noticed they barely shuffled as they passed the yellow painted front door, casting a glance through what appeared to be a lounge window facing the street and then the window following, a study of some sort. Thankfully nobody paid them any attention. It was the day after barrels and everyone was quietly going about their business, some no doubt with sore heads. It wasn't exactly a busy street, but busy enough so they didn't stand out.

'Looks quiet, Harry.'

'Looks don't mean a thing and there could be a dog. Keep going five minutes and then we'll walk back on the other side.' They got to a side road, Chapel Street, and decided that should do it, crossed the road and began walking back the way they'd come but on the other side. This time as they passed they were sure there were no signs of life from the house.

'Stu, go and ring the bell and ask if they need a window cleaner.'

Stu knew there wasn't a choice being offered and after a moment's hesitation whilst he summoned up the will, he duly crossed the road and pressed the door bell. Harry meanwhile had wandered a discreet distance away to come to a stop opposite a Post Office and then duly crossed back over the road once again to look in the shop window. It seemed hardly any time at all when Stu rejoined him.

'House is empty, Harry. I rang twice. No one in. Now what?'

'I break in. You act as look out.'

'Hold on! That's serious, Harry. Prison serious. The street is in full view! You're mad Harry!'

'OK, calm yourself. You go and wait at the bus stop by the Barrel. I'll join you there in five. Can you let me have a tissue before you go?'

Stu reached in his pocket and thrust what was left of the pack into Harry's open palm and headed off. He needed no second bidding and slouched away, not bothering to turn round, mindful that any visible link with Harry over the coming minutes might ultimately prove costly.

Harry took his time going back to number 40. He was watching everything and everybody like an animal hunting. He knew he needed to be calm and focussed and so, he consciously pulled himself together, riding the surge of adrenaline now pumping him up. He chose his moment of approach very carefully – when there were no people nearby and no vehicles passing in either direction. By the time he got to the door he was holding two things, one in each of his hands. The moment had come.

Anyone looking might have thought Harry was ringing the bell, but in reality he was both ringing the bell again and removing Stu's finger print with the tissue. He put the screwed up tissue away in his Barbour jacket pocket, took one final look left and right, then he moved closer to the window. It was an easy-peasy sash window and he slid his penknife blade firmly along to release the centrally located sash mechanism in one swift movement. He felt the well worn arm slide and the window rattle loose. No second security lock, he could tell, it was so easy!

Before doing anything more, he turned, his back to the window facing the road and took off his rucksack. Reaching inside it he pulled out a small black zip case. Turning again, he eased the window up ever so slightly, then in one quick movement he reached an arm inside and dropped the pouch carefully on the centre of the settee where it would be seen. He carefully pulled the window down the few inches or so needed to ensure it was back in place, closed. Could reaching inside a window be considered burglary? He wasn't sure. He looked quickly around again and, once satisfied no one was looking, he walked steadily down the street to rejoin Stu in The Square.

Fortuitously there was a single decker bus waiting. It was blocking a good part of the road much to the annoyance of traffic in The Square that had been forced to wait. Stu was looking anxious at the tail end of a bus queue, wanting to get on. The bus was covered in mud, the lanes so wet from the previous day's rain. They knew once they were inside no one would be seeing in or out of the mud splattered windows.

'Ready?' Stu asked, nervously sliding Harry a fiver to pay his own fare. 'We have to change in Exeter for Plymouth,' he added. They climbed on the half full bus to find there were other returnees from tar barrels making a belated exit from the town. It was good cover not to be the only strangers in a small place. Sitting to the rear, Stu was keen for a briefing.

For the moment Harry was sending a strong do not disturb signal and Stu sat quietly, biding his time.

It was only when the bus twisted and turned through the new Cranbrook housing estate near Exeter, Harry suddenly nudged Stu wanting to speak.

'Mission accomplished,' he said.

'What? What do you mean? You've lost me,' Stu muttered, ruefully rubbing the graze on his cheek, 'accomplished what? What have you done Harry?'

'We went to Ottery for some fun. And I think I've found the place to relaunch, my political campaign. It's time the people's voice was heard. I've just sprung the trap to catch us our first party workers.'

'What have you done this time, Harry? What have you done?'

At that point Harry went quiet and stayed that way until some minutes later the bus pulled into Exeter bus station, the first part of their journey home complete.

Stu was much puzzled, but as he watched his friend he noticed something. Harry was nursing his black rucksack on his lap as if it were something precious. He realised in that moment he'd surreptitiously used in Ottery St Mary whatever he'd carried there inside it.

Harry had planned something since they left Plymouth the previous morning and Stu, had foolishly failed to notice. He might as well have 'sucker' written across his forehead. Harry was never one to lie down, he'd been planning a moment of resurrection, an awakening of his fortunes and from the contented faraway look on Harry's face, Stu realised that a new chapter was about to begin.

6

When Millie Pyneton arrived back home from the school run she got lucky. Yonder Street was such a difficult place to find a parking space, but this morning she'd been able to leave the Peugeot just yards from her door and it could stay there all day. Maybe it was because the streets had been cleared of vehicles for yesterday's barrels and not everyone had brought their cars back, who knows? It was an expected bonus and she happily took the few steps from her car to her yellow front door.

Working from home, running a small card and gift business which more recently had successfully expanded into candle sales, fitted nicely around her family life. Charlie, her long time partner, had a job in a vehicle repairs business on the industrial estate and with the two kids in Ottery Schools, her life centred on the town where nearly all their family and friends also lived, in fact had done so for generations. She breathed a sigh of relief that Barrel night was over for another year. For days it had taken over their lives, put an added strain between them, but things could now get back to normal again, or so she hoped.

It was only after she began tidying up, the kitchen first, then the front room, she noticed it. She didn't recall anyone having left it the previous night and wondered whose it might be. She concluded one of the barrellers had almost certainly forgotten it without her noticing and would call back later, so she picked up the black zipped wallet and stood it behind the clock on the mantle shelf.

Before going to the back room to begin work, her curiosity got the better of her and she looked at the mysterious smart wallet again, but the zipped case was giving nothing away. Perhaps she should open it just to see whose it was, but then the thought crossed her mind that it might be official or private and after touching it, lifting it and tilting it from side to side very delicately, she decided to leave it where it was, and popped it back behind the clock until Charlie got back later in the day. He would surely know what it was. Then she forgot about it completely.

Clicking on and opening her tablet she was pleased to find a series of orders had come in for her products and her mind turned to the task in hand, preparing and parcelling items and dealing with the accounts. Glancing around she realised the back of the house was beginning to look increasingly like a factory outlet with shelves from floor to ceiling and printers, flatpack boxes, wrappers and assorted equipment occupying all available downstairs space. Even outside, the garden shed had been turned into a candle manufacturing zone.

As she worked, gradually stacking a pile of parcels to be taken to the Hermes depot later, she wondered how long it would be before an official from East Devon District Council would come poking their nose in and threaten to shut her down. She suspected she must be breaking dozens of regulations – running a business in a domestic premises, storing in bulk a hazardous material, namely candle wax; employing minors, namely her children. In the meantime, she told herself, needs must and it was a case of making hay whilst the sun shone. The current climate was so antagonistic toward anyone wanting to improve themselves, she thought. It was hard work but flexible as to when she did it and sometimes the family helped her out. At the present rate of product sales they were going to have a very good Christmas, maybe even a foreign holiday before the new school term started in January.

Mid afternoon, she struggled out of her front door carrying all the parcels for mailing to the posting point. She'd totally forgotten what she'd placed on her mantle shelf. Her mind had shifted to the urgent need to collect the children, first Sasha from the primary school and then Belle from the secondary. Timing was tight, but she reassured herself that Belle would wait if she got delayed.

Forty five minutes later, parcels dropped off and children duly collected, the three returned home with the car parked up rather further from the house than Millie had hoped. As she hung up her pink anorak, it was Sasha who called out as she switched on the front room TV, 'What's that Mum?' that the presence of the mysterious black wallet was brought back to her attention once more.

'Something for your Dad,' she answered evading the question, stepping into the room and sweeping the object up taking and placing it on the kitchen table. Sasha seemed happy with that explanation and started watching an American Teen Soap on Netflix.

Picking the object up again Millie sensed that though it looked smartly important there were probably only papers inside and she immediately lost interest. She placed it down carefully, leaning it against a loaf of white sliced bread. Black on white, Charlie couldn't fail to see it when he came in.

Then she had that feeling that something wasn't quite right. Perhaps she'd overlooked or forgotten something, maybe a job still to do. The feeling nagged and she made herself a cup of tea. As she went to the fridge to get the milk she remembered what it was – that big smiling guy, the one who'd flagged her down when she was taking the kids to school. Thinking about it, he'd said he would drop something round for Charlie or was it one of his friends, but he'd never said what it was. It puzzled her that she didn't recognise him, though he claimed familiarity.

Millie put the mug of tea down on the kitchen table and went to look outside the front door. She was sure she'd said leave it at the front door if no one was in, but there was nothing to be seen. She cast her eye in front of the neighbours' doors to see if he'd misheard and got their address wrong and then wondered if someone had taken it in for her. It's not important, she told herself and shut the door. At least she wasn't going mad. She'd recalled what was troubling her in the end even though there was no sign of what he'd promised to drop round. She must remember to tell Charlie.

But as she sat and sipped her tea, she remained troubled. The man's face in the street now she came to think of it did look vaguely familiar, like someone she should know. His face had unsettled her at the time and was doing so now. It was a handsome face full of charm, flirtatious even, yet one mixed with the forcefulness of someone who always got their own way. A bit like her Charlie, she thought.

It was then she heard the sound of Charlie's key in the front door followed by the children's voices raised in excited greeting. The kettle was still hot. That'll please him, she thought.

'In here, Charlie,' she called as she leaned to switch the kettle back on and reach for another mug.

Charlie grabbed her round her waist affectionately as he came in, nearly causing her to spill the hot water as she poured him his tea. It was as they sat down at the kitchen table Charlie's eyes fell upon the black zipper wallet.

'What's this?' he asked.

'Found it on the front room settee this morning. I think one of your friends must have left it last night,' she said passing it to him.

'No, I don't think so. I saw them out myself and don't remember anything being left.' He turned it over, examined it briefly and began to unzip it.

'Do you think you should?' she asked.

'Needs must,' he said, as he pulled out a wad of printed papers. 'Looks kind of political to me. Can't be any of my friends. Are you sure? Kinda looks interesting at first glance. About time someone stood up for the ordinary Englishman. Where did you say you found it?'

Millie felt uneasy. The thought flashed through her mind that someone unknown to them had been in their home without their knowledge; she dismissed the thought as unlikely given she remembered locking the house and there being no signs of a break in. In the next moment her mind went back to the man who'd stopped her when she was driving to school and got her address from her. Somehow she knew the mysterious wallet and he were linked and somehow he'd gained access to their home. Her mouth must have fallen open.

'Tell me what you know Millie,' Charlie said squaring up to her and holding the papers accusingly in front of her face. Millie shared her thoughts and the two fell silent as Charlie began to pore through what he was holding, trying to find out more. It took him nowhere. He looked up, his face that of a troubled man.

'Where exactly did you find them, show me.'

The two walked into the front room. Charlie handed the wallet to her.

'Where? Put them how you found them.'

She told Belle to move herself and then laid them squarely in the centre of the settee, recalling that it was facing her as she went to look at it. Charlie looked up and out of the window to the street beyond as if deep in thought. Then his glance rested on the window catch. When he saw it was unlocked he knew instantly what had happened.

'I shut that window last night, anybody open it today? You kids, either of you touch the window today?'

He was answered with sideways nods all round. He beckoned Millie back into the kitchen, shut the door and indicated they were to sit down at the table.

'I've just twigged it,' he said.

'You gave a guy our address and he broke in to deliver these.'

'That's a strange thing to do. Why would he do that? Why Charlie, why?'

'Try and describe him to me, will you. What kind of bloke was he?'

'Tall, big, smart jacket, cap on his head, big smile. Needed a shave.'

'That's him! We've got a problem. Last night we and the lads were walking back from the Barrel, we were going to pick up the cars to drop people home and to park up on the street again as the barrels parking restrictions from yesterday had expired. Well… there were two guys who followed us and when we turned down the alleyway by the Institute to go through to the car park we surprised them.'

'Oh no Charlie, you didn't, you bloody idiot.'

'No, nothing serious, just gave them the message they were following the wrong people, we just knocked them down, normal like… and they gave up. Nothing bad, it was… nothing.'

'Only they didn't give up, Charlie, because it was no coincidence I was stopped in the street this morning, now was it. He'd seen the car… Big guy, short hair, smiley round face, Barbour jacket…'

'But you told him where we lived, you fool,' he said, raising his voice. Millie patted her hands downwards in the air asking for hush, casting her eyes in the direction of the two girls in the other room.

'Listen. It was put to me like this. This guy had been at the Barrel last night and asked if you'd got home OK. How was I to know? Then he said you or your friends had left some kit behind and could he drop it round. I said someone would be in late afternoon and if no one was in he should leave it on the step. End of…'

'This wasn't him by any chance,' asked Charlie looking again at the leaflets, thrusting one of them in front of her.

It was the same beaming smile, the same man, this time looking handsome and smart in a suit. She knew now why she thought she recognised him. Charlie didn't wait for her to say yes. He didn't need to, her face had gone bright red.

Charlie began going through the papers more thoroughly as Millie watched. He took a sip of his tea and reached for a chocolate digestive biscuit. He was thinking hard. He picked up his mobile and began twiddling his thumbs making searches.

'We've made an unexpected connection with Harry McNamara, you remember the guy, the Britain First Democratic Party politician who caused a stir when he got elected as MP for Plymouth in that by-election. There was lots of controversy over his campaign. He played people's fears when the terrorists came. Not such a bad guy, extreme right, that's what he is. Though he got caught with his fingers in the till and ended up being expelled from the House until they sort out what to do about him. He's a dark horse that one. What he seems to be doing here,' he tapped the paper he was holding with the back of his hand, 'is making some kind of political relaunch, a comeback. I can't make it out.'

'Why's he picked on us, Charlie? Why us? Why does he break in when he could, could just have posted them through the letter box? What about the kids Charlie? I'm scared.'

'Why us? Because he wants us to know that he can. That's why. He delivered me a message.'

'He's a risk taker, a bold one at that. What if he got caught for it?'

'No proof. It won't go anywhere. Nothing to worry about.'

'But we know, and I don't like it. He's picked on us Charlie. Now why would he do that? Does he want revenge for what your stupid friends did last night? Don't you ever stop to think of your family, Charlie. I've had it up to here with you and your mates. I don't like the situation you've put us in. What's this guy capable of Charlie, you tell me?' she said raising her voice and pointing her finger accusingly at the man on the leaflet.

'Hmm. Let's think about this calmly. If he wanted revenge, surely he wouldn't advertise himself to us like this. It immediately puts him in the frame if anything should happen, which is odd...'

'So he has another motive then...'

'Hmm. Maybe he has... He's back to his campaigning ways and wants... to be... in touch.'

Upon that Millie found the conversation seemed to just dry up. Charlie was a man who kept his own secrets and she knew better than to push him too hard. She could read the signs. Charlie had realised something and was not going to be spilling the beans to her. It was always like this, a wall of silence erected to hide any unpleasant truth until the thing came out into the open, usually badly and she ended up having to pick up the pieces and trying to mend things afterwards. There was no further talk to be had and she turned her attention to getting dinner on the table.

Charlie fixed his attention on his mobile. There were other troubling matters in his mind beside that political schemer and roughneck Harry McNamara, foremost amongst them was local news of the discovery of a body in last night's bonfire.

An article on the local Ottery Natters website said the police had no idea as yet who they'd pulled out, or more likely weren't spilling the beans on who it was, but he knew that very soon there were going to be a lot of searching questions asked of those, who like himself, had been responsible for building and organising the fire.

They might have had a good run of looking after things the Ottery way until now, sorting things out for themselves, but it looked like the police would take things on a very different course over the coming days. He had a few phone calls to make, but they needed to be done in private.

After supper, he'd make his excuses and escape the house for a while. Millie would understand, she really had no choice, now did she? She might think he'd got them in danger, but she really didn't know the half of it and he wasn't going to tell her.

7

It was too far to walk from the bus station to Middlemoor Police Station, so they got a taxi. They knew they were early but Harry said, 'They'll see us anyway'. He was right. Once their presence was noted in the police reception by a pen and paper policeman, the same ginger haired, red faced CID officer they'd seen the previous night in Ottery put his head round a door and waved them through. He still looked just as harassed. Harry smiled.

A familiar police interview process followed. They had nothing to hide after all. It was aways easier to tell it how it is to the police than have to make something up as Harry had so often had to do in the past. When it looked to be all done and dusted, and their statements had been duly signed, Harry spoke up.

'I hope you don't mind me asking you a question, officer. But can you tell me who the man was, the guy who died?'

'We're releasing a public statement in a few minutes time. We will be saying that local East Devon District Counsellor, Barry Thornton's body was recovered from the bonfire at the Ottery St Mary Tar Barrels last night and his death is being treated as suspicious.'

'Is there anything else you can tell us, between ourselves, off the record, like?' asked Harry looking for a confidential word in the ear. The officer was not impressed, shrugged, spoke a standard concluding police patter into the nearby microphone and then turned off the tape machine before saying more.

'We may well need to be in touch with you again. This is an ongoing police investigation and we are making several lines of inquiry. Thank you for your cooperation, Sirs.'

He wasn't giving anything more away. It was over and before they knew it, Harry and Stu were outside on the pavement walking back toward a bus stop for the city centre. Harry was beginning to resent not having a set of wheels, but reminded himself the situation was only temporary.

After retracing their steps, seeing to the purchase of fast food, burgers and fries in wing boxes for the journey, they found they had a long wait for the next bus. Food munched, cans quaffed, they sat waiting in the draughty bus station. The two then had an easy, though tedious, second bus journey from Exeter south to Plymouth. By this time Harry had seemed to Stu to be lost in his own thoughts and rather than disturb him, he'd taken the opportunity to make an overdue call to his wife to explain what had happened, why they'd been so delayed and that he'd be back soon.

Then Harry looked up. He'd been going through his own phone messages. Amongst the calls was one Harry had missed which he played back. It had come in from Exeter Police CID whilst they were on the first bus. They were wanting to interview the two of them as soon as possible, interviews now of course done. Nonetheless Harry decided to return that call and using the pretext of the message he asked to be put through to CID and was duly picked up.

'Harry McNamara here. Got your call. How many statements from me do you need?'

Stu smirked… same old Harry, playing games. After a pause at the other end he found he was talking to the same CID man who had actually interviewed them.

'How can I help?' he asked.

'Well, I've just picked up your earlier call asking me to come in to make a statement this afternoon. Just checking you don't want me to get off my bus, turn round and come back again.'

'No, Sir. We have your statement, thank you.'

'Only want to be helpful. Police need all the public support they can get. Oh, did you get anywhere further with why Barry Thornton ended up in the bonfire?'

'We're continuing our enquiries, Sir.'

'He definitely didn't fall in? Someone had it in for him don't you think?'

'What makes you say that, Sir?'

'Stands to reason. Someone had a score to settle. Where better to hide a body and destroy the evidence? He was a Labour man, you said, not a popular wicket to bat on…'

'By all accounts he was a popular man in Ottery…'

'Not with everyone… I expect you've had a look online at his website and the things he's done. I've just been glancing through it myself – all in the public domain, Officer. He was a trouble maker, a thorn in the side. On the occasion someone wanted planning permission to do something

worthwhile it looks like he put his hand up to say "No".
Must have had enemies, don't you think? You mean to say
you haven't a list of them yet?'

'Sir, we have our methods, our lines of enquiry which we are
following and we have our significant witnesses.'

'OK, OK. Only trying to be helpful. I'll let you get back to it.
Goodbye.' Harry cut the call and grinned at Stu.

'I love it! He hadn't a clue. I could tell. When we've got our
set of wheels sorted we're heading back to Ottery and
making enquiries of our own. Got nothing better to do. Turn
over a few sleeping logs and see what kind of creepy crawly
comes out into the light.'

'Do you mean it?'

'Course I do. We've unfinished business with Limping Man.
What else is there to do besides being publicly spirited and
of course supporting Plymouth Rovers?' he grinned.

'Why didn't you tell the policeman about Limping Man?'

'The idiot never asked. His mind's not on the job. Anyway
I've been thinking about that fellow, I sense he was a leader,
other people gathered round him, bit like you and the lads
round me. No, that guy's for me and when I've finished,
maybe the police.'

Harry got out his phone and Stu looked over his shoulder as
he posted a Tweet: 'Local police could and should do
better…'

Stu went quiet. The bus south was making good progress.

On the outskirts of Plymouth, as the bus began its descent into the unexciting modern urban sprawl, a finger of grey estuary indicated they'd returned to the "Ocean City". Plymouth's tourism strap line had been designed to persuade the unsuspecting of its charms, but in today's gloom it looked singularly inappropriate. The bus began to twist and turn. In the few minutes remaining before reaching their destination, Harry made more calls for himself.

After ten minutes, the bus finally pulled to a halt. He'd managed to call round all the old lads from the Plymouth Rovers supporters' gang, those who comprised his trusted and closest core, Harry's own. Arrangements were made to meet at The White Horse later that evening and he'd made it clear it was a three line whip.

Stu was nothing if not 100% loyal and knew he had to make another call himself to further postpone his own homecoming. When Harry was engaged with something, no matter what, it fully took him over, like a dog obsessed with his bone. On this occasion, for some reason, Harry had become a Sherlock Holmes figure, Stu his Watson and the supporters gang would soon find themselves cast as Harry's street runners all working solve the case of – The Limping Man. His thoughts were interrupted.

'Stu, see if there's anything more in social media about the geezer in the bonfire. If the police haven't said anything yet, the dark web rumour mill will be running something by now. See what you can get, will you, you know it's what your good at,' he said with urgency in his tone. A rare moment Stu sensed he'd been praised.

Stu obediently tapped away on his mobile and after a couple of minutes announced with a note of triumph, 'Found something, Harry! He's a thirty-four year old Labour counsellor thought to be taking back-handers over planning matters… Oh yes, spicy! He's been having it off with one of the Tory Councillor wives, Cleo Masters, Jeremy Masters' wife! Even so, seems to have been a popular guy amongst his socialist friends, long-serving local councillor, blah-blah, well-liked and tireless, lots of friends and supporters, blah-blah…'

'Well not everyone was Mr Thornton's supporter now were they? Bet Jeremy was none too pleased with him either, taking liberties with his wife! Planning issues, well… that's like stirring a hornet's nest. Believe me, politicians attract bribes like dogs attract fleas.'

'And… he was on the local Prevent Steering Group… because of his concern at the rise of populist extreme right wing support in East Devon.'

'Huh! Last place anything like that would be on the radar. You sure about that? Ottery St Mary, wouldn't know what an extreme right winger was, unless I've missed something?' Despite his voiced cynicism, Harry felt the murder victim's Prevent connection signalled something significant. Had he stumbled upon something significant in the town?

'He had a habit of putting his nose into things that he shouldn't, it says here.' Then reading from a blog he'd found, Stu added, '"Whether you liked Barry Thornton or not he must have had the DNA of a miner, because he was the digger of dirt par excellence. If it wasn't planning, it was local council failings in education or health. Barry was a hundred percent badger. He dug deep, kept digging and threw dirt everywhere he burrowed; he didn't let anyone get in his way."'

'Interesting… Tell you what I think, Stu…'

'What Harry?'

'First… Find out his private address will you. Tell me who he lived with. Was he shacking up with this Tory bird, Cleo Masters? Where does she live? Dig Stu, dig a bit more… I need to know more.'

Stu lifted his head up with a sigh to find everyone had got off the bus except the two of them. He nudged Harry in the ribs who looked and took the hint.

Out on the street Harry called an Uber and in minutes they were back at his terraced house in Ham Drive, within spitting distance of Plymouth Rovers – home, though to be frank it was nothing like it was when his Mum lived there. It had become an untidy shambles, everything left out. All the shine and sparkle had disappeared.

'Time to freshen up…get a shave,' announced Harry. 'Put the kettle on Stu, you know where everything is…'

With that Harry disappeared upstairs and Stu heard a shower running. Five minutes later he ran up with a steaming mug in his hand, just as Harry had ordered. Harry reached out an arm taking the coffee into the shower with him.

After his shower Harry took a new shirt from its cellophane wrapping without looking down at the growing pile of dirty shirts on the floor waiting to be laundered. His Mum's absence irked him more than he liked to let on. She used to see to all the boring stuff, the washing, ironing, shopping, cooking and the tidying up. He'd never realised just how

72

much she did until she'd gone. Recently he'd got one of the work's girls, Sheena, to come in once a week on Fridays, but it wasn't the same and she didn't have any pride in what she did. Maybe he should pay her for more hours. He had to admit it to himself, since his Mum had walked out, notwithstanding Sheena's help, the place was falling apart. Nothing was in its right place anymore and everything at home felt like an effort. It annoyed him.

'Stu,' he shouted angrily. 'The coffee's cold. Make another you dick head. Try using boiling water.'

Stu hurried up and then down the stairs to do Harry's bidding.

When Harry eventually got down to the kitchen he felt himself a new man, clean and sharp once again. He left his dirty coffee mug with the others. Sheena would see to them.

'Time for the pub,' he announced decisively. 'Let's tell the lads we've something on.'

8

The White Horse was really Harry's second home. Definitely no bouncer on the door here saying, 'no entry, tickets only'. As number one customer, Harry was always made welcome. His favourite pint was invariably put out ready for him on the bar as he walked in, smiles greeting him all round.

Today was no different. There they were – Phil, tall and lean, always with a hungry looking face. He would drive Harry around in his old motor and was his oldest friend. Owen, an obsessive body builder, all bulked out, today in black and white gym gear. Who knew what he was taking to look like he did? Best not to ask. The ceiling light above Owen reflected a shiny white on his bald pate as he hunched over the bar nursing his pint.

Wayne was useful, had an ear for knowing what was going on. His heart was in the football supporters club. Harry once thought he might try and ease Harry out, so Harry had once had to remind Wayne of his proper place. That had settled it, the two had arrived at a mutual respect and understanding even if Harry no longer fully trusted him. Stu stood beside Harry. There they were, five guys, looking to sit at their table, sipping pints, waiting to do business.

Tonight was no different to many nights. It warmed Harry to be on home turf. The place fitted him as neatly as a pair of gloves on a boxer. There was a slight hiccup as Harry was slow in realising why everyone was still standing by the bar. He followed their glances.

Harry signalled Stu to tell the young couple to move off *their* table. The couple were innocents abroad and Harry quickly forgave them their indiscretion; how would they know, but the cheek of it in taking Harry's place. The fact there were five determined tough faces looking across at them led the couple to quickly realise their error. The two swept up their drinks and swiftly moved away into the lounge next door.

Harry made a mental note to self that he must have a word with Dan behind the bar to tell him to keep a better eye on things. Dan needed to find a, "*this table is reserved*" notice or something similar, to ensure Harry was not put to any future inconvenience. Standards were slipping in the pub as well as at home. He put it all down to his being too long away in politics elsewhere.

'What are you all waiting for?' Harry shouted. 'It's not my round! Someone get me another bloody drink and come and sit down.'

Everyone knew something was up. Harry was all fired up and when he was like this, they took it, as they always did, that he had some new idea. The anticipation generated a mix of excitement and apprehension in equal measure.

'OK, listen here,' he said once his next beer had arrived, the heads of his mates and their conversation subsiding in unison. They sat round the circular wooden table as if in a council of war.

'Stu and I were at the Ottery Tar Barrels last night. A right lark! A kind of mad local bonfire night custom – all fire and fury. I'll spare you the details… brilliant it was! I'll just get to the point. You might have seen on the news, there was a body in the bonfire.'

'Yeah! Yeah!' said a couple of voices.

'What you won't know is that it was me who spotted the dead geezer and called the police.'

Harry let this sink in, before adding, 'that was when the fun began to start. Some would say he deserved to die. He was an ignorant lefty. For my part, I think cremating him whilst he was still alive was going a bit far.'

There was raucous laughter round the table.

'What happened next is what's interesting, so listen in. An older geezer, a guy about my height, with a limp, was walking away after, late it was and he said to his mate, Harry began speaking from behind his hand as if sharing a secret, *"He nearly got out. You didn't deal with him. He nearly got out!"'*

'Hell! What did you do Harry? You didn't tell the police did you?' asked Wayne.

'Shut it and listen! So we followed these two into town. They went into a pub. Later, they came out. They're suddenly seven. The odds had changed. I was thinking of taking them on single handed, but I had Stu with me.' More laughter followed, Stu taking it in good heart.

'We followed these seven big fellows anyway. It was dark and Stu and I thought we'd be OK.'

'But, we'd not walked half a mile and we were jumped in an alley. Beaten up, given a kicking. Stu forgot to protect himself, stupid bugger. I was fine. Nothing we could do about it and they got away. Wasn't able to get in a punch or a kick. Owe them one…'

76

'Nooo!....' said Phil. 'Was wondering how you'd got to improve your good looks.' he joked, Stu shrugging, used to being the victim.

'So there's unfinished business. First, we got to show these Ottery lads they don't mess with Harry McNamara. Second, as good citizens we need to have a private word with the limping man and get him to talk; and Third, well, I've got plans and we'll come to those later.'

'With you Harry,' said Wayne, 'Right behind you on this one. We all need to go to Ottery. We'll need to use Phil's car as yours is broke; beat the hell out of the seven guys when we've found them. Find out what the cripple knows using persuasive techniques and then what? Report him to the police or burn him on a fire too? Is that the sum of it, Harry? Do you want me to run with it?'

'Don't like your analysis, Wayne? You're full of holes. Got faults in it.'

'Like what?'

'You need brains Wayne, brains. You march in like a simpleton and you've got a prison sentence written all over your forehead!' said Harry tapping his own temple with his index finger. 'Think, Wayne, think! Yes, that's the general direction of travel, but we have to do some more work first. I'm going back to Ottery with Stu to do the necessary digging and then we'll all go for an outing there. OK? Phil, you'll lend Stu your car tomorrow...'

'Right on, Harry,' said Phil, accepting he'd have to rearrange his own day to fit in with Harry's plans.

Someone pointed out that the pub TV was showing an FA cup match. It was about to start and the pressing agenda now was to get more beer and order some grub from the bar.

Things settled into a familiar pattern. Football the common currency, allegiances in place, eyes turning to the big screen. Meantime a plan was hatching in Harry's mind.

9

Harry stirred in his bed. He turned clumsily to grasp his mobile phone to see the time, which was early for him on a Saturday… 9.06 a.m.. A grey November day was showing through the curtains. He stretched. Memories of a boozy Friday night at The White Horse and a late lock-in brought a smile, but it left him unfocussed, struggling to gather his thoughts. That was two late nights in a row and he was feeling it. In the past he'd been able to shrug off the odd night of excess, now it seemed harder to do so. He tried again to concentrate, marshall his thoughts.

He sort of recalled that Stu must have walked him back home and then he imagined Stu must have got a right rollicking from his wife Penny when he'd got to his own home two streets away. Harry chuckled as he saw the domestic scene play out. He must give Stu a little slack, he owed him that much.

Harry rolled over so his feet fell off the side of the bed and onto the floor. He sat still for a moment thinking how quiet the house was. He spied his set of weights, facing him accusingly, lying unused for several months. What had once been toned muscle now hung as slack fat and his face in the wardrobe mirror looked blotchy, pale and older. It wouldn't do. He wasn't like this when his Mum was at home. He decided to call her.

Unexpectedly it was Nick Grayson from the business who picked up. Something clicked in Harry's head and he ended the call. He needed a coffee and headed down to the kitchen in his T-shirt and boxer shorts. His head began to clear.

A shave and a shower followed. Then he pulled another new shirt from its wrapping, sprayed deodorant generously. He dressed, then waxed, shaped and styled his hair before turning to head downstairs for a second time. Beside him was his unmade bed and his dirty washing draped over his grandfather's old metal chest at the bed end, with still more of his clothes lying strewn across the floor. He shrugged.

Sheena wasn't in until Monday. She did all the domestic stuff. Observing the mess, Harry made a mental note to get her to come in more than once a week. The place was going downhill and with the sad earlier mirror image of himself still firmly implanted on his mind, he knew he was looking worse for wear and in need of restoration work too.

He sat at the wooden kitchen table, a second coffee mug in his hand, gazing out of the window at the miserable back yard. Once his Father's pride and joy, the green lawn was nearly a foot high, its bowling green finish long gone to seed. The roses either side of the single path to the shed and bins hadn't been pruned either and were looking long and straggly, in places falling over onto the path. Harry wondered if Sheena could see to the garden too, concluding probably not, her limited home skills were as far as her abilities extended.

But he had more pressing matters to think on. Why the hell had Nick picked up his call to his Mum? Yes, the two had always been friends, but… He felt caught out and betrayed, then angry, crashing his fist down on the table, making his coffee mug jump, a circular ring of ripples appearing on its surface. Was he losing his edge, missing things too? He should have spotted it a mile off, seen it coming. She'd betrayed him once when he was in the critical final days of his parliamentary campaign, and now she posed a threat to him again. As for Nick, he'd played him for a fool as if he and his Mum didn't have contact with each other. That guy had it coming to him.

His phone sounded. Stu was calling.

'Hi there mate. Did you get roasted when you got in?' Harry teased.

'Yeah, it's no joke Harry. I've just stepped outside to make this call. Penny's seriously pissed off. I'm needed here for a day or two, grounded. You're on your own. Penny's heading for Plymouth shopping and wants someone with her or else. What could I say? Harry, you'll understand, if I can't make it today…'

'No big deal. Give my best to your missus. I'll call you,' said Harry, not wanting his closest ally to feel pressured.

Harry could tell Stu was keen to get off the line and to be fair, Harry knew he owed him one. Stu had been ultra-loyal. Trouble was, he was now one guy down for the trip to Ottery. Phil would be driving. Then there was Wayne, Wayne who was increasingly rattling Harry with his bright, or rather not so bright ideas. Should he come to Ottery for the initial reconnoitre too? Wayne was a loose cannon, a possible liability.

He scratched his head and realised he didn't have the same crowd of mates to call upon as he'd had in the past. Life had moved on, passed him by even. Still more of them, like Stu had opted for domestic bliss rather than football and the pub. There could be little doubt that his time as an MP in London, short as it was hadn't helped. He'd been out of the scene. On return people's lives had moved on, others had been wary of him, steered clear, as if he were tainted goods whereas before he became a Plymouth MP he was the best thing next to white sliced bread. Back then he was everyone's best friend. Now, what was he, a mere footnote in history?

He needed to make more calls. First, he called Phil, only to be reminded that the Rovers were playing at home this very Saturday afternoon and there was no question where loyalty lay when it came to football. Harry told Phil he would see him and the others at the Home Park ground, usual seats, at 3pm, but he decided for his part to be ready with his wheels to get to Ottery straight after the match. Second, he tried to call Wayne, whose phone was switched off, deliberately so as Harry saw it, leaving Harry to conclude, it being Saturday, Wayne was sleeping in.

Harry made himself a third mug of coffee and searched round for some biscuits. This time he had the coffee black, having only now realised the queer flavour was not the hangover, giving him a bad taste in the mouth, but the milk in his earlier mugs had been on the turn. He called his Mum again and this time it was she who answered.

'Hi Harry,' she said in her cheerful voice, immediately putting Harry on his guard. 'I want us to meet up and I've asked Nick to drop me round at your house at 12. You'll be in won't you?' She'd taken control of the conversation which rather threw Harry who'd wanted to quiz her about Nick being on her mobile earlier.

'Yeah,' said Harry, not relishing the visit as his eyes rested on the surrounding detritus and mess, and that was only the kitchen. His Mum would have apoplexy when she saw it. She was the epitome of cleanliness and tidiness. It was in her

DNA. Perhaps she'd help tidy up? 'Ok, Mum, see you at 12. Tell me, where are you staying these days?'

'My sister's…' With that she'd gone.

Things never felt good after a headful of beer the night before, but this Saturday felt unusually depressing. No mates. No help at home. Mum and Nick! Hell, what was that all about? Was Nick after the business, he wondered, by getting in with the family, with his Mum? He should know, the fact was his Dad had left McNamara Metals solely to him. So what was he up to? And what was he doing at his Aunt Zoe's house with his Mum at 9am on a Saturday morning? He needed to find out what was going on and he would when his Mum came round. It was all so unsettling.

Since his Mum had walked out of the house leaving him to fend for himself he'd only had occasional calls from her, polite enquiries after his wellbeing. She'd never once been to see him and had kept a particularly low profile whilst Harry had been in parliament. He'd never understood that.

She should have been proud of him, stood up to the mark and supported him. For his part he didn't want to call her, mainly because he didn't understand her any more, suspecting she'd had some kind of breakdown with their fallout being about the time his Dad had the stroke. His Dad had been next to useless as well, making himself so ill like that, getting a stroke which did for him in the end. No hard feelings, he reminded himself, family is family after all, for better or for worse. Shame he got worse. Glad he lit a candle for him yesterday, the least he could do.

When his Mum called two hours later, she arrived with Nick at her side. The two marched in as if they owned the place and sat down in the kitchen, his Mum announcing they needed to talk. This was a deputation.

'Harry' she said with a confidence Harry didn't recognise in her voice, 'I never liked your politics and I kept out of it. I never liked you being an MP and then stealing public money like that. It made me feel dirty, ashamed.' She pushed Harry's mug and biscuit packet to the far end of the table in a hint of a tidying action. Nick picked them up and put them on the kitchen top.

'Well, Mum…' began Harry, only to be interrupted by his Mum raising a finger.

'I've got in touch for two reasons. The first is so that it's no surprise, so you can't say you heard it first from someone else. Nick and I are… good friends, seeing each other, just so you know. He's been very good to me and I feel much happier now.'

'Thought as…' The finger was raised again.

'And the other thing, the matter which concerns me most, is that your kind of politics is causing me grief, real grief and it's got to stop.'

'What? I'm not in politics any more. Suspended from the House. Read the papers, Mum!'

'You were mixing with the wrong people and now they're calling on me. You're into politics Harry, so stop kidding me. You're always the same…'

'Tell me who it is and I'll tell them to stop,' he offered wondering who was calling her.

'You can't tell these people to stop Harry. These are dangerous fanatics. I've been told to deliver you a message. The thing is, depending on what you do in response to it, it could be bad for Nick and for me. That's what they said. I need you to understand you can't go dragging us into your dirty politics. So do as they ask and tell them to keep away from us Harry… It… it frightens us.' There was a sudden quiver in her voice.

'These guys aren't messing. They want 100% cooperation or your Mum and I are done for,' interrupted Nick, reaching across to offer a comforting arm.

Harry felt a shiver go down his spine. He wasn't sure if it was seeing Nick comforting his Mum or past memories of extreme right wing activists hijacking his political campaign that had come flooding back. Back then they had wanted to use him as an access route to political power. Once he was in London they began making more demands, telling him how his party was to respond to this issue or that. He knew he'd had no choice. Getting caught fiddling his expense had in the end come as a relief, opening up a way of escaping them, offering him a way out. He thought they'd finished with him when he returned to Plymouth, but it looked like he'd been mistaken. This latest matter gave him a sinking feeling in his chest.

'Where's the message?' he asked solemnly, 'let me see it, and to make it quite clear, these people are not as you call them, my political friends.'

A strange expression crossed his Mum's face, a spontaneous mix of relief and worry.

'I was told I am the message and the messenger. It's been made clear to me that no written or electronic trail is to be left, so listen carefully. This is what I've been told to tell you. *"Harry McNamara is to become the South West of England contact for The Circle"*. Got that bit?'

'Yes...' Hearing The Circle's name, Harry saw his worst fears realised.

'I can see you know to whom I'm referring. I can see it in your face but don't ask me about them or how they gave me the message. They made it clear I mustn't say. Just listen as I tell you their words... As if reading from an actual script she continued, *"Apparently you have walked right into a murder investigation in East Devon and we want to recruit your services."'*

His Mum added, 'I don't know what that is, but Nick says that you were in Ottery St Mary for the Tar Barrels two evenings ago and he has since discovered that a politician's body was found in the bonfire. I don't know what you're into Harry, but The Circle had one final thing for me to tell you... *"Await our contact later today"*. That's it. That was all I had to say. I don't mind telling you I'm frightened, so I want you to sort this out Harry. Do the right thing and tell the police everything.

'That won't keep you or I safe, from these people, believe me,' said Harry. His Mum had stopped listening, her attention elsewhere.

'What a mess the place is in Harry. You need to get a grip, at least get someone in to do your skivvying for you While you sort yourself out, Nick and I need to go, no need to show us out.'

With that they abruptly got up from the table, Harry hearing the front door crash shut behind them. Then a distant car engine started up and he heard it pull away as they left the area. He was alone and his past had come back to haunt him.

There weren't many times in Harry's life when he felt outplayed and vulnerable, but his past encounter with the shadowy world of international right wing extremism was in an altogether different league to his dabble in populist politics. They had launched a vicious campaign of terrorism in the South West in the middle of his election campaign, played the politics of fear card to give his campaign a behind the scenes boost. Anti-immigration, fears for public safety, the people's voice not being heard – all on message with his own. And it had paid off, to everyone's surprise, including his own he'd been elected to parliament on a Britain First Democratic Party candidate ticket.

Throughout his time in parliament The Circle had been as close to him as a parasitic leech. They fed off him, they groomed and directed his political life. When a cross-party group was convened to go to the Middle East to look at how best to defend UK naval interests, it was Harry who found himself as a key member on their behind the scenes advocacy. He had to admit, he'd enjoyed visiting the naval base at Duqm, Oman and the hospitality offered by the new Sultan – such a westernised and civilised man facing such barbarian religious extremists at his every border.

But what did they want of him now, and what was their connection to the body in the bonfire? They couldn't know of his involvement in reporting it, or could they? Perhaps left winger Barry Thornton had crossed The Circle's path and had had to be dealt with. So who was the mysterious limping man from Ottery, was this now something more than a local vendetta, was he a member of The Circle?

Harry found he had many more questions than he had answers. He knew that at some point all would no doubt be made clear, but the thought that his Mum and Nick were somehow collateral should he step out of line was a salutary reminder of just who he was dealing with and how high the stakes were.

He got up and for the first time carried his dirty mugs and dropped them in the sink with a noisy clatter, but true to form he drew the line at running any water to wash them up.

10

It was nearly midday and Harry decided to head for the city centre to get something to eat. Owning a factory had the benefit of guaranteeing money in his pocket, not a lot, but more than enough to mean he could always eat out. For a change he thought he'd walk, after all his present physical condition needed some positive input. He made a mental note to rejoin the gym. He reckoned the walk down to the city centre would take him the best part of an hour. It would give him more, much needed, thinking time. The past few days were weighing heavily.

Some female company was needed and without thinking about it he gave Cherry Thomas a call. She'd been a press ally in his parliamentary campaign, an ace supporter, someone he could rely on, but of late their paths hadn't crossed. Why should they, he was old news become no news. She was also attractive, friendly and above all had the ability to brighten his day. To his delight, she replied, 'see you in fifteen minutes.' He slowed his walk.

He found himself at the front of the queue at MacDonald's in New George Street, and rather than wait, he ordered burger, fries and a shake and then tucked himself in a corner to quietly start consuming his brunch. A couple of young teenagers on a nearby table were throwing fries at each other. He stood up and told them to 'behave or get the fuck out of his space.' It was enough.

He returned to his table. He'd only turned his back a second, but as he looked round, there was his media friend Cherry coming across to join him to sit at his table occupying the seat opposite his own. She began stealing his fries until he asked her what she'd like. He went to fetch her order, returning a few moments later to place it in front of her with a smile.

'Why hello, Cherry. Long time no see.'

'Well you know how it is, always chasing the next story.'

'And grabbing fast food. What keeps you to town these days?'

'Nothing today. Day off, time to shop and chill... and...' she said, looking to engage Harry in a more intimate conversation.

Harry leaned forward. He could smell her perfume. He'd always liked Cherry, they had a compatible outlook, she'd a cheery smile, always played it steady. A respected girl amongst his friends with a good figure.

'I don't know how best to say this, Harry...' she said, dropping her voice.

'Say what? I'm all ears,' offered Harry smiling.

'I have a message for you from The Circle.'

Harry hadn't seen it coming. Another "*message*" and via Cherry too. His heart sank, and he felt cornered like a rat in a trap. He stayed sitting, leaning forward, up close, to catch her every word.

'Sorry Harry, but you know I have no choice and I'm only the messenger, nothing personal,' she offered, with a weak smile.

'OK...'

'He didn't give his name but just said he was The Master and you'd know him. He has a job for you. He wants you to go back to Ottery St Mary, go back there and ask for the limping man. That's it. Doesn't make any sense to me, but I expect you know what it's all about, so over to you. I've done my bit. Make any sense?'

'Sort of...' said Harry.

'Now just between us Harry, I don't want to be caught up in any more of this. It's well... unnerving, it comes with threats. I feel as if my own personal space has been invaded, so please, for the peace of mind of an old friend, tell your friends to stay off my back from now on.'

'Of course, Cherry, pops,' he offered reassuringly, her voice echoing those of his Mum and Nick earlier.

'Ottery's where that guy's body was found in the bonfire a couple of days ago wasn't it? It was you wasn't it, spotted it I mean?'

'Yep, I called the police when I saw it... The call on you by The Circle's not of my doing Cherry, believe me,' said Harry trying to look sincere, lifting up his hands to declare innocence. Cherry stood up to leave. He stood up too, adding, 'Any chance we might meet up, do this again, have brunch together I mean?' asked Harry smiling. 'Make up for lost time?'

'I'll think on that one Harry. You still at Ham Drive?'

'Yeah. Just me, my Mum's moved on…'

'Sorry to hear that, so soon after your Dad…'

'No, I mean she lives with her sister… She's fine, really…'

'And when are we going to see the new owner of McNamara Metals at some of the business events? The CBI are wanting to improve local infrastructure. Come along. I'm doing much more around business these days, it's where the money is.'

'And having brunch together?'

'Nice offer Harry. Perhaps somewhere nicer, a restaurant perhaps?' Seeing the puzzled look on his face, she turned with a smile and walked smartly out of the door, Harry's eyes following her trim figure.

Harry resumed his brunch, then went back to the counter to order himself a coffee. He was wondering what The Circle were doing. They'd twice sent him a message to go to Ottery to link up with the limping man.

A couple of things were really bothering him. The Master had clearly put the fear of God into family and friends when they could have simply contacted him directly. He could read gang culture and could see a gloved threat as well as the next gangster. They were trying to intimidate him.

They'd made a slight misjudgement there, a chink in their armour, a failure in their planning. He knew what they didn't. He didn't feel an undying loyalty to protect his Mum, Nick or Cherry. He was absolutely clear about that. To his mind they all had to fend for themselves in the world like he did. His Mum had walked out on him after all. Nick was after the family money and Cherry knew the dirty world she lived in. It was a dog eat dog world out there and only the wolf survived. He was the dominant wolf, a little out of condition maybe, but still top dog.

Something else was bothering him – the limping man. How the hell did The Circle know about the limping man in Ottery? Only Stu and he knew about him. His heart sank, maybe they got a knife at Stu's back too? In the world he was in, he now knew more than ever he was totally on his own. Any family, any friend he ever had was a target. He had to steel himself for what lay ahead, take any losses on the nose. He had a call to make.

'Phil, you made sure you're ready with your car for later?' he asked, 'just double-checking.'

'Sure Harry. See you outside the ground after the game. Usual place. Car's fuelled up and ready. Anyone else coming?'

'No just us,' said Harry, realising he'd just changed his plans and he'd be heading to Ottery in a solo enterprise with a chauffeur, his mission to find and meet the limping man. He turned his attention to the match and made for the ground.

It ended up a 1-0 win for Plymouth Rovers in a tense, nervy game, the result lifting everyone's spirits after a recent run of drawn matches. Pulling at Phil's sleeve straight after the final whistle Harry nodded toward the exit. Phil took his meaning and they drifted away from the others.

Within half an hour they were in the car and heading north, the grey November day already turning to darkness. There was a slight sense of discomfiture as they realised they were driving out surrounded by away fans heading in the same direction. Soon they were out of the city on a dark dual carriageway, the A38 heading north, looking for the A30 and the road to Ottery St Mary. Harry had been summonsed by The Circle and already he sensed their power weighing heavily upon him once again.

11

They travelled in Phil Pott's comfortable white Honda Accord, Phil lost to his music which was delivered almost hard wired straight to his brain through his new white Airbuds. His auditory cortex and temporal lobes located close to his ears – were perfect placed for instantly processing the throbbing heavy metal tunes. It didn't seem to affect his driving ability.

Harry likewise was in a world of his own, fully immersed in his thoughts. The journey should take about an hour he reckoned, but he had no idea what to do when he arrived. The uncertainty was unsettling him and making him fidget in his seat. He'd been caught out once and taken a pasting. If he wasn't careful, next time in Ottery could be much worse. As they were skirting Dartmoor, passing the Buckfastleigh turn off the A38, he interrupted Phil, prodding his upper arm for attention.

'You got your mobile with you? When we get there, keep it on in case I need you, OK?' he instructed.

'Sure Harry, I'll keep my phone on,' he replied nonchalantly before returning to his music which was playing too loud, clearly audible even to Harry. Those temporary lobes must throbbing or frying, thought Harry. Phil would be deaf by middle age.

Harry had a decision to make. There were two courses of action open to him. On the one hand he could risk going straight to 40 Yonder Street and make some direct face to face enquiries of the woman who lived there, but that offered an uncertain and unpredictable outcome. On the other hand, and little better, was the other option, to go directly to the Barrel Inn and start asking after a limping man. Either could backfire, lead to a beating or worse.

He pondered some more. He might have to do both. So which was the best starting point? He went with his instinct which told him to head for the Barrel Inn first, simply because he always felt at home in a pub and there were people about. He hoped they didn't know him in there. Once inside he could sound the place out, keep an ear to the ground, see what came up and have a pint. Anonymity and a pint, taken together – both would help.

Approaching 6.30pm they were dropping down the dead straight two mile run on the familiar Exeter Road into Ottery St Mary. The sign said 40 but Phil kept going at a steady 60. On the bends entering the town he touched his brakes, but not a lot. Then they swung left and right and into a one way system with slight squeals from the tyres, twice. Phil was announcing their presence. Harry would rather he'd didn't but kept quiet.

A supermarket car park showed to the left and at the last second Phil swung in with a third tyre squeal, before he began cursing a slow driver in front clearly looking for just the perfect place to park.

'Get a life, moron,' he yelled in frustration before pulling up in a very tight space next to a shopping trolley shelter. There was only just room for Harry to squeeze out.

'I'll wait here,' Phil stated, obviously quite happy to listen to his music. 'Might pop into the shop to pick up some stuff, but call me if you need me, Harry. I'll leave the motor unlocked so you can jump in if you're back before me.'

Harry headed off, took a zebra crossing behind a garage forecourt and headed up a dark alley which he guessed would take him into Mill St. He kept his wits about him. Dark alleys in Ottery had proved his undoing once already. Safely out the other end, he spied the Barrel just yards away at the near corner of The Square. He took another zebra crossing and with no heavy on the door this time, marched straight into the pub.

He was surprised how small it was. A space for darts to his left where some old cob walling had been revealed to show the pub's great age. A crackling real fire was burning to the right giving warmth and cosiness, the intimate bar not two paces in front of him. People pressed round him on every side, all cheerful. After a quick assessment had been made he concluded it was a typical, old style local, drinkers were mainly regulars on the beer, for the most part old timers. No problem he could spot and no limping man... yet.

Then he spotted the barrels of guest beers, lined up and racked on the back shelf to the left of the bar. His estimation of the pub rose exponentially as he recognised a place that valued its primary purpose – to see good beer was provided.

Harry moved across to eye the choices and after seeking advice from the youngster behind the bar went for a local Otter brewery session beer for starters. He watched as the young lad carefully delivered his pint, served with a decent head in a clean, straight glass. He paid up and looked round for somewhere to make himself at home.

Harry had to decide where to place himself. The place was so busy his options were limited. His eye fell on a corridor beside some stairs indicating there was yet more of this pub to be explored; space opened up as he walked further inside away from the street. There were sounds of a kitchen off to the left and a few gastro-tables set up for dining later, these were to Harry's mind, taking up valuable drinking space.

Sipping his beer, the lack of a second exit, something Stu had mentioned two evenings ago, nagged at him. He didn't like the feeling of entrapment sitting in the back of the pub, but there was nowhere else. Then again there were lots of ordinary local people around; their innocent presence made things feel safer.

He chose a seat in the corner where he could watch. Pub watching is an instructive activity. Small groups of men, a few couples, two young women, a family round the table in the window. After a minute, the lanky young lad from the bar came looking around collecting empty glasses, only to reappear again a moment later looking directly in Harry's direction. He'd been found!

Harry was immediately on his guard, sensing something was up. The lad stepped in closer. He seemed innocuous, no threat there.

Once up close, Harry was offered the lad's mobile with a nod. Not a word was exchanged. Harry took it as the lad wisely backed off a few paces before heading back to the bar, more customers waiting to be served.

'No Caller ID' shown, Harry noticed.

'Harry here,' he announced in as level a voice as he could muster. 'Whose this disturbing my quiet pint?'

'Good,' he heard, but no name was given. 'Bring yourself round to 40 Yonder Street when you've finished your pint.' With that the call was cut.

Progress. My, the local network worked well here. Harry was glad he'd been told to finish his pint. It gave him more thinking time. He decided to call Phil, just so he'd know where he was should either the cavalry be needed or revenge to be meted out.

'Hi Phil, done your shopping?' said Harry.

'Yeah! How long are you going to be, Harry?'

'Just so you know, I'm making progress. I've been called to a meet at 40 Yonder Street. Don't need you there, just want you to know if you need to get me or if I don't show in an hour, you know where to burn. Read me?' It was heavy handed and reckless but he reckoned he had to step up a level in dealing with The Circle.

'Yeah Harry, wait to pick you up or burn the house down in an hour.'

'Exactly.' Call over, Phil immediately went back to the supermarket to buy a lighter, a box of firelighters and an aerosol, just in case. He knew what to do. Keeping his head down, to avoid CCTV best he could, he paid in cash. He'd done it all before.

Meanwhile, Harry turned his attention to the third of his pint still remaining. He'd no idea who his mystery caller was. It didn't sound like the limping man, though he'd only heard his voice once and at a distance. He concluded it was probably just another messenger boy doing what he'd been told.

He didn't yet have a feel of what he was walking into. There was a veneer of local vendetta about things, local Labour councillor done over for messing with Tory wife. But below the surface there was The Circle's dark presence calling the shots and pulling him in. The two were linked somehow, but he had no idea how or what was being expected of him.

Usually, after a pint, Harry felt more relaxed, ready for a second and a third, but this evening he could feel the tension in his face and his stomach. His mind was as taut as a violin string. Even standing up from his chair he found himself trying to see if anyone was watching him.

The only hint of a clue was when he handed the mobile back to the lad behind the bar. He quickly turned away, but not before taking a look at a small row of photos, arranged in three groups – pictures of the try-it-on under agers, those not to be served and then separate, on its own with not a curled corner, his own mug shot. No doubt the lad had just confirmed his ID and he'd earn his reward. As he'd guessed the lad was a messenger boy.

Harry carefully exited into The Square and remembered his street craft. He looked right, where punches usually came from first, then left where a second guy would hang back to follow up. There was no give away whiff of tobacco on the air, no scuffing feet, no sound out of the ordinary. There was no one. He turned right and began walking, not fast but attentively. No one was following behind either.

7 p.m. Saturday night, a few cars on the street, a handful of ordinary pedestrians, a couple of lads and a girl with hoods up and nothing to do. He continued to the chip shop and crossed over, making his way slowly along Yonder Street, waiting for anything to happen. Nothing did.

In less than five minutes since leaving the pub he arrived outside the yellow front door of number 40 and waited again. Nothing. He pressed the doorbell firmly and detected its melodious tune. After six seconds, he counted, the door swung open wide. Standing in front of him, was one of the guys who'd jumped them two nights ago. He stood there like a giant immovable, intimidating statue, built like a tar barreller and probably was one. The higher they stand, the harder they fall Harry reminded himself, and pushed past to go inside.

'The name's Charlie,' he said. 'You'll be Harry. You're expected. Come in, take a seat.' All delivered smoothly and calmly, though there was something Harry detected that was not quite right about the guy. Harry heard the front door click shut behind him. He was inside, with no way out. Had this been wise?

The place looked familiar, just as when he'd leant through the window only yesterday morning. The settee where he'd left his note was just as it was, but he was shown the arm chair in the far corner to sit on. With the fire place to the right, it was the furthest seat from the door and he was firmly beckoned to take that seat. He sat down.

It was the waiting period, the time when pressure is placed using the control of time. It was being applied to Harry right now, but he knew how things worked and saw value in using the opportunity to relax himself, slow his pulse rate, increase his potential for a fast reaction time – something he prided himself on. As he calmed his body, so his mind sent him a message. It added to his sense of personal control – his brain told him they actually needed him.

'Drink, Harry? Understand you like the Otter Beer? Same again?' Charlie offered.

'That was my opening pint, until I was interrupted. I was going to go on to some stout. Got any?' Harry replied as cool as he could. Charlie disappeared into the rear kitchen.

He was left alone briefly. Being a small house, those in the back could not disguise their conversation. Another slight advantage Harry seized upon. He worked out very quickly that unless someone was being exceptionally silent, there were probably just three people in the house and the girl and the kids had been shunted off somewhere else, just to be safe.

Looking around, there was a gift for Harry down by his feet. The fire side set contained a useful metal poker. If required he'd make a grab for it and do some damage if he needed to defend himself. In the tight space, with him in the corner his odds were better than 3 to 1 had first seemed. If they wanted to get him, they could only approach him one at a time in this confined space and Harry was a well practised close quarter fighter. He began to wish he'd not neglected his weight training all these months, but could still count on his size.

The kitchen door opened and Charlie came back in with a full pint glass in each hand. No hostility in that. He offered the nearest to Harry, who gratefully accepted what he saw as his second weapon of choice. Glassing could do serious damage to a man's neck and face. He was not expected to get up, the beer passed down to him as he sat enveloped by cushions in the soft purple chair.

Charlie sat opposite on a simple wooden chair adjacent to the door and began sipping his pint, eye-balling him. In retaliating, the secret was not to eye-ball directly back, but to a spot slightly off line and behind his shoulder. It tended to unnerve the other person. The stare contest didn't last long. Charlie broke off and looked over in the direction of the kitchen. 1-0 to Harry!

Harry heard the distinct walk of the limping man before he saw him, the uneven sound of his pace giving him away. The kitchen door remained open and from where he was Harry couldn't see who had stayed behind, in case… That was unfortunate, a glass and a poker might be useful in most circumstances but a gun or knife trumped both. The balance of control still rested with his hosts.

The limping man had a military bearing about him, and he clearly paid close attention to keeping his appearance smart. Maybe he'd been invalided out of the forces, thought Harry, a man not to be underrated. He looked at the man's face, especially his eyes. It was a square, clean shaven face with deep set eyes and pronounced dark brown eyebrows. There were traces of scar lines down the left side of his cheek, possibly from an old glassing, but it was the eyes that intrigued Harry. They were dead, unusually dark eyes, showing not a trace of emotion, giving nothing away.

'I've asked Charlie to stay, Harry, I know you won't mind,' he said, his words coming out in a monotone line. 'He's useful in case I need anything.'

'So he's good at fetch and carry. Bit like having a dog. Get a drink for him, that kind of thing. They're good with simple commands. Yeah, I can see he has his uses. Let him stay,' said Harry, adding some tension of his own into the mix. He heard Charlie shuffle on his seat.

'Harry, I'm so glad you decided to come over and see me. You see, The Circle has a proposal to make.' He clipped his string of words with a military edge that settled the matter to Harry's mind. Limping man was definitely ex-military.

'Where did you see service?' interjected Harry, as if he hadn't noticed what he'd been told, 'Afghanistan, Iraq?'

Harry had taken an inspired guess as the man's love for the far right had to have roots somewhere and it was probably one of those recent military conflicts that prematurely ended his active days and given him the limp.

'Iraq since you ask. I had the misfortune of being a prisoner of the Islamist insurgency. It ended my military career, just like a Middle Eastern exploit on your part ended your political career, Harry McNamara.'

'Touché,' replied Harry raising his glass. Harry sensed Limping Man was trying to build a conversation intended to go somewhere other than a bruising fight. They needed him, he began to relax.

'You caused us a problem Harry by putting your nose in the trough to illegally help yourself to public funds. We were counting on you to give us more access and influence over the government than you proved able to deliver. Such a disappointment.'

'I've paid the price. It was just a misunderstanding over expenses as you know. All still under investigation, just a temporary setback…'

'But that wasn't how the House Public Accounts Committee saw it. They brought your glorious political career to a premature end, suspended you, chucked you out. Let's let bygones be bygones, shall we Harry. The world has moved on and new opportunities present themselves. We live in a new era of populist politics and this government is embracing our ideas and those sympathetic to us. It's happening everywhere. Lefties are on the run Harry, on the run. There's a mood to protect our borders and look after our people, to make our country great again. England, people have remembered has become a cause worth defending and pride is returning.'

'You could be right there, but before we discuss politics, hadn't we better properly introduce ourselves. You are…?'

'Christian Howard, representing a new more open "Circle" ready for the new age of populist politics. The question is Harry McNamara, are you ready to step into the new age or are you a dinosaur, about to be extinct?' he said, without a flicker of life in his eyes.

'Let's get to the point and cut to the chase Mr Howard. My time is precious to me, but let me correct you on one point. I'm still having the misunderstanding in the House investigated and in the meantime enjoying some much deserved furlough. What is it you want?'

'We'll come to that presently. Tell me, is it true that you wholly own McNamara Metals since your father's demise?'

'Yes…' said Harry hesitatingly, wondering where the conversation was going.

'Good. We will need you to make a few adjustments to your site management arrangements in order for us to do some business with you. We need you to receive some special deliveries, items for secure storage. Are you able to accommodate us Mr McNamara?'

'Well… I leave day to day business matters with my manager…'

'You will need to take a more hands on approach don't you think? It would be prudent to do so if you were to maintain your interest, don't you think?'

'I'm not sure…'

'Don't you think My Grayson is taking advantage of his position? Getting his leg over, pulling a fast one, don't you think?'

'Hmmph… ' was all Harry could manage to say, his mind racing. He was caught on the back foot. He desperately needed to get back some of the initiative.

'This might take a little time, but be assured, we aim to please at McNamara Metals. What exactly have you in mind?'

'I'll take that to be your agreement in principle that we move forward. Excellent. I really think you should go. Your friend might be feeling uncomfortable by now.'

Harry's pulse raced, a real threat lay in those words, menace behind those dead eyes and his mind turned to Phil waiting in the car park. Charlie was getting to his feet. Harry took this to mean the meeting was over and as in these matters, things would follow on in their proper course. He left half his beer un-drunk, a very rare occurrence.

Harry left feeling wrong-footed, the underdog, manipulated and vulnerable. Charlie, looking smug, moved and stood in his own doorway making Harry squeeze by into the dark street.

As Harry walked he hoped Phil had kept his wits about him, but feared he'd be oblivious to the world around him, his white Airbuds anaesthetising his awareness of what was going on. Harry had one thing on his mind, to get back to the car park. The words, "your friend might be feeling uncomfortable by now", ringing loud alarm bells in his own ears.

12

Harry walked briskly, full of apprehension. It took two minutes to get back to The Square and as he swung right between an Estate Agents and a needlework shop heading for the car, he sensed something was very wrong. This was the worst moment, the period of anticipation.

Ahead of him in the one way system, waiting to turn into the supermarket car park there was a stationary queue of vehicles. Nothing strange about that as such. However, a few paces on and he could smell it, fire, always fire when he came to Ottery. Not bitumen or bonfire this time, but the smell of plastic and cellulose paint accompanied by the warning shouts of people. These were not the excited shouts of barrel night, but cries of alarm and fear for personal safety and property.

Edging his way forward and fearing the worst, Harry could see that a fire tender was already at the scene spraying down a row of cars and what was left of a still smoking plastic trolley shelter. In the centre of all the mayhem was Phil's Honda Accord, barely visible through the hissing clouds of smoke and water spray.

Supermarket staff in hi-vis jackets from the store had been recruited to strengthen a protective cordon and were urging people ever further away under the watchful command of the lead fire officer. Some in the crowd were taking selfies. Where was Phil? Harry wondered. He couldn't see him and pushed himself ever closer to the Honda. At first his eyes tricked him, but the white of the car wasn't polished paintwork, but bare, hot metal.

Harry knew this was no accident. The words hurrying him back were still ringing in his ears, *your friend might be feeling uncomfortable*. Harry couldn't see into the car, he couldn't make out whether Phil was inside. The night was dark, the smoke intense, the crowds and stewards obstructing his view. What the hell, he gave a shoulder shove and got himself to the front.

A heavy arm grabbed his own shoulder, and someone began pushing him back with a restraining hand. Luckily Harry checked himself from retaliating and hitting the policeman just in time. In seconds Harry was back on the road nowhere near being able to see Phil's car.

Still no sight of Phil. Then another, lighter tap on the shoulder.

'What's happening Harry? Where's the action?' asked Phil, standing beside him, having appeared from nowhere.

'Your car's… a write-off,' said Harry hesitatingly, pointing though the smoke.

Phil was dumbstruck. 'I just popped over to the pub. You were taking so long, I just went for a pint and a piss. I left it open like you said. Lucky we weren't in it. What the fuck happened? Did you see?'

'We've been sent a message,' said Harry.

'What do you mean?' asked Phil.

'In my experience this town uses fire instead of conversation, that's all. You'd better go and talk to the firemen and explain it's your motor and you've no idea why it caught on fire.

Don't go mentioning me, I'd rather not be asked why I'm near two fires in two days. Police don't like those sort of coincidences. Then you'll need to arrange to get it cleared. The supermarket will want their carpark back. Guess it'll be so hot you can leave your pile of metal there until morning. Try and line up a breakdown truck or maybe a skip would be better. Good luck! I'm going back to the pub. Find me there when you're done. I'll be in the Barrel.'

Harry had no wish to be identified. Hanging around the fire served no useful purpose other than to draw unwelcome attention to himself.

Phil ambled off toward the mayhem. When Harry got to the pub he found it was still pretty full, now with early evening restaurant goers outnumbering the beer drinkers. There was a lot of chatter going on. His seat in the corner was still free. He took his beer over and made himself at home, relaxing knowing there shouldn't be any more trouble.

As he ordered his next pint he confirmed what he'd suspected that there was no local taxi in the town. He then asked the lanky barman the time of the last bus to Exeter. The off-hand reply, 'ten past eight.' He clearly wasn't wanting to engage in further conversation. That gave Phil under an hour to sort things. Harry sent him a text message with his deadline for departure.

Sipping his beer slowly, Harry kept a careful eye on everyone and everything. Most people could be forgotten about in an instant, only one or two were of interest. A Saturday night drugs sale was being quietly transacted between two young guys, careless as to whether they were being observed. There were two other men, football types, drinking after a match and two young women casting occasional gazes in their direction.

A horrifying thought struck Harry, that it could so easily have been Phil Potts burned to death in his car like Barry Thornton was burned to death in the bonfire. There were expectations being underlined, hard messages being sent, that Harry himself would deliver what was being requested of him or else. He understood the language of ruthlessness and fear. It was what he himself had grown up with as a football supporter and politician. You did what was necessary. It was what he called, human economics, a very basic but effective transactional approach to getting what you wanted from people. He knew full well what was going on and the stakes were high.

They'd be counting on him reading the car fire as a warning, a shot across the bows. It went along with all the other intimidation and subterfuge that had filled the past two days. He didn't expect any more trouble tonight and settled into what remained of his third Barrel Inn pint of the evening before going over to the bar get a fourth. The lanky lad had good survival instincts and was deliberately keeping well clear of any engagement with Harry.

Harry had to think hard. The Circle had expectations of his business, but both they and he knew he wasn't exactly running it. That was all left to Nick. The assumption being made was he would step up to the mark and take over. Easier said than done. He'd need to have a meeting A.S.A.P. with Nick and tell him his intentions, the bad news. How he'd achieve this would need careful planning. Maybe Nick was anticipating Harry would muscle in at some point which partly explained why he was trying to secure his own position by sweet talking his Mum.

When push came to shove, Harry knew he himself held all the aces. So that part of things should prove manageable. It might be simply a matter of telling Nick he was giving him a paid sabbatical in recognition for the sterling work he'd been doing. There must be a way…

His mind turned to Phil. Phil's car was nothing. He'd just need to sort it through the insurance and get another. Phil was naive, knew nothing, probably best kept that way. Harry had told him to explain it as a simple car fire, bad luck, it happened all the time, Phil should know…

Harry didn't like being pushed off his pedestal. He was used being top predator. His feeling was he needed to get back onto his home turf in Plymouth and start thinking how to stay safe and regain control. He didn't like The Circle pulling all the strings, using the people close to him. He'd best start thinking about how to defend himself once back home, back at base.

He wanted or rather needed his own wheels again and soon, so his next call was to Ian Drake, the body repair man who'd taken his red Audi in his workshop yesterday morning.

'Yes', Harry told him, 'I'm not stupid, I realise its Saturday night, but if you still want McNamara Metals' business in future you needed to get the dents in the Audi mended pronto and any respraying done by Monday. I need my wheels.' After all the difficulties had been voiced and Ian had fully appreciated Harry was taking no prisoners, it was agreed, and Harry smiled with satisfaction as he was told he'd get his car fixed as requested.

It was nearly eight. Harry called Phil and told him to come to the bus stop outside the butchers next to the Barrel. 'Make your excuses and get over here or you'll be walking back to Plymouth on your own.'

Five minutes later and Phil was next to him at the end of a small queue of people.

'Bloody lost my Airbuds too,' said Phil, as the mud splattered single decker bus pulled to a halt and the queue slowly shifted inside the half empty bus.

'They started asking me if I'd set the car on fire myself. Who do they think I am, some kind of insurance fraudster? I told them what's what. Trouble was they reckoned there was some kind of accelerant used to start the fire. I've left them to it. Fire's out now and there's tape going up around the site to keep people out.'

'Did you do what I said? Keep me out of it?'

'Yeah… yeah… no worries.'

Harry was getting fed up with bus travel. It was all too slow and by the time they got back to Plymouth after a cold wait in Exeter it was late. Once Phil had gone his separate way home, Harry phoned Nick Grayson.

'Yeah, I know it's late, but business is business and it can't wait. We need to meet first thing… I know it's Sunday tomorrow… Too many people don't seem to know the days of the week! Be there! Be at the factory first thing for 9.00 a.m.. We'll meet in your office.'

Harry could feel the raw edge of power being exercise and Nick Grayson crumbling at the other end. He had really no choice in making the call, now did he?

13

At 8 a.m. Sunday morning Harry put on his last, new, clean shirt. Striped and business-like, it had remained unopened for months, but today it was just perfect. He made a call to Sheena and succeeded in getting her to agree to come round that morning whilst he was out. She promised to clean up and as she was out shopping herself later, would be sure to buy him a fresh supply of shirts for the coming week and drop them by. He called an Uber and waited. Hungry as he was, he'd wait before eating and planned to start his meeting with Nick by getting him to sort coffee and croissants.

Feeling he might be out of his depth at a business meeting he grabbed his tablet, opened a fresh page and began listing all the things he wanted from the forthcoming session. Looking down the completed list, he knew for certain Nick wouldn't like it, not one bit. Too bad, needs must.

Then Harry searched for and found his Father's set of keys to the office, they'd lain untouched in the sideboard drawer ever since he made his final visit to hospital a year ago. As for security, he'd always known the alarm password. He counted on the fact that most people were too laid back about passwords and never bothered changing them. Harry was confident that when he tapped in the 6 digit password, 230640 he'd get into the offices. Until now he'd only ever gone into the business as a curious visitor. Today already felt very different.

As he recalled the alarm number sequence he remembered the numerous past factory visits with his Father. They were made in the days when his father entertained the forlorn idea that Harry might one day join the family firm his grandfather had established. For some reason the six number code going through his head seemed vaguely familiar, important even. The sequence certainly must have meant something to his father, why else would he have chosen them? However, for the moment, he couldn't for the life of him think what their significance might be.

He had organised himself to get to the factory early and the Uber dropped him outside at twenty minutes before nine. He used the padlock key on his Father's key ring to open and then re-lock the outer metal gate. Walking the thirty metres across the yard used for parking he made straight for the offices. He found the front door key opened the main entrance door as he knew it would.

Once inside, the alarm beeper began its insistent electronic two tone call clamouring for attention. Thankfully it fell silent as soon as Harry hit 230640. He then made his way upstairs, pushed open Nick's office door, then paused to stand still on the threshold and look around.

Harry had always been a strong believer in careful observation. He sometimes thought that in another life he might have made a good policeman. Rushing in meant important things might get overlooked. His instinct for observing things had meant he once spotted trouble at a football stadium in Turkey, a crucial moment that had prevented a terrorist incident and had gone on to shape the future course of his life. For the first time here he was keen to closely observe what he saw in the factory, bringing to the task his fresh set of eyes.

Ahead of him was an old oak desk. It had been placed centrally, its top clear of all pen holders, paper clip trays and other office bits and bobs. It reflected a tidy and organised mind perhaps. It was probably his father's and grandfather Michael's desk before him – it spoke of a strong sense of unchanging continuity and loyalty within the firm. It was the factory nerve hub, its centre of control, and the boss's throne.

A large Chinese wall painting, with elegant white cranes in a rural landscape standing by flowing water, graced the wall ahead. It was tastefully done, probably an original art work, maybe a gift from a grateful client. It possibly reflected the new direction business had taken in recent years since they started sending metals for recycling to China, using shipping containers.

A tastefully, and he guessed expensively fitted, new wall to wall suite of office cupboards and cabinets graced the left hand side of the room. Opposite, to his right, the slatted blades of a light blue blind shuttered the wide window, a window looking over the newly gated entrance, yard below and main factory site to his right. Prosperity and security, he thought.

There was a single small table to the right, just inside the office door and two smart black office chairs either side which could be pulled forward for the use of visitors. The floor was still the oak parquet of old, but looked like it had been given a recent makeover and shone brightly. It was another sign of business prosperity. In sum, the heart of the business exuded a prosperous feel, it was evidently going well. Something was missing. Harry looked round again and wondered where the IT was.

He got up and walked slowly round the oak desk and sat himself down where his father and grandfather had sat before him. A sudden feeling of destiny and power took hold of him and he clenched the desk firmly with both hands. It was like being at the football or in politics. He suddenly made a connection – business meant power. For the first time in his life business held a certain, though as yet unformed, attraction for him. He sat and waited, feeling like a king on a throne.

He looked down. There was a drawer pull. He put his hand to it and smooth as a Rolls Royce, a clever, hidden mechanism silently rolled out a lap top on a working surface right in front of him. Nice, he thought, I like it. Just the thing to impress visitors. He touched the handle again and the device folded and retracted back out of sight.

In the quiet something clicked in his head. It was a date, the 23rd June 1940, the alarm numbers, 230640. It was the date Grandpa Michael sent his first letter home from the German POW camp signalling he was alive. The letter was with his stuff, in the metal trunk at the end of Harry's bed. He'd often read it. Got it! That's why the alarm had that number! It felt good to know his memory and sharpness of mind were working, but he needed that coffee. He checked the time. Good! Nick was due any minute.

Then he heard the metal factory gate swing open and a car sweep in and park down below. He got up and peered down through the slatted blind. It was indeed Nick, in a smart dark blue BMW. His footsteps echoed across the yard as he walked toward the front door. Then there was a pause as he no doubt registered that Harry had disarmed the alarm and was already in the building.

'Harry,' he heard him shout from the stairwell, 'You there?'

'Up here, in your office,' he replied, sitting down once again, leaning back in Nick's surprisingly comfortable black leather chair. He carefully placed his own tablet on the desk top with his prepared agenda displayed.

When Nick saw Harry had invaded his space, he was totally bewildered and at a loss what to do. Harry for his part, couldn't but enjoy watching him, seeing the slow cogs turning in his head, Nick floundering with his mouth opening and shutting like a goldfish, uncomprehending with nowhere to go except round and round in circles. It was Harry who moved things on.

'Come on pull up a chair, we've things to do,' said Harry taking the initiative and beckoning him forward. He was beginning to enjoy this. To Harry's surprise Nick did as instructed and pulled up one of the chairs from beside the door and sat in front of his own desk waiting to hear what Harry would say next.

'Nick, what do you do for coffee and breakfast round here? Can you sort something?'

'Uh! Coffee and biscuits may be. Over there…'

Nick obediently stood up and opened one of the swish cupboard doors. There was an inbuilt coffee machine in bright red. A minute later it began to hiss and bubble as Nick rattled a couple of cups. Harry sat quietly.

'White without sugar?' interrupted Nick.

'Black, no sugar.'

'Will chocolate digestive biscuits do, it's all there is?' he added.

'I was hoping for croissants, but fine…'

Five minutes later they both had their coffees. Only Harry ate the biscuits, crumbs scattering over the clean desk. He eyed Nick carefully.

Nick went to sit back down in front of the desk. He looked at Harry drinking his coffee and waited.

'Nick, I want you to give me a quick heads up on how the business is doing. You know, turnover this year compared with last year, projections for next year, plans you have, you know the kind of thing. Just the important headlines Nick, not the detail, right.'

'OK, off the top of my head. Business figures this year are based on the projections we made a year ago. We're ten months into the year and turnover will be around…'

'What's turnover?'

'Our gross income before profit, i.e. all the money coming in from our contracts.'

'Understood. So what's the projected ball park figure for turnover this year then?'

'We've two months left and turnover looks set to touch £450,000, maybe a little bit more, but I'm being conservative. I don't like to count chickens…'

'And after all the bills are paid and the employees are paid what kind of profit is the business making on that £450,000?'

'It's not that simple to say…'

'Try me. Start me with a gross profit figure, before we have to pay all the insurance and bean counters…'

'Around £80,000, leaving us with a healthy net profit margin of around £45,000.'

'That seems OK. But being prudent and conservative must mean you keep sensible reserves to meet unexpected shortfalls and expenses. How much are we holding in the bank so to speak?'

'Well, your grandfather and father were always very careful not to over-extend the business. They'd known good times and bad, the booms and the crashes, so they built up a capital rich business, to protect it, and there's a cash wall so to speak…'

'Yeah. Does that mean the business has no debt?'

'Not exactly. Look at it like this. The business owns outright the site it sits on, the buildings and plant and the extensive area of land where we handle all the scrap metal, some twenty acres of prime industrial land. In addition we've more than enough cash in the bank to cover us for at least six months ahead if revenue suddenly stopped coming in.'

'And why "*not exactly*". Are there some debts somewhere in the business? Tell me.'

'Yes, when new machinery is bought it is often beneficial for business tax and other reasons… to take advantage of purchase arrangements by lease or loan. We have some of those.'

'And how many employees do we have currently?'

'Thirty one, maybe thirty two.'

'So I'm right in thinking we're doing nicely?'

'Yes, but every business has to look to where it grows next'

'Which means…'

'We're heavily reliant on trading scrap metal from the UK and selling it on to China. But… the Chinese economy is slowing, for various reasons and there are new competitors entering the field. Our supply side looks at greater risk with fewer motor vehicles being scrapped, less metal on the market for us to sell on.'

'Plymouth is a naval city. Plenty of scrap at the dockside isn't there?'

'Yes, but we've never had a look in there. Maybe with your political experience and naval connections you might…'

'No chance… Any plans looking ahead?'

'We reckon we might make a good arrangement with a South Wales based company. I've done the sums. If we sign off before Christmas it can kick in from 1st Jan. Could add another 10% to turnover next year, so long as the Chinese market stays stable…'

'Ever thought of selling the business?'

'Never! Your grandfather and father would turn over in their graves at the very thought.' The look of horror on his face at the very mention of selling was genuine enough.

'OK. What about buying up any competitors, expanding the business that way…?'

'We keep an eye on that but no opportunities worth taking have arisen, well not yet…'

'Can you do more coffee, Nick? Rustle up another will you. I need to think,' said Harry, once more throwing Nick off track.

Nick busied himself as before, giving Harry his coffee before returning to his seat.

'Nick. As sole owner of this business I've a proposal to make to you, you can take it or leave it.'

'What is it Harry?' Nick asked, shuffling uncomfortably.

'I want you to take a three month sabbatical starting tomorrow, well right now, this very minute to be precise. I may need to call on you from time to time, so keep your mobile handy.' Nick's jaw dropped. This was totally unexpected.

Harry continued, 'You've earned it… the sabbatical, I mean. It seems to me we can afford to keep you on and you'll be paid whilst you're off. It'll give me a chance to get the feel of things, what it's like to take the reins of my business.' He let the final two words sink in.

'But Harry, you don't know anything about running the business…' he pleaded.

'We'll see about that. Everyone has to start somewhere. Grandpa Michael started from nothing. It's in the DNA. No worries there Nick. If it goes down the pan, you'll need to put it back together again. But if you're saying you've no confidence in the future of the business we could look to terminating your employment forthwith, if that's what you're wanting…'

Now Nick was squirming in his chair, sweat appearing on his pale brow, his little moustache jumping at the corner. A rabbit in the headlights.

'No, no. That's fine,' was all he could say mumble, a bundle of nerves.

'First, what's the password for the laptop here?' he asked pulling the desk handle to allow the equipment to glide into place… and do tell me the name of your PA these days. Father talked about… Elsa wasn't it? Is she still working here?'

Nick nodded, 'She's in tomorrow. The PC password is Chinesecracker99, first C is a capital. Elsa's been with us several years… She'll help you. Can I just collect one or two things?' Harry's instincts were alerted and he fired back.

'Afraid not. Call Elsa tomorrow. Take yourself off site. Leave now on your sabbatical and you can come back in three months. Piss me around Nick Grayson and you're fired, understood?'…There was a pause before Harry raised his voice, 'I said, understood?'

'OK, Harry. Yes, understood. I'm going.' He put his half drunk coffee cup down on the little table by the door and turned to look back at Harry. Perhaps it was a last look at the world he was losing control of. It was a mistake, it gave Harry a further thought.

'Oh, and before you go Nick, leave your car keys on the desk there will you. It's a works car and I'm working today, you're not. I need it. You're on sabbatical.' Rain was beating hard on the window. 'It's only a shower. I hope you have an umbrella with you.'

The key's jangled as Nick dropped them on the table. His footsteps retreated down the stairs and Harry heard the front door open and close behind him. Nick had been disposed of.

That turned out better than I could have imagined, he thought. After what I've just done, The Circle should be well satisfied!

14

Nick left the building with no umbrella, his head down and suit collar turned up. It was more than a shower, it was a downpour. His upturned collar was a futile gesture against the heavily falling rain. A cold wetness was already seeping down to his skin.

Harry knew full well Nick would be getting very wet; tough! His echoing, footsteps could be heard retreating across the puddled yard; the gate clanging shut and then silence. He was literally out on the street, gone.

Harry knew Nick would be feeling unhappy, angry even, but he would either have to adjust to the new realities or get out. Working with clear binary options had always served Harry well and if Nick didn't get it, too bad. He told himself that the first lesson of business was one had to be sharp and on top of the game. Sitting in the executive chair he felt very sharp and every bit in control.

He thought he'd spend a bit of time whilst he was in the office seeing what was on Nick's laptop. Then he'd set an agenda for Elsa ready for Monday morning. He had in mind meeting her first thing tomorrow at 9 a.m.

The coffee machine held a certain fascination and Harry quickly mastered how to operate it, a freshly inserted executive pod of Columbian finest grounds was soon steaming, sending him a quality aroma as he made his third cup of the day. Going back to his desk he sat again in the soft but supportive black leather executive chair and reflected on his new position.

Some things were very good, others not so. He was in control. That was good. He wondered whether he should have challenged Nick about his relationship with his Mum whilst he was on the back foot, but business was business. This unresolved issue would need to wait to be dealt with, certainly until he knew how best to approach it. Relationships, he knew, were not his strong point.

That he'd discovered the company was basically thriving and profitable was a bonus, something exceptionally good. He told himself he couldn't go wrong now, could he? He was in a strong position to go back to The Circle and see what was required of him. It had all happened so much faster and with much less hassle than he could have possibly anticipated.

He pulled on the desk handle and Nick's laptop swung into position. He flipped it open and typed in the password Chinesecracker99. It burst into life with a desktop papered with blue envelope files, all clearly labelled and lined up in neat rows like soldiers on parade. Harry scanned them in turn. Boring, boring, boring. How could Nick stand the job unless he was boring too? Probably was.

Next, Harry went into Nick's email box and began a search, not for business messages, but for any that he might have sent to his Mum. There was nothing in either the inbox or sent box. He was about to forget the idea when he spotted the junk, trash and archive files and switched his search there. Bingo!

Deleted files stay in the trash until the inbuilt programme removes them some months later; there they were, numerous personal messages, maybe sent once or twice a day, going back over three months. Anything earlier had gone into the ether. He began to go through them. He realised he was prying and it felt like going through a dirty laundry basket, a world he was reluctant to enter.

It was so uncomfortably personal, he could hear their voices in his head as the two exchanged ever more personal messages making evident their growing affection for one another. After a few minutes he didn't want to read any more, so much so that he was on the point of shutting the laptop down, but something else caught the corner of his eye.

An exchange of emails dated 12th October, not a month ago, pulled him up short . He'd spotted his own name:

"My dear ......, since you ask, I feel very happy running the firm and Harry seems content enough to have it this way. He has never once meaningfully shown his face here or indeed shown the slightest interest which is just as well, though it remains of real concern that I still have to get his periodic signature for this and that. Thinking ahead, perhaps we could arrange for him to receive a little more of an honorarium than he does presently and in exchange sign the whole business over to us. I'll see if our company secretary can get the ball rolling and draw up the necessary paperwork for him to sign himself out of things..., it would secure our future together, your dearest, Nick"

in reply his Mum had written:

"Dear Nick, I never understood why my late husband made the firm over to Harry. Harry never had any flair for business, he only ever cared about football. If you think it would be for the best, do go ahead and make the arrangements. As you know, Harry and I are not in communication, yours, ..."

127

Harry crashed his fist on the desk with such force his coffee cup clattered. It was just as well Nick had left, how he was feeling toward him right now, he could have happily smashed his fist into his face. The thieving, conniving bastard! His next thought was that Nick was going to be facing more than a sabbatical, the guy was deserving a more permanent exile.

The email discovery meant Harry's resolve to get to grips with running the business only strengthened. If his grandfather and father had managed to do so, then why the hell shouldn't he? He quickly scanned through the remaining emails between Nick and his Mum but they were of no consequence. Against his natural inclination, he looked again at the neat rows of blue files on the desktop and decided, boring as they appeared, to systematically work through then one by one.

He had to skim over masses of stuff to identify what was significant. It was the only sensible thing to do, he just didn't have the time to read everything. The more recent files were the ones he more carefully scrutinised and gradually over the next hour and a half, fortified with still more coffees, he found he was gaining a picture of what was his.

His conclusion was that it seemed Nick had given him a pretty accurate picture of things earlier and everything appeared to be as reassuringly prosperous and successful as he'd said it was. However, what Nick had omitted tell him was that there had been an approach from a local major land owning company, OKEL (Only Kernow Estates Limited) who were wanting to purchase part of the prime business land they owned. So far as Harry could see McNamara Metals were not using that area of their extensive site and to sell it could make a tidy sum judging by the figures being offered. So why wasn't Nick selling? He'd need to do some digging around.

There were two other potential problems Harry noticed. The first was the need to re-negotiate the scrap deal with their Chinese scrap recipients and the second to deal with a personnel issue. One of the crane operators had been accused of bullying one of the female office workers. It appeared Sean Murphy had a group of other employees all lined up to say he was as innocent as a nun.

Harry wasn't good at reading accounts but he had a quick mind and soon seemed to find his way around. He quickly found he had a list of questions for Elsa for the morning. One of the key questions he had was who did what round here? He need her to provide him with a list of names and job descriptions against them. A strong believer in delegation, he wanted to be sure to have the key people running the place briefed by him A.S.A.P.. He'd need to see them in turn, another item on the list for Elsa. Finally, he added to his list, see Sean Murphy. He wanted to know what kind of guy this alleged bully was, maybe someone he now had leverage over, someone he might recruit to the cause?

By 1 o'clock he'd had enough, but strangely felt a new sense of purpose and power. The business was all of a sudden more than it had been cracked up to be. It was his to control. He could call the shots. Then he recalled the limping man, Christian Howard and his interest in the firm. Harry had secure control of his domain, he needed to get the measure of Christian Howard who had, so far, called all the shots. Harry liked to be the only top gun.

He felt it was worth doing some more homework on what he had stumbled into in Ottery. He had gone there to enjoy a night out, but also to begin his local recruitment drive to revitalise his flagging Britain First Democratic Party. People had short term memories when it came to political misdemeanours and his plan was to get himself back in the House at a future date. Over the coming weeks he intended to get out to a number of the local Devon towns to see what the political landscape looked like and see if he could recruit supporters to the cause.

Becoming a reputable businessman at the helm of McNamara Metals could only strengthen his new political campaign. Local talent in Ottery St Mary had a raw appeal. He'd seen the barrellers, how they worked the crowd, how they'd bundled Stu and himself in that alleyway. They were just the kind of popular grass root guys he needed and nothing had changed that first impression since his first night in the town. What bothered him was the cuckoo in the nest – Christian Howard. What on earth was he doing there and what was he up to? What were The Circle up to?

Harry definitely needed to do some more digging. He decided it was time to find Stu and picked up the BWM car keys off the table with a smile and a swagger. He flicked a switch and watched with satisfaction and amazement as the laptop disappeared into the desk.

Downstairs, he re-set the alarm, locked up the office door and two minutes later was smoothly pulling away in a luxury motor, insulated in the warm and dry, the wiper blades silently, efficiently, sweeping away the lashing rain.

Harry felt a new day was dawning, he was on the up, though there was much to be done to be certain he had secured his rise.

15

No one was more surprised than Stu when Harry pulled outside his house in the smart BMW.

'Jump in,' he told him without a word of explanation. 'We've got things to do.'

They drove down to the water front and found a space near West Hoe Park. Harry took Stu to an upbeat bar in Grand Parade where they could look out over the grey waters of the Sound as they sipped their beers and had a meal in a basket lunch.

'I've taken over the day to day running of McNamara Metals. Decided it was a useful move. It protects my interests and gives me a base.'

'And the car?'

'Comes with the job. I can put the red Audi away, keep it for special occasions. But there are things I want you to do…'

'Yeah, Harry.'

'The party's been neglected of late, so there's things to fix. First though, I need some intel.'

'Yeah, about what?'

'Like why local lefty, Barry Thornton ended up in a bonfire; like why Limping Man Christian Howard is flexing his muscles; how's that for starters Stu - mastermind in the dark arts, social media whizz!' he teased.

'I'll get right on to it, ask about, make a few searches. It'll take some time.'

'You'll need to be very discreet,' said Harry with a steely gaze, 'These guys don't mess around. I'll drop you home. Then we're going back to Ottery tonight. I'll pick you up around 6-o 'clock.'

'OK, Harry.'

It was just after 2-o 'clock when Harry dropped Stu back at his house before driving himself the further five minutes home. The BMW, like his Audi was German engineering. That fact appealed. It was a solid, reassuring, superior car. The smooth comfort of the new BMW just did not compare with his old Audi. The BMW's extra electronic gadgetry significantly improved his driving experience. He thought he'd put it through its paces, see what it could do when he took Stu to Ottery later.

Back in Ham Drive, he pushed open his front door and was pleasantly surprised. There was a perfumed smell of polish which to his mind even added a clean sparkle to the air. Looking around, he could see, joy of joys, Sheena had been in. A pile of new shirts was stacked on the hall table. The washing machine could be heard quietly whirring out at the back. The sink and worktop were clear of dirty crocks and the kitchen had been swept clean, giving the spacious appearance that came with order once again. The interior space had been restored. Harry's spirits further lifted.

He made himself a coffee and then phoned Cherry.

'Hi Cherry, babe. Harry… I'm after an update on the Barry Thornton killing in Ottery. What can you tell me?'

'Harry, you're full of surprises. I thought you'd have moved on from that. As far as I've heard there's no news. Everything's quiet. The police have not issued any further statements and I've not heard anything from anyone except polite condolences. Like you, I smell a story here, but I've found nothing out to tell you yet, Harry.'

'But there must have been some big reason why someone wanted him dead. He didn't crawl into the bonfire because he was drunk or homeless, a man waiting to be barbecued, now did he?'

'I think you could be on to something there, Harry. People say Barry Thornton was a thorough nuisance. When he got his nose into something he never let up. He'd find out what was happening and bring it to light. He was straight Labour; if he found a Tory taking advantage, be it planning regulations, back handers, whatever, he'd go for them and nothing would get in his way. So I guess he had more than a few enemies.'

'So the police will have a few lines of enquiry to follow up then?'

'Sure… but you know what, it's impossible to believe anyone in East Devon would go so far as to murder a political opponent, it's so out of the ordinary Harry, it doesn't fit with the local scene as we know it. Something else is going on… You're right to ask questions. I've always thought you had a good nose, Harry.'

'And a good body to match the nose, eh! What are you doing later? Got anything on? Fancy a trip out to Ottery, dig around a little, I'll help you get your story. Might even treat you to a drink in a nice little local pub? How about it? What else has a girl got on a wet Sunday?'

'Well, OK Harry, you're on. Just like old times, eh? What's the plan?'

'I'll pick you up at yours around 6, maybe just after,' he said, remembering, but not acknowledging he was picking up Stu too.

Harry liked Cherry. He could picture her now with her neat blond bob of hair on top of her head and trim athletic figure. She'd always bubbled with energy, the epitome of what a hungry reporter should be, ever chasing the next story. They'd always been good friends and had a lot in common in how they saw the world. They'd actually known each other at school, though Harry had had no time for her then, obsessed as he was by football.

More recently if he'd needed sympathetic news coverage for his political progress Cherry had delivered it. He wondered whether he'd imagined it, but he felt there was a spark of something between them and hadn't she just jumped at the chance to come to Ottery with him? Bugger, he thought as he remembered Stu; he might be a gooseberry. He should have mentioned him to Cherry. Perhaps he'd need to ditch him out somewhere, not sure when, whether before or after the evening in Ottery. Can't have him spoiling things…

His mind turned to Nick and his Mum. The thought troubled him, not just the very idea of the two in some kind of relationship. He imagined Nick had left the office and gone straight round to see her to brief her on the day's turn in events. No doubt his Mum would be as surprised as Nick had been to discover that Harry had shown such an interest in the business; he imagined they would even now be plotting afresh as to how to redress their new misfortune at being squeezed out and how Nick might recover his position. No chance.

He considered whether to call his Mum, but quickly decided he stood to gain more by leaving her to stew in the juices of her own making. He held all the cards, a handful of aces. He considered the two would have little option but to eventually come back to him when they'd decided what they would do. He pictured some cringing and wringing of hands, Nick desperately pleading, wanting his old position back. Definitely not happening.

To Harry's mind, it was too late for that now and maybe Nick would have to be given his cards sooner rather than later. That was another bit of power play Harry held in the situation and good finance play after the figures he'd seen as to Nick's salary and bonus. Business, he realised had finally felt like something worth taking up his time and trouble. It might be a sabbatical for now, but he already knew Nick would have to go. He himself was on the up.

Just as people seemed to have written Harry out of business, it was the same story when it came to politics. When the expenses scandal had come to light last year, he'd been suspended from his parliamentary seat and become tainted goods. From the moment of his meteoric rise everyone had wanted to be seen with him, then suddenly after his fall absolutely no one wanted to know him. A fallen star, he had slipped from the sky and been lost from sight. He hadn't a friend anywhere, except on the street back in Plymouth.

Their mistake! They'd all made a very big miscalculation, it was all going to turn out very bad for them! No one wrote off Harry McNamara.

For some months Harry had been quietly formulating a return to politics, but this time he was making his way following a markedly different route. He didn't much care for Parliament with its old school set of ways and predictable mix of left and right politicians. Politics at the top table had looked bland and disconnected with what people were feeling and wanting on the ground and anyway he was barred, for now, from going there.

Rather, Harry was set on resurrecting a revolutionary, New Britain First Democratic Party, but at a local, community action level. Knowing full well that the public memory of the disgraced was an incredibly short time frame, he was already ready to move on again, climb out of the shadows and set up small cells of committed activists in every local community, starting in Devon. In fact it amounted to a new political awakening, something he sensed was on the cusp rising up internationally as well as at home.

With no party office as yet, he'd been working from out of the upstairs spare room at home and had begun to assemble ideas and materials to bring his phoenix-like aspiration about. He considered himself to be sharper and wiser from his recent foray into mainstream politics. The spare room had become his den, with every wall and surface, even the ceiling, now covered with his ideas and heroes. He was surprised at just how many people out there thought like he did and in recent days his new Instagram account had started to hum with all the attention it had been getting. It was time.

His first move back into politics had taken him to Ottery just three days ago. Knowing that the place would be full of people for tar barrels, it had promised to be fertile recruitment territory. He had gone with a rucksack of leaflets but without any plan except to keep his eyes open. Then, by the end of last Thursday night he knew he'd found the kind of people who might be approached. He'd seen guys to enlist, but then The Circle had... well, had got there first. Limping Man had stolen his party night. He'd been scuppered and the tables turned on him.

Always when Harry met an opponent he had two options – smash or grab. Either Limping Man had to be smashed and stopped or he had to be stopped and recruited, only under Harry's control and command. This was the way things worked, it was the first law of the street.

Harry's recollection of The Circle was that it was international, a distant, shadowy right wing organisation using social media to reach its tentacles into every corner of the globe. It watched from afar the right wing political parties' efforts and then like a parasitic insect jumped on the back of any potential success upon which it might feed and thrive. Then it would lend its weight and muscle and follow up by trying to get some political gain for itself from it.

He'd experienced it all first hand for himself. When he'd set out in politics in Plymouth it was The Circle who, initially unknown to him, had set a series of terrorist attacks in motion during his campaign with the result that people became more scared, more anti-Islamic and piled their votes behind him when it came to the ballot box. The very first thing that happened after the Returning Officer had declared Harry as winner was The Circle had called him and from then on they instructed him on his political career in the House. So what was Limping Man doing in Ottery?

This was a puzzle Harry couldn't for the moment unravel and he had to let go of the matter for now. This evening he decided he'd pay another visit to Charlie Evan's house at 40 Yonder Street, this time with Cherry and Stu as company and together they'd start digging. Something usually came to light when stones were turned over. They wouldn't be expecting him and that would give him the advantage of surprise.

He chuckled at the thought that Stu ought to team up with Cherry as her junior reporter, he'd be good at it. That could be his excuse to her for bringing Stu along this evening, if he needed one. Stu had better come up with some useful intel before they set off.

Harry went upstairs to the spare room. He looked around him at all his weeks of work. One could be mistaken for thinking of it as a control room. Neat rows of recruitment packs in their black zip wallets were lined up. A map of Devon on the wall had localities marked with numbers identifying where he was going to build his bases. Photographs of possible personnel he might recruit to the cause were posted on the right hand wall as a series of mug shots. This was the beginning of a revival, something big. It would be a great awakening, his chance to save the British people.

16

Stu took ages to come to the door. Harry had messaged him to say he was outside, but nearly three minutes had passed as Harry waited impatiently in the car tapping the steering wheel with his thumbs. He didn't want to keep Cherry waiting.

'What kept you, you slow bugger?' he chided, as Stu slowly made his way into the front seat.

'I was doing what you asked Harry, digging around for the stuff you wanted, err, nice new set of wheels…' Stu protested innocently, his eyes still glued to his phone, typing fingers and thumbs working away frenetically.

'Find anything?' asked Harry having calmed himself.

'Yeah! I think so. Don't know what to make of it though.'

Stu went quiet as he studied his phone. Harry put the BMW into Drive and smoothly pulled away.

'We're collecting Cherry Thomas,' he announced. 'I think she needs to help us uncover the story here. I think you should help her get the facts.'

'Well, OK, Harry. But you may want to hear this first.'

'What?'

'I've got info on Limping Man, your Christian Howard. Think you'd like to hear this…'

'Come on then, spill the beans…'said Harry excitedly.

'I'm pretty sure this is the same guy. Born in Exmouth, Devon, served in the Royal Marines. Last based at the Commando Training Centre Lympstone, near Exmouth. Captured in Iraq, injured in a botched rescue attempt and hospitalised out of the action. But, Harry, he was subsequently dishonourably discharged after a tribunal case! He'd killed, or allowed some Iraqi prisoners to die, in circumstances that are not entirely clear. It's been very hard to find out things, it reads like the military's reputation was at stake here.'

'Is that it?'

'No… I struck lucky on another dark web site. A couple of his former marine colleagues felt so dissatisfied with the handling of the tribunal case they posted some pretty dirty stuff on our Christian Howard straight after the tribunal had washed their hands of him. That says something don't you think?'

'What were they saying?'

'In a nutshell, that he was a hateful, bullying, murdering bastard. I get the impression he was somewhat unhinged and unpredictable, always plotting some scheme behind people's backs. He had a nasty set of friends who'd soon as put a knife in you as look at you. Oh yes, he was once done for helping himself to weapons and ammunition from a munitions store. That time he tried to explain the thefts away as some kind of system test, an educational exercise and he was let off with a short spell in the glasshouse. Again, former colleagues lambast him as dangerous trouble.'

'How long ago was he let loose on society?'

'He came back from the Middle East to Exmouth in late 2012. An extended period of sick leave and rehab followed which left him with a permanently disabled leg, his hallmark limp. So by the time his tribunal case was over, he seems to have re-entered civvy street sometime in 2015.'

'You've done great Stu. Bloody marvellous! What happened to him next? What's he been up to? Do we know? Got anything?'

'Nope! Not a thing, since then he's been under the radar, that is until you spotted him, in Ottery, three days ago. Couldn't find anything at all, until…'

'Until what?' shouted Harry, taking his eye off the road ahead briefly to turn to Stu.

'Until I started looking again on the dark web and asked a couple of geeks I know to help me. He's definitely doing stuff. You wouldn't call it a job exactly.'

'What then?'

'He's The Circle's South West of England Leader and he lives, wait for it, at Broadhayes Manor Barn on the outskirts of Ottery St Mary. He's been renting it.'

'Stu, I owe you! Keep all this under your hat will you.'

Harry slowed the car to a halt.

'Look there's Cherry, ready and waiting at her door. Jump out and let her in the front Stu will you. You can carry on your research in the back… more room.'

'OK, Harry,' Stu answered, so much feeling the warm glow of Harry's praise resting upon him, he didn't think to question his relegation to the back seat.

Cherry hadn't recognised the car as Harry glided to a halt. She remained standing there playing with her phone by her front door. Finally, Stu leapt out and called to her. Recognising him, the penny dropped and she came over and joined them, carefully climbing into the front next to Harry as he'd planned.

'Hi Cherry. As you can see Stu's coming along. This afternoon he's proved himself a very useful guy, to the point where if he could help you in some of your investigative journalism, I think he'd prove himself incredibly useful,' he said tantalisingly. 'Been waiting long?'

'No… I didn't recognise the car. New is it?'

'Sort of. I've taken over the family business and this is part of the deal. Like it?'

'Nice, Harry, better than mine,' which was the reply Harry hoped for.

'We should get to Ottery before 7-o 'clock.'

'What have you in mind for this evening, Harry?'

'You know me. I've an idea, then it becomes a kind of work in progress. Let's just say we're going to begin with a visit to a couple of potential supporters.' He reached the touch screen in the dashboard and organised some modern jazz. Ella Fitzgerald was singing *Dream a little dream of me*, her sweet silvery vocals generating a calm atmosphere as they motored on. Everyone settled into their seats and relaxed into the journey.

Leaving Plymouth behind they were soon on the duel carriageway heading north, skirting Dartmoor, grey low hanging clouds reducing visibility on the dark road still further every time they gained any altitude. There had been moments when Harry had played with the car, checking the acceleration and braking, provoking reaction from his passengers. A high speed was maintained on the largely traffic free road and they pulled into Ottery within minutes of 7-o 'clock, just as Harry had predicted.

This time Harry decided to park up in what he hoped would be an anonymous side street opposite the old refurbished Mill. He decided to leave the BMW discreetly in a row of parked cars up a steep hill, well away from the supermarket car park where Phil's car had been torched.

'OK, we'll leave the motor here. It's just a short walk up Mill Street into town,' he announced. Everyone clambered out.

'Cherry, there's the possibility of a real news scoop for you tonight. You could be the one to get the inside info on Barry Thornton's murder. What's more you could find yourself hearing about a resurrection in grass roots politics. There might even be more for you on extreme right wing development in Devon. I assure you, whatever happens you won't have had a wasted evening,' he smiled mysteriously.

'Being with you Harry, time is never wasted,' she said cheerily, Harry knowing a flirt in his direction when he saw one, and not minding it one little bit.

'We're heading for Yonder St first,' he stated, waving his arm vaguely up ahead. Harry was back to being smartly dressed, wearing the jacket he last wore when political campaigning in settings where appearance counted, like the business centre and the hustings. One of Sheena's newly bought shirts had been called into action, though he'd decided against wearing a tie. He felt he looked important, precisely the image he wanted to convey.

Harry was counting on surprise and when he pressed the musical bell push at 40 Yonder Street he got it. A young child opened the front door and seeing Harry took a step back. Without any hesitation, Harry moved inside and beckoned Stu and Cherry to follow.

'Who is it?' a woman's voice in the kitchen called to the child.

'It's Harry, following up on some papers I left here for Charlie the other day.'

He heard a gasp, then there was a moment's silence before Millie put her head round the kitchen door, a look of startled puzzlement on her face as she saw Harry in style with two others. She herself was dressed for homely tasks, all grubby jeans, baggy T-shirt, an apron, with her hair falling all over. Harry could cut a commanding presence when he needed to and it was working a treat.

'What do you want? He's not here…' she said with a distracted glance, first in the direction of upstairs and then toward the kids in the kitchen. Harry could read exactly what was going through her panicked mind. Contrary to what she said, he knew Charlie was upstairs and that she'd been undecided whether to call him or not. Her glance to the kitchen also meant she had the safety of the kids playing on her mind.

'Call Charlie down and then go and see to the kids in the kitchen,' Harry quietly ordered, choosing to stand this time, his back close to the front door .

'Charlie, come down will you, it's for you…' she cried.

There was a steady heavy clomp as Charlie descended. Harry enjoyed seeing the look of surprise when he saw their faces.

'Calm yourself, Charlie. Nothing to worry about,' he said pushing his outstretched palms downward in a gesture of cool.

'Let me introduce my friends. Cherry Thomas is one of the South West's leading news reporters, a big friend of mine and this is Stu. He's well, let's say he's very useful to have around. Come and sit down a minute Charlie, I have proposition to make, an offer if you like.'

Charlie hesitated, but soon realised it was prudent to sit down. He ended up where Harry had sat last time, low down and in the corner. It was as if the wind had been taken out of his sails. A big man, he looked crumpled up somehow and Harry knew he had the upper hand. It was time to land his catch.

'Like I say, I think you are in a position to help, to do some more good for your community. When I first came to Ottery three nights ago I was impressed, you and your friends are what makes a place like this great to live in. Loyal, strong, looking after your own, family first, that kind of thing. I respect that, I really do. Did you look at the information I left with you Charlie? My invitation. Did you think it over? I thought I'd come over in person to cement our deal. Alright with you?'

'Yes, I saw that, but things are… complicated.'

'You mean Limping Man, Christian Howard?'

'I shouldn't really be saying this, but Christian has already signed me up with his outfit and I'd need to talk it over with him. I'm not sure he'd like what you're proposing, could lead to a conflict of loyalties and so forth…'

'Well, interestingly enough I think Christian would like to be brought into our conversation. I've things to put to him and I know he'll want to take our earlier conversation forward. Why don't you give him a call and get him to pop over. We'll be down at the Barrel this evening. Tell him I've asked you to bring him along, just the two of you mind, no one else and tell him if he doesn't show, we've an interesting tale to tell the police. We'll leave you to it Charlie, see you later.'

Harry waved his two friends to the door and they let themselves out. It was raining again and they increased their step in the direction of The Barrel Inn, less than a five minute walk.

'I'm not sure I followed all that,' said Cherry, her heels clicking along on the pavement.

'I'll explain over a pint, Cherry. All will be made clear, believe me.'

'You want to work with them both don't you Harry,' said Stu, spotting the characteristic way Harry went about things. 'You're back into politics again Harry, and you want Cherry to be the first to know…'

'Something like that Stu, first round's on you,' he announced as he pushed open the pub door. Sunday night at the Barrel Inn seemed quieter. Having scanned the place, Harry led the way to the table in the window near the entrance door leaving Stu to handle the drinks at the bar.

It took less than thirty minutes before Charlie's head appeared looking for them. He nodded on establishing contact and leant on the bar chasing to the lanky young bar tender as he ordered his drink. He only turned his head as the door opened again, as just paces behind him Limping Man walked in. He didn't wait at the bar but came straight across to Harry's table and sat himself down saying nothing until Charlie had brought the beers over before taking himself back to the bar.

'We've a few things to sort out, rules of engagement and the like,' he said, 'but first, I want a proper introduction to your two friends. She's a reporter or something, that right?' he asked, as he picked up his pint and took a sip. He waited on Harry's reply.

'This is Cherry, top drawer investigative reporter, absolute whizz at getting the best stories around. Read the papers much, Christian? No? Well, no matter. This is Stu, long time colleague and friend of mine. We're here to tidy up.'

'Get to the point, Mr McNamara.'

'Loose ends. You know what those are? No? Well, let me tell you then.'

'A guy gets kicked out the army after a tribunal. He's pretty aggrieved after a life time of service in the Marines and he's feeling ditched, dumped, blamed… And he wants pay back. His military and political masters don't see what he's been fighting for and have no idea what pain they put him through… How am I doing Christian?'

'Go on…'

'He finds The Circle, or rather they find him and make him an offer. *"We understand you,"* they say, *"we know how you feel and we want to help. In fact we'll offer you a valued position and work, real work that counts for something."* They are very direct, very persuasive, believe me, I know from past experience Christian Howard. You're not the first to be recruited.'

Christian seemed to relate to what Harry said and when he twigged that Harry had been through The Circle recruitment regime his face eased a little. Harry was reaching him.

'Would you like to tell me or shall I tell you what really happened to Councillor Barry Thornton, just so we have no misunderstandings between us? Then perhaps we can talk about the real matter to hand, the collaborative political initiative I'm proposing, the bit where we need to see eye to eye and be 100% sure neither of us get it wrong. Follow?'

'Barry Thornton died in unfortunate circumstances… He'd seriously pissed off someone,' he said quietly.

'Tory Councillor Jeremy Masters,' interrupted Harry.

'Yes, him. Barry had been indiscreet.'

'He'd been fucking Cleo Masters,' added Harry.

'Just shut it and listen, you cocky bastard,' said Christian getting angry and raising his voice. 'He died in bed with her…'

'Nope,' said Harry. Christian cast him a withering look.

'OK, he had some kind of fit, a stroke, whatever. He couldn't move, unconscious in a coma even. Cleo stupidly called her husband Jeremy who called me, who called Charlie, who happened to be the man guarding the bonfire last Wednesday night, the evening before Tar Barrels. Some people were told to lose Barry's body in the fire. It was clumsy, impulsive, but the guy was a gonna anyhow and no one wanted to be associated with all the shit that would fly if things were done any other way. Something to add McNamara. You look like you're about to lay an egg!'

'Yeah… One thing you overlooked, he wasn't dead when he was put in the fire.'

'Come on…' said Christian. Charlie's face had gone as white as a sheet.

'I saw him reaching to get out. I was the one who called the police. Watched them get him out. Yeah… it was me! And I know you did it in for him because I heard you talking as you made your way into town later that night. Idle talk… thought the marines would train that out of you, carelessness costs lives…'

'I've warned you already about your mouth...' rasped Christian, stung by Harry's comment.

Charlie strolled over, his big bulk towering over the table. 'Everything alright boss?' he asked. Christian flicked his thumb dismissively sending Charlie back to the bar. Perhaps he was annoyed at a job badly done, thought Harry.

'Or what, Christian Howard? I'm sure Cherry can write a nice little story, exclusive they call it, with all the details I can give her.'

'There's certainly quite a story here Harry,' Cherry piped up.

'On the other hand a more considered approach might be to keep this to myself and for us to think about what we might do to help each other, politically. Charlie, providing you keep him on a tighter rein, seems to have all that it takes to get local action off the ground and you, well I think if we get The Circle to assist rather than undermine, I really do think there's a future in collaborative politics in the South West, don't you?'

Harry watched as the cogs turned in Christian Howard's head. He knew Harry had seized the balance of power and didn't like it. For his part, Harry felt a glowing sense of self-satisfaction building, he'd baited the trap, they'd taken the bait, he was reeling them in. Life didn't get any better.

17

'It'll be three months tomorrow since Harry sent me on sabbatical and I'm supposed to be back Monday,' surmised Nick Grayson. He'd heard nothing from Harry in that time. Sitting in the kitchen facing Bev McNamara at his Plymouth home, hunched over the breakfast table, he gripped his coffee mug in two hands, the all pervading smell of burned toast hanging in the air. He was gazing up at the McNamara Metals promotional calendar held on to the fridge door by a *Visit Dartmoor* magnet. The picture showed a heavy duty crane astride a mountain of scrap metal being sorted into concrete walled bays ready for shipment to China. He'd personally supervised the photo shoot. Today was Friday 7th; Monday 10th February was ringed twice in red biro.

'It's gone very quickly. I think we both enjoyed the mini-cruise to Santander with Brittany Ferries. You really needed that break. But I can see you're itching to get back. You don't like having nothing to do and there's only so many golf rounds you can play, especially in the winter months,' said Bev McNamara. To be frank she was a bit puzzled that Nick had taken so many days out on his own 'to relax', but he'd always returned looking chilled. 'How are things looking for the morning? Has that son of mine Harry been in touch yet?'

'No. Not even replied to any of my emails. I tried to get back to work sooner than this but he's blanked me out. I really don't know how he and I can work together. We're... so very different. It may take a while to get the company affairs sorted as we'd hoped.' Nick brought his mobile to life and scanned for new emails. It took a moment for them to arrive into his Inbox. When he looked again he saw one from

Harry, sent from harry@mcnamarametals.com. Clearly he'd set up his own email address at the company.

'My God! Harry's actually written,' he announced in a mocking tone. Bev paused at what she was doing at the sink, sensing its importance.

'What does he say?'

A long silence followed as she watched Nick reading carefully with a look of shocked seriousness on his face.

'He's called me in for a 9am meeting with him on Monday. *In the light of events*, he concludes, *I'm not to be building up my hopes*. That's it. What does he mean?'

'He's sacking you,' Bev answered. 'He's getting rid of you. I know Harry. It's so obvious.' She walked across grabbing a kitchen towel to dry her hands and put a comforting hand on Nick's shoulder.

'*In the light of events*?' he repeated, 'What can he mean?' He looked crestfallen.

'He's manufactured some reason to be able to sack you, I know it. You need to think about what you can salvage from this. Harry, being Harry, don't be surprised if he tries to see you off with no pay, no reference, nothing. But if you fight back, he'll give you something, but mark my words, he won't ever let you work there again. Have you an employment specialist solicitor you can speak with? You're going to need one.'

'Yes, but I need to see what Harry has in mind first. In spite of what you say, he's very vague. He also says, I'm *not to be building up my hopes.* It might mean he doesn't want me to take full company control any longer. He might simply want to share the CEO position, do some kind deal or make some other kind of arrangement. It won't be what it was, but it will be something…'

'No, you're finished Nick. You'll need to move on, to salvage what you can from the situation and find pastures new. At the very least you have to consider taking him to the Employment Tribunal for the way he's handled you. You shouldn't be walking away with less than a generous golden handshake and a glowing reference. You're owed that much.'

'I need to see what he has in mind Bev. I can't believe it's as bad as you say.'

'Believe me, it is!'

'I'll just give Elsa a quick ring at the office and confirm I'm coming in to see Harry and I'll see if she can throw any more light on things.'

He tapped in the familiar works number followed by Elsa's extension.

'Elsa speaking, how can I help?' she answered chirpily.

'Nick here, long time no contact, how are you?'

'Oh… Nick. Yes, fine. You enjoying your sabbatical, lucky fellow. You'll be pleased to hear how quickly Harry has got into things, it must be in the McNamara family DNA. He knows how to strike a good deal, I'll say that for him. We've managed very well whilst you've been off. I hadn't realised the three months were up.'

'I'm calling because Harry's called me in to meet with him at 9am Monday.' replied Nick coldly, not wanting to hear how well Harry had been managing things.

'One moment, Nick. I'll just check… Yes, that's right, you're booked into Harry's office, your old office… 9am Monday morning. Alright for it are you?'

'Yes… Anything you can tell me about the agenda, Elsa?'

'No, this is something Harry arranged. I know nothing about it, until I'd checked the diary just now I didn't know he had arranged to see you and so far as I can see there's no paper work or agenda files unless he's sent them to you directly. Tell you what, I'll touch base with him and check that one out. If there's anything further I'll send it on. Otherwise I may see you when you're in. It'll be lovely to catch up and hear about your time away. Have a great weekend. Bye.'

'Nothing…' Nick announced to the waiting Bev who had heard every word.

'He's definitely sacking you Nick,' she repeated, 'and you need to fight him, every inch of the way. He only understands battles, does Harry, it's what he does, who he is. Get a grip, he's writing you off.'

18

'Ah Nick, prompt as ever. Glad you got my email. Sorry to keep you waiting. Did Elsa get you a coffee? Excellent! Bring it in with you. Have seat,' said a magnanimous sounding Harry, extending a hand of welcome, looking sharp in his pressed suit and new, fresh from the packet, white shirt.

Just as he was three months earlier, Nick found himself shepherded into the hard seat placed in front of what was his own desk. Looking around he couldn't help but notice Harry had made some changes. The desk was cluttered. It had a small red Audi die cast model sitting on the one corner and a miniature presentation banner from Plymouth Rovers on the other… no taste.

On the wall facing him behind Harry, placed centrally, was an unmissable large new picture frame featuring a colourful photograph of a smiling Harry on the pitch at the football club's Home Park making community awards. Nick recalled that Harry's picture had been taken at the event in his parliamentary campaign a couple of years back. Either side of Harry's picture were the matching but slightly smaller pictures of Michael McNamara, company founder and the late Patrick McNamara, his son. He looked around, but of his own picture there was not a sign to be had. Nick chose not to mention it.

Nick felt the clean edges to what was his space had been marred, the order he'd created, the self-discipline he'd exercised over his realm had slipped. He couldn't help but make a sneer of disapproval at what he saw as this violation, realising as he gazed around him, it was true what Bev had said, he'd really lost control of what was his own office. Difficult as it was, bile rising in his throat, he tried to focus his thoughts. He heard the familiar sound of the car crusher at work in the yard and imagined the vehicle being dropped by crane into the box before the hydraulics crushed its designer shape slowly, popping the windscreen at some point, to leave a small metal cube ready to be parked up with all the other small cubes ready to go to China. Each block was cash. He'd missed the sounds of the business, how he loved to count the cubes as promises of more profit.

'I was wondering if there shouldn't have been an agenda attached to the email you sent me, Harry. I can't say I'm feeling prepared for a meeting I haven't been briefed on.'

'No worries there old chap. It is all very straightforward. Short agenda. One item... you. No easy way to say this, Nick, but we're letting you go. After a lifetime's faithful service we're having to let you go. Lucky fellow! You'll be able to play all the golf you want.'

'Letting me go! I'm not wanting to be let go. I've a job here,' he heard himself say in a tone half a tone higher than usual, a voice that didn't carry the slightest conviction.

'You know how it is. It's about economics and efficiency, Nick. It's the accountants, the bean counters that rule us all today. They tell me we really can't pay for two CEOs. The business doesn't warrant it. See it from my point of view. Fair's fair, you've done your bit, it's my turn to do mine. Don't worry, I'll make sure we give you a proper send off, you can choose a watch or timepiece... you know the drill better than I do, that kind of thing... McNamara's is a caring family business... it's what we do.' Harry was able to make his voice sound oily without even trying.

'I'm only in my 50s... Do you hear me, I'm not wanting to be let go?' retorted Nick shrilly.

'You may say that Nick. But don't force my hand. Be gentle on yourself and take what's offered.'

'And what are you offering as severance?'

'A good reference if you think you have a few years left in you. I'd really like you to do what you want to do for the future. As I say, we can give you a good reference to help you secure a new position. I'm getting to know some of the other Plymouth firms, I'd be happy to put in a good word here and there. The McNamara family are really most grateful.'

'And cash?'

'Oh, I think the three month sabbatical took care of that. You really shouldn't be greedy, Nick.'

'See you at the Employment Tribunal Harry, this is constructive dismissal at the very least,' said Nick angrily as he stood up, determinedly making to leave.

'Oh, I wouldn't call it that. I really don't think you'd be best advised to go down the tribunal route if I were you,' said Harry menacingly. 'If you stop and think about things when you've calmed down and talked it over with my Mother you might see reason. I'm sorry but you presently have a red mist of anger obscuring your normally keen sense of judgement, Nick. I'm sure she will help you see sense. Oh, and do ask her to say hello sometime. How I miss her,' he added, betraying not a hint of the slightest warmth.

Nick turned and was all ready to storm out of the door when Harry spoke up. 'Think carefully what you do Nick. I think I have enough evidence to get Devon and Cornwall Police to launch a criminal proceedings against you for seeking to steal my business. What do you have to say to that?'

'You bastard,' he muttered as he summarily left, slamming the door hard behind him.

Elsa put her head round, 'Everything alright in here,' she asked Harry, sensing atmosphere.

'He didn't even ask after the car,' said Harry, 'otherwise our meeting went extremely well. Get me another coffee will you, there's a girl.'

'Glad to hear it, Harry. Of course. Coffee coming up just how you like it.' As she walked over to the red coffee machine she wished Harry would stop referring to her as 'a girl'. He was young, energetic, taking the business forward, but he could be annoyingly patronising too.

19

Harry had hoped Nick might have put up more of a fight. He was disappointed his Mum had shacked up with such a wimp. That interview with him was all rather flat and low key, not fists at dawn, nothing that got his blood flowing. Nick had even turned up in a grey colourless suit.

Sometimes office work was so dull. The business kind of ran itself and for all Nick's character weakness, Harry had to admit Nick had run a tight ship with able people appointed, each doing their bit. Apart from Sean Murphy. Sean had been too bullish but after speaking to him recognised someone who got things done and led the yard. He'd learned that Sean's father had been just the same. A quiet word in Sean's ear was all it took and things had settled down. The whole workforce did their bit and the cubes of scrap kept being produced. Knowing this to be the case he could leave it all ticking over as a nice cash cow. Scrap came in from a host of regular suppliers who were only to glad to offload their waste metal and create space for themselves. Firms in China paid to take the sorted metal off their hands. Some of the more valuable reclaimed metal, aluminium especially and the lead from old batteries were separately retained and turned a tidy earner.

In the daily life of McNamara Metals, underlings came and asked for Harry's backing when they required it; when an exceptional item of expenditure needed to be approved or a new contract signed, that kind of thing. It all seemed very straightforward. And yes, they could manage without him much of the time, certainly long enough for him to give his time and attention back to the pressing matter of politics.

Over the past of three months he'd been able to do quite a lot to mobilise things working from his new office. He picked up his mobile.

'Stu, all set for this evening?'

'Yes, Harry. Everyone's replied. The first meeting of the New Britain First Democrats is an all seats taken affair. It'll be my first visit to your conference room at McNamara Metals'

'Limping Man's replied in the affirmative.'

'Did you speak to the new Exmouth guy, Adam?'

'Yeah. He knows the score. He and Charlie from Ottery seem to be shaping up nicely as local leaders.'

'Can you get Cherry to come, bring a photographer too? Phil Potts is useful that way if she hasn't anyone else,' Harry suggested.

'I'll get the firm to lay on a hospitality spread, sandwiches and pasties, beer… Elsa will source it. Leave that to me.'

'I thought you'd have spoken to Cherry yourself Harry since… you two are, well… close?'

'Nope, not yet. Pleasure and business are separate things Stu, remember that. You should have invited her along with the others, but now you mention it, I'll give her a call myself. I need to see that she actually comes, no last minute excuses about a bigger story elsewhere.'

'OK, Harry. Any need for someone on the door, hospitality?'

'Good thinking. I've employed someone new here on Night Security. You might remember him, Dan Cash?'

'Yeah, yeah. Bodybuilder, he got done for anabolic steroids, it ended his career. Good guy to have around at the football or in town late at night.'

'Yep, that's him. Found him in a coffee shop a couple of weeks ago. He'd fallen on hard times so appreciated a leg up. When I showed him a picture of the black uniform, tough guy outfit he'd be getting, he was up for it like a shot. Just like that. I find uniforms give nobodies a purpose. I also gave him a couple of self-protection items I sourced on the internet, just in case of trouble. He'll be on the gate all tooled up. We don't need him at the yard all the time, so he just comes in when I tell him to.'

'Does he need briefing about tonight, Harry?'

'Send me a typed attendee list by email Stu, something Dan can use to check everyone in from. I'll brief him properly myself later, tell him to be thorough, get him to do some body searches in the mix. He'll like doing them and it'll impress.'

'I love it Harry. You really are bouncing back. All in just three months. The Party's back up and running, albeit with a new name. What swung it for us last time Harry was you got the social media thing happening when everyone else was still in the world of knocking door to doors and handing out pieces of paper. Old methods are shit. Do you think we're ready to get someone to do our media stuff again, get someone in for that tonight, Harry?'

'Bloody hell Stu, you're brain's fired its second grey cell! Not yet Stu, not yet. I'll say something about that tonight. We've an empty office next to the conference room and I was going to recruit a couple of extra IT-media people, base them in there. I've been meaning to speak with you about that Stu, bringing you in, but not right now. I'll tell the factory the new IT people will be working on a project for me. Seems a good way forward, but too soon to do that by tonight.'

'OK then, Harry. I'll send you the email list of attendees and I'll be along early.' With that he'd gone.

Harry picked up the coffee Elsa had made him. It was cold. She was only in the next office and he knew if he shouted she'd come running which was exactly what he did and how she responded.

'Coffee's cold,' he growled as she came in, nodding disapprovingly at it.

'I'll fix you another one, Harry. Don't forget to drink it this time,' she chided. The machine hummed and hissed and the steaming cup was placed in front of him. Elsa disappeared again as quickly as she'd come. Useful, she is, thought Harry, turning his attention to the next call he had to make, to Cherry.

'Hi, Cherry. How you doing babe? Monday morning and all that; lots of weekend stories to follow up?'

'It's really quiet actually, Harry. People's minds are thinking toward Valentine's Day,' she hinted.

'Huh! I need you here at the business tonight,' he said. 'Got an event needing news coverage.'

'You do have such a way with a girl, Harry. How could I refuse? What have you in mind?' she teased.

'An evening at the factory, but we could go on somewhere after,' he added as a sweetener.

'Sugaring the pill, Harry?' she added, 'What am I having to go to first?'

'More work for you I'm afraid. Popular local politics is on the rise again and my own political career is back on track. There's a story here for you and you're the first, well only, reporter to know. The inaugural meeting of the New Britain First Democratic Party is tonight in the conference room at McNamara Metals. We kick off at 8-o 'clock. Some of the lads can't get off work any earlier. Can you get a photographer along? He need only stay five minutes, to get a shot of everyone, people like pictures…'

'I'll see what I can do. You know Andy Stone, he should be free.'

'Perfect. Let me know if he's not and I'll get Phil Potts in,' added Harry.

'I'm sure it'll be fine. Yes, I'll let you know if not.'

'I've been meaning to ask. What's the latest on the Councillor Barry Thornton story?'

'Well, the police let what was left of the body go to be buried last week. Actually, I went along. Funeral was in the parish church then a short ride to a quaint little cemetery behind a line of yew trees on Higher Ridgeway. They buried him in the far north east corner, a discreet plot. It's run by the Ottery Council.'

'He might get a discount as a councillor, don't you think?' quipped Harry smiling at his own dark humour.

'Surprised to see how many Labour people turned out. Some had to stand outside the church in the rain. People seemed very upset at losing a guy who worked hard…'

'No, no, I mean the police inquiry. The real story…'

'Funny you should ask. I had a chat with the DCI from Exeter who was also at the funeral. Funerals always get people to say things they might not at other times. He was happy to tell me stuff, off the record, like…'

'The ginger guy, Holder. Him?'

'Yes, and…you need to be careful Harry. The police, they're looking at The Circle. I'm pretty sure they interviewed Limping Man last week. They think The Circle were behind it because Barry had some kind of undercover knowledge about them. The first post-mortem showed up strangulation prior to being placed in the fire. The DCI told me they'd stripped down Barry's computer and they'd found stuff, lots of stuff and they were still sifting through it. It's even more complicated than they first thought, the word, *"blackmail"* came into the conversation and he thinks maybe Barry was being blackmailed about his affair with Cleo Masters. So the main thing is, be careful Harry.'

'You mean Barry Thornton was threatening to expose The Circle to the authorities… and to stop him they in turn were turning to blackmail?'

'Yes, that seems to have been the case.'

'And what about the info on The Circle? Do the police actually have anything?'

'Not that he was able to tell me. I think he would have done if he knew anything… so I'd say not, or nothing much…'

'Hmm… Thanks for that. See you later, chick.'

Harry turned to his coffee. He had to think. He'd need some time on his own with Limping Man later. The guy seemed to be playing ball with Harry, but Harry needed to know he wasn't exposing himself to a black hole of trouble waiting for him just when things were taking off politically. Nor did he want the police knocking on his door because of what Limping Man or The Circle were up to. He called Stu.

'Stu, tell Limping Man to get along early, for 7-o 'clock. Tell him for a meeting, just the two of us, we need a private conversation before the meeting. A pre-meeting if you like. No need to say more. Got me?'

'Yeah, Harry. I'll get right on to it.'

Harry was finding he had a good deputy in Stu, and although Stu was claiming benefits, Harry kept him well in funds by slipping him £20 most days. He and his missus Penny were happy enough with the arrangement. Stu's cash worries would disappear soon when he took on some social media work for Harry.

'Elsa,' he yelled, 'In here.'

A rapid scurrying of feet and then the diminutive form of Elsa ready to do his bidding appeared in the doorway.

'Need you to organise the food and drink for tonight's meeting in the Conference Room.'

'Oh, I didn't know there was to be a meeting…'

'No, and you don't need to know. All you have to do is set it up just as I say. It's my bloody meeting not yours!'

'Yes, Mr McNamara.'

20

For several minutes Harry stood going down through the slatted blind of his strategically placed office window. Good, he thought, seeing that Dan, with his back to Harry, had duly clocked on at 6 p.m. He had his legs apart, standing with attitude like a guard dog, monitoring the metal gate as if his life depended on it, as indeed it did. Harry noticed Dan had added to the black uniform a new, shiny pair of heavy duty boots. He wondered whether they had steel toe caps – probably did. Dan was measuring up nicely. Dan and Harry watched the last of the factory staff leave at 6.10 p.m. Harry then turned away to return to his desk.

Earlier, he'd jotted a memo list on his tablet. He glanced through it, then added Stu's reminder to get the social media side up and running A.S.A.P.. The Conference Room would need one or two final preparatory touches, so locking up his office he descended the stairs taking them two at a time and headed straight there. It was a functional space, but nicely proportioned. Elsa had organised the chairs as he'd requested, two semicircles facing the projector screen at the front.

There were two black tubes lying on the floor either side of the screen. Unzipping each in turn, Harry carefully erected the banners he'd ordered, one for either side of the screen. They'd taken him a while to design and get right. The first carried the words, "National: Quest for Power" the other, "Local: South West England's Awesome Pioneers". The imagery in support of the headings had been tricky too and he'd eventually settled on an iconic but grainy picture of British troops raising the Union flag on the Falkland Islands for the National banner and an equally grainy but flattering picture of Charlie carrying a flaming tar barrel on Barrel night. Harry wanted both Limping Man and local leaders to feel the cause. He had found a couple of side spotlights which completed the platform party image nicely as he directed lights on to the two banners.

The food and beers Elsa had ordered arrived at 6.30pm, Dan calling Harry to ask if it was alright if he let the suppliers deliver their items. Harry supervised with a careful eye to detail, the items going to the back of the Conference Room on the tables set aside for the purpose. The family business was an excellent secure base of operation and his intention this evening was to create a seductive atmosphere of solid confidence for the two factions as he sought to bring them under his wing. The room itself would work. Harry then took himself off to freshen up, slipping the bill for everything into his wallet to be paid from the firm's hospitality account in the morning.

The next call came from Dan again, at 6.45 p.m. to say he had 'a cripple' asking for entry. 'The geezer's name's on the list is a… Christian Howard, but I thought I ought to double check as I didn't see you'd have been letting disabled people in – just checking…' he added.

'He's OK, let him through, Dan. Show him a bit of respect. Direct him to the Conference Room and tell him I'll meet him in there.'

No sooner had Harry pulled two chairs together at the front then Christian Howard arrived. Disability or not he could move quickly if he wanted to, Harry thought.

Harry offered a hand. 'Nice to see you again, Christian. Let's talk. I thought it would be profitable for both of us to meet privately beforehand. To sort things. There are things you want and there are things I want.' Harry turned on the charm offensive, doubtful that it cut ice with this hard-nosed guy.

'Just the right kind of set up you've got here Harry. Nice touch, the lad on the gate, but he's not hard enough. You need to rough him up, send him to one of our weekends for real men. I'll send you the link. He could do well, he's got the build and the attitude, wants to please. Tell you what, seeing as I'm generous, I'll pay for his first weekend's training. How's that for an offer.'

'He'll do alright,' said Harry, not wanting to take crumbs thrown his way by Christian Howard.

'Let's get straight to the point. When The Circle's path first crossed with mine a couple of years ago I think you got it all wrong. You didn't work with those of us in the Britain First Democratic Party, you just played the terrorist card and that fed people's fears and they trusted me. I've been thinking both our ends are much better served if we play the game together, get on the same side. Follow?'

Limping Man sat still, what was going on behind those dead eyes Harry could only imagine. So he pressed on. 'It would be a great help to me to know what The Circle can actually bring to the table, personnel? Resources? Finance? In fact I was counting on you coming up with something useful. I know we got off to a rocky start. You lost your man in Parliament.'

'Too true. You blew it.'

169

'I was misled, I admit, and then the government stole my clothes, taking a more populist line, even signing up my supporters… But you and I know that won't cut the mustard. It simply won't do. It won't make this country great again. I believe you've shown up here in the South West to rebuild the cause, yes?' This time Harry waited for a response.

'Look, The Circle's an international body of sympathisers. As such it is hard to get agreement on what we should and should not do. As to deciding on when and where… Our strongest member groups are in the USA and parts of Eastern Europe and they naturally enough see their own homelands as their first priority, and so leadership is sometimes, well less than focussed.'

'I understand that, but you remain committed to the English and people here don't you?'

'What we do internationally, do very well, is work together to promote the cause through social media. We can educate minds and promote the image. What's more we draw in the young and those who are otherwise disillusioned with politics. You'd be amazed how easy it is to manufacture hate and create trolling armies. Much harder to get actual boots on the ground, but the current thinking is there's a link to be built at grass roots between boots on the ground and the virtual forces we amass today, which is why we need you, and yes, I'll grant you, you're right about the South West, it shows promise.'

'Can I show you something? Come, have a look.'

Harry led Christian to the next room, opening the door to reveal a suite of laptops and wall screens in pristine condition. 'Business can be usefully paternalistic like it was in Victorian days, taking an active interest in the lives of local people. This room is just waiting for some software gurus to move in and get to work. Do you know anyone? Can The Circle meet us 50:50 if we take on four people? But, I want to be very clear, I'm not interested in the USA or Eastern Europe except in how it serves us, for me it's all about England. I'm not wasting my time. Get me?'

'Who looks after them?' asked Christian, ignoring Harry's question.

'Christian. I'm a people person not an AI accessory. I can't do that stuff. Hear me out. This private space is available. I'm offering it, they'll need someone to lead them, what can you do to help us? Let's say I'm testing The Circle's commitment here.' He saw Christian go quiet, thinking the offer through.

'Of course and I'll provide two people. You'll need to find two loyal people, experts in social media, but there will still need to be international engagement. Remember they are people who think like you and me. They are our brothers. England has its place, but can't go it alone, The Circle has loyalties too…'

'When can you provide your two? How soon?'

'From 1st March. Is that soon enough for you? Does that pass your test?' he growled. 'I'll want to see forums and chat rooms with a South West focus up and flourishing quickly. I want to see your results or I pull the plug, pull my people out. People don't realise how fast you can do things online. It can be done very fast. We'll see all kinds of events happening by the summer, I promise. Your, our, campaign will take off or I'm pulling resources and I'm off.'

'My campaign is premised on relaunching a New Britain First Democratic Party with myself as leader. I'll be working to get British business on side using the success of this business as a springboard. I'll be wanting to tap into the populist and nationalist agenda protecting British lives and livelihoods and sending foreigners home.'

'That's not enough.'

'How do you mean? Are you wanting to strong arm the agenda again? Last time your lot got it wrong, infighting, failure, attacking British treasures and killing British people. Marks out of ten, I'd give your lot about two. Blunt instruments, you'll need to do better this time, sharpen up what's in your tool box.'

'You forget our attacks got you elected. We learn. Yes, we need to be more measured, more precise in the dark art of persuasion and I agree with you we will achieve far more if the two of us work together in setting the agenda.'

'Well, finally, that's music to my ears.'

'There's a little matter of a small request I have. Something I've been meaning to ask…'

'Yes,' said Harry wondering what as coming.

'We need a secure store room in the South West, here in Plymouth would be ideal. Have you somewhere? I mean you were kind enough to meet my offer of a 50:50 on the personnel side of things, how about we offer you 50:50 on the costs of providing a secure lockable, isolated storage facility.'

'What have you got in mind?'

'Three empty shipping containers. I noticed you already have quite a number of these on site. Surely making three more available for our joint enterprise, located here wouldn't attract undue attention, would be possible?'

'I don't see a problem, but I'd have to talk to the site manager about it and devise a suitable solution, but no, in principle I don't see as there would be any problem. What do you want me to store and when do you want to deliver?'

'First delivery of military grade equipment arrives 1st March. Containers to be ready and in place ready to receive it. How does that sound?'

Harry's phone rang. He ignored it. He was thinking hard.

'Get your phone Harry, take the call,' Christian said.

Harry ignored him. Harry had a surge of well being charge through him. Power from business and politics was becoming tangible. Adrenaline coursed through his veins, but his brain cooly reminded him to be careful, so he pulled back. He was not one rushed.

'You're asking a lot of me, Christian. You and I will need to talk again after the meeting. You're too guarded. You want my help, then you need to tell me a lot more. I'm taking a huge risk here if I let you in. I'm the first one left exposed when someone gets fingered. Come on, our first guests are arriving. I need to be persuaded of your methods. I see success as taking the mainstream with us and I need to be sure we will achieve precisely that. And I haven't forgotten that Councillor Barry Thornton died at The Circles' hands and I want a good explanation for why that was necessary. I'm a man schooled on the football terraces and I know the difference between a yob, a thug and someone whose ideas are ideologically pure and practical. So we'll talk again, but later.'

Harry stood up, ignored his companion and walked toward the door to take Dan's latest call.

'Cherry Thomas coming across, Harry.'

21

At 7-o 'clock precisely, Harry stood up in a room full of
people, a sea of white faces in front of him, twenty seven to
be precise. To the one side of him sat Christian Howard, to
the other and a little further away, Charlie Evans from Ottery
St Mary and next to him, Gavin Wilson from Exmouth. The
four of them were in effect, though there wasn't officially
one, the platform party. Harry was in the chair. He noticed
only three were women – Cherry and the two trusted girls
For a moment he wondered whether gender inequality was
an issue, but quickly dismissed the notion. Cherry was in for
the press story and he'd asked the two other women to help
with the gene swabbing later and to serve the refreshments.
Being practical, that didn't make him a sexist misogynist did
it? Satisfied on the point, he began speaking.

'Welcome. We'll do half an hour's business and then have a
break for food and beer, or just beer, whatever's your
preference.' Applause followed. A good number were
football supporters he guessed from the rapport he was
building. He felt connected.

'Welcome to the party. It's a party for we're celebrating the
kick off of the New Britain First Democratic Party. I'm going
to introduce you to these important guys in a few moments,'
he swept his arm in Christian's direction first, then the other
arm toward Charlie and Gavin. But first, Andy here is going
to take a team photo. Andy's a good local lad and this is all
about promotion of the cause and marking this auspicious
occasion. So don't mess about and just do what he says and
then we can let him get on his way.'

Harry waved Andy over. With Harry looking over his shoulder he soon got everyone lined up, a row seated, others behind, the four key guys exactly where they should be, around Harry. Andy cheerily took his shots and left.

'OK, down to business. Politics today is boring. Politicians don't tell us the truth, they don't have the confidence of the people and don't deliver what's needed. So it's time for something radical and different. It's time to do what's required of us, to do our duty as English patriots. You've heard it said, "America first", you may have even heard it said, "Britain First" but I'm saying England First and the white working people of this great nation come first.'

There was a murmur of approval. Harry gave the two local leads, Charlie and Gavin a call and got them to stand either side of him. He put one arm over each of their shoulders. Three big men together, brothers in arms.

'I want you to know these guys are the most important people in our movement in the South West. They hold respect in their communities. They are defenders of tradition and culture and all that is valuable to us. They are true English giants. Over the coming weeks we will recruit similar such guys from the towns and cities across Devon, then Somerset and that foreign land they call Cornwall!' Catcalls followed.

'Now I want you all to stand for a moment as a mark of your promise of loyalty to the movement and to these two men. On your feet or out the door. We have no hangers on. We are going to reshape politics and take the country forward with us. If you don't stand, you're out.' Everyone stood. This was serious. Harry made it so.

'OK. The Ottery Chapter is led by Charlie and he's got nine guys; Gavin has eleven with him from Exmouth. Each one of you are to leave your contact details for Party registration before you depart today and an email will be sent to give you an access code, a route to view your membership of the party. Within two months you will be joined by many thousands!' A cheer followed.

'I'd like to invite Christian Howard to speak. I want you to listen very carefully to what he has to say. Christian, over to you…'

'Let me begin by congratulating Harry on his massive achievements. He is a pure Englishman, a man who promised himself to us and our cause, a man who is bringing all the resources he can muster to take us forward. We are not a party for compromise. All migrants must go or be dealt with. We cannot tolerate people who are leeches, sucking the blood of our nation's health and draining our public services dry. I represent the international side of our campaign and through The Circle I will be bringing its considerable influence to support this initiative in the South West of England. We need to back our leader, with our blood, with iron and if need be our tears.' Then Christian sat down and folded his hands together. It was neither an act of prayer or humility, rather it signified self-control. Applause followed and Harry enthusiastically joined in realising he had just been given Christian's public endorsement.

Harry stepped forward. 'Many of you will have checked your ancestry before coming, but we want to keep a genealogical record along with your membership. We don't want to find underlings trying to get in and pollute the pure blood line we share. Let me show you.' He reached for a pack.

'Before you fill your mouths with beer and pie go to Tracey. She'll use a stick like this taken from a sterile pack, wipe the end thus on the inside of your mouth and then place it in the tube to be sent off for analysis by our gene testers, *23andMe*. Make sure your name's on the tube label, sign off and we'll get your results for you. Clear?' There were nods all round. 'Genetic purity tests over here, then refreshments after,' Harry directed.

Soon the formal start to the evening dissolved into lively informal conversations as food and beer were heartily consumed. Boisterous banter and a noisy crowd gathered round the laden table. To the sound of clinking glasses the atmosphere was transformed from that of the office into one of a pub.

Ten minutes in and Harry's phone buzzed in his pocket. He ignored it. It persisted. He took it out and glanced at the screen. It was security, Dan on the gate. He picked the call up and moved outside into the corridor where it was quieter.

'Harry, thank God. I've got Nick Grayson here. He's been ordering me to let him pass. I told him he wasn't on the list for your meeting and he couldn't go in. He got that near to me clocking him one, Harry. He asked me all kinds of questions which I wasn't going to try and answer. I said I'd call you if he wouldn't mind waiting. He's sitting in his car outside the gate, well he says it's his, a silver-grey Ford. Can I let him in?'

'Nope. You did exactly the right thing. Keep him outside. Did he say what he wanted?'

'No, not really. Some personal effects to pick up, he said. But I get the impression he's also really interested in your meeting, being nosey. Kept asking who and what for? My guess is someone's told him about it.'

'I'm coming out to speak to him Dan. You did good to hold him.'

Harry was rattled. He felt vulnerable and betrayed. Nick had been sacked, given his marching orders, but wasn't going away. The guy's turned out to be a bloody nuisance. He hadn't got it. Harry thought he needed to be given a firm lesson to ensure that he wasn't to try to come on site again or contact any employees. He guessed Elsa was to blame for telling him about the meeting. He'd deal with her in the morning, but first he had to decide what to do with Nick. He stepped back into the room.

'Charlie, Gavin, come with me. There's a guy at the gate who shouldn't be here. You don't think you could come along with me and make sure he understands he's made a big mistake coming here tonight and make it 100% certain he won't make that same mistake again.' He saw a smile grow on both their faces.

'Sure boss. It's what we do,' said Gavin nodding to Charlie who put down his pint glass.

'Anything we need to know about first, Harry?' asked Charlie.

'Like what?'

'Does he have a weak heart or… Are there any passing police patrols ever come this way?'

'You worry too much Charlie. Make it look like an accident, just so he understands, but keep your eyes open.'

The three arrived at the gate. Dan looked relieved to see them.

'He's over there, in his car, on his mobile I think,' said Dan pointing to the Ford parked up under the street lamp.

'Go back inside the gate, Dan, those two will sort it,' ordered Harry, ensuring Dan wasn't going to witness what happened next. He turned to Charlie and Gavin to speak to them.

'When he's finished his call, I'll get him out of the car and get him to come over to me,' said Harry.

He walked slowly over toward Nick who had seen him approaching, a solitary street light casting long shadows against the factory wall. He watched Nick cut his call. Harry didn't need to tell Nick to get out the car, he was so furious he was already out and closing the twenty paces between them fast.

'What the hell's going on Harry? I just called in to collect a few personal effects and I find what? Who have you got in there Harry?' He registered that Harry was not alone. Who are these guys with you? I don't recognise either of them.' Harry had never seen him so wound up. For a quiet, grey man, this was an attempt at going purple.

'Nick, things have changed round here,' Harry said quietly and calmly. 'You were told to leave and not come back. If I can find that photo of you I'll send it on, together with any other personal effects. I thought I'd made it perfectly clear when you saw me first thing this morning, you have no access to IT or other areas like accounts. In fact I'll tell you again, you are not allowed on site and Dan on security was properly doing his job, acting on my orders to ensure you or any other unauthorised person is kept out. Dan did as he'd been told.'

'You can't treat me like this. I've given my life to this business...'

'You don't mean that do you Mr Grayson,' said Charlie menacingly moving between Harry and Nick. Like a wild cat, he'd slunk in close without being noticed. He moved in still closer and Nick's demeanour suddenly changed from anger to instinctive fear. Harry knew it every time he saw it, everyone recognised a loser at that moment when their face showed they knew they were about to be taken down.

Harry saw a look of panic cross Nick's face as his eyes searched left and right for help. He looked at Harry making a last ditch appeal. It wasn't heard by Harry or anyone else. There were just brick and concrete walls and three menacing guys. Gavin grabbed both Nick's arms and forced them behind his back. In a flash Charlie took the car key fob from Nick's one hand and his mobile from the other. Harry watched as Charlie walked over to the Ford, climbed in and started it up.

'I think we're going to see Mr Grayson off for you, Harry. We'll be back very soon,' Charlie said in a matter of fact kind of voice. Harry watched as he nodded to Gavin who dragged an upright Nick to his car and pushed him into the back seat of the car with himself next to him. A moment later Charlie had spun the car wheels and they were moving away into the night, soon to be out of sight. Harry gave an oh well kind of sigh, turned and headed back inside the gate.

'Problem solved,' he said to Dan, 'Well done! If anybody asks, nobody called this evening, definitely no-one in a silver-grey Ford called Nick. Let Gavin and Charlie in when they come back will you.'

'I've got you, boss,' he replied with a grin, repositioning himself, legs astride, as he stood guarding his gate.

22

Cherry approached Harry as he re-entered the Conference Room.

'There's a slight gender imbalance in here Harry,' she said, looking around her, 'and where did you disappear off to?'

'That's two questions, Cherry. Firstly, I didn't have time to get any more girls along much as the guys might have liked that and secondly, I had to attend to a matter of site security. You know how it is, the buck stops here, with me. All sorted. Only took a moment. System's working fine now. Time for a beer. Want one?'

'So Harry, tell me where's your campaign headed next? You're clearly on a big recruitment drive over the coming weeks. With no elections coming up, what's the plan? What's the story here? You hoping for a parliamentary comeback?'

'We build up the movement. The first bricks have been laid, we add to them incrementally, maybe it will take years, hopefully less, but we will be ready to take power... Christian here brings considerable assets and I'm hoping to build our online base very quickly, if necessary piggybacking on one of the sites he's already working with. You watch, this is going to be big. You won't have seen anything so huge before,' and then he burst out laughing. Cherry looked at him as if he'd gone mad, but in reality he was having such fun. 'Come on,' he said, 'chill, have a beer why don't you? This is the start of a new adventure in popular politics. Who knows where it will lead?'

'Harry, your chat up lines aren't improving any,' she said smiling at last and reaching for a bottle, but your developing line in politics is intriguing me. It has a kind of basic appeal to grass roots people who fear they might be losing out.'

'Yep, something along those lines. But I want to give people a sense of community, fun and hope. The politics I believe in is making things happen, you'll see. We're appealing to the instinct for the self-preservation of one's own people. Life with me is not the humdrum life of losers, not boring…'

Harry's phone was ringing silently, vibrating in his pocket. He excused himself to take it wondering whether Dan was having more problems. No, not Dan. It was Gavin.

'We're on our way back, walking. Won't be more than five minutes. Just want you to have the heads up. Nick sounded off big time and well, Charlie was holding tight, very tight to quieten him down.'

'How was he holding him, Gavin?' asked Harry worried at what might be coming.

'Round the neck, Harry, round the neck. The guy kept shouting and wriggling.'

Harry went quiet. He recalled Barry Thornton's body in the bonfire and the indications that Cherry had reported from her conversation with the DCI that Barry had been strangled and then placed there in the flames. Harry needed to think fast, but needed more facts to go on.

'Where have you left him?'

'He's in the driver's seat of his car. We cleaned off all likely areas where there might be fingerprint points. Made sure only his own prints were left on the wheel. The car's half a mile away, further along Shapters Way, left as if he'd pulled over to the side of the road. The industrial estate's quiet at night. No one saw us, didn't spot any cameras, no other vehicles. Left his car keys in the ignition and his mobile in his pocket.'

'Is he… is he dead?' Harry felt he needed to ask.

'Probably. We didn't stop to check for a pulse if that's what you mean. Charlie just wouldn't let up, holding him I mean, and then he went limp,' said Gavin. We're just arriving back at the gate. Charlie's talking to Dan.

'OK, you two, get back inside, quick as you like, act as normal. I just need to brief Dan so he understands that Nick did call here, but wasn't let in and then he drove off. It's just that they may trace his visit to the factory gate from his mobile, so we need to be up to the game as the cops will certainly come calling. Nothing will happen this evening, that's for sure, so go and get yourselves a beer. No one's to know you've been off site. Mingle, mingle. If anyone wonders why you were out of the room it was to have a conversation with me in the corridor about politics… and keep that pretty vague, make it about choosing a leader… OK?'

The two did as they were told. Harry was left wondering how many people Charlie would strangle given half the chance. The guy he'd just given backing to on stage was a liability. Charlie Evans had gone too far, created an unnecessary problem. He'd need watching, had his uses though, he thought, like a half-tamed wild dog does.

Harry stood just inside the Conference Room to make his call to Dan who quickly grasped what his new on-message line was. It would be easier, always was, thought Dan, to be telling the truth when it came to telling lies.

Cherry was approaching him with two bottles of beer. It was time to give her attention, but then at some point Christian Howard needed a briefing, not least to advise him that his right hand man, Charlie, was literally, keeping a too tight a grip on things and needed watching.

Cherry sensed Harry was distracted and Harry for his part felt uncomfortably vulnerable. He had no wish to tell her anything. Right now he wasn't sure how to handle her. One solution was to offer to take her on somewhere after, to make her feel special, but his mind was racing thinking about Nick Grayson. Why the hell did he have to turn up and spoil the party?

'We'll find somewhere quieter later, Cherry. I've still some loose ends to tidy up here,' he offered, in carefully moderate tones. 'Look they need calling to order. Excuse me a minute will you, love…'

Harry moved swiftly to the centre of the room and hit his bottle on a table top with an attention seeking wallop. It had the desired effect, everyone's conversation levels dropping and heads turning in his direction.

'There are just a couple of things more tell you before we wind up. The first is that our future meetings will always be here at 7-o 'clock on the first Monday in the month. Tonight, being our first get together has been brief, just to give you a flavour of who we are and where we are headed. I've got a brief presentation to show you before you leave, so bring your drinks back to your places and don't fall asleep.'

Harry used the remote control device to dim the lights and start up the projector. He had promised and checked the system earlier and knew it would perform as required. There was a short slide showing a set of constitutional ideas, attributed to a guy called Covington. It clarified the geographical area for membership, three counties in the South West, and a racial agenda restricting it to verified pure white, Caucasians.

He then flashed up a series of quick cartoons poking fun under the heading, "Not Like Us" which released much mirth. Finally, Harry showed a short film listing some of the patterns of behaviour expected of members in the New Britain First Democratic Party. Obedience, smartness of dress and appearance, unwavering belief in a new white nation, fearless cleansing from all foreigners and other malign influences.

When it was over he checked the time. His plan was to get people safely on their way back to Exmouth and Ottery, well away before any police came calling. He guessed the road north from the factory would be blocked off once Nick's body was found which could be anytime soon. It was time to see everyone off and tidy up. He could afford to leave nothing lying around. Normal factory life had to seamlessly follow as if the meeting had happened by 8am tomorrow morning.

To his relief he'd managed to slip a quiet word in Christian's ear about Charlie and a looming problem. Christian indicated that concern about Charlie's performance was a shared worry they would need to come back to. There the matter was left, for now.

After everyone had gone Cherry came up to Harry's office with him. Harry knew Elsa would see that the rest of the tidying up in the room downstairs was cleared first thing.

'Like a coffee?' asked Harry, eager to enjoy showing off his coffee maker.

'OK, black expresso,' she answered, walking across to sit on Harry's chair and then eyeing him intently. 'So this is what it feels like to run a company. I still can't believe you're the same Harry,' she laughed.

'The very same…'

'One minute you're one of the lads, a football mad guy who's never lost his obsession for the sacred game. Then there's Harry the Plymouth Parliamentarian, a man with a silky tongue who persuades people to see things his way. And now, what do we have here, Plymouth's newest entrepreneur and one of the youngest too? Will the real Harry please step forward and identify himself!' she jested playfully.

'Here's your coffee. You won't sum me up that easily, Cherry Thomas. And you forgot, at this precise moment I'm your barrista. Will this do?' he asked cheekily, handing her her drink.

'You're no ordinary guy, Harry. Sometimes a loner, often surrounded by groupies. You hold something of a fascination for a girl. I can't help wondering what will become of you. I'll give you one thing, you're never boring!'

'Hmm! And you're someone special too. Always smart and sharp, always vivacious and focussed; always ready to tell my story. Can you, I wonder, play the supporting journalist part, at a time when I need to rely on you?' he said leaning over to look into her eyes.

'Harry, you know that deep down I have a lot of sympathy for the cause. I've watched this country being sold down the river as, in the name of austerity, public services have been reigned back and undermined. Too many outsiders have been allowed in and diluted what was once great. You're the only person I know who has the guts to name what's truly going on and fight the cause. I think you know you can count on me, Harry.'

At that Harry kissed her on the mouth and she in turn wrapped her arms around his big frame to hold him there. Harry knew, even as they kissed, it was time to get away from the factory. The timeline for escape was closing fast, otherwise he'd face a closed road and police questions if he wasn't already too late.

'We have to leave and leave now,' he told her pulling away. 'Did you come by car or cab?' he asked.

'Uber…'

'I'll give you a lift, come on, we need to make a move.'

Surprised, she looked at him afresh realising that she didn't know Harry as well as she thought. What was it, she wondered, that was driving him now? Why this impulsive urgency? There was something manic as well as controlling about him, it was in his eyes.

A moment later they were downstairs, outside in the car. Then Harry was locking up the yard gate behind them, Dan having finished his shift. He climbed back into the BMW and they headed north. As they passed a parked up silver-grey Ford, Harry gave it a very long glance.

'Do you know that car?' she asked.

'Can't say that I do?' he lied. His gaze returned to the road ahead. 'OK if we head back to my place, I've got some good pink gin to try,' he grinned.

'OK by me,' she said, feeling the heated front seats beginning to warm her.

A quarter of a mile on and a police car with its blues and twos flashing passed them going in the opposite direction. Cherry glanced at it, Harry took a deep breath and sighed with relief. A little local difficulty, he thought, had nicely just resolved itself.

23

But it hadn't entirely. As he led Cherry back into the house at Ham Drive, his mobile pulsed in his jacket.

'My Mum,' he said, 'Excuse me a minute. Help yourself to a drink in there,' he offered, pointing her in the direction of a row of bottles on the side. 'There,' he pointed to the pink gin, and there...' the tonic water beside it. 'Won't be long.'

Harry made an exit to take the call in the kitchen.

'Harry, I'm worried. You haven't seen Nick have you? Said he was popping into the business this evening to pick something up, but he's not come back and I can't reach him. It's not like him. His phone just rings out. Wondered by any chance whether you'd been there or might have heard from him?'

'Sorry Mum, Can't say I can help. I'm actually at home... entertaining company...'

'Oh, sorry to disturb you. Call me if you hear anything. Promise me, Harry,' she said, her voice quivering with emotion.

'OK Mum, I'll ring if I hear anything. I promise.' With that their conversation ended. Harry felt as if a dark shadow had descended. He was living in a world where truth was a casualty of convenience and deliberate lies came naturally, even when chatting to his Mum. All the same, he reasoned, she had betrayed him, run out on him when he most needed her support in his parliamentary campaign. It had almost cost him. He owed her nothing and his feelings for her had long ago shut down entirely. A bit of fake news was the new normal, what was so wrong with that? He determined to forget about the nuisance call.

Harry strode into the front room where Cherry had made herself quite at home and was half reclining on the sofa. She'd closed the slatted blinds, put on the table lamp and poured herself a very large gin and tonic. Harry smiled, she smiled back, conquest beckoned. It had been a while. He went over and helped himself to an equally large whisky and then flopped down beside her, throwing his jacket on the floor as he did so.

'We've fired the starting gun,' he said.

'And you're on your way up again, Harry. Congratulations, resurrection man! I know of no other politician with your charisma or grasp of contemporary realities. I think once you get your campaign rolling out it will certainly build and you're right, today, online is the only place to be.'

'And here's to my favourite press agent. Cheers!' he said, clinking his glass against hers.

He could smell her perfume and it did something intoxicating to him. He reached down, placed his glass on the floor and reached an arm around her pulling her toward him, but it was clumsy and desperate and she spilled her drink on herself.

'Oh no! My new top!' she explained in panic. She wriggled free from him, stood up and pulled away.

'Sorry, I'll get something you can dry that with from the kitchen,' he offered. 'There should be some kitchen roll somewhere. I'll find some.'

In the kitchen he searched frantically. Sheena's tidying had confused him, nothing was ever to hand.

When he returned Cherry was no longer by the sofa. She was standing by the TV, looking business like once again. She'd put her jacket on, zipped it up high and was speaking into her mobile. She looked up as he approached.

'I've an Uber arriving any moment now,' she said.

'Oh!...'

'Something's come up. My editor wants me down in Shapters Way, some breaking news. That's where we just came from isn't it, down near your place...?'

'It's a long road. Did he say where it was... What's it about?' asked Harry.

'No, just said look for the police road block and you won't miss it.'

'I could drive you,' he offered without enthusiasm, not really wanting to take himself into the danger zone.

'No, thanks... Sorry, Harry, must fly, yes, my taxi's outside already. Need to flag him down. Bye...'

When she'd gone Harry flopped down in the settee, retrieved his whisky and felt something was not quite right. His instinct made him wonder if Cherry was playing him.

He should have had her there and then, but the spilled drink, the sudden call, the departure... all too inconvenient.

'Bloody women! Thanks Mum! And sod you Cherry Thomas,' he murmured out loud reaching for the whisky bottle to pour himself another big one before mockingly toasting them both.

Harry didn't like it when things were untidy. Tonight had brought other people firmly into the heart of his future plans and things had gone both well and badly. He wondered whether Charlie Evans from Ottery was a psycho. The guy would definitely need careful watching, there were two strangulations that he knew of. That big man from Ottery would need to be kept on a tight leash.

And Cherry, he felt like she had been stringing him along, sweet talking him. Maybe she was only after his story and the free drinks, not really wanting to be his girl. That departure had been genuine enough on one level, the story of Nick in the car would prove real, but the gin and tonic down her front? He knew an evasive swerve when he saw one and now he was convinced that she had duped him and he threw his tumbler furiously into the fireplace in a fit of frustrated, impetuous rage, with a harsh crashing of splintering glass.

He stretched out on to the sofa. Some girls liked to play hard to get, he mused. It wasn't over. He'd send her some flowers tomorrow and leave her a message asking they meet up. He'd need to play a more gentle game. That would work, it had to.

His mobile rang. It was his Mum again.

'Harry, Nick's been found, in his car. There's a police woman with me. She says, she's telling me… Nick's dead and they suspect it wasn't due to natural causes.'

'Sorry to hear that. I'll send an email round at work tomorrow morning. I'm sure people will want to express their condolences.'

There was a silence at the other end.

'Is there anything else? I mean, do you need help or something? I'm sure you'll get over it. People are very resilient… I'd come over but I've been drinking. You are a very resilient…'

'Harry, Nick's dead…' she interrupted him. Then he could hear her tears.

What could he do but end the call. It was his Mum's emotional problem of her own making. It wasn't as if he could bring Nick back, even if he wanted to which he realised, he didn't; notwithstanding Cherry had earlier called him the resurrection man. Nick was history and his Mum just had to come to terms with the fact.

24

It was the end of the working week, Friday morning, Harry was drinking coffee alone, sitting at his desk in his office. It had proved to be a difficult and frustrating week for him since the previous Monday evening with all its promise of a new beginning, a new dawn, albeit with the Nick Grayson incident throwing a dark cloud across proceedings. He also had his personal life and police encounters competing for his attention. He reflected on it all and tried to collect his rambling thoughts.

First thing Tuesday morning he'd discovered it had indeed been Elsa who had secretly contacted Nick to tell him there was a strange meeting happening at the business on the Monday evening and he had told her that he was coming in regardless of the fact that he'd been sacked.

He'd also said he wanted to collect his photograph of himself and collect a file of items he'd instructed Elsa to keep by for him in a folder in her office. Harry had subsequently relieved her of the said items, reasoning that now he was dead he no longer had need of them and Harry would know what to do with them. She meekly accepted this, fully expecting another stern rebuke for going behind Harry's back.

Suitably chastised he'd told her to think on her situation. He had given her a lecture on loyalty and decided on balance that he would be better served keeping her in post than losing her. He could understand her loyalty to Nick after so many years working for him, but now he'd gone, a similar problem surely wouldn't arise again. Besides, he counted on her to do his running around and she did that very well.

Of course he had gone carefully through the file she had passed over to him. Most of it he tipped straight into the recycling bin, but in and amongst the paperwork there seemed be some interesting material Nick had deliberately failed to mention, in fact one big fact deliberately concealed from him.

The firm had, back in his father Patrick's day made a number of significant cash payments, all carefully recorded to various members of Plymouth City Council. What they were precisely for he couldn't make out, but he reckoned he now had enough leverage with Elsa to get the truth from her. Whatever it was had the distinct smell of corruption about it.

Next day, Wednesday, two days ago now, he'd done just that. He'd called her up to his office. She had indeed expected the summons and stood sheepishly in front of his desk as if she was in court awaiting a sentence. He didn't offer her a chair, choosing to make use of the theatre of the situation to ratchet up the pressure. It felt like it was when he had been in the headmaster's study as a schoolboy, bizarrely he was now the head.

Some people just needed to get bad things off their chest. She, unlike Harry himself, was one such person. She almost seemed lifted, relieved even, when she told him, and there was no holding her back. She spilled all the beans. Patrick had bent the ear of councillors over the years and Nick had fixed the payments. Harry listened as she told him how business tax, planning exemptions and business enterprise awards had come the company's way simply by quietly sending money into certain councillors' accounts. What

Harry realised was that he had unexpectedly ended up with what was a blackmailer's gold mine, a treasure trove for him to exploit when he was ready. He locked the incriminating papers in his office wall-safe, securely hidden behind the picture of himself.

During the week the police had also been in to see him to interview him. The local police DC was pleasant enough. It had all been so pedestrian, the officer simply and unimaginatively churning the paperwork. There hadn't been a single difficult question. 'Yes, Nick Grayson used to work here. No, he hadn't seen him this week. No, he had no knowledge of any financial or personal enemies Nick might have had. Yes, he was so much an ordinary man, always in a grey suit, a stalwart of the company in his day. Yes, he was fondly thought of by all in the business world and would be missed…' Then it was over.

However, a day later a DS had come back. That was more tricky. The first pathologist report had shown a similar pattern on Nick's neck to an earlier murder on the file, that of Barry Thornton, a murder Harry himself had been interviewed about as a significant witness only three months earlier. 'Did he have any comment to make? Did he not think it rather a coincidence that the two murders placed him in the frame as a double significant witness?'

Harry had played straight bat, looking every bit the sharp cut professional businessman and politician he had become. He made every effort to be helpful and even made the DS a coffee. In the end the DS had gone away. The man was inscrutable and Harry had no idea what the police were really thinking and fully expected they'd be back again with yet more questions.

He remembered Cherry had had access to the man he nicknamed 'Ginger', the Exeter DCI, and thought it was worth chancing a call through to her for an update on police intel.

'Hi Cherry. How did you get on Monday night? That new item you had to dash off for in Shapters Way? It was Nick Grayson who used to work here, wasn't it? I've had the police in a couple of times, making enquiries, such a shock for us all…'

'Yes, reckon we saw the police going to the spot when you drove us up to your house. Sad business, a murder. He must have had enemies…'

'I've got something for you Cherry, phoning to give you the heads up on a possible story. When I had a second visit from the police on Wednesday, I was told the police forensics reckon Nick was murdered in the same way as that guy in the Ottery bonfire. Don't ask me how they tell one strangling is similar to another, but it's strange don't you think? Weirdly it places me near both which is… well, to say the least, uncomfortable…'

'Yeah! It sure is weird…'

'You might want to chat to your DCI friend in Exeter again. He might know more than they told me.'

'Will do Harry.'

'Any chance you can keep me posted on this one, Nick being an old family friend and a key figure in the business over so many years. More than that I'm finding it a little unnerving having spotted one body in the bonfire then finding out it could be the same murderer killing Nick. All a bit too, well close to home… So anything you can find to help me put my mind at rest would be good. Knowing there's a vicious strangler out there is bad, really bad…'

'Yeah, I'll call you. It's a live story, I'll copy you in on updates. Watch my news blog.'

'Oh Cherry, you know you once said you'd like to go to a nice place to eat out, well more upmarket than MacDonald's. How about it? Tonight? It being Valentines Night… My treat…'

There was a pause on the other end. Harry waited.

'OK, Harry. No more spilling drinks down me, right? What time?'

'I'll text message you, make arrangements later…'

Harry felt lifted. It was back on. Having a girl alongside him was important politically. It would reassure the movement. He'd make sure he got some pictures taken of them both tonight, ones he could post on Instagram, Twitter and in other social media. It would flatter his image. Besides, he didn't want the party to think he was queer. There was a strong party line on that kind of thing.

Head down, Harry found it impossible to write any kind of tribute to Nick to send round on the office email, so he called Elsa in and told her to see to it. The good thing was she seemed flattered to have been asked.

'Let me see it to sign it off before it goes out will you,' he said, adding, 'And send a copy to my Mum, Bev McNamara. She'll only ring for it if she doesn't get one.'

'No sooner said than done,' Elsa chirped.

Later that day three empty shipping containers were being delivered as new storage facility. The first of three articulated lorries was carefully negotiating the tight entrance. It made Harry excited, the risk, the stakes were rising. He'd told Bill, the site manager, where they were to go, the far end of the parking area away from the others. 'A forward looking investment, ready for expansion,' he'd told him. The lie worked a treat. The guy couldn't be more helpful and would personally supervise their arrival and siting.

At 3.10 p.m. Harry looked out of his office window between the half opened blind to see if all had arrived and whether they were being directed as to where to go. There was no Dan on the gate since Monday night, as Harry had thought it prudent to keep him off site for a few days until things quietened, leaving the site manager a free rein. Harry could see him swinging open the double gates himself. Two in place, one still to go.

An hour later all the trucks had gone and there was a quick call from Bill sounding pleased with himself for having seen to things just as Harry had wanted. Harry sounded appreciative. It was time to let Limping Man know he already had his storage. Harry wanted to know more about the proposed contents and to be ahead of the game when it came to risk managing their arrival and safe storage.

The second part of the task list, outstanding from Monday evening, was to find the right quality people to meet his 50%

quota for the new IT suite. The easy bit was calling Stu with the job offer. As for the other person, he'd begun by making a few enquiries of the usual staff recruitment sources – the Job Centre and an employer's website and in both areas had drawn a total blank.

'Stu, I need another person, good at IT, to work here on the political side. We had a small team when we ran the parliamentary campaign and they did us proud. Can you see what you can do to find me someone? The main thing is that I need to be able to 100% trust them as being on message. There'll be some reward in it for you.'

'Harry… I was just thinking Keri could do with the work. I can do all the stuff Harry, you know it, access the dark web, create the videos, source and write the right text, evaluate the gaming apps, all that stuff. I'm pretty sure Keri can too. Presently, she works from home, but she'd be good.'

'Stu, I'm more than happy to take you on, but isn't Keri black or maybe just mixed race? That could be problem don't you think?'

'Nah. She's Irish, just swarthy with it. She's a good lass. She voted for you Harry, I know she did! Don't let a good sun tan get between Keri and making a good employer happy.'

'OK then. Both of you are to come in on Monday. Arrive about 10-o 'clock. Report to my office. I'll make sure you're expected. I'm not giving anyone the usual, regular paperwork at this point, you understand… Let me know if there's any problem with Keri. Tell her she'll be well rewarded. I'll fill you both in on what's required when I see you.'

He had one last call to make before he went off to get ready for his night out.

'Hello Christian. Three containers on site and two back office staff lined up to start Monday. How's your side of the bargain coming along?'

25

It was Friday 3rd April and at 2 p.m. Harry joined others to attend Nick Grayson's funeral, held at Ford Park Cemetery in central Plymouth. It seemed ironic that he'd died parked up in a Ford and here they were at Ford Park, it was a fitting end.

The quaint Victorian chapel easily accommodated the few mourners, amongst whom was Harry's Mum, Bev McNamara. Duty required Harry's presence or he wouldn't have been there. In recent years he'd only ever been to two funerals, his grandfather's and then his father's, but truth be told he found funerals distasteful. The platitudes were grating, the heavenly pleading empty, and tears hypocritical and sentimental. He had no time for all that.

What he did like was a tidy performance provided by the undertakers and vicar all smartly attired in their immaculate black uniforms. He appreciated seeing these street theatre cultural events conducted with precision and respect. Today's service for Nick was short, if not perfunctory and clearly the elderly officiating minister knew Nick even less well than Harry himself, so hardly at all. Otherwise the working officials did their jobs as they should.

Two thirds of the thirty or so comfortable chapel chairs were taken up, though none of the mourners chose to sit near the front. Harry thought the grey slate wall of remembrance in front of them, which had been inscribed with the names of deceased servicemen was a nice touch – Nick liked grey, it suited him in life and death.

Harry had chosen to accompany his Mum and stood and sat beside her as the service required. At a couple of points she was tearful but appeared to be holding herself together well. It felt strange to be almost in intimate reach of his Mum after their falling out, or rather her abandoning him. Neither seemed to know how to react toward the other. First she reached to hold his forearm, but then let go as Harry thought she realised what she was doing. For his part, when later she became tearful again he felt in his pocket for tissues, but they were never offered. There was an awkwardness in their being together, like oil and water they could never find a way to be as one. He looked at his watch. It had been going on for half an hour, should be over soon.

Earlier, Harry had felt it was only appropriate he should offer the business Conference Room for the reception afterwards. He'd sent all but the most essential staff at McNamara Metals off home for a half-day's leave as a tribute to Nick. It wasn't entirely an act of generosity, Elsa had pointed out that the noisy crane and car crusher, the fork lifts, the vehicles going in and out of the yard all had to be silenced if the atmosphere was to be anything like respectful.

Harry had reluctantly agreed to some work being done as overtime on Saturday morning to make up for lost production time.

The gesture to give a half day's leave to the yard staff had been well received. Harry had additionally sent his now up to complement, four person IT-social media team who just happened to be occupying the room off the Conference Room, away for the afternoon too, reminding them to make sure they locked up after them to keep out prying eyes.

In the event, just Elsa from the business had chosen to pay her respects in attending the funeral service and wake. To Harry's mind it seemed disloyal that everyone else had simply bunked off, probably to go fishing or head down to the pub. Personally, he might have had no time for Nick Grayson, but Nick had run the business with his father Patrick and served alongside him in the firm all his working life, so the fact only Elsa had come along filled Harry with a kind of resentful loathing for his own employees. It was a matter of duty and respect, values he cherished.

Whilst in the funeral limousine, Harry and his Mum had travelled back to McNamara Metals sitting beside one another. It was she who had taken the conversation initiative and began firing questions at Harry.

'I was very fond of Nick. He'd become a real friend after your Dad died, even before that if I'm honest. Your Dad lived for the factory and nothing else. It was his first love, before you and certainly before me,' she said. 'He left it entirely with me to bring you up and I'm going to tell you straight Harry, in the time I've been living at my sister's and then at Nick's, I've come to realise I did you no favours, none at all.'

Harry was taken aback by his Mum's frankness and didn't know how to respond. It was delivered without the slightest hostility in an even tone of voice. Perhaps the occasion had unsteadied her, derailed her off her normal emotional tracks, thought Harry.

'You walked out on me you mean?' said Harry.

'No, I mean I should have walked out of that house a long time before I did. My one regret is I was so slow in realising my mistake.'

'What mistake was that then?'

'I continuously spoiled you like you were for ever a baby. I never let you grow up. You were given everything you wanted, spoiled and never disciplined, as a result you were never given a chance.'

'Bullshit Mum… You're upset… Look,we're nearly here. Calm yourself. You need to come in, sit yourself down and have some tea…'

They were almost there. He spotted Dan, suitably smart, on gate security duty this afternoon ready to check all the mourners in and out. He'd recently been issued with an official clipboard to fasten his lists to. Harry knew such little gestures easily pleased people like Dan.

His Mum looked at him, now with fury in her eyes, their conversation stalling as Harry lowered his window and spoke to Dan on the gate, who with a knowing nod let them into the yard. The two walked silently side by side into the main door of the offices then along the corridor into the Conference Room.

'I've not been here before,' she said breaking the silence. This surprised Harry who realised in that moment that his parents had indeed lived in two watertight separate worlds – work and home.

'I could get someone to show you round,' Harry offered rather bluntly.

'Another time, maybe, Harry boy.'

Naturally there was tea for his Mum and a bottle of St Austell Brewery, *Tribute* for himself. As tea and beer were served by the two waitresses in black uniform and white pinafores, Harry and his Mum separated as they went to speak to different people.

Looking around him Harry realised he didn't know these people, an oversight on his part, so he made straight for the person he knew to be Nick's sister. He ought to speak to her, he thought, it was expected.

'Hello, I'm Harry McNamara,' he said offering his hand.

'I know who you are, it's Samantha King. Thank you for laying this on,' she said cooly, waving her arm and hand expansively and definitively not taking his.

'The least we could do,' said Harry, mindful as he said it, it was in fact the cheapest spread the caterers were prepared to offer him.

'I hope you don't mind me saying this, but you treated my brother like… he was a piece of shit!' she said, her voice rising with every word.

Harry was taken aback and looked around him to see if others had noticed.

'You might well worry that others hear, but I really don't care. Nick toiled all his working life for you and your family and what happens, the prodigal returns having been squandering his life with the pigs and takes over as the favourite. Nick meantime, having run this place and made it what it is, is booted out without a by-your-leave. You were responsible. Do you know what that did to him?

'I expect you're about to tell me,' he said quietly.

'You're dead right I am. You destroyed him. He came to see me a broken man at a complete loss what to do next. He was lost…'

'I'm very sorry for your loss,' Harry ventured, 'and I need to say how grateful we all are for Nick's long and worthy contribution to this business.' Upon which Harry turned briskly, making his escape, and found himself making straight for his Mother.

If Harry thought an easier conversation would follow he was quite mistaken. His Mum was picking up where she'd left off earlier.

'Harry, you and I are family. There's only you and me left.'

'You've my aunt, your sister… '

'Look she was kind enough to take me in, but you are my flesh and blood, you are my son and a Mum never forgets her son…'

'You did! You left me to fend for myself. Everything needed doing and nothing was done. You left me to suffer, that's what you did,' said Harry realising it was his turn to be raising his voice.

'Not here, Harry. We need to sort out a few things, outstanding business, but not here, not now, Harry.'

'OK, Mum, I'll call you,' he said touching her arm so everyone could see they were apparently on good terms.

Harry made an effort to circulate and got bored. In the end he ended up talking to Elsa and decided now was as good a time as any to see what he could learn from her.

'Elsa I'm very grateful you came. There really isn't much other business representation apart from you and me to keep the side up,' he said affably. It seemed to work.

'Harry, it's so sad. Nick was good to work for, even if he did slip a few bribes. He was kind, regular as clockwork and did what had to be done. Loyalty and hard work count in a place like this. Do you reckon one of the people he'd slipped money to was behind his death? I've been losing sleep over it. What if they go further and go for me or you, because we know what he did? What do you think? Are we safe, Harry?'

Harry immediately regretted coming to speak to her. This was not the conversation he envisaged, so he tried a different line. 'Where do you think his strengths really lay? On a day like today we need to think about what he was good at, don't we.'

'Well, he was very good at accounts, watching the expenditure to see nothing was wasted, checking invoices were sent promptly and that we were getting paid. You know, the basics of business life. He was a penny pincher, never spent money unnecessarily… if I wanted to raise the height of my PC on my desk to avoid back strain it took him months before he'd agree to spend the ten quid to buy the new part. You'd probably call him a bean counter, but it's what makes the difference in a small business like ours, that's why your Father had such faith in him. I never understood why you got rid of him like you did…'

'What did he do when he wasn't working? Did he have any interests? Family? Friends? What?' asked Harry, glancing round the room to see his Mum was happily sitting down with a paper plate of cake in front of her in a lively conversation and Samantha King was talking earnestly to a tall, lean bloke by the window.

'He liked sailing and had a small yacht,' Elsa added. 'He kept it at the Yacht Haven on the Plym estuary, The Mount Batten Marina I think it's called. I've often wondered if you could see it from the bottom of the road here. That was his main interest. He called his boat his sweetheart, named it "Scrapfish". Never spent his money on anything else so far as I know.'

'Did he have a social life sailing? Any friends you know of?'

'I'm sure he knew people down there, but he used to sail alone as far as I know, then meet people at a club house somewhere.'

'What do you imagine will happen to his yacht now?'

'No idea. The boat keys are probably still in his locker.'

Harry hadn't thought to check whether Nick had cleared his locker. Perhaps that was why he had come in that fateful Monday evening to allegedly clear his stuff. He'd wondered what he'd meant by that ever since, not believing it was just a photo of himself he'd wanted. He kicked himself, how stupid to have not thought to check.

'Do you by any chance hold a key to his locker?' Harry asked.

'Yes. I keep meaning to go through it, but can't bring myself to. I'd be glad if you would do it when you have a moment Harry. It's locker 2 in the works corridor. Your Dad was always number 1.'

'Fetch me the key will you Elsa, I'll check it over later.'

Elsa nodded, put down her now empty cup of tea and disappeared, returning a few minutes later to slip a small bottle opener key ring in the shape of a yacht with two keys attached into his hand.

'Don't know what the other key is for,' she added as she went over to talk to the now idle catering staff. Harry smiled to himself. He'd always fancied getting his hands on a yacht.

Harry was getting impatient. What had these people got to talk about? Their inane conversations seemed interminable. Just what did they get from it? It was nearly 5-o 'clock and he wanted to see the catering team cleared up and off site. There were half a dozen mourners still chatting away. Hadn't they homes to go to? The weekend was approaching. It was time to bring things to a conclusion and he cleared his throat before striking his desk loudly with a spoon. That did the trick.

'Can I thank you all once again for coming to Nick's funeral and supporting those who were near and dear to him. Very shortly the factory will be closing up for the night and we need to allow the catering staff to get away.' A round of appreciative applause interrupted him, '…and then, then the cleaning team have to come in and do their job, not that

you've made a mess.' A ripple of polite laughter followed.
'But I do need to ask you all to begin to move toward the
exit. Elsa will help you retrieve any coats or belongings on
your way out.'

Harry began working the few who remained toward the exit,
like a sheepdog circling and driving forward a small flock of
reluctant sheep. Among them were his Mum and Samantha
King, so deep in conversation with each other, it was as if
they were old friends. His Mum had never properly moved
to Nick's flat and was heading back to her sister's place. He
had a feeling that Samantha lived over the Tamar, just in
Cornwall. He asked Elsa to ensure he had her correct
address and contact details before she left.

Then they'd gone, caterers and Elsa too. The mention of
cleaners had been a lie, an invention of his to get them
moving. Lies seemed to come so easily to him. He wondered
if people noticed and if they did whether they cared. They'd
probably be glad he'd used any excuse available to bring the
miserable proceedings to an end. Looking out of the office
window he could see that only Dan remained on duty at the
gate, quietly sitting in the dim light of his security kiosk,
looking down at his mobile reflecting white on his face.

For a moment Dan's face looked ghostly and he thought of
Nick in the cemetery. It made him stop and think – having to
attend three funerals was more than enough in a lifetime.
They were inherently miserable and given half the chance
he'd avoid attending any more.

26

The following Monday afternoon, Harry looked at the time on his phone. He had two hours until the evening attendees arrived for 7-o 'clock, maybe less and he'd been notified to expect a delivery arriving at 8-o 'clock, items to be stored in the containers.

He felt Nick's keys in his trouser pocket and decided to do something he'd foolishly overlooked earlier, to search Nick's locker. Every employee at McNamara Metals had one. Never having thought to use a locker himself he'd walked past the row of yellow doored lockers numerous times without a second glance. Perhaps he ought to check his father's locker too.

When he got to the corridor he saw locker number 1 had no padlock and could be swung open. His father's locker was empty. He pushed it shut again. Then he tried the key in the lock of locker 2. It clicked open. Opening the door wider he found it contained two yellow box files, standing vertically together. On the spine of one it said, "Scrapfish" and on the other, "Accounts". Harry pulled them both out, closed and then re-locked the locker, before taking the two bright yellow files up to his office for examination.

Harry had an instinct for things, he had it now, like a scented trail with him as the hunter, he'd hit on something important. Placing the files on his desk he checked his excitement, time to make himself a coffee from his personal machine. The coffee would help him focus.

He pulled open the "Scrapfish" file first. A picture of a boat had been glued to the inside of the cover. A pile of letters and documents lay to the right. Harry began flicking through them before he suddenly stood up grasping and waving one paper in his hand. 'You thieving bastard,' he shouted out loud.

The document was a two year old paid invoice for £45,000, the price McNamara Metals had paid to buy a Hunter Legend 360 yacht. It's a company perk! Nick's careful accounting was so he could have his own private sailing boat paid for by the company! No wonder he was so determined to come in and collect a few of his personal things.

The red mist cleared from before Harry's eyes as he suddenly realised his stroke of good fortune. This magnificent boat was now actually his own! It little mattered that he might not know the first thing about sailing but the boat strictly was and still did belong to McNamara Metals and it was therefore entirely his own to do with as he pleased. He'd landed on his feet, first a profitable business, second a nice BMW car and today, a superb looking yacht.

He smiled contentedly and placed the yacht ownership document back in the file on top of the other paperwork taking another look at the glossy photo of a fine looking vessel. What else there was remaining didn't interest him. He glanced through the wad of paperwork quickly. There were invoices for servicing the engine, the purchase of new sails and charges for mooring fees. A small booklet served as a kind of on shore ship's log and he could see it had been written in Nick's spidery hand. Harry saw the reports as typically Nick – containing boring accounts of the weather and sea conditions and details as to the routes he'd taken out of the estuary and back again, even on one occasion venturing east as far as the Isle of Wight. He then flipped the lid of the box closed and turned his attention to the other one marked, "Accounts".

Harry pulled out half a dozen sheets of account papers. Glancing from one paper to the next they were all very similar, but he couldn't make either head or tail of them. The six sheets were headed, *Alabama, Alaska , Arizona, Arkansas, California* and *Colorado*. All American States with a list of figures in pounds sterling, not US dollars, with no individual amount shown exceeding £1,000. Most entries were for very small sums and no sheet totalled more than nine or ten thousand pounds. The total of the six sheets came to around £35,000. To what these accounts referred Harry had absolutely no idea. Flicking the sheets over, there was nothing else on the reverse to help solve the mystery. He resolved to ask Elsa about them tomorrow.

He then removed all the paperwork from the two files, having decided to lock them in his office safe. The empty yellow box files were then placed into his office cupboard. His attention then switched to the need for an agenda for the forthcoming evening meeting. The now regular contingent from Ottery and Exmouth would be joined tonight by new recruits from Plymouth and a further two guys from Exeter. The cause was building.

After their previous Monday meeting on 2nd March, Limping Man had been in touch. He was always brief when he phoned. He'd asked that Harry saw to it that the four geographical area leaders should stay on tonight after everyone else had gone. They would need to help with the delivery needing to be stored away in the shipping containers Harry had organised. He'd also insisted Harry ensure a fork lift truck was available.

In addition Christian had phoned to say he wanted some statistical feedback as to what the four newly appointed social media team had achieved, especially as he was meeting half the cost.

'Make sure we get some data feed on new subscribers, membership growth and so on,' he'd ordered. 'If these four don't deliver, we lose them.'

Limping Man didn't mess and he didn't waste words. Harry reassured him, 'it's all in hand'.

Christian said he himself would arrive with and take personal charge of the lorry shipment taking place later in the evening and so would not be in attendance and would miss Harry's pre-meeting.

Harry had another coffee and by the time he'd drunk it he was ready, a check list agenda on his phone as to the night's proceedings. It was time to go down and check the Conference Room out to be certain as to its readiness for the evening.

Sure enough Elsa had done her thing, the refreshments team had been in and made their delivery. She'd also organised Dan to come in off the gate to set out the furniture. It was now laid out just as Harry had wanted it, with fewer seats than the earlier meetings, because he'd decided to restrict attendance to two guys per area and only one person from the media team. It had been bothering him that large numbers of attendees carried additional unwarranted risk, so he'd cut it back to the core. A quick scout round to see there were enough beers and Harry was happy.

First to arrive, ten minutes before anyone else was Marcus from IT, who was making the opening presentation. Harry had asked him to show something that would inspire the cause as well as provide feedback on the work the media team had been doing. Harry had decided not to include Cherry in his invite list tonight, wary of her running a story over which he had no sanction. He thought he'd try and catch up with her later. She was always busy and they seemed to be drifting apart, he couldn't have that.

By 7.05 there were ten people in the Conference Room, all with a bottle of beer to hand in an atmosphere of camaraderie and hushed seriousness. Harry glanced outside to ensure Dan was at his post; there he was, the dutiful sentry at the gate. Harry had the thought that Dan might have been born with a key hole in his back. Wind him up and he moved mechanically just as he was programmed to. He was an ideal worker. Harry turned and called the meeting to order and introduced Marcus Harrison.

Compared with everyone else present, Marcus was the runt of the litter as Harry saw him. He wondered if he was a half human of some sort. Standing straight and squinting through his glasses he couldn't have been much more than five foot tall. But what he lacked in stature he made up quickly with a show of tech competence. The ceiling projector flashed into life and the wall was illumined by a gripping action show supported by high quality sound.

To Harry's mind it neatly summed up many of the recent developments in his own political thinking. The pro-immigration, pro-abortion and pro-LGBT activists of the time were creating conditions in which the white English populations were on a course for decline and replacement. He'd heard it all before, but the way Marcus presented it this time with sharp imagery as if put out by a Hollywood film studio, backed up with tight graphics and clear charts made the evidence irrefutable. It was exactly what he had wanted to see and hear. He was glad he'd not invited Cherry along. She wouldn't have much liked the bit about alpha males ruling and the role of women being relegated to providing sexual and reproductive services. Harry knew what Marcus meant, but it had been bluntly stated, rather too obvious and crudely put. When the initial presentation came to a close, Marcus went on to deliver an analysis of their "reach" after just one month "live".

Harry was unexpectedly gripped. An astonishing number of links had been made with other far right groups and online *comments* received had already exceeded several hundred. The *membership boxes* had started to pull in daily applications and these were being vetted as they arrived, granting temporary membership status until confirmatory DNA genealogy reports were back which in turn triggered the progression to full membership procedure.

Marcus said many of the comments were from people wanting to know what they could do, asking how they could help support the cause. It was especially pleasing to be getting financial support, the US proving particularly lucrative. After thirty minutes without interruption, the screen went blank, the room fell silent and Marcus sat down. He'd done a good job and Harry felt able to invite questions.

'How do we use your stuff to put actual boots on the ground?' asked the new guy from Plymouth. Toby Grant was a usefully big fellow Harry had known for years, they'd grown up together rising through the ranks of the Plymouth Rovers Supporters Club. Toby's question was a good one, but outside Marcus's field of expertise.

'I think we'll hold that one until later,' interrupted Harry, 'excellent question Toby. Any one else?'

'How precise are we being about DNA? I mean some people say we've all got some undesirable traits in our ancestry?' asked Charlie's deputy from Ottery.

'DNA is a most interesting subject in its own right. Of course some of the lefties are trying to blur the science. What we do is check for purity. Look at any silver or gold ring, it will never be 100% without impurity, but we're looking for a high, good enough, standard. We're following American far right practice and guides on this one. Let me put it like this, if someone's DNA comes back who is out and out Ashkenazy Jew that would be very clear and you know what we'd tell them.' There was a knowing guffaw.

'But we can live with a few imperfections and I don't envisage us having to turn people away. Having said that we are always on the look out for the infiltrator, those who might damage out movement, so as well as DNA scrutiny we have a second level of admission to membership testing built in to our membership protocol.'

Questions went on for a quarter of an hour more. The effect seemed to Harry to be one of bonding to the cause. People were lapping up what Marcus was telling them. It was like music to their ears. This cheered him and he hoped when he reported to Limping Man later he'd be happy.

Harry glanced at his watch. 'We've just a few minutes before we all go outside. Toby asked a question about what we can all do in a practical way as boots on the ground. What you will be doing shortly will make what you do next with your white brothers become self-evident. We will be fighting for the cause.'

The group time broke up and Marcus began to clear and lock away his things. 'You can go home now Marcus. You did a good job there. See you in the morning.'

'Thanks boss,' he said, sweeping up his jacket under his arm and heading for the door.

Not long after Marcus had gone, Dan called Harry to say the evening's shipment had arrived. Christian was asking for them all to assemble at the storage containers Harry had specially ordered, that had been sited at the far end of the factory yard. Harry briefed everyone and they set off downstairs in an atmosphere of eager excitement.

The smart looking tractor pulling the first artic trailer carried a huge red-brown rusty container on it. It drove in, swung round and reversed up into the yard, slowly approaching the nearest container. With a hiss of brakes the engine died. The driver stayed in his cab. The two rear doors creaked as they swung open, the driver quite unable to see what was going on.

'He knows nothing and it's best to keep it that way. I told him to stay in his cab and paid him well to keep his mouth shut. Can you get your container doors open, find someone to use that forklift, organise a human chain and get this thing unloaded. Quick as you like. We don't want to take too long over this. And tell your guy on the gate to be as sharp as a

cat on heat tonight. Anything twitches out there he's to jump
to it and let us know, right?'

Harry nodded. He'd just heard the most words ever from
Limping Man's mouth in one go, perhaps he was anxious?
Harry called to the guys, organised them and stood back to
observe progress. It was only clear what some of the items
were from the shape of the boxes. Harry was certain that a
substantial supply of light arms and ammunition were
included. These were stacked first at the far end of the open
container. Other square boxes had what looked like Russian
text printed on them. Christian whispered in his ear, 'high
grade military explosive. Make sure they're handled gently.
And those,' he indicated with his thumb, 'mortars, British,
best quality L16 81mm, standard army issue, but not these
babies, they're ours,' he grinned. Harry sensed the man's
familiarity with weaponry.

When the last of the items had been unloaded and guys were
beginning to complain with the effort involved, the job was
done and the doors padlocked shut. The forklift whirred and
spun round on its axis to disappear and be parked up for the
night. The cab driver was waved on his way, Dan opening
the gates to let him out as he approached. The truck pulling a
now empty rusty container soon disappeared into the night.

Everyone else got called back into the meeting room for a
brief final resume. This time Christian Howard did the
talking. What he had just brought onto the site earned mega
respect in terms of brownie points and everyone was
standing before him as if he was a sergeant major, which to
Harry's mind, he might well once have been.

'OK guys, a good job well done. I get about, but I can put my
hand on my heart and say, *The South West is Best.*'

Those were familiar words to Harry's ear, words which had come from the 1930s far right news sheets his own grandfather had left behind. Headlines on paperwork in his own bedroom, kept in a metal trunk. He wondered if Christian knew of them and felt a moment of paranoia. Christian was still speaking.

'I don't need to say this, but I will and only once. Traitors get burned.' Christian let the words sink in and then he looked across at Harry who was just then thinking of Barry Thornton, the one time labour councillor, strangled and then burned in a bonfire. A cold shiver went through him, but he was not going to let it show.

'Thank you Christian. I think we can let the guys go now. We meet here next, on the first Monday in May, same time, same place. There will be more news then. In the meantime, follow the websites, all of us keep building momentum where we are, but I want no private initiatives. I want to know every breath you take before you take it, which means you keep 100% quiet on everything. Thanks guys.'

Only Christian and Harry remained on site. Harry felt a deep loathing like bile in his throat, making him catch his breath, but knew he had no option but to work with this dangerous guy with whom his political future was now enmeshed.

27

There were just the two of them left in the Conference Room, only one light remained on. Harry felt for an instant as if he were lost in a dark cave, only a hint of daylight from somewhere high above. It was time to turn it out and go. Harry watched Christian carefully.

'I need a lift back to my car Harry. I'd be obliged if you'd take me,' said Christian.

'Where did you leave it?'

'Exeter, Sowton Services, M5. The rendez-vous point with the lorry…' he offered by way of explanation.

Harry knew an order when it was given. Limping Man had told him to serve as his driver. He was pushing it, but Harry took it on the chin. Tonight the man had gained a lot of kudos with the lads, a very significant amount of weaponry and explosives had been delivered, just like that. It was an impressive achievement worthy of huge respect. He knew better than to ask its source.

But, the two were supposed to be partners and Limping Man's attitude was that of a man trying to take charge. Harry had to be careful, it wasn't going to happen. To his mind there was something distinctly unhinged about the guy, cold, he'd soon as have you killed for amusement as look at you. In that moment Harry instinctively knew for certain that Limping Man had put Charlie up to the murder of Barry Thornton. It was time to push back a bit, assert himself, to re-dress the imbalance in the so-called partnership arrangement they had, to keep himself in the reckoning.

'Sure Christian, a lift's no problem. Sit yourself down for a minute. I'll be right back. I need to make a call before we leave.'

Taking his time, Harry walked out of the room and up to his office where he made a long overdue call to Cherry, wondering what response he'd get. He quite fancied some down time with her and asked her if she was free later. He couldn't help but recall Marcus's presentation and think of himself as an alpha male, Cherry as his sexual plaything. The image didn't sit quite squarely with reality just yet. He couldn't bring himself to think he was not an alpha male… Logically, the problem the two had in getting it together had to lie with her. She just needs more time.

'Sure Harry. I'm off home soon. Fancy a take-away? Indian?' she cheerily answered.

'OK, but I'll be about an hour, maybe a bit over. I'm still at work…' He didn't feel the need to explain further. It was complicated.

It was done. He closed his office door and went back down to Christian who was drumming his fingers impatiently on the arm of his chair. Harry gave a superficial apology for keeping him waiting, but inside felt he'd pushed the guy back and gained himself some ground, a little breathing space.

Once both inside the BMW Harry drove slowly to the gate. Dan opening it for them, his wave more like a salute, as they approached.

'You think he might want to work more hours, Harry?' asked Christian. 'Keep an eye out, deter troublemakers, burglars and the like? He looks useful.'

'It costs, Christian. I'll think about it.' Harry was pushing back some more. It was a tried and tested route to get respect, pushing back. He thought he could well afford to pay Dan more hours, it seemed a good suggestion, but he wasn't going to show he would act on it, because Christian had said so.

'I want to talk about the future,' Christian began, as the car began accelerating up the A38 dual carriageway running along the edge of Dartmoor. 'The future…'

'I expect you have plans. What do you want to say?'

'You never ask me about my colleagues Harry, the people who are our masters. I know you know they are there in the shadows, and if you did ask you know I wouldn't tell you. I respect that, you not asking that is.' He clearly wanted to talk about them.

'They are very determined men,' he continued. 'They're watching out for us and they're telling me what they want done. Unlike you and me, mere minnows, they grasp the bigger picture, they see the whole pond.'

'And what, in their collective wisdom do they propose?'

'The summer, Harry, the summer. That will be the time for an ideal storm.'

'And…'

'And that's when we make our move…'

'I may only be a probationer in the world of business, having unexpectedly stepped into being an entrepreneur, but I do know one has to have a vision, a goal, a clearly achievable target and a series of do-able steps identified to be able to get to where one wants to be. The risks and the costs have to be worked out beforehand. We can't afford to fail. You'll need to convince me,' Harry stated, again prodding Christian for more.

'Can you be ready to receive a small fleet of vans at the factory, arriving over the next month or two?'

'I expect so, but questions may be asked,' answered Harry, 'questions like what are all these vans to be used for? We don't need vans in the business, that kind of questioning.'

'You'll think of something, Harry…'

'OK, but that's logistics. What are the vans actually going to be used for and when?'

'Each of our district teams will need to be trained up to do their job and they'll need the right transport for it, the vans, but more about that later… they are just a smoke screen, Harry. The truth is, what we're really about, and only you need to know this, is supporting the increasingly right wing factions within our government.'

'No way…'

'For the first time we have a platform of insiders in government, in the military, even in MI6. Think Harry, I couldn't just help myself to all the ordinance we've stashed away at McNamara Metals tonight. I rely on loyal insiders who in turn are counting on us to deliver. We have powerful backers, we're not alone.'

'I'm impressed,' said Harry, trying to concentrate on getting past some slow traffic whilst wondering who some of these people might be.

'The other thing is, through your team's work, we've a growing network between us of online sympathisers and activists. That membership list we're building needs to be carefully prepared. They are in their own way a weapon and we want to get them loaded, like we so excite them, they act for us as a huge pack of lone wolves. We just pull the trigger when we're ready and away they go, bang, bang, bang all over the place.'

'It's good you're bringing all this to the table, Christian,' said Harry, realising that Christian was letting his guard down. Harry wanted to appear to be lapping up every word, the impressed suppliant. It wasn't difficult to do, indeed he was truly impressed, which in the light of what he was hearing wasn't hard to be.

'The weak link as I see it are your guys in the back office,' said Christian.

'They know stuff,' batted back Harry deensively.

'We're too vulnerable to have them blabbing to their spouses, feeling self-important, letting their guard down. I need to count on you to man them up, Harry. I'm leaving you to do this. It's a matter of trust…'

Harry saw Christian pull a gun from somewhere under his jacket. He kept it low, the pointed end waving unsettlingly in Harry's direction.

'Ever used one of these, Harry?' he said cooly.

'Nope. But needs must, as you say, Christian, needs must. How about a quick lesson. Given your own military background, that shouldn't be hard to do now, should it?' Too late, he wondered if he was being too subordinate.

Harry remembered the info Stu had found about his Royal Marine background. Even in the semi-darkness of the dashboard lights and that of the ongoing traffic head lights, he could read military so very clearly in the man's face.

'Did you happen to bring any ammo?' he asked.

'Box on the floor. It's simple really. Do this, hold like so, pull here. Everyone knows what the trigger does. It'll kick up. Always look what's beyond the target and what direction a ricochet might take. Bullets take a long while to stop. I've seen too many idiots using guns, yes even in the military. You need somewhere secure for this. The cloth's to keep it wiped of prints and any forensics. You must be ultra-meticulous. It's untraceable, the serial number's been removed.' Christian opened the glove compartment and placed the gun, duly wiped, inside the black velvet cloth and together with the ammo from the footwell wrapped them both up in a tight bundle. This was placed inside the glove compartment and shut away.

'Your own little political campaign gave us a great practice run two years ago. Yes, there were glitches, set backs, but with hindsight, it all helped. You achieved a populist move to the right and the creation of a strong right wing presence in politics today. What some don't realise is just how right wing some of those in the House now are. The campaign we have in mind for the summer is simply to do enough to tip the waverers over the edge. Just like we panicked the population to dare to vote for you, so we are now going to spook the government itself into taking lasting steps to put the far right in the driving seat. Once done, that's where things will stay, believe me.'

'Wow, I'm impressed,' said Harry.

Swinging off the M5 motorway just before Exeter, Harry dropped Christian on the service station forecourt and watched as he disappeared inside. He would not be wanting Harry to know what vehicle he was using and Harry knew he himself would be watched to ensure he left first. So he turned, drove away, went round a couple of roundabouts and headed south again heading for Plymouth, two things on his mind, Cherry and an Indian Take Away, and how the hell he'd ended up with a lethal weapon in his glove compartment.

28

He called Cherry as he dropped down into Plymouth, the BMW easing back into the late evening light city traffic. Harry took the unusual step of watching his speed, keeping securely within the limits, he couldn't afford unnecessary extra entanglements with the law. It was getting late, just after 11. She asked him what he'd like to eat and he asked for it to be delivered at his place. She said it'd be there in 30 minutes. Playfully, she said she'd arrive after he'd opened a bottle and paid for the take-away. His mood lifted.

No sooner had Harry entered his front door than the take-away arrived. A smiley-faced looking young Asian guy held out a brown carrier bag in the one hand together with an empty palm for his money. Harry paid up on his card reader and slammed the door shut. He noticed Sheena had been in again, made the place tidy, nice job. Someone had once said her Dad was Polish and Mum Czech. He wondered whether it mattered and preferring not to know more, pushed the memory to the back of his mind. She knew how to clean, that was what mattered.

The take-away brown bag, full of plastic packs, was placed on the kitchen table whilst Harry looked for a bottle. He had some Prosecco somewhere. He judged it to be a girlie drink. She'd like that. He found it in the bottom of the fridge, nicely chilled and pulled it out, placing it on the worktop. He went to find himself a beer.

The door bell rang and Harry went to let Cherry in. She was dressed like a flamingo, all pink and with a fluffy collar.

'What the hell?' he couldn't resist saying, as he leant forward to kiss her on both cheeks. 'Where did you get that outfit?'

'You're such a charmer, Harry. Now, where's the curry? I can smell it from here and I'm starving!'

'Come on through. The kitchen. The Prosecco's chilled. I'll pour if you want to start serving up.'

'You're working long days Harry McNamara. Not like the fun loving lad you once were. How's business?'

'Well you know me, a natural everything I turn my hand to! It's in the blood anyway! My grandfather established the company, my father developed it, I reap the benefits of their hard work! Simple really. Here…' He filled full to the brim a fizzing frosted glass flute, placing it into Cherry's waiting hand. He lifted his beer and their glasses clinked. 'Cheers! Here's to success and prosperity!'

It was as the tandoori chicken had almost gone and all that remained of the peshwari nan were a few crumbs, Cherry said, 'I can't believe you're doing all this business stuff. Why?'

'It's not so bad, really. I get to play god in my little kingdom down town. Power and profits! We've around thirty five employees. It's a small family business, it works, it pays the bills and I have a nice car, well two cars actually.'

'Tell me Harry, what's your ambition? What do you want from life? I mean, are you really content with the way things are? You never struck me as the kind of guy to ditch politics altogether. You used to have such strong views about things, about the way the world was and what needed to be done to change things. Where has all that side of Harry gone? Will the House forgive you and let you back?' She pushed the nearly empty plate to the far side of the table to concentrate on her topped up glass of Prosecco.

'You wouldn't be much of a reporter if you hadn't got a good nose for things, Cherry Thomas. Of course I'm following the politics, but at a distance these days. I'm biding my time, watching the government come round to my ways thinking. What's so wrong with that?'

'You're being bloody evasive, playing with me. I asked you straight. You swerve left and right and leave me guessing. Come on Harry, you've never been shy!'

'It's been a long day at the office, Cherry. I've been out of day to day politics since parliament suspended last year, keeping my head down for a bit. I wouldn't do myself any favours to put my head back up above the parapet too soon now would I?'

The clock in the hallway quietly struck midnight. Harry thought he ought to make a move on Cherry. Truth to tell he didn't know where to start. All his previous advances had gone horribly wrong. Alpha male, no, clumsy oaf, yes.

'Cherry, you're a nice looking girl and we're friends and I...'

'Harry, you're very sweet, but I've an early start tomorrow...'

'You could stay over...'

Cherry got up and reached down for her little bag, also in pink. 'No, I really ought to go. I'll get an Uber...'

'No, no. I'll run you back now, door to door. Not a problem. Come on…'

'They climbed into the BMW. It smelled musty from the drive with Limping Man. Harry turbo boosted the aircon in an attempt to freshen it up and take away some of the alcohol fumes. He watched as Cherry also noticed the air as she sat inside.

As he pulled away, she opened her bag and he watched out of the corner of his eye as with a couple of sprays she applied more perfume. He wondered whether she was teasing him, trying to get him back to her place for the night. She reached up and pulled down the vanity mirror behind the sun visor and poked around at her eyes.

She appeared to look round for an interior light switch and the glove compartment dropped open at her touch. Then she saw the unmistakeable shape of a wrapped up gun. That was when Harry swerved, leaned into her and reached his hand across silently and deliberately slamming it shut again. The stupid cow!

29

'I wish you hadn't,' said Harry, thinking hard. She stared at him.

'Sometimes in the scrap metal business you come across things and then... you have to decide what to do with them.' The lie rolled off his tongue so easily he almost believed it himself.

Cherry wasn't speaking. It was as if she was looking at him as a gangster. She'd turned in her seat and was looking intently at him, with a stone cold sober gaze. In his eyes, the serious look wasn't working. Dressed in the very image of a decorative gangster's moll in her stupid pink flamingo outfit, how could he really take her seriously, but he had to. He concentrated. This was a crisis.

'I'd rather you forgot what you saw and just let me dispose of it in the estuary,' Harry added lamely but creatively. 'I'm only sorry I hadn't done so before you came round. It's just... I've been so busy. You know what it's been like.' The lies kept coming.

'Harry, you can't chuck it... It's not responsible. I mean it ought to be handed in. There might be history behind it, a link to an armed robbery or something...'

'Look, I don't want my employees getting into any trouble over what they found. I owe it to them. It's more complicated than you know. The guy who found it has had a run in with the police over domestic matters and he begged me to just get rid of it.' More lies upon lies. 'It'll disappear, don't you worry, I'll see to it as soon as… Just don't want things being made any more complicated by you speaking out of turn.'

'Speaking out of turn? Come on Harry, that's a flaming gun, you've got there!' her voice strident.

Harry was in trouble, Cherry wasn't giving up without a fight. He was flummoxed. He fell silent. They'd almost arrived at her flat. His time was nearly out. He was feeling undecided about being at her flat too. Any hopes of sexual conquest had faded. Then he saw a way out.

'Tell you what. I'm dropping you off and then I'm driving straight to the estuary, right now, end of. I've decided to put an end to the matter, the proper thing… You can come with me if you want…' He offered enthusiastically, gambling, in the event rightly, on her declining the offer.

Cherry, having to think about what he was saying let the initiative in the conversation shift back in Harry's direction. They pulled up and he walked straight round to her side, opened her door.

'A gentlemen always sees a girl to her front door,' he said with a smile.

She hesitated again and Harry knew he had won out. She fumbled for her keys still uncertain. But Harry, leaving her there, kept moving on and was back in his driving seat and on his way before she could think of anything to say or do about it.

Of course he had no intention of driving to the estuary. He drove calmly straight back to his place and thought hard what to do with the weapon that had already almost caused him a major meltdown. What if Limping Man got to know of this carelessness, he thought. He'd be the next strangled man for sure.

Whilst he was sitting outside his house pondering what to do next, it came to him. He started the car again and drove the few minutes it took to get to McNamara Metals, let himself in the gate, disabled the alarm, went straight to the lockers and taking a key from his pocket placed the wrapped items into the currently empty Nick Grayson locker with a heavy metallic clunk. Thankfully there was absolutely no one around to hear it. Sorted. A dead Nick Grayson had his uses. He smiled with satisfaction.

He drove home. Calculating how much time had passed since he'd dropped Cherry off, he decided the travel time sums worked out just fine and sent her a simple text message: *Lovely evening, shame you couldn't be with me on the estuary. Such a romantic setting. See you soon, H. xx.*

It was the early hours of Tuesday morning but after all that had happened he thought he'd have a large whisky and watch some football before going to bed.

30

Harry drove into work early next morning. Elsa had for some time ensured there was snack food to supplement Harry's coffees on such occasions. As he checked in everything seemed reassuring normal. The three containers at the far end of the site stood there immovable, looking as if they'd been part of the industrial furniture for eternity, attracting no interest from anyone.

Inside, number 2 locker looked just as he'd left it in the night, the Conference Room was neat and tidy ready for the day and the IT suite was closed up until the four guys arrived shortly. All was well with the world as Harry settled into his office, sipped his coffee and opened his lap top on the old oak desk.

There was a message waiting for him, from Limping Man, brief and to the point:

Four white Ford Transit vans are being delivered to McNamara Metals late on Friday afternoon, 10th April.

Harry made a mental note to self to be around when they arrived. There was plenty of space for them to be duly parked up beside the shipping containers. Placed there they'd be out the way. He decided he'd personally look after the sets of keys. Dan would need to be alerted to the delivery. In fact he could oversee it, supervise the parking and bring him the keys after. He gave Dan a call and briefed him.

Also in his inbox was an internal email from the firm's accountant, Glenda Hill. The heading was '*1st Quarter Accounts*'. Harry thought he'd better take a look. It occurred to him he'd been running McNamara Metals since the previous November. The 4th Quarter had brought the previous year to a healthy, profitable conclusion. Sums had been set aside for a few bad debts and tax, but Glenda had been quite upbeat about it all and he felt he hadn't needed to pay the accounts much attention since, but just to be sure…

Opening up the 1st Quarter current year accounts file it all looked rather confusing and after struggling to make sense of what he saw for several minutes, he called Glenda to come and talk him through the figures. Five minutes later she was in his office standing in front of his desk. He waved her round to his side, telling her to bring a chair round with her.

Glenda was a female form of Nick Grayson, dull and wearing grey clothes. Probably in her mid 50s, prematurely greying hair, she'd been another lifetime employee of McNamara Metals. Harry realised he knew nothing else about her. Perhaps, he thought, a good boss should take an interest.

'How are we today Glenda?' he ventured.

'Fine, thank you Mr McNamara.'

'Harry, please… You've been with the firm a long time. Must have seen a few changes.'

'Yes, for sure. I guess in Michael's day it was all very hand to mouth, irregular. Lean times more than profitable ones, but he got the company established and invested in the site. It was a good time to buy back then. Your father Patrick, well, he got things straightened up on the business side, had a flair for networking and building the business to what it is today. I dare say you'll take it to the next level, Harry.'

'OK, I called you up because I'd like you to talk me through these first quarter accounts. It's the first quarter I've been totally responsible for, so I'm interested to take careful note. What's the score Glenda?'

'Turnover remains stable, cash flow is fine, reserves adequate to meet foreseeable contingencies. With Mr Grayson's departure there's been some small saving, but we've spent more on staff. I was meaning to ask you about the Security man and the IT workers you've taken on. Income has come in to cover half the cost which is a real coup on your part Harry. However, I'm not sure the company is seeing any benefit from their work, unless I'm missing something, in fact I'm personally not sure what they are doing for us at all. That is a matter for you, of course. But, in my opinion, such a significant extra investment needs to be off set by new income being generated, so we will need to watch that it starts coming in in the next quarter don't you think?'

'You're absolutely right, Glenda. The thing is they are doing some excellent market research, but we need to be patient. They know if they don't show results their posts get terminated.'

'The other thing is, we make an annual stock take shortly and I notice you've ordered three storage containers, the ones at the far end of the yard. Are we to expect a rental or other charge for these?'

'That's me, Glenda. I saw an opportunity to acquire these and snapped them up. No costs, no invoice coming. We're always needing somewhere secure to place the more precious metals and we need to make forward provision for growth. As regards Dan Cash, I think we've probably been very lucky in the past in respect of organised crime, so I've taken an interest in site protection. Putting Dan on the gate at key times was my idea too.'

'Yes. He seems a very diligent young man, smartly turned out too.'

Harry ran his fingers down the lines of figures on his lap top calling for explanations as he did so. At the point where he lost interest he thanked Glenda for her help and let her go, telling her to send Elsa in on her way out. She and her junior handled all the finances, he gathered, and an external firm of accountants produced the final year's accounts sent to Companies House.

Harry walked over to get himself another coffee. That was enough time on accounts. Overall, things were as they should be, the business was running itself and producing the cash, though he didn't like the questions Glenda had asked relating to his extra staff, the storage containers and Dan's appointment. She'd probably be straight on to him when the four vans appeared on Friday. He resolved to keep a sharp line between support services like Glenda and operational matters that he would keep firmly under his own control.

Elsa knocked and entered.

'Ah, good morning Elsa. How are we today?'

'Fine, Harry. How can I help?'

'I'm not sure. I came across one piece of paperwork of Nick's. I think it was some accounts, but maybe not. The sheets were headed up with the names of American states. Do you know what they might be?'

'No, Harry. No, we don't do any business with the USA. It must be something private, something of Mr Grayson's. Sorry Harry… I can't help there…'

Harry's phone rang. It was his Mum. He waved Elsa off so that he could take the call.

'Hello Mum. You OK? You've caught me at the office.'

'You remember we spoke at Nick's funeral…'

'Yeah…'

'You were going to phone me.'

'Sorry Mum, been pretty busy…'

'So I thought I'd call you. We've things to talk about. Can I come over later, to Ham Drive I mean?'

'Sure, I'll be back around 6-o 'clock.'

'See you then, Harry.'

Harry was feeling ambivalent about his Mum. Duty required him to look out for her, but she was, well an awkward burden to him. It felt like she was making demands on him, but to be frank he couldn't quite see what she was after. He thought she'd taken off and left him to it, but now she was at his back. It made him feel uncomfortable.

Perhaps she was fed up with living at her sister's and was angling to move in back at home. No chance! Sheena was proving to be pretty good at sorting out his domestic stuff and he preferred the clear contractual relationship he had with her. Mum back, it would be a major interference in his life again, it was not going to happen.

He had a couple of business calls Elsa had asked him to make. Nothing much to them, one an invite response to a Chamber of Commerce event, a breakfast at the Duke of Cornish hotel. 'Would Mr McNamara be attending?' He signed up, why not? The next was an enquiry from a car scrapping firm in Somerset and Avon wanting to talk about new business through a joint venture. Harry wasn't sure about what it meant and redirected the call to Glenda. Then Harry had time on his hands. He felt listless and bored. He needed an excuse to get out of the office.

Harry remembered "Scrapfish" down on the Plym Estuary. It was time to take a look. He decided to pop into the IT office and drag Stu away from his laptop for an hour. It would do them both good.

Ten minutes later he'd told Elsa he had business to see to in Plymouth and would be back later and he headed off in his BMW with a smiling Stu beside him.

'Why the outing? Something on your mind Harry?'

'I've a surprise, but it's a secret, something just between the two of us. OK?'

'Yeah, sure Harry. You know me.'

'Well, this car came as a nice business surprise. I've got another. You'll see in a few minutes.'

Harry idled the car through the busy city streets, gained a little speed up to 40 mph in the dual carriageway alongside the estuary, took a couple of roundabouts, headed south and then swung into the marina.

'Look out for a yacht called "Scrapfish" will you,' ordered Harry. 'I'll park up over there'. Harry checked he'd got the boat keys.

A crusty old sea salt, looking about 80, wearing dark wellies, jeans and a sailor's jacket, eyed them suspiciously. Harry gave him a confident wave which only half satisfied his hostile gaze. They began their search, Harry realising quickly that this method was hopeless. Given the large number of boats out on the floating moorings looking at every boat to try and read its name was not going to yield quick results, so he called after the the old man.

'Excuse me,' said Harry, walking quickly to catch up with him. 'How do I find a boat here? I mean what's the best way to find my boat when I've not been here before?'

'Ask the guy who sailed it last where he moored it up,' he replied in a flat Devonian drawl.

'But, that's the problem. He died recently, he kindly left it to me and we need to find it,' said Harry trying to look sad at his recent supposed loss.

The man relented, he had a heart. 'Come with me,' he said, leading them toward a small office. 'What's the name?'

'This is Stu, I'm Harry,' said Harry puzzled.

'No, the boat's name,' he said, opening a large, tattered notebook, corners curling with age.

'Oh, "Scrapfish". She's a Hunter 360.'

'Nice model,' he said, warming to them and flipping the book shut. You should have said that to start with. You were after Nick's boat. Terrible shame what happened to him.'

'Absolute tragedy,' added Harry, looking sideways at Stu to try and get him to stop grinning. 'It's a sad way to inherit a boat.'

'It's not far. Come with me.'

'That's it, there,' he said pointing out a sleek white shiny vessel sitting proudly on the water at the quayside. It had three small oblong windows set in the side of its hull and a canvas protected cabin area toward the rear.

'I'll leave you to it, I've things to do, this time of year, always gets busy, everyone wanting their boats ready for the new season.'

Harry and Stu approached the magnificent looking yacht like boys with a new toy.

'Harry, who'd have believed this is yours?' said Stu.

'Sure is. Comes with the factory. Have you ever sailed Stu?'

'Never. You?'

'Nope,' said Harry, 'but can't be difficult. We need to look it over, come on.' They carefully stepped down on to the boat and began manoeuvring themselves round to access the cabin area. Harry fumbled in his pocket to find the boat keys. He opened it up and they both stepped down inside.

'Looking first at the array of technical equipment and some sort of screen and radio system, he immediately realised he'd need someone with sailing knowhow to give him a briefing, but he couldn't think of a single person he knew. A rolled up chart of the estuary lay to one side, but again it defeated him. Perhaps that crusty old sea dog might help, at least point them in the right direction for some tuition. All they could do today was look around.

Harry led them both down into what was a spacious lounge area. There was a central dining table with grey soft-cushioned furniture circling around it following the contours of the boat. A decorative non-slip floor carpet made it all look very comfortable. There was a singular lack of fuss, no ornaments, nothing personal, no wine or beer bottles left lying around. It looked to Harry's mind rather soulless, like its last owner.

Harry began looking around to see if there were any signs of its former user. Small cupboards and stowaway compartments could be seen everywhere. Harry got Stu to help him.

'What are we looking for, Harry?' he asked.

'Just looking around, Stu. I don't know really. Don't you think it's rather empty, nothing to suggest anyone actually ever lived on the yacht? See what you can find. You start up there, look in those compartments where we stepped on board.'

Harry began feeling round the interior lower walls, under the cushioned seats. He found life jackets. He found waterproof clothing, size alright for Stu but too small for himself. There was nothing, all very strange. That was until Stu called out.

'Here, Harry.'

The two stood side by side before the yacht's wheel and engine controls. Stu had used the keys to open a small cupboard. There was a heavy duty plastic or was it a rubberised cloth sack with a zip fastener. Stu pointed to it. Harry pulled it out and took it down into the lounge area and placed it on the table. From the weight and feel of it, there was certainly something inside. He unzipped it slightly and looked in. Envelopes and papers he surmised.

'I'll look at them when I get back,' he said chucking the pouch on to the table. 'How about taking it for a spin, just on the engine?'

'Are you sure, Harry?'

'Let's see what the engine's like. There's a fuel gauge here. If it's empty we'll ask old Captain Haddock about getting some more. Pass me the keys again. One should be for the engine.'

Stu pulled them from the locker door and threw them to Harry who had put on a peaked captain's cap he'd found. 'This lever will be forward, back and neutral and the wheel should be just a wheel, what can go wrong?' he announced grinning. 'Here we go,' he said as he switched her on. The engine turned over, but nothing fired up. He tried again, same result.

'Stu, have a look under there and see if there's a fuel on/off switch, will you.'

Sure enough, there was one and Stu moved it across. Harry turned the key again and this time the diesel engine sprang to life, a gurgle of bubbling water and some white smoke emitting from the rear as it did so.

'Untie the ropes Stu. Time to see what she's made of. Tank's nearly full. Excellent! Come on, let's go!'

Stu scrambled back on to the quay and untied the ropes throwing them back on to the deck.

With Stu back on board, Harry noticed the boat was already being moved by the strong tide pushing it backwards. He quickly pushed the gear from neutral into forward and levered in some power. "Scrapfish" responded immediately and surged forward. Harry was worried. It didn't respond like a car and he needed his front end away from the quay side. Fortunately, it swung away and they pulled out into the estuary missing the moored boat in front by inches. Harry adjusted his cap and stared out ahead. There was another boat approaching in the channel but well away from them. So this was what Nick did with himself, he mused.

'Let's see what she can do,' said Harry pushing the throttle forward getting a rewarding ramp up of power from the engine somewhere below decks. 'Why's that guy getting all excited?' shouted Harry, as the distance between the two boats seemed to be closing all too quickly.

'He's wanting you to move out into the estuary, Harry.'

'He can bloody well keep left,' said Harry, 'He needs to calm himself. At his age he'll do himself a mischief. Why doesn't he change course?'

'Harry, look over there. Different rules, boats heading down estuary are on the right hand side, different rules Harry. You need to move and quickly.'

Harry responded in an instant, and waved dismissively in the direction of the passing yacht only feet away. Harry looked over his shoulder, the guy was moving into a quayside space not far from where Harry had been moored up only moments ago.

The boat was moving along, but not nearly as fast as Harry had hoped even though he'd opened the throttle wide. Maybe the engine wasn't really anything but ancillary power. He really must get the hang of how the sails worked. Before turning back he thought he'd just head over to see if he could see McNamara Metals near the opposite shore and then it would be time to return.

In the end the two were out on the water over an hour, by which time Harry had at least got the measure of operating on engine power. Before returning he decided he'd let Stu have a go at the wheel which went down well, and then Harry took it back. Facing him was the tricky business of getting back alongside the mooring jetty.

It took Harry a couple of attempts to get the approach just right. In the end he discovered by trial and error that it was best to come in against the current which gave him more control. Stu was sent up on deck to tidy the ropes and grab the forward end one ready for him to make an exit and secure the boat.

Half an hour later, after gently clipping the quayside a couple of times they were safely moored up, any rise and fall in tide levels accommodated for with slack lines.

Back in the BMW, the boat locked up, the mysterious pouch Stu had found thrown on the back seat, they set off to leave the yard. They were flagged down. Old Salty was waving with a non-too friendly look on his face down by the gate. Harry slowed up.

'Reckon his constipation's playing up,' Harry said to Stu before lowering his window.

'There's been a complaint about un-seamanlike behaviour. Apparently you took your boat out without due regard to oncoming vessels, nearly caused a collision. It'll be reported to committee,' he added.

'The guy must be due for another eye test soon,' said Harry cooly. 'I was nowhere near him…' he added, not waiting for a reply.

Within a quarter of an hour they were back at the business and Stu disappeared into the IT suite. Harry went upstairs, taking his mystery pouch with him, putting it unopened on his desk before making a coffee. He felt uplifted by the whole sailing experience. In the time he'd been out of the office he'd forgotten all about the business, the cool wind had freshened him and salt spray was still to be tasted on his face. He thought he should do it all again and soon, but next time get some sailing tutor to come along and show him the ropes.

Tipping Nick's envelope and papers on to his desk he instinctively knew they were Nick's secret. Why else keep a pouch secreted away on his boat? The first envelope he opened contained a wad of £20 notes. Harry flicked through them like a bank clerk, the notes fluttering between thumb and forefinger. He estimated they ran into thousands rather than hundreds of pounds. He slipped them back inside out of sight and reached for the next envelope.

It was the same again, all twenties but slightly fewer of them. In all there were six envelopes. One envelope contained a note book. Harry realised immediately he opened it that its contents were linked with the sheets he retrieved from the "Accounts" file he'd taken from Nick's No. 2 locker. The six pages were headed up exactly the same: *Alabama, Alaska, Arizona, Arkansas, California* and *Colorado.*

He went to his safe and retrieved the "Accounts" papers laying them out alongside the notebook. This time everything fell into place. The little bribery and corruption number Nick had been running produced a tidy cash flow and he'd kept it and the supporting documentation down on the boat. The sheets Harry kept in his safe were anonymous summaries of the more detailed information naming names set out in the little notebook all written in Nick's spidery hand.

Harry smiled as he read the names of political figures and council staff and he set his mind to work to see if he could resurrect a couple of the scams as little earners on the side. Twenty minutes later, he'd sent a couple of short to the point emails to a couple of prominent Plymouth City Councillors to test the waters, asking for a more modest cash donation in a sealed brown envelope to be made by the 30 April, delivered to Dan on security at McNamara Metals with

251

Harry McNamara: For Personal Attention printed on the outside. Harry smiled as he locked all the papers and the cash pile in his rapidly filling safe.

Things were looking to be on the up! A business, a car, a yacht and now a stash of cash with more to come. There was just the little matter of Cherry to sort. That shouldn't be difficult. He had an idea and went on line to send her a special delivery of red roses, no expense spared.

31

Friday's were when everyone at McNamara Metals had their thoughts on the coming weekend. Harry had noticed there was a general slowing down, a dissipation of energy. Even the noises in the yard with the cranes, the fork lifts and the crusher slowed. It was as if lethargic tiredness was a catching disease for both machinery and men, all winding down to a complete halt by the end of Friday afternoon.

Harry had received a message from Limping Man to say he was sending across four vans for storage and they would be arriving during Friday afternoon. He required Harry to send two messages, the first that all was ready to receive them, the second to advise when delivery was complete.

Harry made a call to Dan and arranged for him to be on site from lunchtime. He explained the factory were receiving some additional vehicles and that initially these were just to be parked up over by the three storage containers. Dan promised to see to it. Dan was told that keys and any paper work should be placed on Harry's desk. The matter was solely for his personal attention.

A telephone call came in… Cherry.

'Hi Harry, that was so sweet of you. I've just received the biggest bunch of beautiful red roses. They're so wonderful. I've not time to arrange them now, so I've left them standing in a sink full of cold water. No one has bought me flowers for ages.'

'Glad you like them. I thought I owed you.'

'No, don't be silly. You did the right thing Harry, I'm sure, going down to the estuary.'

'I was wondering if you'd heard any more on the grapevine about the the police investigation into the Ottery bonfire case and Nick? I've not heard a bean.'

'I was looking at a blog and someone says the police have so far drawn a blank. They're pursuing their enquiries is how they describe their activity, which as of now means doing nowt.'

'I can think a stirring labour councillor might have enemies , but do you think Nick had any?' asked Harry. 'He was such a mild mannered guy. Grey Man I called him, he wouldn't stand out in a crowd, wouldn't upset anyone I can think of.' Then Harry's mind turned to the blackmail sideline Nick was managing and he added, 'but I did hear he might have lent on a few people in the city council to try and get favourable planning and other outcomes.'

'That's always going on Harry. Not something you can get to the bottom of easily. It's all backhanders and unless someone is stupid, nothing gets proved, no one gets prosecuted.'

He let the subject drop.

'What are you doing this weekend? Any time off?' asked Harry fishing for a date.

'Well Harry, a guy who sends me such lovely flowers deserves some attention.'

'Are you free at 8?'

'Can be, what are you thinking?'

'I'll take you to a pub in town. Leave it with me. We never made it last time. I'll book a table for two.'

'Sounds good to me.'

'Pick you up just before 8 then,' said Harry, beaming at his own good fortune as he ended the call.

Harry had a two mugs of coffee lunch and was looking out through his slatted blind window when the first of the vans arrived. It was a clean looking newish nondescript white Ford Transit. It couldn't be anything but the first of the four. Dan was there, talking to the driver, explaining where he was to park up and instructing him to bring him the keys on his way out. Nods of understanding were exchanged between them. Dan was proving to be a really good asset. Harry made a mental note to ensure he slipped him an extra cash reward on his way out later.

No sooner had the first driver disappeared off site, then the second van arrived. This time there was a longer altercation between the driver and Dan. Harry guessed the man was wanting to use the toilets and Dan was telling him that wasn't possible, but probably not very politely. In the end the driver's need won over Dan's resistance and the man went into the factory toilet block before leaving.

Harry missed the next two van arrivals. However, he knew all was complete when Dan knocked on his office door and placed the labelled set of four van keys on Harry's desk.

'All parked up in a row by the storage containers, Harry.'

'Any problems?'

'No not really. One guy was wanting the wash room, but no, seemed pretty regular guys, all with London accents.'

'So not local then?'

'I'd say not.'

'You've been doing a great job, Dan. Look take this and have a treat over the weekend, you've earned it.' Harry slipped fifty pounds into Dan's hand.

'Thanks Harry,' he said beaming at his good fortune. 'Call me any time I can help.'

'Will do, Dan, and thank you once again.'

Harry had a number of routine office chores to see to before he left for home at the end of the afternoon. Glenda needed a number of accounts to be signed off. Elsa had left letters for him to sign for her to put in the last post and he had decisions to take as to which contractor to employ for the relaying of a concrete roadway at the city side of the yard.

Once all was done, Harry locked up at 5-o 'clock, climbed into his BMW which Dan had just hosed down and polished for him and made his way home.

As he drove he realised work was not so bad, and now Cherry would be waiting for him. Having a good time with a woman was long overdue and it was, after all, Friday night. Things were looking good all round.

That was until he remembered his Mum's call earlier and his heart sank. She was coming round to see him at 6. He wondered what she could possibly want, but any thoughts on that completely eluded him and he knew if he were to get a shower and be ready for Cherry her visit would have to be brief.

When he pulled up at Ham Drive, he had no sooner gone inside when the front doorbell rang. He opened the door.

'Hello, Mum. I've not got long, but do come in,' he called and wandered off in the direction of the kitchen. 'Tea?'

'Tea, alright, yes. I came to say I'd like to move back in here,' she announced. 'I feel a certain rootlessness. Staying at my sister Zoe's is fine, but it's not home. I'd like to move back in here.'

Harry didn't answer, just watched the kettle boil. It made quite noise. He reached for one mug, teabag, milk and spoon. She wasn't going to like what he was going to say next.

'Sorry, but life move's on. I can't handle having anyone else around. When I get back from work I need my own space. It's the only way I can deal with the pressure. I've moved on and so have you. It won't work having you back.'

She turned, left the tea on the side and walked straight out of the front door.

32

By the beginning of May Harry was finding life had never been so good. He'd even got Cherry into bed, albeit they were both drunk and he didn't think much, if anything, had happened between them. In his mind it was a conquest, something ticked off on his bucket list and he could chalk it up as a sexual victory of sorts. He'd been to bed with Cherry, hurrah!

The May Bank holiday weekend had been good springtime weather and he'd found a guy at the yacht club to take him down the estuary and give him some instruction in "Scrapfish". He hadn't known there was so much to learn and attend to. It was just like the football or driving, there were rules. It had given him a real buzz and now he knew what was what on the water it was entirely up to him what rules he chose to obey and which he ditched.

That weekend had started well. On the Friday, Dan had called him to say he had had two sealed envelopes delivered to him at the gate. When Harry opened them later in his office, both contained £500 in twenties, all self-explanatory, cash he simply locked away in his safe alongside the many thousands of pounds already sitting there.

Even though it was a Bank Holiday, Limping Man had insisted that there should be a regular first Monday meeting in the Conference Room. He was desperate for the IT team to provide updates and sounded like he was being pushed by someone else to get results and soon. Harry had agreed because there were no security issues, the factory being closed for a long weekend. Limping Man had told Harry to check the second on-site shipping container could be opened up as it was to receive the next delivery of munitions at 8-o 'clock, with the same arrangements applying as before.

Harry could see no problem. The only difficulty he had had was to persuade Elsa to set up the Conference Room with beer and refreshments which had involved her coming in on the bank holiday Monday afternoon. A generous extra payment in hand seemed to settle her reservations. Harry was finding the strategic use of his cash pile always got him his way, achieving what he wanted with the minimum of hassle. Simple transactions between humans, he reckoned, always worked best.

Dan was on the gate when the guys started to come in just before 7-o 'clock. The evenings were light now and it struck Harry that these arrivals were very visible to anyone looking out for them. They were not part of the regular work force and he was surprised no one had asked him about his monthly Monday evenings. He had some patter lined up if they did – he would say it was a business development training evening. As he watched Dan let them through into the yard in turn, he thought again. Maybe it really did look so very ordinary seeing men going into a factory, even if it was a bank holiday Monday evening. Everyone was well used to the 24/7 economy and factory hours were totally at his call. Just maybe no one would ask awkward questions.

There was quite a camaraderie building between the guys. He greeted each as old friends, they were now part of a team. Gavin Wilson, with his side-kick from Exmouth arrived first. Gavin had the handshake of a rugby player, a domed bald head like a world wrestler. He squeezed his hand hard, Harry reciprocated. Mutual respect flowed like electricity between them.

Then Charlie Evans strolled in accompanied by a different deputy from Ottery St Mary this time. Charlie was sporting a black eye. Harry wondered whether his other half, Millie, had socked him one, but wasn't going to ask. He never quite knew what reaction he would get from Charlie, never completely trusted a strangler. Clearly Christian still got on with him, they were always whispering together, thick as thieves.

Marcus hurried in apologetically, more like a hobbit among giants. He tried to explain to Harry how the bank holiday traffic had slowed his return journey from Newquay, but no worries, he'd have the IT report up and running in no time and he was as good as his word.

Limping Man, Toby Grant from Plymouth and Mash Tooley, the Exeter leader all arrived simultaneously. When they were all gathered, Harry on a nod from Christian, called everyone to order. The atmosphere felt relaxed, but workmanlike.

'We're taking another artic delivery in an hour, so we need to press on. Can you guys help yourselves to something from the beer and pasty table, then come over and join us. Make it snappy, yes. Marcus is all set up and ready to go.'

Five minutes later, Marcus was presenting his update. All the graphs were moving in the right direction, the Twitter, Instagram, and web hits were growing exponentially and Marcus was on this occasion more worried about the added potential for security breaches to arise. Their closed chat room was proving particularly time consuming and tricky to manage and difficult to monitor. He'd more or less had to allocate Stu full time to it to keep an eye on it. Soon more staffing help would be needed if they were to cope, Marcus added.

Gene testing was proving a very popular activity and the attachment of a Paypal facility was proving financially lucrative. Marcus asked for guidance where to direct the significant funds coming in. Donations to the cause had also been made, mainly from overseas, particularly the US. Harry looked over to Christian who stood up and said that he'd have a word privately with Marcus outside the meeting.

Nearly all gene testing results had resulted in automatic membership eligibility being initiated. The few dubious test results had been followed up and waved through as explained by probable gene blips which Marcus was happy to go along with. Marcus shared that gene testing had provided most contacts with a lot of fun and had a cementing effect on the sense of belonging to the campaign.

Marcus was certain there had been a couple of attempts by official or not so official hackers wanting to get inside things to find out what was going on. He was pretty confident that they remained ahead of the game, but warned that with the increasing size of the operation it would get ever more difficult to maintain all round secrecy for very much longer. They may yet have to close down and relaunch by the end of the summer.

As before, Marcus took questions. He put up a short film clip from the States on weapon handling, Marcus making the point that actual weapon drills needed to be organised before the summer and Christian would be saying how this was to take place. Then Harry gave Marcus the OK to leave for home ahead of everyone else, not that anyone thought Marcus would be any use lifting crates of weapons.
Just after 8-o 'clock the call came through from Dan to say the expected artic had arrived and he had the fork lift over

by the containers ready for unloading. Harry heard the lorry's reversing bleepers sound as it made its way cautiously across the yard, the truck snaking left and right to gain a straight line backwards.

The arsenal seemed to include a lot more high explosive crates this time and Harry felt a tinge of concern that so much dangerous material was on the factory site. It surely had a huge potential for disaster if anything, even a lightening strike, should disturb things. He quickly dismissed the thought. A lifetime of practise told him it never did any good to dwell on fears. He saw that everything was safely stored, the doors locked tight and he knew it wouldn't be for so very much longer.

By 10-o 'clock there was just Harry in the building. He went back to his office to grab a final coffee and take some cash from his safe before heading home. As he sat there quietly sipping from his mug, he reflected on all his good fortune.

Here he was, all powerful in a profitable business, a respected figure in his own community, the BMW car, the Hunter Legend 380 yacht, a safe full of cash, and the girlfriend in tow.

On the back of this personal success his political ambitions were rising from the ashes and very soon with the help of all his allies in Devon and internationally he'd be able to call the shots once again.

The far right wing which he represented would not be written off lightly, nor could it be swallowed up in in some insipid Tory mainstream populism. The true party of the future lay with him and the people. Once the news was out that he was taking control, everyone would come rallying to the cause. He was on a roll, he was back, things were coming together and by God it felt good.

33

It was now the beginning of July. Most unusually for Plymouth, a persistent heat wave had been stuck in place over the South West for two weeks and sweat was on everyone's brow at McNamara Metals.

Harry had insisted Dan start up the engines and check the four white Ford Transit vans every week. He wanted to be sure they were kept in tip top condition, ready for the day they were needed and that was going to be very soon. His sense of anticipated excitement was being tempered by a certain tension, something Harry put down to the weather. Stress was in the air. A good thunderstorm would clear things.

It was up to Limping Man to give the final go ahead. Perhaps he would do so at this evening's meeting. It frustrated Harry no end that Limping Man kept thing so close to his chest.

Harry felt he was the fall guy, the man first in the firing line, exposed to all the risks. It was McNamara Metals, on his say so, that were looking after the three shipping containers filled with enough ordinance to run a small war. He felt for a moment as if he were a blind man walking to a cliff edge. Beads of sweat ran down his brow. Harry got up from his desk with a deep sense of unease, then frustration, then anger boiling within him.

'Elsa,' he yelled, more loudly than he'd intended. She came running into his office.

'Get the meeting sorted for tonight will you, usual arrangements for our monthly Monday evening training do.' He'd got used to calling it that. The euphemism avoided any awkward questions.

'Yes, Harry. It's already in hand. I meant to tell you, I had a phone call about the meeting earlier.'

Harry felt a cold shiver run through him.

'What? A call? What call? Who was it?'

'Yes, he didn't give his name. Just asked if the meeting was on tonight. I told him it was. I did right didn't I, Harry?' she said, seeing the look of puzzlement on his face.

'Did he say who he was, leave a number?' enquired Harry.

'No, he was very polite and just asked if he might confirm the time it started.'

'And you told him?'

'Yes… 7-o 'clock.'

'OK, OK, thank you,' he said, waving her toward the door, as if shooing away a troublesome fly.

Back on his own, Harry was bothered. No one had ever phoned the office about Monday meetings and no one would ask what time the meeting started, would they, unless they were spying on him? He needed to think and act and do so quickly. It was already early afternoon. He grabbed himself another coffee regretting he'd turned down the offer of one of those iced water machines for his office. Hot coffee on a hot day was bad, but not as bad as the situation his imagination was conjuring up for this evening. He decided to give Dan a call at the gate.

'Dan, I'm wondering if you've had any unusual callers recently, anything that's made you wonder what someone might be up to? Anything, Dan, anything at all?' He heard Dan's mind turning over in the silence.

'Well actually Harry, one thing. This morning, a woman pulled up in her car at the gate, just to chat. It's never happened before and I wondered whether to call you there and then, but she said, not to trouble anyone. But then she asked if you, Harry McNamara, worked here and whether I knew if you were in. I went to call you and again she stopped me. Twice, odd that. That was it, she just left. It was nothing. No message left, and she's not been back.'

'Never said what she wanted.'

'No, nothing.'

'So with hindsight she was fishing for information about my whereabouts?'

'That would seem to be the sum of it, Harry, nothing more. I didn't think anything of it at the time, maybe she was a journalist or the like?' he said, now feeling he might have missed something important.

'OK Dan. Be on extra alert for the rest of the day. Let me know if anything happens to concern you. Watch everything, check everything, even look at who's parking up or cruising round by the gate, OK?' He heard Dan's 'Sure thing, Harry,' before the line went dead.

He could trust Dan. Harry knew that someone, probably police or counter terrorism had started poking around. Marcus had also been voicing worries about hackers getting into his IT programmes. This, the call to Elsa and the caller at the gate meant three separate attempts to prod Harry's defences. He needed to contact Limping Man as a matter of urgency. Harry's trusted instincts were running round inside his head ringing alarm bells.

'Hi Christian, we need to think twice about tonight,' he fired off. He waited as Christian listened whilst Harry went on to explain the new scenario. Christian remained quiet. His throat eventually cleared and he replied.

'This is what we'll do,' he said. 'Marcus, you and I still need to meet, together with the four area leaders, but I think not at the factory. Can we use your place, Ham Drive?'

'Sure, not a problem, I take it, we'll meet at the same time, 7-o 'clock?

'Yes. I'll get off the line so you can get in touch with the others. Simply tell them there's no meeting tonight, nothing more.'

'I'll do that.'

After he'd gone, Harry made his calls and was in luck. All but Charlie picked up. A text message left for him was quickly responded to. All was re-arranged. Harry called Christian back.

'Harry here. The new arrangements are all sorted.'

'Good. You were right to call. We do have a problem. I've made some enquiries of my own. My contacts in The Circle are telling me that the authorities have an inkling something's up, so they're out looking with a sense of urgency. Turning over stones, seeing what they can find underneath. We've had a few random things happening at our end too, so we all need to be extra vigilant. Nothing to be unduly worried about.'

'That seems manageable then.'

'Furthermore, just so you've got the heads up, the police in Exeter are probably going to give you another questioning about the two murders. It bugs them you are linked to both, but aren't, if you see what I mean?' Harry heard him chuckle at the other end. This was something else Harry could well do without. He wondered where Christian had got his information.

Christian off the line, Harry shouted for Elsa again. She came running into his office.

'Tonight's training meeting's been cancelled. Insufficient takers to make it worthwhile.' Lies came so easily, ever smoothing his path. 'Cancel the refreshments would you. Any further calls about tonight, I want them to be put straight through to me. Oh, and can you see to it that Dan knows of the cancellation down on the gate.'

'Yes, Harry, will do.'

Harry sat down again at his desk. Occasionally he was in the practice of taking a walk around the scrapyard site. He'd put on a bright yellow hard hat and a matching hi-vis vest and set off. He never announced he was doing it, reckoned it kept the workers on their toes. He thought now was a good time to do it. He went over to his cupboard and pulled out his yellows and hard hat. Like any manager's hat, they looked as if they were fresh out the box and had never seen a day's real work.

Five minutes later he was crossing the yard toward the cranes lifting cars and vans into the crusher. He got cheery acknowledgements. The guys are appreciating the show of interest, he thought. He looked here and there, exchanged a brief word with the site manager, Bill, strolled through the area of sorted reclaimed metals and thought things looked quieter than before. Indeed the whole yard seemed to have a sleepy summer air to it. He was told by the export clerk the next shipments to China had yet to be scheduled and before that took place they needed to source and sort some fresh metal. Harry took note and then headed over to the three isolated containers and four parked up white vans.

It was a quieter area. Usually there were seagulls screeching overhead but the hot sultry weather seemed to have tamed even them. There was an annoying buzz from somewhere and Harry looked up to see a black drone a few hundred feet directly above him. He immediately adopted a continue as normal mode, and kept swinging his head here and there so as not to indicate he'd located it. His ears continued to monitor the steady whirr just above him.

Harry felt his adrenaline begin to rush. The authorities were on to him. No one normally sends drones to spy on a yard full of scrap metal. He thought he might give his cursory check of the shipping containers a miss and swerved his path to make for a path that took him round to the back door to the offices. He listened out for the drone. It seemed to have changed path in order to keep him in clear sight. He tapped in the number on the door keypad and moved inside.

Back in his office, he called Dan.

'Dan, there's a drone above the yard. Do you see it?'

'Yes Harry. What's it doing?'

'I think it is taking a close look at us. Industrial spying I'd call it. Please ignore it, but keep half an eye on it. Let me know when it disappears.'

Harry got a call five minutes later to say that Dan could no longer see it. Harry sat at his desk not quite sure what he should do next. What was left of the coffee in front of him was tepid, but he sipped at it slowly, it seemed to help him gather his thoughts.

A few minutes later and things were clearer in his head. The authorities were seeing him and McNamara Metals as being at risk and worthy of close surveillance. It was likely what he had observed was only the tip of an investigative iceberg.

He wished he'd thought about his mobile phone use earlier, but what could he have done? They probably had some knowledge already of his contacts. Who could tell how much of the IT operation they'd picked up on? He was troubled, unnerved.

Truth to tell, the window of opportunity to launch a successful attack was closing in fast. The meeting at his place tonight would need to decide to proceed or abort as a matter of urgency. No way, thought Harry, could the incriminating arsenal in those containers continue to remain on his factory site. Tonight's meeting with Christian was going to be critical.

34

As Harry drove home he made a detour to a small corner shop and invested in a new pay as you go mobile. It was a sign of his insecurity. In the car again it was but a few minutes to his front door. As he went inside he felt paranoid. All the way home he'd kept looking up at the sky and checking for more drones, even wondering if the odd rooftop seagull was not a disguised camera. He knew he had to be careful, but it was getting to him, and in relocating the evening meeting to his home he'd belatedly realised, that this was not without risk either. Constantly fighting a welling sense of apprehension, he'd known better days. It was hard to remain positive.

Stepping inside the house, the warm air felt stuffy and close, but he was definitely not going to open any blinds or windows. He couldn't help himself but wandered around looking for evidence of anyone having been in beside Sheena. He even picked up the house phone and turned it over in his hand, looking for listening devices, but not having any clue as to what he might be looking for put it down again on its stand. He was on edge. There was probably an hour before people began arriving. He went to the kitchen cupboard and pulled out a box of bottled beers for later.

Christian was the first to arrive and when Harry opened the front door to him, he looked skyward and then up and down the street. Christian noticed.

'Calm, Harry, calm yourself man,' he said, placing a hand on Harry's shoulder.

'It's alright for you to say that, the first line of any attack comes to my door. The munitions, the location, all with my name on it. Your shadowy Circle friends are probably well hidden out of sight. I'm the one who's had a fucking drone over his head this afternoon.'

'Calm, Harry, calm. It's OK. Everything's under control,' he said, still with his arm firmly placed on Harry's shoulder. 'No one knows anything. They're fishing in the dark.'

'But they're near us and one slip, one lucky break on their part and we're in deep shit, and you bloody well know it. As I see it we need to be either acting quickly or abort the whole thing. We can't wait until we're found out. If that happens we'll all be done for and nothing achieved.'

'You're thinking along the same lines as our friends in high places. I'll be saying something to the meeting later about what's going to happen. Don't lose sight of all the good work, the thorough preparation that's been done. Secure foundations have been laid for a successful coup. We've an important night ahead of us and we both need to put some confidence into our troops. So stay calm and carry on. How about a beer, Harry?'

They moved over to the beers and took a bottle each before going into the lounge and sitting down.

'This place reminds me of the time we first met over at Charlie's house, Harry. A nice cosy home, not something I know anything about.'

The comment made sense. Harry could never imagine Christian Howard as even having a home. If he ever had a home it was with his Royal Marines, everywhere else was just a shelter.

'Last November, Ottery, I remember it well,' Harry replied.

'We've come a long way since then.'

'Why did Barry die, Christian?'

There was a silence and Harry wondered whether Christian was going to say anything at all about the matter, but he did. Maybe he needed Harry more on his side than he was letting on. Maybe… he just knew Harry was in so deep, so what the hell?

'No harm in you knowing Harry, since I've grown to trust you and like you. That man had gone too far. Like a terrier with a rat, he kept pursuing our guys with a determination that knew no bounds and that was his undoing. He'd even started digging into my background where he had no business to be. The Circle jealously guards the privacy of its members. Our lives depend on 100% security. Barry Thornton made it his business to compromise us.'

'I can understand how that would be totally unacceptable. So it was nothing to do with him having an affair?'

'Absolutely not. Charlie was sent to give Barry a clear message about poking his nose in. He was told to back off or else. The trouble was, Charlie's grip of the situation, well let's say, it was too firm, over tight, if you follow… That night Charlie phoned me to say he thought Barry had died when he'd put our concerns to him. As Charlie was looking after the bonfire, guard duty, later that evening at Ottery, the night before the big event of the 5th, he had the ideal opportunity to place the troublemaker in the middle of the fire, which he did. Well, you know the rest.'

'You and I both know Charlie's a liability,' said Harry. 'He needs watching. I've met people at the football who don't know when to stop and he's one of them. He's got a screw loose. It's a character defect. He's a liability.'

'He's been told. He's been spoken to. We have to keep him on side, for now,' said Christian, shrugging, but doing so without real conviction.

Harry felt he had no choice in the matter, but was pleased to have been given the truth behind Barry Thornton's death. He wondered at the terror of the man coming round in that bonfire as it was lit a day after being left for dead, him getting so near to getting out, but dying in agony, in hell. Then there was Nick Grayson, Charlie's hands had closed round his throat too long and too tightly.

Charlie Evans was a psycho, a dangerous killer, yet Christian had merely talked to him and was trying to say he was being kept on side. Harry felt uncomfortable. He liked to run his own outfit, Christian was too bullish, too pushy and Harry knew he might yet have to deal with the bastard or bastards for himself, but not right now. What could he do? Nothing but wait.

At which point the front door bell rang and over the next ten minutes the core team arrived and congregated in Harry's front room. A couple of extra chairs were purloined from the kitchen to ensure the seven had somewhere to sit. The relaxed atmosphere was entirely at odds with how Harry himself was feeling. In an effort to share the easy team spirit, he shed his jacket and rolled up his shirt sleeves. It was his home and he made it known he was both host and in charge before handing over to Christian.

'Thought it best to meet at Harry's, moving around is a good security move, and believe me, we all need to attend to security at this time. I say this in all seriousness. We've had a number of significant, too close to hand, security incidents in recent days, including a drone over Harry's factory today which is why we've suddenly relocated to the comfort of Harry's home. I'm afraid his personal beer cellar will feel the cost.' Laughter all round followed.

'Harry and I have been considering our options. The position is this. We need to be as tight as a duck's arse as to security. No careless talk, no careless phone calls, no trusting anyone else, 100% looking around when you're asleep as well as when you're awake. We begin our final week's preparation two weeks today, Monday 20 July. You'll all need to book time out from work, from family and tell them you're on a ten day training course. I don't care what you say – come up with something…. say the Job Centre are telling you to do it, your boss has told you… Whatever you tell people, stick to it, but say it's residential, that it'll mean staying away from home and you won't be around. Tell them it's about training for life and no one will be allowed to bring or use mobile phones. Clear so far?'

'Yes,' came back the answers in ones and twos as people began to work out what Christian was telling them.

'Nope, that won't do guys. You'll all answer in unison, clearly and loudly, "Yes, Sir!" Is what I say clear so far guys?'

'Yes, Sir!'

'I know this will come as a bit of a surprise Harry, but tomorrow you are going to send a notice to all your employees at McNamara Metals which will make you the most popular manager since the factory opened.'

'I'm already that, Christian, but do continue…' said Harry smiling.

'The idea of a workers' holiday week is back in fashion at McNamara Metals! The whole place will be shut down for the works summer holiday from when the gates are closed at 5 p.m. on Friday 17 July until you reopen for business on Monday 27th. If anyone notices the place isn't entirely empty and asks you why Harry, tell them you're hosting a training conference at the works, otherwise it's shut to everyone, even cleaning and service personnel. There's one exception to the holiday plan for all, and that's Dan…'

'Dan?'

'Yes, we need Dan on security at the gate for the whole time of the training conference. I think he might need some additional personal training to make sure he can deal with any callers, expected or otherwise. Call it up-skilling. And if you don't mind, I'll take him off site myself for a day next week if that's OK with you Harry?'

'OK, I'm sure he'll be agreeable to that and the extra workload…' said Harry, thinking that yet a little more cash from the safe was going into Dan's open hand.

'Parliament begins its summer recess on the 21st. By then everybody will be thinking of going on holiday, that is everybody except us! It's all going to happen boys. It is finally kicking off. The final weeks and then victory is ours.

In the meantime it's blood and iron. You need to keep working at personal fitness, and in tiptop fitness for what's required, each and everyone of you.'

Marcus had been standing quietly at the back by the window nursing a bottle of beer, looking every inch the opposite of a perfectly fit specimen. Tonight he had none of his projector equipment with him. However, he knew what was expected of him and when Christian paused, Harry nodded in Marcus's direction, giving him a clear signal his moment had come.

Marcus was a master of information, super fit when it came to data and IT. He seemed to have all the numbers in his head and at his finger tips. He reeled off the impressive growth in membership figures as indicators that populist support for a clearly expressed right wing agenda was being well received. There was a downside. During the past month, he reported, they had seen a serious hacking attempt to get into their data, but it had been spotted in time and seen off. He warned of the need for increased IT vigilance as the operation continued to grow and further hacks were certain to be attempted.

His final remark, made after a prompt from Christian, was to say that the state of operational readiness they had now reached meant large numbers of people could be crowd managed to turn up at specific locations and be called upon to do so at relatively short notice. All the software was in place to run the operation. Marcus just needed to know when and where to place people. In the meantime, he added, he had lots to do to keep him and his team more than fully occupied.

Harry couldn't resist the urge to take a glance through the window blind to the open street, just to check there was nothing untoward happening outside. He felt twitchy and jumpy. As he looked up and down Ham Drive, all seemed quiet, a few people strolling in T shirts and shorts in the evening sunshine and no sight of a drone. He brought his attention back to the very different world inside his front room. Christian was flapping his outstretched arms in exaggerated downward movements, much as a swan seeking flight. He wanted everyone quiet and with their undivided attention focussed on him. The arms began to move less quickly as the action gradually achieved its intended result.

'I've a lot of relevant past experience that you'll just have to trust me in claiming. To start with, just believe me when I say Harry would not have made it into parliament two years ago without help from us at The Circle. Behind the scenes, even without him knowing it, we pulled all the strings, caused the pops and bangs and gave him his parliamentary seat on a plate.'

'Mainly without me knowing it, but thank you all the same,' interrupted Harry, smiling.

'We'll move on, if I may. You are aware too that as your ordnance procurement officer I have, with your help unloading it, managed to assemble a useful war chest and the time has arrived for us to familiarise ourselves with what we have and to be prepared and briefed as to how to put it to good use. You will have no doubt guessed that my past military experience at home and abroad has helped us both acquisition the necessary hardware and enable me to kick you guys into shape. That's exactly what I'll be doing on site during our *holiday week* at McNamara Metals. I don't want you to have any false illusions about what you're getting into. The training will be hard, military hard. It'll be what's needed to ensure we get the job done.'

He paused as he assessed how the guys were receiving him. He had them, they were hanging on his every word. Harry imagined he could see these men as having being pulled out of the humdrum, from having nowhere to be or to go existences, being handed something so much better. It was like Christian had given them a cause to believe in and unite them.

'There's no need to underline how important it is that our interests at this critical stage are protected. Careless words and actions cost lives in a war, and let me make it clear, so it comes as no surprise, our own disciplinary code requires that I exercise corporal punishment if serious failings occur. Understood?'

'Yes, Sir!' came back the reply. Things had definitely stepped up a gear. Harry sensed a new military discipline had entered into things.

Harry said that he wanted to be certain that during training the factory remained a safe place for them. He'd personally do his best to ensure there was no outsider interest in their training week. The Conference and IT suites were theirs to use as were the offices, including his own, on the first floor.

If Christian could brief him what was needed in terms of hospitality, training resources, etc. he'd get on to it during the coming days. No one was to ring or otherwise communicate with the factory and any vital personal calls were to be made directly to himself and only then if absolutely necessary. Harry read out his number, the one for his second mobile, his new untraceable pay as you go phone and he insisted that if they had any other number for him it was deleted from their list of contacts.

Then Christian wanted detailed reports from each of the four regional leaders. He wanted to know how many guys they each had in their units. The figures ranged from fifteen to thirty three. He got them to work in pairs to whittle down their local numbers to just eight, eight with two held back in reserve. It was then it occurred to Harry that Christian would be using the transit vans to carry men and equipment to where they were needed and there was no room to carry extras along for the ride. Only the best men were being selected. Whilst all this was going on Marcus was sent off home.

Charlie and Gavin were assigned to work together with Harry engaging in their work and decision making. Toby and Mash, the Plymouth and Exeter guys respectively had Christian listening in on them. The four local leaders were tasked to each produce their written lists of eight plus two names for Christian within the next twenty minutes.

Most argument seemed to be made by Gavin who found Charlie difficult. The guys Gavin said he trusted and wanted to include, Charlie would always find some objection to. Charlie wanted ruthless rather than understanding guys, fit guys rather than people readers. It troubled Harry that the two were at loggerheads. Success would ultimately depend upon everyone working well together. It wasn't going well. However, in the end, with half a minute to spare they settled on their lists and handed them to Christian. Harry felt that one useful person had been ditched because Charlie felt he was psychologically unfit, defined by Charlie as weak minded. How ironic, thought Harry. Perhaps it took one to know one.

To round the evening off, Christian told them that each unit would be issued with battledress fatigues and he needed to know specific sizes of all the men before the end of the week. Christian said he would source the military attire and it would be issued during the first training day. It was up to the four area leaders to tell their ten guys to be at McNamara Metals for 08.00 on Monday 20 July. Dan would have a complete list of attendees on the gate. Everyone would have to be checked in by him.

A brief final question and answer session followed and then the evening was over. By 10-o 'clock Harry was alone in his house, empty bottles and ruffled cushions the only sign of the council of war that had taken place.

He thought he'd give Cherry a call, he needed some empathetic company. He tried to reach her several times, eventually leaving her a message. She never called back, so he reached for his Laphroag whiskey bottle and poured himself a generous glass. He fell into the sofa, switched on the TV and slumped, spread out, his day done.

He was half asleep and there was a distant ringing. He glanced down at his phone, one in the morning. Hell, it was the front door. A raid? Suddenly he panicked, thinking everything was over. The adrenaline kicked in and he jumped up, his head a fuzzy fog, a glass tumbler falling to the floor.

The bell rang again. He tried to cool himself as he tried to collect his thoughts, realising belatedly that no self respecting raid on his property would ever involve multiple rings of the door bell. Cautiously, shirt tails out, he opened the door.

'Hello, Harry, thought you'd like some company.'

It was Cherry with a big smile on her face, and as she stepped inside she added, 'and what was it you had in mind this evening?' Harry's anxious look melted into a broad smile as he opened the door wide and fixed his eyes on his welcome companion.

35

Cherry never stayed as long as Harry had hoped. By 2 a.m. she had left him sleeping in bed and made her exit, so silently that he had hardly heard the front door shut after her. Still it was nice whilst it had lasted. If only he knew how to keep her around more. Harry was quite unsure what kind of relationship they had, that was if indeed they had one at all. With that thought he fell deeply asleep.

Back in the office drinking coffee next morning, Elsa put her head round the door with a worried look on her face.

'Harry, Glenda wants to spend some time with you this morning. She says it's urgent. She's presently putting together something to show you but asks if you can be free to see her at ten?'

'Sure, I'm around. Tell her to come right on up when she's ready.'

Elsa disappeared to relay the message, leaving Harry to ponder what was on Glenda, his accountant's mind. She'd never asked for an urgent meeting before. They had routine weekly conversations with occasional paperwork for Harry to sign, but nothing was ever urgent.

An hour later there was a tap on his office door and Harry called Glenda in. She was carrying her laptop under arm, wearing a careworn worried look upon her face.

'Good morning, Harry. I'd like to show you something if I may.' Harry pulled a chair beside his as she opened up her laptop to throw up a huge spreadsheet.

'What am I looking at here, Glenda?' he asked.

Glenda was sitting close and Harry noticed how out of fashion, indeed old and worn her clothes were. She had no taste, no dress sense. Looking closely at her hair he thought it was going grey, wispy, even unkempt. She was getting more than middle aged, characterised by self-neglect and her skin was going blotchy, pasty even and he wondered how long it would be before he too began falling apart. But there was no time for more distraction, Glenda was pointing animatedly with her index finger at the figures on the screen before them. She was a figure obsessed by the dancing numbers on the spreadsheet.

'We have a cash flow situation,' she said. With our Chinese contractors "Amoi Lin King" paying late, in fact they haven't paid us at all in the last quarter, this is a big hit and we need to take some ameliorative action.'

'Take me through it slowly,' Harry pleaded. Glenda flicked back to another screen of figures.

'These are the last quarter accounts, 1 January to 31 March. It always takes a little while to pull them together even with the accountancy software we use. They show a marked deterioration in our turnover. I thought it would all be fine, our Chinese contractors "Amoi" have been late payers before but they've always paid up. So I thought the figures wouldn't be so bad if they paid up by May. The thing is, Harry, we've been shipping them our scrap since last November and they still haven't paid us a bean since then! I tried chasing them yesterday, but I can't get any reply. I've emailed and phoned Shanghai and nothing has come back.'

'Not good then?'

'No.'

'Can we get advice, intelligence from somewhere? Chamber of Commerce, the DTI?'

'I've done what I can. The reality is I think "Amoi" are in trouble themselves. There has been global slowdown in trade and the industrial sector has been affected more than others. Trading conditions in China are under pressure from all sides… cutting carbon emissions, a health scare causing factory shut downs, moves against corruption and a general slide toward recession with added pressure from an aggressive USA squeezing the Chinese economy.'

'What happened to good old fashioned debt collectors? Send round the heavy mob,' chipped in Harry.

'You don't understand Harry. The bottom line is we are in big trouble.'

'We've a good reserves situation haven't we?'

'They're being used up and we've some big bills from our own creditors to pay very shortly.'

'So you need to put a cold flannel on your forehead and go back to your office and put everything onto a single sheet of paper to tell me what we need to do to get through this mess. Why the hell am I only being told now?'

'But Harry, I send you accounts summaries every week!'

Harry knew that because they didn't interest him he hadn't even taken the trouble to look at them. 'OK, my fault,' he said lifting his hands, 'but it would be very helpful to me, to us all, if you could put together that action sheet summary A.S.A.P. and come back to me with it. OK?'

'Yes, Harry,' she said dutifully, though Harry detected a distinct lack of enthusiasm, or was it hopelessness, as she set off to tackle the task.

With Glenda and her depressing laptop gone, Harry strolled over to his coffee machine and set it into action. As he stood there waiting before his steaming, hissing, aromatic coffee, watching the brown liquid gradually filling his mug, he thought, what the hell?

Even if McNamara Metals crashed to the ground at the end of the month it will have served its purpose. It had given him a position to run things and a political platform. He thought nostalgically of his old red Audi, nicely repaired and currently stored away in his garage at home whilst he raced around in the works BMW. Maybe he'd be back driving the Audi again soon – life could be worse! Maybe he could make the works holiday one to be taken by all on unpaid leave given the state of the company accounts? Well, he'd wait to see what plans Glenda came up with. To protect his own financial position he needed to make sure car and yacht stayed his and he'd be certain to get all the cash out of the business and into his own account before it fell apart. These were the important things…

Back at his desk, Elsa put a call through to him from Exeter police. Harry had been half expecting to hear from them. He answered warily.

'Harry McNamara, McNamara Metals here. How can I help?'

'DCI Holder, Devon and Cornwall Police, based at Middlemoor, Exeter. I'm in the area presently. Would like to come and interview you if that's alright with you. Expect to be with you in fifteen minutes, Sir?'

'Of course. Anything we can do to help officer, we will,' said Harry. The day wasn't starting well. He had never been a great fan of Tuesday's, rarely any football and the weekend too far away.

Harry had only ten minutes to gather his thoughts before an alarmed Dan called him from the gate to say the police were here asking for him.

'Sorry Dan, I should have told you. I was expecting them. Show them every courtesy and bring them across. I'll come down and meet them. It's all routine…'

Before setting off downstairs, Harry instructed Elsa to come in and see to the refreshments for their visitors. He left her fussing around the coffee machine and opening some biscuits as he made his way downstairs.

It was another warm July day and the mid-morning's heat from the sun made the enclosed yard feel claustrophobic. The officers were in white short sleeved shirts and looked smart, fresh and young. The shorter one looked Asian. Harry wondered whether they were being provocative sending the fellow, but prudently he just bit his lip. They greeted him with a professionally administered smile and steady gaze. After the handshakes, he turned, Dan returning to the gate.

'Follow me,' Harry said, feeling he should have some advantage being on home ground. 'We'll use my office.'

As they stepped into the shade of the office block corridor, Harry leading the way, Marcus was approaching, clearly wanting to have a word with him; when he saw him with two police officers, he froze, turned and started walking away. Harry responded quickly as the officers missed a step and looked at each other.

'He's our IT man,' Harry explained, 'a total geek, he'll pop back to see me later. Come on up,' he added, cheerily.

Elsa had pulled two chairs in front of Harry's desk and did the dutiful hospitality thing asking the two if they would like tea or coffee and then went about serving them, biscuits too. Harry still had half a mug of cool coffee waiting to be drunk on his desk.

'Thank you Elsa,' Harry said, moving across to show her out of the door and to ensure it was firmly shut after her against any prying ears and eyes. He sat down back at his desk and looked up at the officers wondering how they were going to play things. The ball was in their court. He didn't have long to wait until he found out.

'Harry McNamara. You have some explanations to offer, some explaining to do...'

'Anything I can help you with?'

'We have you placed near two murders; both victims were strangled. The first was Barry Thornton. It was you who called us late in the evening when you were at Ottery St Mary on 5 November last. Yes?'

'I did what any decent person would. When I saw the guy I immediately called for emergency help. There were crowds of other people, but I responded first I believe. The poor man…'

'We're grateful for the call. But, the worrying thing is you were there at the scene and the forensics make it quite clear that the second murder victim Nick Grayson, who ran this company until just before his demise, was strangled very near here and in the same manner as Barry Thornton which makes you a person of interest to us.'

'You mean they were the same killer's handiwork?' replied Harry, feigning a look of surprise.

'That would be correct… and the murder of Mr Grayson places you very much in the frame for both murders, Mr McNamara. The identical method, the close association, the location of Mr Grayson's body in this very street, you being personally present at both murder scenes…'

'Not quite true, officer. I was not exactly present at the murder scenes… Am I the accused here or am I being invited to help you with your enquiries?'

'Mr McNamara, we need a DNA swab from you.'

Harry was troubled by this. He'd heard police plant DNA evidence. There was every chance some of his DNA would be near Nick or possibly on him. However, he had little choice.

'Of course. Have you one of your little pots and sticks? Let's get it done. They'll be plenty of coffee mixed with this sample,' he joked.

The Asian officer who had said nothing so far produced a test tube and took a mouth swab, screwing the lid closed and putting it away. The questions continued.

'Can we go through the events on the day of Mr Grayson's death once more, just to be sure we've got it right.' He didn't wait for Harry to agree, but pressed on.

'Nick Grayson came here to see you on a day when the business is normally closed, Sunday 8 November last year.'

'Yes, that was when he began his well earned three month sabbatical.'

'And then on Friday 7 February this year you sent him an email to tell him he'd been sacked?'

'Correct, but I'd need to check you are right about the date.'

'Believe me, I'm right about the date. Then, after the weekend, on Monday, 10 February, tell me what happened, on the day he died. Start from when you got up that morning. Take your time…'

'I came in early, and had a meeting with Nick at 9 a.m. who saw me here in this office. I had to tell him he was being let go. One of the worst jobs a boss has to do, believe me. I sensed he was genuinely disappointed to be leaving the company. He looked kind of lost. I thanked him for all the years of loyal service and said we would want to make sure his contribution was properly recognised at an appropriate time and place and I'd be in touch. I remember him mentioning, or was it me, a timepiece for him... He seemed happy with that... and that was about it. We did some reminiscing, about my grandfather and father and we discussed the company finances I think, but then he was keen to play golf or something, and that was it.'

'Anything else.'

'Oh, Elsa, my secretary popped in and out, made sure he had a coffee...'

'But he wasn't happy, was he?'

'I'm no psychologist, what makes you think that?'

'He was very unhappy with the way he'd been treated.'

'I don't know about that. What I do know is that he was very much in need of a sabbatical. After that we just couldn't afford to keep him on. People get burned out, start losing their motivation... he was like that...'

'Let's talk about motive. Could Nick Grayson have been a threat to your interest in the company?'

'No. Absolutely not. We both understood this is a McNamara family business and I am the sole proprietor. Nick was our employee. What possible motive could I have? If we could have afforded to I'd have kept him on, but as our accountant Glenda advised, we cannot pay for two managers. Sadly, he had to go...'

'Well tell me about his car. The one he drove on two occasions when he came to see you on Monday 10 February.'

'His car? He didn't have a car to my knowledge, but I could be wrong there. When he left the company for his sabbatical he left the work's BMW car parked in front of the offices. That's what you'll be thinking of, yes. I've been using the BMW since. He may have had a personal vehicle but I never saw it. He probably parked it up on the road outside, most visitors do…' Harry looked rounded plaintively.

'Immediately upon leaving here, before driving away after being told of his redundancy, he sat in his car and contacted the Employment Tribunal to see if he could take action against you. He also consulted his solicitor. Did you know that Mr McNamara?'

'No, but as I said, he really did need time to sort himself out. That was the purpose of the sabbatical in the first instance, to help him. And when I had to make him redundant, it is normal practice in business that people try and see what they can salvage from their situation. Maybe he felt our generous settlement wasn't enough. So far as I'm aware neither the Employment Tribunal nor his solicitor have been in touch, so I guess he never followed that through… may be had second thoughts. We try to be generous.'

'He was murdered… dead… he couldn't follow anything through. But we've had a close look at his communications in those hours, on that last day of his life. What do you think that tells us, Mr McNamara?'

'His golf score? I've absolutely no idea. I guess you're about to tell me…' This policeman was starting to annoy him.

293

'Let's talk more about his second visit here to McNamara Metals that day.'

Harry had felt as if he'd been winded by a blow beneath the belt. He had to think fast.

'Second visit?' he repeated, 'that's news to me. What time would that be?'

'In the evening, around seven-thirty. Where were you at that time?'

'I'm not sure.'

'We have you located here, Mr McNamara.'

'I may have been working late, I often do.'

'What were you working on and who can corroborate this?'

It was warm in the office but that didn't explain the perspiration on Harry's brow. He was thinking hard. He didn't want to involve Dan, but he had little choice. His presence on the gate offered him a ready alibi. But Harry was blowed if he was going to tell them until he'd had a word with Dan first, just to be sure he had his lines straight.

'I worked until the middle of the evening. Then I drove straight home. I think I was working alone, usually do…'

'Which route would you have taken to get home?'

'I tend to turn right out the yard and go straight along Shapters Way.'

'So we have you placed at the scene and the time of the murder.'

'What? If you're thinking I'm party to this, then I think I need to have a solicitor present. I don't like where you are going with this. Nick Grayson was a loyal and faithful employee of this company and I had absolutely no wish to see any harm come to him.'

'He came to the company that evening to collect personal effects.'

'Did he?'

'But we didn't find any on him or in his car? Can you explain that, Mr McNamara?'

'Maybe he changed is mind? You're trying to pin his death on me. I have a right to remain silent.'

'Don't get up. We'll see ourselves out. We will be in touch. Do not leave the area.'

After the two had left, Harry sat quiet thinking hard. Then he called Dan up to his office.

36

Twenty four hours later, Wednesday morning, Harry was feeling more back in control. The previous day, immediately after the police visit, he'd spoken to Dan on the gate, firstly to reassure him and then to brief him. The reassurance was the easy part.

Getting Dan to understand what he was to tell the police took rather longer for Harry to be certain he'd get it right. Eventually he understood he was to phone and tell the police that Nick had called at the gate on the evening of his death asking to collect some of his personal things from the offices but in fact Dan didn't let him in as Harry had told him that he was not to be admitted. He was to report that Nick hadn't liked being refused entry but had more or less immediately driven off and that was the end of it. Nick had definitely not been allowed on the site, he'd not seen Harry and Harry himself had remained in his office all evening, only leaving in his car around 9-o 'clock.

Harry left Dan to make his call to Middlemoor Police Station and after he and the police had had their telephone conversation around lunchtime, Dan duly reported it all back to Harry and everything went quiet again as he knew it would.

Early afternoon, Glenda asked to see him. She'd produced what she called her Action Plan. She'd made some enquiries and had been in touch with their business contractors in China. In return she'd been given some assurances that a large payment in settlement of amounts owing would be made into the company account later in the week.

'Any chance of making them pay sooner?' asked Harry.

'Not for all the tea in China,' she declared. 'Even then, I'll only believe it when I see it.'

After chewing over what this all meant for the solvency of the business they agreed they had little option but see what transpired.

There was more in the Action Plan. One item required Harry's agreement to sell off some of the valuable land the scrap yard owned in this prime area of Plymouth. There was little business sense in tying to retain it and Harry conceded there was no alternative but to sell. Glenda would get back in touch with Kernow Estates or OKEL as it was called who had shown an earlier interest.

It bothered Harry that the area to be sold was immediately adjacent to his three containers and he didn't want any site investigators wandering around any time soon. Land deals and the like would inevitably take a while to be sorted and he anticipated that by then, the time they needed to use the containers would have long passed.

Glenda suggested that until the land sale deal was done, they could probably secure a short term bank loan facility if things continued to slide. Glenda went back to her office. She had something to work at for now but she was far from being a happy lady and seemed to Harry to have further aged even since Monday.

Harry himself still felt unsettled. Memory of the earlier police visit stayed with him. It bugged him all the more because he was innocent. How ironic, when he hadn't done anything, he wasn't a strangler, that they should try and get him for those two crimes!

His composure was further disturbed when his old mobile buzzed around lunchtime. It was his Mum. Now what could she possibly want when he was busy at work?

'Harry, how are you?'

'What do you want, Mum?'

'Afternoon tea with you, Harry.'

'When?'

'Today at 3 p.m.. Meet you somewhere? Where do you suggest?'

Harry took a deep breath. 'Boston Tea Party, Vauxhall Street down in town. Do you know it?'

'Yes, Harry.'

'OK. I'll meet you there at 3-o 'clock,' he found himself saying.

Harry's Mum Bev didn't ring him without a purpose. Since she walked out on Harry two years ago, she'd changed. Once mild and helpful, she had gone all self-assertive and strong minded to Harry's mind. She used to be the home maker, manageable, but she'd rebelled against all that. Now she was just the bossy Mum, all unpredictable as she entered her older years. He had to admit, most of the time he was lucky. She kept out of his way. What, he wondered, was she after this time, money perhaps? He might take her some from the safe. A simple solution to keep her quiet for a bit. He had enough weighty matters on his mind without needing to worry about her. She could fend for herself, like she had left him to. Tea at three it was, duty called.

Sometime after 2-o 'clock, Limping Man phoned Harry on his new mobile number. At first Harry couldn't put his hand on the phone. When he did, Christian announced he'd be collecting Dan at 9-o 'clock next morning for his personal training session. Harry of course agreed. Dan would enjoy the attention and hopefully the training. Harry didn't ask any more about it as he was far more preoccupied with having a conversation with Christian about the morning's police visit.

It seemed that Christian wanted Harry to recount the whole interview with DCI Holder and his side kick, word for word. Every now and then he'd stop Harry and ask a point of clarification. In the end he told Harry he'd done exactly the right thing and the police hadn't anything on him to take it further so he was to rest easy, which Harry was ready to believe.

Their conversation lasted for more than twenty minutes. By then it was time for Harry to head into town to meet his Mum. He shut down his laptop and watched it smoothy put itself away. The sun fell hot on the yard as he walked outside and got into the BMW.

It took a while to find somewhere to park up. Eventually there was a metered space a couple of streets from where he wanted to be. When he arrived his Mum was standing outside looking at her watch. She spotted him and smiled. What was she up to?

The place was quiet, very quiet. The middle of July, a Wednesday afternoon on a very warm day, who else would suggest tea, except Bev McNamara? Even the nice tea room refurbishment hadn't brought in the crowds and the waitresses were bored with too much time on their hands and too little to do.

Tea for Bev and Coffee for Harry were ordered and taken by Harry on the tray to a table upstairs where it was quieter still.

'Harry, you well know I didn't come just to drink tea, so I'll cut to the chase, Dear and tell you what's on my mind.'

'No surprises there then, Mum,' said Harry frostily, 'but as I said before, you're not moving back into my place.'

'No worries on that front Harry. Let's talk big picture. I told you on the day of Nick's funeral that I thought I'd failed you, I'd spoiled you too much. That and your Dad's neglect of both of us did you no favours, Harry. You were always bright, but you used your smart mind to suit yourself and I let you get any with it. All too often I put your football supporter scrapes down as high spirits, but in fact they were the naked aggression of a spoiled kid. I see it so clearly now and I wonder how many kids you hurt, how many kids you sent home to their mums bleeding and bruised.'

'You really don't need to blame yourself on that score. Have you been seeing a psychologist or something? Where's all this coming from? More to the point where is it all leading? Look those kids got what they deserved, I never sought a fight with anyone. It's dog eat dog growing up. You never had to worry about me looking after myself. I did it. When I was small the other kids had their dads take them to the

300

football. Mine was always working. I was on my own, had to fend myself. I always have. I'm a survivor. No one took the piss and got away with it, nobody. That's what made me strong, made me somebody.'

'Dad's big mistake was to always put his work first. He saw life as a duty to provide and he did, he did it well. We never went short, except in terms of… love. He used to buy you the best. Like me he spoiled you. He thought giving us things… would be enough.'

'We never went short.'

'When I watched you set out to become a politician, at first I was proud, I thought wow, you're making something of yourself. You had a following. That was when I saw clearly for the first time that what we'd done for you wasn't enough. All that doing everything for you just like Patrick and I did, in the end did you no favours Harry. We brought up the most selfish spoiled person, but I never think it's too late Harry, never too late to change, it's a matter of personal choice… Dad even gave you that Audi of yours before you'd even passed your test, but you never once thanked him for it. Took it like it was expected, took it so you could be one up with your mates. We were never able to get you to settle into work, even into the business, so I was very surprised when you decided to give the business a go. In fact I was so surprised I've not stopped thinking about it since last November.'

'It's in the DNA, Mum, in the blood. It's my turn to do my bit.'

'I don't believe you Harry. And that's the other thing, Harry, you don't know what telling the truth is. I blame us on that front too. Not that we didn't know, but we let you get away with whatever you wanted to say or do. Being an only child didn't help you either, Harry. No, you've never had any real genuine interest in the company, so pull the other one. For some reason it suits you to be there...'

'You'd be surprised. The business has been a real heart warmer for me, all kinds of unexpected benefits. I thought you'd be proud that for six months now I've been head of the family firm?'

'I first knew you told big lies when you stood for parliament. You told people whatever you thought you could get away with, and developed an excellent line in telling everyone what they wanted to hear. You also allowed your vindictive side to find expression in those hateful policies you backed, the anti-Muslim, the anti-foreigner, the anti-migrant line you kept trotting out.'

'What's brought all this on Mum? I thought we were having a nice afternoon cup of tea and you give me a character assassination with a proper slagging off.'

'There's more. I've had the police round.'

'What for?' asked Harry, feeling a sense of alarm.

'They asked me about Nick, a lot about Nick, everything about him, what kind of person he was, his lifestyle. It was then the penny dropped. That's something you never did, ask me about Nick. And they quizzed me all about his movements on the day he died. You don't want to talk about him or that, do you Harry?'

'Well... It would upset you...'

'More lies, Harry. Just be quiet and listen.' she said raising her palm toward him. 'The police asked how Nick felt about being sacked. They asked if he went to the yard on the day he died and what he was going back there for.'

'And what did you say?'

'I told them he was unhappy at losing the only job he'd ever loved. He was going back that day to collect some personal items from his locker and take a last look round. That's what he'd told me earlier in the day'

'Did he say what personal things he wanted?'

'That's something you know about Harry, that's something you know about my lad,' she said, pointing her finger at Harry accusingly, her voice rising and her face reddening.

'I think you should… calm down, Mum. It's all water under the bridge now, Nick died.'

'No, he was murdered, and what do you know about it?'

'What?…'

'What do you know about Nick's murder? He didn't just die, he was murdered and you know it, I just know you know and so do the police.'

'Look if it helps, the police came to see me earlier, a DCI Holder and his colleague and I'm helping them too, so we'll wait and see, but you do need to calm down, Mum. Believe me I had nothing to do with any murder.'

'Harry, I know you through and through. You're my only son and by God I'd stand by you and want what's best for you. You can be a hero, like you were once in Istanbul. You can be loyal like you are to your mates, but when I know you're lying and you let that nasty side come out… that hurts, it really hurts,' she said, going all quiet. Harry thought she might cry. It was getting embarrassing. One of the table staff kept looking in their direction.

'Don't you worry about me. I think tea's done Mum. I need to get back to the office.'

Harry was feeling churned up by his Mum. Deep inside he knew she understood some of the darker things about his character and he felt exposed and vulnerable. It worried him that she might talk to people and that his hidden self might suddenly be exposed. His Mum had always had a soft spot for his Grandad and what also unsettled him was that he had just seen a glimpse of him in her. She seemed to be making some kind of appeal to what she saw as his good side, but she wasn't being real. Life wasn't really like that was it, he'd made his choices and had to live with them, so had she. Surely it was all about being practical and doing what it took to survive? The thing was she just didn't understand him.

Walking back to the car, Harry couldn't help but glance back over his shoulder every few minutes, once more needing to check if he was still being followed.

All he saw was his Mum, standing still, alone, poised on the pavement outside the tearoom, watching him walk away up the street. It was like when he was little and she'd watch hm carrying his school bag as he went to primary school. He thought he ought to give her a wave, which he did, he always did. She waved back just before he headed round the corner and back to find his car.

37

By the Friday, Harry was so twitchy he felt he needed some down time. The news that there would be a works holiday for a week in a week's time had had a mixed reception amongst the thirty or so employees. People liked to know where they stood and didn't like sudden changes to their plans. His announcement made this odd quirk of human behaviour abundantly clear. To Harry's great surprise, this change, a free holiday for all, made everyone at McNamara's suspicious rather than happy. They, like Harry himself were anxious and he resented them for what he saw as their lack of gratitude.

Harry decided to escape the febrile atmosphere of the factory yard and decided he'd put his recent sailing lessons to good use. The weather forecast looked favourable. He called Cherry and put the idea of a sail to her.

'It's not something I've ever done, Harry. Are you sure? I might be sick or something.'

'We'll only go where it's calm, up and down the Plym estuary. It gives you a very different perspective of the city, from the water.'

'I didn't know you sailed, Harry?'

'That's me, a whole side of my life you've yet to discover! How about it? I need to chill out and the weather promises to be glorious. You'll love it. I'll pick you up at 9, tomorrow. OK?'

'Alright, Harry. I'll need to think what to wear…'

'I'll bring the life jackets.'

Life seemed better when there was something good to look forward to and his few times on the yacht in recent weeks had taught him one thing if nothing else, there was freedom away from it all on the water.

On Saturday morning the sun burned in a still sky. Harry knew an offshore wind would pick up later, but if it was too light he'd use the engine to cruise them to somewhere quiet. Cherry was ready with a small day bag. Harry thought they needed to pick up some provisions for the sail, so they called in at a local supermarket en route. By 10-o 'clock they were clambering onto the yacht, Harry giving orders, Cherry trying her best to do what was expected, but clearly enjoying the novel experience.

'Flake the mainsail,' he ordered. She looked puzzled. 'Look fold it in pleats and lie it along the boom… there… ready for me to hoist. Don't bother with any ties to hold it, there's not enough wind.' She began trying to do what was expected, frequently firing questions to check if she was doing it just right.

Harry turned a blind eye. He'd hoist the mainsail himself a little later. 'Hoist the foresail now,' he ordered, pointing toward the prow. She clambered round and began pulling on a rope Harry nodded toward. He watched her begin pulling finally making it secure before smiling at him. Further down the estuary he would cut the engine.

He was loving this. He was in total command, she was his crew, taking his every order. His world was his boat and all else was forgotten in the moment. Only it wasn't.

As they pulled away Harry saw a police car approaching the marina. He tried to avoid glancing too obviously at it, but he knew instinctively from their approach to the waterside they were trying to catch up with him.

No way was he going back now, and with every passing second, the current and soft breeze were taking him further down the estuary and further away. They'd literally missed the boat and he chuckled to himself, double checking to ensure his phone was switched off to any incoming calls.

Harry realised they must have been following or checking on his movements somehow because only Stu knew about his yacht until today and Stu would never grass. He didn't like this sense of always having to look over his shoulder. Life was becoming more stressful by the day, but not for much longer he told himself, not for much longer.

'Harry, can I use the cabin, it's a cool breeze up here?'

'Sure, make yourself at home in there. Should be some wine and glasses. See what you can find.'

A minute or two later she had made her way back from the cabin clutching two full glasses of sparkling Champagne. You certainly know how to do things in style, Harry McNamara. You're full of surprises,' she said beaming at him.

They were set on a course which meant that even in sun glasses Harry was being dazzled by the sun, still lowish in the sky ahead reflecting off the water. He called Cherry to take the wheel. She was nervous about it, so he wrapped his arms around her and for a few minutes they were directing the boat together, the throb of the engine vibrating through them both. Harry quietly slipped instructions into her receptive ear. She soon got the hang of it.

Next, Harry had in mind getting the mainsail up, but as he'd only done this once before he needed to think carefully how to set about it. He looked around to read wind strength and direction. He yelled at Cherry to go harder right as he finally got the mainsail up and the boat began to respond in different way. It was time to cut the engine.

Soon the estuary opened up into Plymouth Sound and Harry's next challenge was to read what the other yachts and bigger vessels were doing. "Scrapfish" leaned into the wind and picked up speed, a spray splashing up into the air as she began to race ahead.

Harry was issuing more instructions to Cherry now and she was looking across nervously for Harry's reassurance. Harry hadn't experienced quite such a turn of speed as this before and he thought he might slacken off to be certain he could retain control. Ideally he would have liked at least one other sailor on board. As they got further out so the waves started to build and the splashing became hard hitting reverberating thwacks as the hull coughed into darker seas. He let the boat forge ahead unchecked.

With the Mount Batten Tower to their left he took a bearing south but began to realise there was a very large continental ferry coming from their right. He took a course nearer land not wanting any entanglement with such a big vessel with a threatening wake.

They made good progress and once in calmer seas he got Cherry to take the wheel once again. Harry looked at the map Nick had left in the boat to work out exactly where they were. Soon he had a plan. Passing the village of Wembury he aimed for a small river estuary, the Yealm, which would let them access the village of Newton Ferrers where he knew there were at least two good pubs. Where he would moor up would need to be resolved when they got there. He knew that in busy periods the Yealm estuary harbourmaster would turn boats away, but he chanced that they were early enough in the summer season to get lucky.

As they headed landward and into narrower waters it was time to take the sails down and get the engine into action again. It was all very physical and time passed quickly. Harry was beginning to understand why Nick liked it so much. The engine came to life at the first turn of the ignition and he asked Cherry to keep an eye out for vessels or obstacles on her side as he slowed the yacht and idled it inland.

The land either side gradually enclosed them and Harry began to wonder whether the water depth was sufficient. He picked up his mobile to call the Harbourmaster, who unusually did not operate by radio VHF contact. He asked for a visitor's mooring and was directed to come right in and raft up by the clearly marked visitor's buoys.

Finally, they were amongst other vessels and once secured to their mooring, fenders in place between them and a larger vessel, they settled on the Ship Inn for something to eat.

Food was ordered and eaten outside a soft warm breeze making life feel good as lunchtime spilled into afternoon. Only it didn't, didn't continue to feel good that is.

Or strictly speaking it did until 2.30 and then things changed. Harry saw a police car arrive at the pub and he watched as one officer got out and went inside, the other following soon after. He could see a brief conversation taking place with one of the bar staff and then the moment of truth, a hand waved in the direction of the outside seating area where Harry, in a crowd of other Saturday sightseers, was sitting. There was no direct route to him from where they were so he would need to judge his timing to perfection if he were to avoid them. That they had him in their sights he had not a shadow of a doubt.

Cherry was quite oblivious at this turn of events, her dark glasses covering her closed eyes, her body lying back allowing her to comfortably absorb the sun's warmth. Leaving her undisturbed and without making a sound, when the police were out of sight inside the pub, Harry stood up and walked quickly away and down to the quayside.

He pulled himself onto the yacht, started its engine, cast off the mooring ropes and quietly slipped away, trying to disguise his appearance and keep low in the cabin. Once in mid-stream, he found the ebb tide current was taking him fast toward the open sea. It felt safe enough to steal a glimpse back. The two police men had left the pub and were now walking along the quayside looking this way and that.

He picked up his mobile and called Cherry.

'You're where?' she said, Harry having disturbed her reverie.

'On the river, just testing some things out on the boat. You'd dozed off! I'll be back shortly, enjoy the sun.'

Then he cut the call, swung the boat round so that it clung to the near bank and slowly made the return journey, mooring up again once he was certain the coast was clear.

'Come on Cherry, settle the bill, we need to get back. There's a fast tide to take us down to the open sea. Come on!'

For much of the return journey Harry was thinking hard. He knew it wasn't his own paranoia. Time and again there were signs that the authorities were on to him, whether for the two murders or the political cause about to come to life. He felt equally vulnerable when Cherry observed and commented on his change in mood.

'What's up Harry? You seem to have lost your mojo. This has been such an unexpected pleasure. Are you sad the day's nearly done?'

'Suppose so,' he said in a rather downbeat way. 'It's a busy time and there are some issues at work. You know how it is, sometimes life can be very pressurised.'

'Don't tell me about it. Fortunately for me my editor has told me to chill this weekend and that's just what I'm doing.' She reached for him and held on to him at the wheel, the lively sea throwing them against one another.

'I'll need to moor up and get back to the business later. Quarterly accounts time,' he added, to satisfy any curiosity.

'You're a very different Harry to the one I used to know. You were so carefree, so up for it and sat so light to life. I'd never have thought a set of accounts could come between you and a girl,' she teased.

'Take the wheel, Cherry,' he ordered, 'I need to take in the mainsail.'

Harry quite liked being in charge of his yacht. On a boat, he'd come to realise, he gave orders and people obeyed them. It was a near perfect pastime!

38

Harry dropped Cherry at her home and headed straight back to Shapters Way swinging left at the closed metal entrance gates to McNamara Metals. Dan saw him coming, his vigilance warming Harry. As Harry entered the yard he pulled up and dropped the passenger side window to speak with him.

'Hi Dan. Hot day for you. How's it been?'

'Fine. Surprised to see you here on a Saturday boss. All quiet here.'

'That's good. Glad to hear it. I need to catch up on some paperwork whilst it's quiet… Oh, how did your security training go with Christian on Thursday?'

'Hell Harry, that was something else. Took me to a farm on Dartmoor, not allowed to say where. Had a personal instructor with me all day. Taught me how to spot things, size things up, how to make a measured response, weapons training and all!'

'Weapons training too?'

'Yeah, but I'm to keep hush about that bit, but thought you'd like to know. Between you and me I've even got my own tool issued to me by Christian, a Glock, keep it in a special holster inside my jacket.' Dan patted his chest proudly.

'Well, we should all feel safer knowing that Dan. I'll leave you to do your job. Now the works are closed for a week there should be no one about, not a soul anywhere near the place, only trainees… follow me? Otherwise I need to know if you see so much as a trespassing mouse.'

'OK, boss,' he grinned. Dan had proved an excellent choice for a security man, his black uniform was always immaculate and he cut a sharp image. From his build, Harry was convinced he was now working out at the gym, hopefully not pushing the steroids too hard. In sum the security work perfectly suited his personality.

Harry drove the few remaining yards across the yard and parked up adjacent to the door to the offices. The fact that Dan was now armed and it had seemed so normal was both OK and not. Christian had taken it upon himself to give Dan weapons training, issue him with a serious piece of hardware and station him with it at his factory gate. Harry felt sidelined, annoyed and at the same time realised that the stakes were high, things were moving on and some of it was outside his control. At least Dan looked more than equipped to deal with any expected security issues. Perhaps Christian was simply protecting his investment.

Once in the office, Harry could taste the sea salt on his lips and went to the toilet to wash his face, arms and hands. He returned feeling much refreshed. Coffee came next and then as he went to sit himself down at his desk, he paused to look at the three mug shots on the wall.

His grandfather Michael, who had founded and built the business from nothing, then his father Patrick with a rather dour expression on his face. It said everything. Patrick had built on his own father's legacy and given his life to the business but, as his Mum had reminded him, this had been at a cost to the rest of the family. He couldn't think that working hard had made him a cheerful soul.

Then there was the smiling picture of Harry himself, youthful and carefree in the middle, looking every bit as if he was the master of all he surveyed. The picture already felt strangely out of date. He was now a man who felt he was carrying the world on his shoulders. The business was at risk, the political campaign was on the cusp of success but on the edge of being thwarted. The Circle were once again driving a campaign as only they saw fit. Such stress felt too much. He knew what the phrase, the burden of history meant. It lay across his own shoulders.

Another coffee was required and he helped himself. The quiet of his office made him realise he had his own space in which to think and then put the world to order. With each sip Harry felt himself getting increasingly angry. For one reason after another there was pressure being put on him. It just wasn't fair!

Firstly, Christian was pushing him around and it wasn't him alone, it was his shadowy international Aryan master race network. It was The Circle who were pulling all the strings and he was being controlled, manipulated. As before, two years ago, he was the puppet, they were the puppet masters and his sense of impotence got to him.

Secondly, the police were on his tail for something he knew about, two murders committed by Charlie Evans from Ottery, but this was so unfair, since he himself had absolutely no responsibility for either death. Harry began to blame Christian for protecting Charlie all the way through and wondered if he'd missed chances to shop the nutter to the police long ago. Now Charlie had bargaining power at

Harry's expense. How long would it be before they came knocking on Harry's door blaming him for the murders, arrest him even? It felt like they were well on the way to taking that course of action.

And thirdly, there were those two women in his life… Cherry – too independent by half, but maybe coming round to his way of thinking and then there was his Mum. She should be supporting him like she used to in the past, instead of asserting herself the way she'd started to these past weeks, accusing him, denigrating him…

In sum, Harry felt he was far too much out on his own and exposed to who knows what. It was all his struggle. He needed to find ways to overcome all these obstacles and if they didn't play ball with him, there'd be hell to pay and he'd take the fucking lot down with him. He startled himself by crashing his fist down on the desk.

That's when he first noticed the file sitting there. He recognised Glenda's handiwork. She'd left some paperwork on his desk for his attention. Opening the front cover, he found himself running his eye down it. Her handwritten memo stapled to the top stated that before going off on holiday the previous afternoon she thought she ought to let him have an up to the minute accounts briefing given how precarious the business's finances were looking.

She'd factored in the loss of productivity from closing the factory for a week. Yesterday, she'd been in touch with the company's bank and agreed a short term loan facility provision from the end of July. OKEL had responded to her enquiry about the land sale only to be told that the industrial land market had entered a new degree of uncertainty with figures being revised downwards for this year. Currently they had no interest in buying land from McNamara Metals. She hadn't been able to identify another interested party and had got an estate agent on the case. Glenda hoped Harry would be able to come up with some creative ideas by the time she came back.

Harry had no creative ideas. The figures needed to pull the firm back, if no payments came in from China, looked astronomical and he thought he might end up having to lay people off when they returned. That's what managers did wasn't it? He'd need to find out how to make redundancies happen. He opened up his lap top and drafted an email instructing Glenda to start thinking along those lines and to come back to him with ideas as where the knife should make the first cut.

Then Harry thought of himself. It never took long. Self-preservation had always been a priority. If the company looked like foundering, he needed to get more cash set aside for himself as and when he could. He instructed Glenda to transfer £20,000 to his personal bank account in lieu of management services provided. That was the second email drafted.

Harry walked over to the safe and opened it up. The cash pile inside had reduced over the weeks, but he imagined there to be several thousand pounds in twenties he could take away to see himself through for a while. He looked at the blackmail accounts and considered his option on making a future income built around them. Then he sat down again at his desk and wrote another email, also to Glenda, telling her to make arrangements for the BMW to be made over to him from the company as his personal asset. Maybe there were other assets on site he could acquire if the ship looked like sinking. He'd speak to her personally about that when she was back.

Things were beginning to look better, coming under his control. Some might call it asset stripping, but he thought of it as precautionary measures. He got up, walked downstairs with his bunch of keys. He opened number 1 and number 2 lockers. The wrapped gun and ammunition Limping Man had given him on that drive to Exeter were wrapped as he'd left them in number 2 locker, the piece Cherry had discovered and believed he'd thrown into the estuary.

Harry thought it needed a more secure hiding place. But where? The bottom right lockers, numbered 36 to 40 were unused, anonymous, their keys in the locks. He moved the gun and box of ammunition to locker 40, locked it, found he could switch keys 39 and 40. New key from 39 wouldn't open the locker when he tried it. Job done. Suspicion moved that bit away from him. He didn't want any gun found with his own name against it.

He went back up to his office and began putting some sort of order to what he thought the coming week's training programme should look like. He didn't want Christian to be calling all the shots. His personal aim was to ride the revolution, like a surfer on a wave. At least he was the political figurehead for what had been hitherto an underground movement. But what if Christian sought to dispense with him too? From what he knew of The Circle it was a dog eat dog organisation, no mercy shown. They'd cast out any one person, rightly or wrongly, for the greater good of the cause. That was how it worked, that was how the football supporter lads worked. Harry understood it completely.

The more he thought about things the more he realised the week ahead posed by far the biggest risk to him yet. He had a week of intense operational preparation happening out there in his own yard and there was the growing feeling that the authorities had some inkling, were trying to see what was happening. Were the plans he and the The Circle drawn up fatally compromised, the powers that be just waiting to get them all red handed? Harry didn't want to be caught with his trousers round his ankles.

It bothered him that a balance had been tipped and Christian was in the ascendant and made all the decisions. He would know what would be happening with Harry just a follower. So, he told himself, if they were approaching wartime he should show some personal leadership and initiative. He began to formulate a list of his own before making a long overdue call to Christian Howard.

'Hello, Christian. Got a moment?'

'Yeah. What's up?'

'This coming Monday. You've not sent anything through to me yet… '

'It's all in hand Harry. I've got two ex-military guys coming to facilitate things. Served with me here and in the Gulf. It's sorted. During the week the four teams will be put through their paces and brought up to the mark. They've a lot to do, they don't know it yet, but they'll be different by the end of the week… become men, real men. Trust me, I've got worse teams than these up to the mark before now.'

'So what's the programme you've given these two army extras, Christian? It's all happening on my watch and we're partners in this together, right?'

'Sure Harry. In the hours of final struggle, people start worrying, get tense, show it in different ways, I understand that. We're that close to victory, Harry, that close...'

'Christian, I'm a guy who only takes so much on trust. I want you to send an email or better still an encrypted phone message with the programme and I want it this afternoon. Right?'

'I don't work like that Harry. When I delegate a training event, I give to the guy who knows how to do it to deliver the programme, I don't do it for them...'

'OK, so just let me have something on the brief you gave them to deliver.'

'OK, you win. I'll copy over what I asked them to do. Just so you know, we'll be using the vans and some of the stored equipment, all the guys will be issued their military uniform and going up onto Dartmoor for some of the time. My problem Harry, has been and still is, what to do with you this week...'

'How do you mean?'

'Well, you'll be pleased to know I'm not involving you in the field training programme, but the political side, your side, needs taking to the next level too. I need Marcus and his team to be working more closely with you to bring the public space campaign to a climax and I want some assurances that you've mobilised all the support out there, otherwise it doesn't matter a fig what I do with four teams of guys with guns and explosives, if the political side is useless we might as well surrender. Do you get me?'

'I was thinking along the same lines myself,' Harry lied, agreeing to what seemed a sensible approach. 'But to date I feel like I'm the only political element in all this, all The Circle's work has been off limits and I need to know from you what that side of the campaign is going to look like, otherwise, being totally frank with you, the whole thing is going to be nothing but a fucking disaster!'

'Tell you what Harry, I know Wednesday is a Dartmoor day for the lads. How about I bring a couple of the other political guys down to your office for the day. That would enable all of you to work together and make a timely appraisal of where things are and how we can get this thing done. I think my friends would agree to that. I can be in on it too if you think it would be helpful, include Marcus…'

Harry felt he'd been organised into a situation not of his own making once again, but could see no other way forward than to agree with the proposals, which is what he did before ending the call.

Afterwards he felt a bit better about things. In retrospect he'd put some pressure on Christian and got something out of it. He knew what the guys would be doing in the week ahead and how it was all to happen. Clearly Christian had access to professional help – fine, he had to trust him on that. As for his own political role, he had secured an agreement to bring the wider political wing together for a critical meeting on Wednesday. He felt he could live with that and went to get himself another coffee.

For some reason the conversation still left him feeling personally vulnerable and without thinking about it properly he went downstairs, exchanged the keys in lockers 39 and 40 and opened locker 40 to retrieve the gun.

He locked up and carried it to his office and placed it on his oak desk with the solid clunk of metal meeting wood. Unwrapping it, he picked it up, nursing it in his palm and felt its cold weight in his hand. He no longer cared if his finger prints were on it. Then he opened the box of ammunition and began loading pieces as Christian had told him. It felt awkward and slow, so he took them out and did it again, faster this time, as if he were practising for a showdown like they did in the old western films. Then, holding the gun firmly in both hand he lifted it deliberately toward the closed door to his office and pointed it imagining a target in his sights.

'Bang,' he shouted, lifting the point of the gun, before standing up and wrapping the still loaded weapon back in its cloth.

He turned, opened his safe, re-wrapped the gun and cartridges and put them away; he was now fully convinced the time was nearing when he might have to use his weapon. After all he couldn't expect his guys to be trained to shoot to kill and not be prepared to do the same himself. That was how it was, how leadership from the front worked. He understood it. No doubt about it, he was in far too deep for any messing around. Do or die, there was no way out.

39

'Harry, I want you to take me to church.'

It was 8-o 'clock on a Sunday morning and his Mum had woken him up, placing a direct command directly into Harry's left ear. These days she'd taken to getting straight to the point.

'What the… Do you know what time it is?' he asked her, his eyes squinting open.

'Yes, and if you can get over here in half an hour I'll have a full English ready for you before we go. There'll be just enough time for you to enjoy it without bolting it down.'

Harry was completely thrown. He'd plans in mind to take "Scrapfish" out on the water again, but he parked that idea up immediately, put it on the back burner until later. Just recently, his Mum could be very insistent.

He'd succumbed before he knew it, probably because she'd promised a breakfast just how he liked and remembered it. He rolled out of bed to face the day. His Mum's change of heart struck a discordant note. He couldn't understand her any more. Perhaps she'd also signed up to the radical #*MeToo* movement that was giving so much trouble, too much of it about.

Then it dawned on him why she'd called. It was his Mum and Dad's anniversary. Even since his father's death two years ago she always went back to the church on their anniversary or the Sunday nearest. He felt the sense of duty pressing down as he got dressed. Hurriedly, he grabbed his keys and mobile and headed out of the door.

Harry hadn't been to his Aunt Zoe's house for years, but he knew exactly where it was. Its location had been indelibly laid down in his mind in childhood, memories which included regular Sunday lunch visits, boring as hell. It was one of those semi-detached 1930s houses, three up, two down with a manicured square lawn on the front and a narrow driveway made of two rows of paving slabs to the side providing just enough space for two cars. The house had been spared the bombing of Plymouth in WW2. Why had Hitler spared it? The house was remembered for its enduring boredom, its neutral and pastel colours and the unexciting, make do and mend behaviour of his long widowed aunt.

As soon as Harry pulled up the front door swung open. His aunt took him in and sat him down alone at the kitchen table, his chair looking out onto the back lawn with its bird table and hanging feeders. Harry had a horror of ever finding himself trapped in this kind of domesticity.

He heard his Mum busying herself upstairs as he was handed a white ironed linen serviette which he tucked into his collar before tucking into the spread laid before him. The food was good and needed, all washed down with coffee, which was as he remembered it… instant and disappointing. He left half of it, a thin brown sludge ready to go straight down the sink.

Mum in her dark blue Sunday best coat stepped into the room. She had one of those old Lady Thatcher style handbags grasped firmly in her right hand.

'Good morning, Dear,' she said, stooping to disconcertingly kiss him on the cheek. He got up and they left Aunt Zoe to clear up. She didn't do church. Harry went round to open the passenger door of the car.

'Let's go,' she said, 'I'd like to park up at your place and we'll walk to St Martin's from there like we always used to.'

'There's no "always" Mum. I can count the number of times on the fingers of both hands.'

It didn't take long to get back. They set off together walking side by side. Harry had a sense of deja vu, suddenly feeling uncomfortable when they passed the spot where Harry's friend Cathy had been killed by The Circle two years previously. He shuddered at the thought of possibly more perilous times to come before quickening his pace, only to find his Mum lagging behind. He slowed, 'Come on, you know how much you hate to be late,' he urged.

They walked into church and the elderly man, more bent over his stick than he remembered from before, said a polite, 'good morning,' and handed them both a service booklet.

They shuffled down the central aisle to where they usually sat. Harry remembered to switch his mobile to silent and settled himself down, leaning against a stone pillar, feeling his breakfast settle. His Mum next to him had dropped her head in an attitude of prayer.

For his part Harry's eyes wandered to survey the scene. His gaze fell upon the brass plaque on the wall. Last time he was here he hadn't been able to read the small lettering beneath the title, *"Michael McNamara"* from where he sat. Now, the words were so engraved in his memory he could make them out clearly from where he sat. He read, *"In eternal gratitude by Michael's friends in Plymouth for his support of the Jewish Community and its ancient Synagogue."*

Harry thought he'd have a word with the vicar after the service to see if he could have the plaque removed. Nice man that he was, his grandfather Michael had lost his way later in life. Once a staunch nationalist he had allowed a woman to turn his head. There was no need for everyone to be constantly reminded of his mistake, least of all his own family.

Harry went through the motions of standing, singing, sitting, listening and praying. Most of it he just didn't get. He wondered how such places continued to survive with a couple of dozen mainly older people turning up once a week. How did they generate any turnover? He began thinking of it as a business, something he realised he knew something more about than he did last time he was here.

By the time of the sermon, he wasn't listening to the vicar, he was thinking about how to turnaround the finances of McNamara Metals. 'We need a bloody miracle,' he muttered under his breath. His Mum nudged him under his ribs to quieten him. It was just like when he was a kid, he thought.

Soon it was over and a watery brown liquid in a green enamel mug was offered him in the name of coffee. He took it anyway, second mug of sludge in a day. As before he left most of it.

He recalled he'd made his last visit here in the midst of his political campaign to become an MP and it had caused quite a stir, some people taking issue with his sensible policies. This time no one bothered to engage with him. He realised that a disgraced past politician was a forgotten nobody, but they'd soon sit up and notice when he was back.

He managed to place himself in line for a conversation with the vicar. When he was greeted, his hand being warmly shaken, the vicar announced how pleased he was to see him here again after so long and how sorry he'd been to hear of the death of his father, Patrick. Harry remembered they'd been at the church for his grandfather Michael's funeral prior to that.

'Humph!' said Harry, before adding, 'any chance of removing that plaque?' pointing with an outstretched arm at the offending brass plate. 'I can send a man down from the yard if it would help,' offered Harry.

'Is there a problem with it?' asked the vicar puzzled.

'Of course there is. The family don't like it.'

'But the family should feel proud of the good he did… It's very modest, indeed humble that you should wish your grandfather's good works to go unremembered, unrecognised…'

'No, you misunderstand me. He was a very much mistaken old man. The Jews should leave this country and all their synagogues be pulled down, likewise the Muslims should return to Arabia and their mosques confiscated, along with every other unfaithful, heretical immigrant who dares darken these shores…' said Harry with increasing feeling in his voice. This man was such a soft target.

'What! I can't believe you mean it… Jews, Muslims and people of so many different faiths and none make our country the great place it is… besides, it is our Christian duty to welcome the stranger, the foreigner and the alien… '

'There are too many Guardian reading lefties like you, but back to the point. When can I send a man down to have that plaque removed? He'll leave it tidy, won't know it was there…' Harry offered more quietly.

'I'm afraid you can't do that. I don't really know where to start…'

'Try me…'

'Well, any changes here require a legal faculty, a permission…'

'You can get that…'

'But, it's more complicated than you realise. For a start, the plaque isn't the McNamara's, it was presented to the church by others and I fail to see what grounds you have for making such a petition…'

Harry's Mum had joined them.

'What's he arguing with you about this time vicar?' she asked smiling.

'Harry wants the Michael McNamara plaque removed and I've told him my view on the matter.'

'There's some churchy red tape to get round first, Mum.'

'It's rather more than that Harry…'

'He's winding you up, Vicar. I love that plaque. It's a wonderful tribute to a fine man and the man whose factory has done so much good for the area.'

That killed the discussion. Harry had no wish to argue with both his Mum and the vicar and reluctantly let the matter drop. He reasoned there were bigger battles to fight, but he wouldn't be forgetting whose side the vicar was on any time soon. He would have loved to have the backing of the church behind his current right wing campaign that he was in the midst of building, so he thought he'd try a different approach.

'I think you're right vicar, at the end of the day the plaque itself isn't the important thing here, it can stay if you say so. What is important is the need to get unemployed young people good jobs, to cut crime and build our hospitals and care services. Don't you agree if government were to prioritise these things it would make a real difference in people's lives? After all our community needs to strengthen the ties that bind it, don't you think?'

'Why, yes, of course Harry…'

'Then I can count on your support?'

'Well, yes, on those things, yes…'

'Thank you. Well, Mum it's time I got you home.'

It was as they were leaving the vicinity of the church, Harry's phone vibrated in his pocket and he pulled it out to see Dan was calling him from the factory. He told his Mum to walk on ahead whilst he took the call.

'Hi Dan, what is it?'

'We've had an intruder. I made a walking patrol round the perimeter just now. I've been doing them how Christian taught me, making the rounds at irregular times. That's how I found the guy.'

'Where was he?'

'He was at the back door to the offices trying to get in. He looked at me twice, I think he even thought of taking me on. When I drew my Glock and aimed, or rather waved it at him, he legged it. He had a folding aluminium ladder by the back wall. Just saw him disappearing over the top when I got near. In his haste he left the ladder behind. Must have bought it specially for the job. Brand new it is. Got it down by the gate house now. I ran straight back to the front gate as I reckoned they'd drive back that way.'

'And?...'

'I saw the same guy being driven off. They were in a Land Rover Defender, Harry, strange, not your usual burglars. Thought you ought to know. It's all quiet now, nothing to worry about. Don't think he got in. Left emptyhanded. Shall I call the police?'

'No police, Dan. Are you quite certain you disturbed him before he got in?'

'Yes.'

'I want you to do two things and then call me straight back. Go into the offices and check all the doors. I especially want you to check my office door and also, all the locker doors on the ground floor. Then go over to our three containers and four vans. Check they are all secure. It'll take you a few minutes, by which time I'll be back home. Call me then. OK?'

'OK, Harry…Will do.'

After Dan had gone to make his checks, Harry was left with two nagging thoughts. The first was that this was an official investigation by MI6 or counter-terrorism, another 'fishing' visit because they thought something might be up. If they hadn't found what was inside the containers then he wasn't too worried.

The second thing about Dan's call that was troubling him was that Dan had brandished his pistol. Very stupid! What kind of normal factory security guard waved a pistol? They'd be on to that and they'd be back. There seemed little point in getting Dan to ditch his weapon. It was too late for that. They'd seen it. What Harry needed do was to get down there and give Dan a de-brief so that he had an unshakeable story line ready for when the authorities next came calling, which couldn't be long.

'Mum, something's come up at work. I'm going to have to drop you straight back at Aunt Zoe's and go straight in.'

'OK, Harry. Sometimes I forget what you've taken on. It was like this with your Dad. I was thinking about him just now. Even on our wedding day, he popped into the factory to see about something. It set a pattern of behaviour he could never shake off. It meant a lot that you came with me today, Harry. Don't forget you need time to relax too, Harry. I'll call you later.'

And so it was, with his Mum dropped back at Aunt Zoe's home, Harry drove into work, pulling up at the factory gate just forty minutes after Dan's call. Dan was duly back on the gate having made his tour of inspection.

'No problems Harry, everything as it should be,' he announced reassuringly.

'We have got one problem, Dan and that's you and your gun. I want you up in my office in five minutes,' he ordered, driving his car swiftly over to the other side of the yard by the offices. He went inside, made himself his first decent coffee of the day and sat down at his desk to await Dan. The next fifteen minutes were spent giving Dan the third degree. His foolishness in producing the weapon was made absolutely clear to him.

In the end, suitably chastised, Dan even offered to hand the gun over to Harry. Harry, however, said it was far better that Dan kept it, but that he should know how to respond to any official enquiry. If that happened he needed to simply say the weapon was given to him by a friend in the gym where he works out… no names of this "friend" were ever to be provided. The weapon was to be handed over to any police with the minimum of fuss and maximum of cooperation. Any further outsider intrusion was to be immediately reported to Harry.

Before Harry sent Dan back to the gate, he added with a knowing smile, 'You did well though Dan. Made the guy run. He'll think twice before messing with you again. And the other thing, I want you to keep your weapon because there may come a time when the best men, like yourself, need to stand up and fight for the cause. So well done. You'd better get back to you station.'

'OK, Harry.'

Harry was about to open Glenda's file, still sitting on his desk, waiting for that miracle financial input to save them. He had to admit, things were looking challenging, to put it mildly. When Glenda was back, he'd get her to fix it, but there was nothing more he could do about it in the coming week. To be honest, a lot of the technical stuff, just passed over his head. He needed her experience, maybe get the contracts guy in for a three way meeting. So he fired up his laptop and sent them both an email for a meeting for Monday week, to meet first thing when they were all back.

Then his mobile rang. It was his Mum. He'd not that long ago dropped her home. What could she want now?

'Harry, I've just been chatting to vicar Stephen at St Martin's. He was pleased to see us both this morning. He told me about your views on the family tribute plaque. Why didn't you ask me about it?'

'I hadn't got round to it,' he lied, 'knowing his Mum would not have shared his views on the matter.

'Well, I've got to thinking I just don't know where you are going with all this right wing politics stuff. He told me you were anti-Jew, anti-muslim and pretty well anti-anyone you might think of as an outsider. You seem to have forgotten the point of the plaque, Harry. Your grandad Michael, whom you always loved, he turned his back on all that Blackshirt stuff and that plaque is a reminder to me and everyone who cares to look at it that even when someone sells out to hateful politics they can sometimes still find a way back and do something good.'

'OK, no big deal, the plaque stays. Was there anything else? I've heard one sermon already today.'

'Yes, Harry, I don't know what's got into you lately, but I don't like it. You lie as easily as you tell the truth, you've got the gift of a silver tongue, could sell sun tan lotion in the arctic. But it'll do you no good, you'll be found out, Harry, mark my words.'

'You worry too much and tell that vicar friend, Stephen, he needn't think he can go behind my back.'

'Now that's unfair, Harry. He was concerned for you. He and I are old friends. We were chatting. I told you because he made it plain as day that you're in a bad place Harry. I've been trying these past days to build bridges with you, so that we can at least meet up, have a conversation together from time to time. But I fear we're just going to end up arguing.'

'Looks that way…'

'We fell out over politics two years ago, but it was more than that. I realised I'd done you no favours spoiling you and I feel much better about life and that I'm doing the right thing by you if I tell it how it is. So here it is Harry. Whatever it is you're up to, whatever the scheme or ruse you've got running, the thing you're definitely not telling me about, but I see it in your face, in Stu's face too, I don't like it. It feels to me that you're slipping beneath the surface into some deep and dark waters, just watch you don't drown Harry.'

With that she'd gone, leaving Harry looking at his mobile in disbelief. What? Who? And how does she know all this?'

40

'Stu, it's Harry. Fancy an evening at the White Horse? We could get a few of the others in, have a few beers. Sunday nights, nothing much else on. I'll give Cherry a call, see if she can make it too? Bring your missus, Stu, time you took Penny out, don't want Cherry to be the only chick,' he jested.

'Don't think she'll come, Harry. We've some news actually Harry, she's kinda… well, expecting.'

'Stu, you've done it now. You've got to come, we want to celebrate with you. Tell her…'

'She keeps being sick, Harry…'

'Well, get her Mum to sit in with her. If not bring her anyway. Shall we say around 8-o 'clock?'

'OK, Harry, I'll see what I can do. Catch you later…'

'Oh, and congratulations! I think that's what people say.'

'Thanks, Harry.'

Harry got up and made another coffee. Maybe he shouldn't have so many mugs, he was on edge, hyped up, maybe coffee didn't help. He had another anyway. He rang Cherry, she picked up immediately. She was doing weekend catch-up chores at home and more than happy to come out later.

'There's some stuff I need to go through with you, Harry. News stuff… before I put it out. Can we grab a few minutes? Say 7.45 p.m.?'

'Sure, do you want me to pick you up? We can chat in the car. I can leave the car in the Black Horse's car park overnight and you can take an Uber home, yeah?'

'Fine, Harry. Love you!'

She'd gone. What did she just say, "Love You". He'd have to watch this emotional attachment stuff.

He made several more calls and the prospect of a good night out with banter, laughs and plenty to drink seemed settled. The Black Horse had for many years been a second, no, his first home. He thought it was time to get back to Ham Drive, change into something more relaxing, ready to let his hair down, relax.

Yachting was never going to happen today, in the week maybe, well he was the boss, he'd take "Scrapfish" out some other time, when the weather seemed good, why not? Might have to wait until the coming week was over with. Cherry would be up for coming again, perhaps they could sail west next time, he mused. There were some good upsides to his life.

When he got to his car, Harry saw Dan had already left. His security kiosk was dark, no one at home. He cast his eye round the yard, it all looked as it should and he got in the BMW and felt its reassuring soft surge of power as he set off for home. Tomorrow was a big day, training on site for the whole team. Things were on the cusp of happening, he could sense a big moment.

Back at Ham Drive, he found some live cricket still in session on the Sports channel. It was a county match, Lancashire versus Yorkshire, limited over, a close finish in prospect and he settled down in front of the TV to catch the final overs of the day.

He had a couple of hours to kill before going out. After only two overs he began to fidget. He got out of his chair and went to peer out of the front window like a nosy elderly person, looking one way, then the other, checking what was happening on the street. An ice cream van came by playing its overloud music. At least it was a piece of patriotic, "Greensleeves" albeit the van's name was in Italian. The van disappeared round the corner and the music stopped.

Then it struck him, he'd been quite strong in what he'd said to the vicar that morning, expressing his feelings toward foreigners. Seeing the Italian name had reminded him. However, Italians had been on the German side in the war, which meant they weren't so bad were they, but did that mean they like all the other foreigners have a right to live here in Plymouth? No way. He'd thought leaving the EU might have settled such issues, but that hadn't been the case. It all seemed very complicated, past and present dividing people up the way they were. His own party were trying to get a handle on the issue and through what Marcus and his team were promoting, wasn't it clear that the only ones who really mattered were people like us? He concluded it was the only straightforward position to adopt.

Harry was startled. Cries of "Owzat!" There had been a wicket on the TV and everyone was excited. He tried to re-engage but found it impossible. His mind was full of ideas and fears. The umpires final word, "Out!" kept echoing through his mind like a political statement. That's what he wanted, all the outsiders out whilst looking after the interests and well being of one's own folk. That was a right thing to do wasn't it?

'So what was that vicar doing trying to make out those foreigners had a place? It felt like the plaque was a desecration, he'd need to come back to the matter and ensure that somehow it was removed, and what a legal faculty couldn't grant, a crowbar from the work's yard could fix in a matter of seconds. He'd send round one of the lads, slip a few fivers from the safe. Max had done some work in the past, he'd do anything for a price. First things first, he needed to watch out for unnecessary distractions in this final week. It would have to wait.

At precisely 7.40 p.m. Harry stepped out of his front door in pressed jeans, a white new designer T-shirt and expensive trainers. His hair waxed and deodorant on, he was ready and set off for Cherry's.

Upon arrival he didn't need to get out of the car, the front door opened as he brought the car to a halt and there she was bouncing down the path toward the car with a smile on her face and a spring in her step. She looked neat, her hair nice.

'Hi Harry,' she said, leaning across to peck his cheek.

'Whoa, there Cherry,' he said, instinctively pulling back, before adding, 'I've waxed my hair.'

'It's nice on a summer's evening to chill out. Shall we drive out to the Hoe before we head for the pub?' she suggested.

'Why not. I like the place.'

Cherry talked about what she'd been doing, her work at the paper, her time with girl friends out at the shops earlier that day, catching up with house work. Nothing she said was of any interest to Harry. He pulled up not far from Smeaton's Tower, the red and white painted historic lighthouse that symbolised his city.

Crowds of other people were also enjoying the evening sun, walking or sitting on the grass, the blue sea shimmering beyond. Harry wondered if it were possible to see "Scrapfish" from the top of the tower. Cherry had been talking all the time her voice buzzing somewhere in the background, but Harry's wandering thoughts were suddenly interrupted by something she said.

'Harry, prepare yourself... I'm pregnant.'

Instinctively he knew this was significant. His head swung round to face her in alarm. It was as if the sea out there had suddenly swept up and over the Hoe taking him and throwing him violently head over heels. He must have looked shocked, no words came out.

'It's OK, Harry, I'm OK about it,' she said patting his forearm.

'Well, congratulations!' he muttered, not quite knowing what to say next.

'You are sweet,' she said, reaching further across, this time to embrace him.

Harry let her, he didn't know what else to do. His mind was racing. Was it his? Of course it bloody was, must have been that night they were both drunk, when was it, around six weeks ago? She must only just be pregnant. Not too late to do something about it, perhaps, not that she was thinking that way.

'Are you sure?' he heard himself say.

'Well, we were a bit drunk but it definitely happened. It's early days, so no public announcements yet, OK? Don't go telling everyone tonight. I haven't even told my Mum, only my sister Cleo and best friend Jackie.'

Suddenly Harry felt he'd been thrown a lifeline. Space and thinking time were needed and he'd been given it. It didn't have to be made known for a while.

'Time to get to the pub and I shan't say a word,' he promised.

Long shadows were forming, the lighthouse had an unnatural orange glow to one side and the grass looked oddly dead in the light, somewhere between green, gold and brown. Harry felt his whole world had changed, he couldn't see it how he saw it before.

Five minutes later they were pulling up in The Black Horse car park. Hell, he was going to be a dad. He needed the time she had given him to process the implications. How the hell did this fit in with everything else in his life at that moment? It could be politically useful. And what was he to do about Cherry? He walked round to the passenger door and offered her a helping hand to get out of the car, as if she were unwell.

'Treat me as normal you idiot,' she said, springing out. She looked every bit the happy party girl, Harry for his part had seen the whole complexion of the evening ahead change in a few minutes.

They went in, both Stu and Penny were there. Now that was a surprise. She'd decided to come after all. She didn't look very pregnant either.

'Hi Stu, Penny. You remember Cherry… Can I get anyone a drink?' he offered.

'Tonic water,' said Cherry.

'A pint of best for me,' said Stu, 'and Penny will have another Appletise.'

'You pregnant too, Cherry,' jested Stu.

Suddenly Harry watched his whole world unravel before him in social confusion. Looks said everything. Harry felt he'd been left stranded at the bar like a beached whale.

'Hi Harry,' said Keith behind the bar, 'so you'll be wanting champagne!' he teased.

Harry realised he'd been rumbled and had little choice but to go with the flow. He stuck with the earlier drinks order adding an order for four flutes and a bottle of champagne. Returning to their table he did the expected thing, put his arm around Cherry and let the baby talk flow.

Cherry seemed happier at every expression of affection, every look in her direction, that Harry gave her. At first he felt OK about it, but as the minutes ticked by he began to feel a sense of entrapment, the same feeling he had at an away football match when the away supporters had outnumbered and surrounded Harry and his mates after a game. Only this time he didn't know how to fight his way out.

In the course of the next hour the pub filled up, the initial group of four became the centre of a party of nearly twenty people. The banter and the drinking began to reach a crescendo and Harry ended up buying four more bottles of champagne. As Harry moved toward the bar to order yet more drinks, Stu offered to give him a hand and the two moved away from the noise.

'Harry, we need to talk,' said Stu in a desperate but quiet voice Harry barely heard.

'You want to talk?'

Stu nodded. 'Let's take them the drinks and then we go out to the gents.'

Five minutes later they were side by side at the wash basins.

'We've a problem with the IT, Harry. It's Marcus. He's disappeared.'

'He was there Friday. How do you mean, disappeared?'

'I know where he lives. I wanted to check something out for Monday so I went round to his digs. He wasn't there.'

'He'll have gone away for the weekend.'

'No, his flat is totally empty. It's ground floor, I walked round, looked in through the windows. He's done a runner.'

'Are you certain? Have you tried calling him?'

'Yeah. He doesn't answer whatever method I use… He's totally silent on social media and for a guy who's been posting a minimum of twice a day for months something's very wrong. In every sense Harry, Marcus has disappeared, done a vanishing trick. I don't like it.'

'What about the other two in IT?'

'Nah, they're fine, but they've heard nothing of Marcus either. Apparently he was the last to leave on Friday. He was still messing around finishing something, he said, before he could leave.'

'You need to come with me to the factory and investigate. I need you with me. I haven't a clue with your computer world, so I need your help. We can't leave ourselves compromised at this stage, we need to check things out, our security…'

'OK, but we can't drive, we've both had a skinful already.'

'I'll get Cherry to drop us, I'll tell her to wait, shouldn't take us long, I'll think of something, come on, no time to waste. I'll do the talking.'

Back with the others, Harry had to shout into Cherry's ear, but she got the message. Penny asked if she could come along too for the ride. Harry thought she would be company for Cherry and agreed. Leaving their drinks on the table, Phil Potts was ordered to guard them with his life, to which he simply said, 'Oh yeah!'

Cherry took to driving the BMW like a natural, Harry mistakenly thinking at first that he'd have to give her a lesson on the basics to get them under way. Fifteen minutes later they pulled into the McNamara Metals yard. Harry had had to unlock the gate to let them in and the two men walked across to the offices whilst Cherry turned the car round and parked up. All seemed just as he'd left it a few hours ago, only it wasn't.

He sensed rather than knew that someone had been in. Maybe molecules in the air had changed. He sniffed like an animal hoping to detect its secret. Nothing, but he knew.

With Stu walking silently at his side, he stopped by the lockers and looked. The keys were all vertical in the locks. He'd not left them like that. He thought of the gun in his safe, glad he'd relocated it there. His instinct to check it was still there proved irresistible.

'Stu, you go into the IT suite and just satisfy yourself all is in order, how you left it. I just need to pop into my office, then I'll join you.'

He watched Stu head for the Conference Room and the adjacent IT suite nearby.

Harry took the stairs two at a time, wound in the number combination, first clockwise, then left, then back and finally right again. He pulled open his safe door. The gun was still there together with Nick's papers. He felt the weight of the gun through the black cloth wrapping it, not daring to bring it out, before pushing it back in, shutting the door, spinning the locking wheel and heading downstairs to rejoin Stu.

'All OK up there,' he announced.

'Wish I could say the same in here,' said a downbeat Stu.

'What is it?'

'Looks like a major data loss, a hack and a half. I can't even get into half our stuff. Hell. I need to spend some time on this.'

'Tell me what's going on Stu. Look at me, talk my language.'

Stu swung round, his eyes ablaze.

'Someone's hacked our system. Some of the basic protection we've built in place over all these weeks has been taken down leaving us wide open. We're bloody sitting ducks. It looks like the wall was breached late Friday. We're in trouble, deep shit. We won't be able to mobilise everyone this week, Harry. Someone knows what we're doing. I can't stop this Harry, I can't fix this, even if we get everyone in. I'm going to have to secure and shut down what's left.'

'Marcus?'

'Guess so. Come on Stu, can you access his personal stuff and see what's there?'

'He never gave me his password.'

'But you'd know it Stu, you know it, don't you?'

'Yes… but…'

'I'm telling you to access his personal spaces and bloody well find out what's going on here. Then make sure that he's locked out of the system, permanently. I always knew there was something geeky about that half-built fellow. That

Judas, he's betrayed us… I've got a call to make. I'll be upstairs.'

When Harry got to his office, he made himself a double strength coffee and sat down at his desk. He needed to ring Christian Howard, but didn't want to do so until he had all the facts he could muster at his fingertips. He'd wait until Stu had finished. He needed to think. The women sitting in the car outside would just have to wait a bit longer.

In a few hours time, Christian would begin training the guys. He'd also want to be up to speed on the social media campaign that was supposed to offer the critical momentum to guarantee success. Now it looked like someone, quite possibly GCHQ in Cheltenham, had had a lucky break and could access their files. This could only mean an early visit from Counter Terrorism and the end of all their dreams. Maybe it wasn't as bad as he feared, but only Stu could confirm this. He was so desperate to have an update from him, when he had finished his coffee he went back downstairs to find him.

'Harry, I've some good news and some bad.'

'Try cheering me up.'

'It looks like although the firewalls we'd put in place had been turned off allowing open access to our site, in fact the firewalls had been deliberately removed, we could still be OK. I've created some new software and encrypted access so that I'm now the only one who can get in, no one else. I can't find any wholesale loss of data or corruption of our data now I've had a deep look round. That's the good news.'

'And the bad news?'

'Marcus.'

'Marcus what?'

'He's a gambler with debts, big debts. His web history, email folder and message box all tell the same story. He was being chased for money, a lot of money. I think he's done a runner. Why he left our site insecure I don't know, but on Friday night he was busy with his gambling before he left.'

'Any chance he has data with him he might try and sell on?'

'I can't tell.'

'We have to assume the worst. Could you find any indication as to where he's gone?'

'Well for a geek, he's typically so very predictable and easily traceable. He's got his find a phone switched on in Settings and if we click on it, like so, look there's his phone and probably him holding it!'

Harry looked at the map page with clear blue dot pin pointing exactly where he was located, Union Street, Plymouth.

'He'll be at the Grosvenor Casino, look, near the Barbican. That's where he is. You and I have a job to do. The girls need to deliver us there. Explanations? Leave it to me. Cherry still needs to drive.'

Harry decided he needed to take care of things before any call to Christian. Sending Stu downstairs, he went back to his office and stuffed the gun in his trouser belt under his T-shirt. It looked too visible. He took a box file and found it just fitted inside. A couple of added rubber bands made certain it remained shut. It looked like paperwork. It would have to do.

Back in the car he nursed his file on his lap, passing no comment. He didn't need to, files are what business men do.

Cherry knew where the Grosvenor Casino was and cheerfully headed there commenting on what fun it was to drive a top end BMW. Well, it took her mind from noticing Harry and Stu's worries. Upon arrival, Harry told Stu to wait in the car. He carried his box file in with him under his arm.

At reception he simply announced he was wanting to deliver some paper work that had been requested to a punter called Marcus. A big yellow box file held high did the trick. Would she mind calling him over to reception. He didn't mind waiting a few minutes. Before she had time to argue he found himself an easy chair and made himself comfortable, ignoring the security man eyeing him strangely.

Harry saw Marcus first which gave him the advantage. Harry got up and intercepted him before he even got to the receptionist where they might be overheard. A hand was extended as Harry took the advantage that came with surprise.

'Marcus we need to talk, privately. Come with me. Harry opened his box file, the lid shielding the contents from reception. He saw the gun work its persuasive power even without being drawn and pointed. Marcus began walking, his shoulders dropping even more than usual. Harry closed the lid and put the box under his arm.

Once outside, the car was about twenty paces away and Harry had to think fast.

'We need to drop some girls off first, then Stu and I need to have a chat with you. Say nothing for now. In you get, in the back, next to Stu. I'll do the talking.'

'Cherry dear, one more little journey to do, then you can return to the champagne, or the tonic water… Stu, Marcus and I need to have an urgent business meeting at my place. It shouldn't take long, then we'll join you.'

And so it happened, just like clockwork. Cherry drove first to Ham Drive dropping the three guys off, then with Penny beside her in the front, left to return to the pub.

Once inside the house, the three of them in the living room, Harry turned on the charm sensing Marcus was feeling very vulnerable and rightly so. He placed his very visible box file on the arm of his sofa chair.

'Marcus, this is no time for beating about the bush. I need you to tell us straight out what's going on with you. We're at a critical point in our campaign. This coming week is when it all happens and you go AWOL with all kinds of gremlins coming out of the woodwork. What the hell's going on? Explanations please.'

'Sorry, Harry. I can't do it. I don't like some of the stuff I've been having to circulate, it's too vile and violent for me. I've been working too hard and it's happened before, I go into a downward spiral.'

'What's that, a spiral?'

'I go down. I shut down. I start gambling, big time. I'm pretty good normally, it picks me up, I stop after a bit and… but it's been a disaster this time. I've been borrowing everywhere and I need to pay back, so I've gambled more. I left my rented place, got my deposit back.'

'So where are you staying. Which rock have you been hiding under?'

'Back at my Mum's in Stonehouse.'

'Look, I reckon Stu can fix most of what damage you've done, but I want to know if you've told us everything. We need to know. Just sit there a minute will you and don't move.'

Harry got up and went into the kitchen. When he came back he saw Stu flinch. Stu had seen the kitchen knife Harry was carrying. He came up behind Marcus and laid it across his little finger.

'Now for a guy who spends his time at a keyboard, losing fingers one by one could bring a promising career to a premature end.'

He saw the colour drain from Marcus's face, beads of perspiration appear on his brow. Even Stu had blanched. The stakes all round were very high. Marcus was frozen in his seat waiting on Harry's next move.

'Start having a conversation with Stu here about what you've been doing and with whom. You get things wrong, forget something important I start cutting off fingers, one at a time. Harry move the knife very slightly to give Marcus the message and he flinched. A little blood flowed. He talked and kept talking.

Half an hour later Stu announced that he had got the full picture and Harry stepped away from Marcus.

'Just going to get you a plaster,' said Harry smiling as he disappeared into the kitchen with the knife. He was back in a tick with the plaster ready to apply. He pressed it in place.

'Marcus, now you can go home to Mummy, but make 100% sure you turn up for work before I do tomorrow morning. With that Marcus got up and shuffled out of the front door.

'He'll come round,' said Harry to Stu. He smiled, 'Let's get back to the party. They'll be missing us.'

41

Monday morning, 20 July. Dan was first to arrive at McNamara Metals at 6-o'clock. Harry followed him in just after 8-o 'clock. Dan knew what the coming day held, but Harry reminded him anyway before going across the yard from the gate to park up. At 8.30 a.m. Christian Howard was let through by Dan. Christian thought he knew everything, but he didn't know what Marcus had been doing and Harry intended to keep it that way, for now.

It was ironic really, considering Marcus was one of Christian's own appointments and paid for by him, along with Marcus's colleague Nicki of course. Harry began to wonder as to her loyalty and reliability. He reassured himself with the thought that Stu would have told him if anything had shown up, besides, worries like that were all too late now.

By 9-o 'clock the whole team were assembled in the Conference Room. There were four groups of eight with, in addition, Charlie, Gavin, Toby and Mash as area leaders, each to drive a van, keys to be collected from Dan on the gate. The four person IT team, Marcus, Stu, Keri and Nicki stood together in a separate huddle, each fiddling with their mobile phones. They'd be staying in the IT suite working. Harry and Christian stood side by side at the front ready to call the shots.

In the few minutes Christian and Harry had had before everyone was on site Harry had quizzed him to find out more about the programme. It was with some relief he was told that after an initial short briefing the four groups of eight and their leaders would be using the four white vans to head out and onto the north side of Dartmoor for the day. Christian had primed two guys to be in place to run things. They'd be using some of the military training area and firing ranges out of bounds to the public, familiarise themselves with arms and explosives. Access and permissions were all taken care of Christian said, with a dismissive sweep of the arm. They'd be taking with them kit from the shipping containers and wouldn't be back until around 20.00 hours.

Half an hour later, the vans loaded with equipment and men, they could be heard leaving the yard in five minute intervals. With the factory closed for the holiday, suddenly it seemed all very quiet once more with only Christian, Harry and the IT team remaining on site.

'Now the foot soldiers are away doing their thing the rest of us need to get to work,' announced Christian. 'Marcus, you come and sit next to me.' Marcus's eyes almost popped out his head as he was steered to the head of the conference table. The other three in the IT looked on. Harry could see his self-confidence had taken a noticeable battering and he looked wary, like a frightened rabbit caught in the open.

'Come on, sit yourselves, settle down, gather round. This is what we've got to do in the week of the Big Awakening.'

'"The Big Awakening", you make it sound like D-Day,' said Harry.

'It is. The Big Awakening is the opening battle in our world campaign and it starts here, this week. All eyes will be on the South West of England. So listen in and listen carefully. Today we begin our guerrilla war in digital space and your task is to go for the targets I give you. I want each of these listed people to feel so attacked they can no longer function. This is about embarrassing and undermining key officials, discrediting them to the point of resignation or worse. This will be like … like a cyber 'air strike' and they won't know what's hit them. Your trolling will require you to be so fleet of foot you will need to be constantly shutting down and opening new accounts to avoid detection like there's no tomorrow. If you like gaming, today will be the best day of your lives. You'll fight hard to keep up with the pace, believe me it will be your longest day. Follow me?'

There were nods all round.

'In The Circle we've identified who and where to attack. There are MPs and councillors, celebrities and cultural leaders, leading industrialists and academics, all are included. For the rest of this week we are going to troll-blitz and destroy what remains of any opposition to our cause. At the same time you are going to go on message promoting the true British citizen's fight against the evils we face. Those virus-like foreigners who drink our life blood, the Jewish financiers who fleece our wage packets and the news commentators who push out lie and after lie. '

Harry had never seen Christian so wound up. His dark eyes almost flashed, but Harry for all his looking, couldn't see any light there. Your job will be to overwhelm them with what they see as "hate speech". I want their media hashtags filled with so much of our stuff they don't work for them any more. I believe in you, the work you've done to build our capacity in recent months, we can do it, we can!' he said, forgetting himself and striking the table with his fist.

'I sort of get all that Christian, but there's something I'm not seeing here. What's the end game? What do you want to see happening by the end of the week?' interrupted Harry.

'Harry, boy...'

'Don't bloody patronise me with, "Harry boy",' he retorted, shocking both Christian and all those round the table.'

'Harry, Harry, you asked me a question... Let me give you an answer. You deserve to know.' Inside Harry was still feeling riled and angry. Christian was taking him for a ride, moving him like a disposable pawn on a chess board. What did he mean saying, "You deserve to know", that he had earned some kind of approval rating from Christian? The two were meant to be partners weren't they? He didn't need to earn anything. Harry bit his lip, held his tongue and listened to what Christian had to say. Every now and then this guy Christian really, really, pissed him off.

'We're a catalyst, a trigger to a bigger gun. Our job is to seed the conditions to allow other things to grow. That's how it works. We achieve most when we unsettle and cause fear and panic in other places. It doesn't take much. Human beings are pretty simple creatures really.'

'I agree with you there,' added Harry, private sarcasm partly driving his remark.

'They like to be led by their superiors, have strong leaders. They really want to be proudly patriotic. When they are given the truth about things, they see sense. This week is about winning the information, hearts and minds war. And the good news for you four guys is that our international friends have set aside this week to lend their support to our

UK war. Everything you do will be backed hugely by our collaborative effort. You will be receiving direct support from several hubs in Europe and the USA. The Circle's leadership group met over the weekend to finalise and coordinate all our efforts.'

Christian turned to Marcus sitting silently next to him. He reached across and put an arm over Marcus's shoulder. Harry could feel how heavy it was as he watched Marcus's wary face and the detectable flinch as he tried to move away but didn't.

'Marcus, when you check in, in a few minutes time, you will find supportive and informational messages awaiting you from all our overseas IT leaders. They've orders to join and support our battle under our command, prioritising the mobilising of their overseas servers and operational units to the one cause. England is seen as a key location in the global war.'

'OK,' said Marcus.

'And where do I come into this?' interjected Harry in a lull in the conversation.

'These guys need to get to work, so much depends on them in modern war. Then you're absolutely right, you and I need to talk about what we're doing this week,' said Christian, releasing Marcus.

'OK guys, off you go, any problems I want to be the first to know,' Harry announced directing his eyes at Marcus. Once they were out of earshot, Christian began talking again.

'There's a public and political side to this campaign too. By Friday, we need you to be back on the news programmes and calling the political shots. There's a lot of preparation to be done here. I've some pull with a couple of key programme producers, but you're going to need to get up to speed with giving on-message presentations by the end of the week.'

'Fair enough,' added Harry, waiting for some sort of punch line as to what exactly he'd be doing.

'We're wanting you reinstated in parliament. An essential part of the programme this week is to galvanise that to happen. The Circle are counting on you to front The Big Awakening in the public's eye and they want to see the strongest case made for your wrongful, politically motivated dismissal of someone who was the people's choice… over turned. This is your route back into politics but not like it is, the best politics has always ever been when patriot populist leaders call the shots, which is why we need you there.'

'I'll believe it when it happens,' said Harry. 'Haven't you forgotten, I'm suspended from the House?'

'You understand politics instinctively. You're the best prospect for a right wing leader we've had in a generation, Harry. By Friday, I assure you, you will be on all the main news channels. They won't be able to stop the momentum of your campaign. By then we won't need to find you news coverage, they'll come looking for you, they'll be clamouring at your very door!'

This appealed to Harry. He liked the confidence they had placed in him wanting him to be their political front runner, with international support too. Christian was voicing something he'd wanted to hear for many a month, just how important he, Harry McNamara was to the cause. He knew deep down this was right. After all he had the parliamentary experience. Yes, he had left in disgrace, but that wasn't entirely fair, a book-keeping error by someone else. He was a fervent patriot, loved his country with a passion and he knew what the people really wanted. Harry realised his burst of anger toward Christian earlier had perhaps been premature and had now totally dissipated as he contemplated his own quick return to power with himself at the helm.

'Could you use some coffee Christian? Why don't we adjourn to my office to work on what we need to do?' It felt better to be taking charge, going into his office space added to his sense of personal control.

Harry led the way debating in his own mind as they walked, whether he might sometime use Christian as his personal political advisor. He'd need some assistance when the government saw the error of their ways and readmitted him to parliament, a fixer…

'How do you see things working?' asked Harry, once he had shut his office door.

'Here,' said Christian, reaching into an inner pocket to pull out an envelope. 'This is for you. Call it a battle plan, whatever. Our Head of Strategic Planning in Germany got it approved by The Circle, it's what you have to do, all spelled out as orderly as something coming from the German government office, the *Ordnungsampt*.'

'What was that?'

'The *"Ordnungsampt"*! The German's have their own "Office of Order", that's what it means… In other words they are bloody efficient. Why do you drive an Audi and a BMW? Because they're organised thinking people. They have a lot to teach us sloppy minded English.' He held up the document in his hand.

'Look, it starts where we began with our first meeting here on 10 Feb.' His stubby finger pointed at the relevant section. 'Here's some strategic diagrams and timelines which I found quite helpful and then some bullet point lists specifically for you to follow,' he said, flicking through the first few pages.

Harry took the document and thumbed through it for himself. As he glanced at it page by page, he found some parts had been highlighted in red for his particular attention.

'Bloody hell!' he exclaimed. 'I've got my work cut out. This is as long as the Bible, but from what I've seen already, I like it, I like it a lot. What are you going to do whilst I get on with this?'

'A couple of things. I'm going to spend an hour or so with the IT team. You can see from that document there are critical targets they must hit each day this week. I want to be 100% confident in them that they'll do what they have to. I also want to see what the latest figures are for membership, what support, voices and bodies we can call upon in our hour of need. What was it Horatio Nelson said? "England expects that every man will do his duty."

'Just so,' said Harry

'I intend to ensure they all do just that. Then I'm off to north Dartmoor. I'll join the others south of Belstone. Know the place?'

'Near Okehampton…'

'Yeah, that's it. They've got some regular soldiers with them getting them started, our supporters from the barracks helping us out on the military ranges. They'll check out our guys for any *Bravo Foxtrots*, weed them out. It should be a good day providing the leg holds out.' Harry had forgotten about the limp.

'OK. But what do you mean, check out for "*Bravo Foxtrots*"?'

'Army slang, meaning I check out who are the fucking useless ones who don't help out their brothers and we get them off our backs.'

Harry was picking up all Christian's military background emerging as he spoke. He wondered whether Christian was taking something. He seemed strangely energised and sparky, more aggressive, demonstrative and Harry had a moment of unease, but could think of nothing to say.

He watched Christian make his way downstairs, annoyed that his limp was making him slop coffee from his mug across Harry's pristine office floor.

Harry turned his attention back to the document he had been handed, his orders. On the front neatly typed was the title:

The New Awakening
Mr H. McNamara
Plymouth.

More carefully this time, he began thumbing through a carefully organised personal action plan. It made him feel slightly uncomfortable, it was orders from above, military style, leaving him un-consulted, somewhere below the mysterious anonymous higher ranks, maybe a little above the foot soldiers. He had the feeling that he was being played, manipulated and as he turned the pages the feeling increased as the prescriptive tone of the document irritated him as well as alarmed him.

He needed to read what it said anyway before coming to a premature judgement. Besides it all rather presumed he was an influential politician, whereas the reality was he wasn't that any longer and there was a long road ahead if he was ever to get back.

Half an hour later, he'd managed to reach the end and felt exhausted at what was expected of him. He was no miracle worker, he worked hard but didn't have the tireless German work ethic that lay behind what he'd been reading. He got up from his desk and walked over to the coffee machine, setting it to life and enjoying the reliability of the grinding, hissing, steaming, splashing process as hot brown liquid fell into his cup.

Someone was coming up the stairs. The uneven step told him it was Christian and a moment later he poked his head round the door to announce he was off. Harry had the distinct impression he was checking up on him, Christian's eyes darting upon the document resting on Harry's desk, then back to him.

'The four downstairs are doing fine, told them they were here until late this evening, that there would be a bonus in it as well as the job satisfaction,' he grinned.

Harry once again felt annoyed. He should have checked with him if his employees were required to stay late. Once more he kept quiet.

'Call me if anything crops up, see you back here about 1900 hours.' He dropped his empty mug on Harry's desk and left.

With his office window open, Harry could hear the limping man's stride crossing the courtyard. Harry realised he'd never seen his car. Always parked out of sight, discreet, anonymous. Harry couldn't stop himself casting a gaze up at the blue July sky to listen and look for any drone. Nothing. All was normal, except it wasn't. The site felt odd on a Monday with no machinery crushing cars, no crane squealing, no calls from the men as another wreck was hoisted, no shouts from the foreman, no Elsa or Glenda, just an unsettling silence.

Harry realised that the plans for the week included no time to attend to the family business with its pressing problems of cash flow, land sale and a Chinese contract up for renewal to be considered. If his political world took off he would need to leave things to run themselves as he made his way back to London. That meant he'd need to find someone to run things here, but who?

Glenda was only any good at accounts. Elsa was an efficient secretary and PA but… It would have to be either one of the yard managers like Bill or one of the operatives, but they were mediocrity itself. he'd need to appoint someone new from outside and how long would that take? Harry felt squeezed on all sides, The New Awakening, the business, his Mum and Cherry…

Picking up his document from his desk and sliding it inside his inside pocket he left his office and walked downstairs. He needed some air. He crossed the yard to Dan who put his mobile away and stood up to attention as Harry approached.

'Relax, Dan, I'm just taking a breather. How's things?'

'To be honest, time passes too slowly with the yard closed. Not much to keep the interest. I'm sitting around too much and it gets boring.'

'Well, let's take a walk round the site and see what we can see,' he said, glad for some company, someone who wasn't up to their ears in one part of Harry's worry load or another.

A few minutes later they were by the shipping containers containing the munitions, an empty space to the side where the four vans had been.

'Looked like a military operation the way that guy Christian organised the guys this morning. Stands for no nonsense that man. Quite happy to use a fist or a punch to put people in their place and get them to be serious.'

Harry hadn't seen this side of him but completely accepted Dan's account as true. There was something about the bully about him. It took one to know one, Harry thought, thinking of his own tendencies to lay one on any miscreant.

When they were alongside the giant car crusher, the silent metal plates with their hydraulic pipes lying silent, Dan ventured another opinion. It was then Harry realised Dan was good at observing things but quite naive as to what the full picture was.

'He thinks no-one notices, Mr Christian. He drives this Mercedes SUV but always leaves it where he thinks no one sees it. You can't hide a car like that. When I walk up the road to get my pasty I see it. I've seen it around. He likes to drink at an ex-serviceman's club near where I live, the 1922 Club. Know it?'

'Yeah, does he have mates?'

'Don't know. But he's definitely an old soldier that man. Once a soldier always a soldier.'

By this time they were back at the gate and Harry made his way back across the yard on his own to head for his office, thinking on what Dan had told him. Intelligence, however little, had its value and Harry knew he had something.

Harry was required to begin preparing speeches and thinking about video clips he would need to do in the afternoon for the IT team to edit and use before the end of the day.

His mind went back to thinking about Cherry and what she had told him at the Hoe yesterday. It was information he still didn't know how to process. Last night there had been lots of banter at The Black Horse but he'd returned home confused and uncertain as to what the news really meant.

He had no doubt Cherry had him in her sights. He wasn't too unhappy at that. She was a nice looking chick and easy enough. But did she want him for keeps? The thought sent a shiver down his spine. Then again, there were public expectations of a leader, to have a woman at his side, to be a family man, to look the part for the party. She would do, she had stood by him, she knew his politics. Take a day at a time, he concluded. Maybe he should call her later.

He hated seeing himself on videos, but it was remarkable what a bit of skilled editing could do. The clips were filmed in Harry's office with him sitting magisterially at his desk, the photos on the wall behind him blurred out of focus giving his situation the mix of status and anonymity required. The team satisfied, he left them to process what they had. Soon, he realised, the vans would be returning.

Sure enough, at 7.58 p.m. he heard the first of the vans return and went to watch from the slatted blind window as Dan waved it in. Over the next five minutes the other three were safely back. He heard tired voices and farewells being exchanged as they made their way home knowing they were to return first thing. Then Christian could be heard making his way up the stairs to Harry's office. This time Harry felt his uneven steps sounded sinister to his ear.

'Coffee Christian?' offered Harry as he stepped into the room.

'Yes, great, thanks,' he replied.

'Good day?' Harry enquired.

'They're a bunch of civvies who'll never be ready,' he added with venom. 'Some were jumping in fright when they had to use standard army issue weapons. One or two were pretty good. Charlie has a knack with explosives, a man with no nerves, useful that…'

'More of the same for them tomorrow?'

'Yep. Part of it is getting them used to following orders. Getting there, but they stop and think for themselves. That's no good to us. They bloody well need to obey orders when they're given,' he barked, simultaneously hitting Harry's desk with his fist. The wild eyes were back, the pressure there, the adrenaline pumping. Harry knew he could never trust a man so wired.

'The team here has done everything set for today. Worked hard, videos made and streamed, temperature raising and pressure building nicely moving up toward boiling point,' said Harry in a measured voice. 'Time you got home. Incidentally, where might that be? Exeter?'

'That's personal. See you tomorrow Harry, same time, same place.'

Harry could hear the IT team leaving the building crossing the yard in quiet conversation. With that Christian himself stood up, left half his coffee and disappeared, leaving just Harry on site with Dan at the gate.

Harry called Dan on the phone. Take yourself home Dan, I'll lock up and secure the site. See you here same time tomorrow.'

Harry sat back down at his desk. It was nearly seven thirty. His mobile rang. It was Cherry.

'How's your day been Harry, dear,' she asked.

'Good thanks. I'm still at the office, about to finish up.'

'I'm in Exeter at the police station.'

Harry's pulse started racing.

'You still there, Harry?'

'Yeah. What are you doing there?'

'Another story… However, I did bump into my friend the CID guy, Holder, and you know what, he asked after you!'

'Me?'

'Yes. I told him you and I were friends and he asked after you. We had quite a chat. In fact he bought me a coffee.'

'That was nice of him.'

'He said, he would like to think he might catch up with you again. Asked if you knew a Christian Howard?'

'I said I didn't think so. Do you fancy eating out later or getting a take-away.'

'Can we make it later in the week, got to bring some work home with me tonight? I won't be good company,' he lied. She had just grassed him up whether she knew it or not.

This time before going home, he opened his safe, removed the wrapped gun with its ammunition, slipped the hard gun into his belt and put the ammunition box into his jacket pocket.

The time had come when he needed to be ready for any eventuality. The evening light had a strange orange colour as if the very sunlight had taken on a new hue. Indeed his whole world felt very surreal and extreme.

42

It wasn't what he needed to hear to start his day. Harry took a call from Stu as he was driving to work next morning.

'It's Marcus, I can't reach him. I'm worried, he just wasn't himself yesterday,' said Stu.

'OK, I'm in my car. I'm going round to his Mum's, I know where it is. If I'm late in, tell Christian I'm delayed, but get him to get off with his guys in the vans and not worry about me.'

'OK, Harry.'

Harry pushed the car along at the 30 MPH speed limit, the early morning traffic not dense enough yet to slow his progress. The early morning sun was low in the sky behind him causing problems for the oncoming drivers. It promised to be yet another hot day. He pulled up in a parking lot at the end of Peel Street and walked to the door. A couple of taps and a scruffy looking woman with a tea towel over her arm opened the door.

'Yes, What do you want?' she asked, eyeing Harry suspiciously.

'Marcus,' he said simply.

'Oi, Marcus, get yourself down here, it's for you. Geezer in a posh car, c'mon,' she yelled, turning periodically as she awaited his response. Time passed and she called again.

There was still no reply.

'You think he's left already?' asked Harry.

'Nope,' she said, looking at her watch, 'it's not yet 8-o'clock. Gets up at eight fifteen, he does, can set my watch by him,' she grinned, a missing tooth spoiling the effect.

'Look I'll go and get him. You can come in if you like,' she offered.

'I'll wait if it's all the same to you,' he said.

There was a loud cry from upstairs. 'He's gone, gone…'

A minute she was back downstairs, a worried look upon her face.

'He wasn't in his right mind last night. He wouldn't eat his supper. I'd cooked him fish fingers, good for his grey cells, but he hardly touched them. Sorry, he must have gone out…'

Harry turned and went back to his car. On trying to ring Marcus he just got his answerphone. He decided against leaving a message, turned the car and headed for the office. He had no idea what to do. Marcus was Christian's man, but had turned out to be a liability. What was worse, he'd known that and hadn't told Christian. He had little choice, the venture was at risk, should he tell him now? If he did he wondered what reaction he'd get, probably an outburst of some kind. Then Harry pulled out his phone and did a find my phone search, but it was either switched off or disabled and nothing showed.

As he was pulling up at the scrapyard he saw Christian talking to Dan by the gate. They saw him approach and they stepped apart from each other and waved him into the yard. When Harry climbed out of the car, he called across.

'Christian, here a minute. A word. Need you in my office.'

He'd already made the first of two coffees by the time Christian joined him.

'Shut the door will you,' said a serious sounding Harry.

'What's up? Problem?'

'Could be. No Marcus.'

'He might show later… it's early yet.'

'No, take it from me he won't show.'

'Problem then. He's always had a tendency to crash when overloaded, rather like the computers he works on. We need to find him. I'll send the lads off to the Moor and get on to it. I've got a few ideas. Leave it with me. No other problems, Harry?' he said a strange look in his dark eyes, waiting for a definitive answer.

'No, no other problems. I'll talk to IT while you're gone.'

'Thanks. We'll be back earlier today, nearer five. Can't work the lads too hard. They'll get very warm on the Moor today. To finish earlier, it'll boost morale, you'll see. Catch up with you after five, Harry.'

Christian took a couple more swigs of his coffee and then placed the cup on Harry's desk and headed off and out. Harry felt a mixture of relief and concern.

The day was heavy, the heat turned sultry, the bright sun of first thing had given way to a sapping haze. A storm might be coming and time dragged. Harry was losing interest in what he had to do. There was only so much speech preparation a man could do and he tried to break the monotony by checking on the IT team downstairs. A man down, they were incredibly busy and didn't welcome his intrusion or questions which held them up. He retreated to his office and took more coffee.

Just before twelve he heard something outside and instinctively he knew it was something. He stood up and walked over to the window peering down through the wooden blind slats at an altercation at the gate. There was a police car with two officers talking to Dan.

Harry did two things very quickly. He telephoned the IT room and told Stu there was an emergency. Police were about to be present and they were to shut everything down, then act normally. As he was doing this, his phone to his ear, he walked over to his safe, opened it up and placed his instruction document, his gun and his ammunition safely inside, closed the door and spun the combination locking it. Then his phone rang.

'It's Dan. Police visit, Harry. They're coming across now. No idea what about. Asked for you.'

In less than two minutes there was a knock on his office door.

'Come,' called Harry instilling boredom in his tone.

'We meet again, Harry.'

It was the CID officer, Holder from Exeter.

'Good morning officers. I'd offer coffees but it's the works holiday week and we're light on people to run around. What can I do to help? It can't be a social call, or can it?'

'I'll come straight to the point. Does Marcus Harrison work here?'

'Yes, he's head of IT. Why?…'

'I'm sorry to have to tell you, but we've found a body…'

'He should have shown this morning, you see only the IT people are in. Good time to make changes to the system whilst the factory's closed…' he lied. 'And when he didn't show I went round to his home, to see if he was OK. We're one of those old family businesses who care for our workers. His Mum, she called upstairs for him, but she was as shocked as I was to find he wasn't home. Neither of us had any idea where he was.'

'When did you last see him? Well, he left with the other IT workers last night, around 7-o 'clock, I guess. You could ask them. I could call his team up if you'd like to speak with them?'

'Thank you. We will need to do that, but later, don't rush me, Sir. We'll go to their office when we've finished here if we may.'

'Fine. Can you tell me where, what happened to Marcus?'

'Not presently, Mr McNamara. You will have to be patient. Would you mind accompanying us for a moment please? Come down to the yard.'

Harry did as he was told. This was a really unwelcome development. Things were on a knife edge.

'Is that your vehicle sir?' Harry nodded. 'Do you have your car keys with you please?' Their *Sirs* and *Pleases* were beginning to annoy him, but he knew he had best stay calm. They didn't like him and he didn't care much for them in return. It was as well to know that, but stay the right side of the respect boundary.

Before opening the car door, both officers donned blue plastic gloves as if the car was some kind of forensic evidence. They searched it meticulously and Harry sensed their disappointment when they didn't find anything. He felt a keen relief that he had some time ago removed the gun.

'Please don't touch the car. We'll hang on to the keys if we may. We'd like our forensics to come and look around too.'

'When might that be? Someone will need to be here to unlock, let them in…' said Harry thinking fast.

'An hour's time I guess,' said the side kick.

'We have a situation Mr McNamara and once forensics have given us a preliminary on the cause of death we will be needing to interview you again. Please don't go anywhere we can't find you. Same address is it, Ham Drive?' Harry nodded. 'Now where do we find your IT team?'

Harry led the way, noting the police had deliberately left their vehicle blocking entry and exit through the yard gate. Dan was watching what was happening intently.

'Let me introduce everyone. This is Stu Beamish, and Keri Williams and finally, Nicki Schwarz. Do you want to tell them or shall I?'

'Thank you Mr McNamara. If you'd like to go back to your office, we'll have a few words with your staff, thank you.'

Side kick went over and held the IT room door open, plainly signalling Harry should leave. He did.

Back in his office, he sent a text message to Christian:

C, police visit here about Marcus, now deceased. No facts known. Police still here. Stay away until I say coast is clear - H.

A moment later came a one word reply:

H, Understood, C.

Harry took Glenda's file out, placed it on his desk for its distraction value and went to get himself a coffee, but then stopped himself, deciding he'd hang on until the police had left the premises. He wondered what had caused Marcus' death. Probably he had taken his life given his gambling debts, but he couldn't quite believe it, and yet, he told himself, he'd known such things to happen. He thought he might ring Marcus's Mum, any responsible employer would do the same.

'Hello Mrs Harrison, it's Harry McNamara here again. Marcus never showed at work today and I've had a police visit. Is it true what they tell me?'

He could hear a woman's tearful voice at the other end of the line, someone trying to collect themselves. 'Yes Harry, my Marcus… he's dead. His body was found beside the A38 last night, but they didn't know it was him… not until this morning and they called on me just after you came round. There's a police woman sitting with me now.'

'I'm so sorry to hear of your loss Mrs Harrison. Marcus was such a solid part of McNamara Metals, solid as gold. We send our deepest condolences…'

'Thank you…'

And with that Harry cut the call. He'd learned something more and it worried him. Something wasn't right, his instinct told him. Suicide isn't something done "beside the A38". His thoughts were disturbed by the sound of the returning policemen. He flipped open Glenda's file and pretended to be reading it.

'I'm sorry we are bearers of bad news. We need to be on our way, but as I said a moment ago, forensics will need to see your car, so no one to go near it please. Do thank your IT team. They are a credit to your company, Mr McNamara, helpfulness itself.' Harry wondered whether he could detect a hint of sarcasm in his tone.

Then they'd gone. Harry didn't go to the window, but listened as their car doors shut with a double clunk. After a back and forth as a turn was made, wheels spun as the police car left and all was quiet again. It was only then Harry stood up and went to get himself a coffee.

Harry's mind was in overdrive. First of all he called Stu to come up to his office for a thorough de-briefing on the interviews downstairs but learned nothing new, except the police were interested in Harry's movements the previous evening, which was easy as everyone had been innocently enjoying themselves celebrating a double pregnancy announcement down at The Black Horse, Stu reminded him. Harry let this pass.

When Stu had gone back down to tell the others they could start up again and do their best to try and make up for lost time, he felt some relief that he had not been personally tied to Marcus's death. The second thing he did was call Dan on the gate to alert him to the forthcoming forensics visit.

Then he sat back and tried to ponder the significance of the day's events. He had to, he knew something was wrong and it troubled him. Instinctively, he knew Marcus' death was no suicide and no accident. But why? Who?

Thinking coldly about it as he sipped his drink he had to conclude Marcus had been murdered, his body dumped quickly without a thought as to its quick discovery. And it would be no random murder, only a killing by someone who knew him. Could it be Christian or one of his aides, even Charlie at it again? Maybe Cherry could discover something, she was a news chaser, a fount of information with sources in the police. He called her.

'Hi Cherry, Harry.'

'Hi Harry, shame we never had that take-away last night. How about tonight?'

'OK Cherry. I'll come round. Got a problem with my car, but should soon be sorted, I'll have it back by this evening…'

'How's your day been?' she asked, Harry thinking she thought he was making a social call.

'Once a politician, always a politician,' he said enigmatically, before adding, 'unfortunately there's had been another death in the business. I had the police round here today. A guy from Exeter, the same policeman who was investigating that Labour politician guy's death in Ottery.'

'And the guy who died from your place, Nick Grayson.'

'The very same… Are you still accessing stories from Exeter police? I've been talking just now to our employee's Mum, Mrs Harrison, about her son Marcus. She's very upset and the police are telling her less than nothing. I think that's positively cruel. Don't they teach these people inter-personal skills any more?'

'No problem, Harry. I'd already been directed to it by our news editor. I'll get back to you when I know more. Hopefully before we meet up tonight, if not sooner… You know you can stay over if you want.'

'Must dash, Cherry, see you later.'

He felt a necessary entanglement looming as part of his information chasing. Whatever Cherry found, he still had a problem, there were live and ongoing police enquiries and a murder he felt was inevitably going to be linked with their now vulnerable political campaign. He needed to talk to Christian and lay it straight.

Dan called. His problem was a white van at the gate and a man with an ID claiming to be from Devon and Cornwall Police SOCO.

'Let him in and help him, Dan; he'll want to look at my car,' said Harry, 'Oh, and tell me when he's gone will you.'

It took forty minutes before Dan called back.

'He seems satisfied Harry and he's left your car keys with me. I'll bring them across.'

'Hang on to them, I'll collect them from you when I leave,' he told him, not wanting to be interrupted, but he was.

A few minutes later Stu called up to ask Harry to come down to the IT suite. When Harry arrived it was if all hell had broken loose.

'We've been hacked and everything's in meltdown and there's nothing we can do, nothing,'said Stu in despair. 'The thing is, Nicki's been looking into it and it all comes back to some files Marcus worked on at the end of yesterday afternoon. We think he's tripped a self-destruct button, or he's fed someone else to do it for him.'

'See what you can do. I need to make a call,' said Harry dashing back to his office to ring Christian.

'Christian, you'd better get straight back here, we have a big problem, a problem like you've never seen.'

'On my way.'

43

Just after 4-o 'clock Christian arrived back at McNamara Metals and hastily climbed the stairs to Harry's office. When Christian walked in he looked to Harry every bit a haggard and broken man. He almost fell into the chair in front of Harry's desk, his face a picture of fatigue, his empty eyes betraying nothing and his body weary. He'd not seen him like this before and it alarmed him. Outside, giant sized drops of rain were beginning to fall with beady plops striking melodically against Harry's window, heralding a coming storm.

'Coffee?' asked Harry, his offer followed by distant peel of thunder.

'Yes, thanks. Tell me, what's up?' Christian said quietly with a real seriousness, desperate to hear what he knew would be bad news.

'The IT mission here is seriously compromised. I'll get Stu up to tell you what's what directly. More than this, we're a man down, Christian, a man down.'

'Who? What?'

'Marcus Harrison never showed today. The police came here, said he was found dead by the A38 last night and his demise seems linked to our software malware problem. Let's remember Marcus was your man and it looks like he was a weak link. Our team have been trying to counter this fiasco all afternoon. We're not sure if it was Marcus personally, or whether he enabled others from outside to kick our system into touch. Either way, we're still locked out, our wider political mission is seriously compromised, if not derailed and as things stand the computers have crashed. We're in deep shit. That's my take on it. Our chances of getting back, making any sort of recovery are bloody zero!' The ferocity in Harry stirred something in Christian.

'Hell! I'm surprised your IT team haven't been able to sort it. Are you sure they're up to their jobs Harry? Someone will pay for this?'

'Let's be practical here Christian. We've lost our IT mission which was driving our campaign and it was your man, your lead man, Marcus Harrison who was responsible. It's happened on your watch.'

'You're not over-dramatising here are you Harry? Do we know yet whether counter-terrorism have caught us out?'

'Not yet, but we need to know. We've also got the police on our tail, in addition they've been here twice today following up Marcus. I've just had SOCO all over my car. Who knows when they'll be back and I don't like it. So tell me, what do we do now? Postpone, delay, modify our plans or push ahead?' his voice raise in fury.

At that point there was a knock on Harry's door. It was Stu, who looked at both of them his facing saying, 'Am I interrupting something here?' He then came right in and pulled up a chair. A much louder peel of thunder crashed outside, the rain now hammering down.

'What've you got Stu? Anything?' asked Harry.

'We're trying to bring things back in stages. Not so bad as I first thought, still bloody awful though. We've safeguarded and fire-walled our membership data base which we can utilise through a new server route. So we're back in touch with our people. However, our trolling has been stopped, that's our our targeted leading figure programmes, they're all still blocked somehow. I hate to say it, but I think our site has been leaked, we're compromised as of...' Stu ran out of words and simply opened his palms indicating he had nothing to offer.

'We have a Judas,' said Christian. 'You, Stu, had better get straight back to work and leave us to think about what happens next.'

It was when Harry nodded Stu slid off his chair and quietly left the room. He knew who he took orders from. It wasn't Christian Howard. It wasn't until Stu was well out of earshot Christian spoke.

'Marcus betrayed us,' he said, bluntly and quietly.

'How do you know?'

'I had him watched. He was up to his eyes in debt and would have sold his birthright for a wad of cash. I've had a tail on him on and off and yesterday no sooner had he finished here than he was in some casino in town. There are two things you can't trust in life, one's a leftie and the other's an addict. Deep down our friend Marcus was both. That creature betrayed us.'

'So what do we do?' asked Harry, thinking to himself that he was now more than certain Christian had had a hand in arranging for Marcus's death, '...and has he betrayed us to anyone, which is crucial to know, or let us down which we'll have to just manage and work our way round?'

'I think we'd know about it already if counter-terrorism were on to us. We've still got a core we can trust. I think we press on. The lads from the Moor will be back soon. No problems there, they've done good. Four units of guys who are almost ready.'

'Ready for what? You've never told me what exactly they'll be doing Christian. I think the time has come to let me in on the bigger picture.'

'Every successful revolutionary body has its military wing. We're there to be brought out as and when we're needed. The Circle have identified a number of strategic individuals in the South West whose offices and homes will be paid a visit by our boys during tomorrow and through to the end of the weekend. The noise, let's call it, will herald in The New Awakening.'

'OK... but what do I ...'

'It's your role, as you know, being like a bigger and better right winger than anyone else you might care to name, is to herald in the new world for us. I don't want you to bother yourself with where and what we'll be doing. Think of it as a necessary separation of function... like the IRA and Martin McGuinness. Remember them?' Harry nodded.

'Well, maybe that isn't the best analogy, but you get the idea, the strong arm on the one hand and a First Minister on the other. The two hand in glove though we won't broadcast it. It's a tried and tested model, and it works. The guys are having a final short briefing here at 9-o 'clock tomorrow in the Conference Room and then we set out. They don't know this, but they won't be coming back here again… other than for the occasional collection of munitions.'

'I get the picture. Your guys do some fisticuff, bang bang shake up stuff, personal pressure on leading figures and I'm not to know what so that I can't be compromised. You put the cat amongst the pigeons and I step forward offering the political solution to the people's woes. I think I can handle that Christian. Why did it take so long to spell it out? I don't think I've ever met anyone who plays his cards as close to his chest as you do.'

'I'll take that as a compliment.'

'Doesn't this rather imply you and I will be having rather less direct contact with each other after tomorrow, more of an arms length relationship? You were the one who used the analogy of the IRA.'

'You got it. The Circle work best in the dark, unseen. You won't be seeing me, no one will, but you will be hearing from me and you'll still be able to reach me. Everyone's happier if we keep things at a need to know level only.'

'I'll need my political advisors, a team round me,' said Harry, voicing something that had been on his mind a while.

'We're ahead of you there. You'll find from Friday, your IT team will be supplemented by four more people, you'll just absorb them into your McNamara Metals work force, the perfect smokescreen, just call them Sales!' he joked with a shrill unnerving laugh.

'OK Christian. I'll await developments. No problem,' he said, whilst wondering how many more late in the day decisions would be taken with zero consultation.

Harry thought Christian was beginning to look wired again, excitable even. There was something manic about him, mad even.

Then there was a distraction, a noise in the yard as the first of the vans returned. The storm earlier had lifted and shafts of sun were breaking through. This time the guys were still in camouflage fatigues. They crossed the yard with kit bags, stripping off their military wear as the walked, changing back into civilian clothes before setting off for home – Exmouth, Plymouth, Ottery and Exeter. All thirty six men, he counted them in, seemed weary but purposeful to Harry's eye.

Within half an hour all twenty four guys had disappeared. Harry and Christian were still talking. It was whilst Harry had his back turned toward Christian, making more coffee, he suddenly turned his head and saw him popping a white pill into the corner of his mouth.

'Medication,' he muttered, seeing Harry's glance.

'Something to wash it down with then,' said Harry bringing over the next coffee, whilst thinking, medication my arse. 'So tell me, what happens to the men and the remaining munitions after tomorrow?'

'We need you to retain two containers for our use, but as from tomorrow night you can do what you like with the remaining empty one. The Plymouth van will stay here on site, makes sense to use the security of your yard for it, the other three will be with the men in Exeter, Exmouth and Ottery.

'And the IT team, now a man down, what happens to them?'

'Marcus will not be easy to replace, but we'll find someone new and slot them in. Maybe it'll take a week or two, but we're committed, the virtual society we're creating is as important as the real one you will be leading, if not more so. The political scene is changing. I don't pretend to know how it works but let's be quite clear that the real future is a web world.'

'So tomorrow things will get quieter here. When do I start getting my political team of four you're sending me? I need them A.S.A.P..'

'The Circle have been preparing your support team in London and they will be arriving tomorrow afternoon. You see everything's being taken care of Harry. We've rented a couple of furnished flats round the corner from here, walking distance. Want to keep them low profile, no traceable vehicles, that kind of thing. I met them, had to brief them about you last week. Had a morning with them and an afternoon with The Circle big shots, in London... a five star hotel... There aren't many perks in my line, but a night there was one of them. You'll do alright, you'll be back in parliament again, be able to rent a London pad, stay in good hotels paid from the public purse...'

'We're not there yet,' Harry remind him, thinking Christian was way ahead in a dream. Maybe is pill was beginning to take effect. 'So I may not see you after tomorrow?'

'That's the plan. A final briefing with the guys in the Conference Room tomorrow morning then that is it... Time I went,' Christian announced looking at his watch before getting up from his chair.

Harry realised that things were about to move to a new level. Soon, but he was not sure quite when, he'd be back in politics, invited in like a first minister. The Circle knew what they were doing, directing and moving pieces from the shadows, powerful ghosts he would never see. He had every confidence they would make the necessary lever pulls behind the scenes on his behalf. They were proving to be his guardian angels from the dark side, catapulting him back into power, this time with real clout.

He wondered what the political aides team he'd be sent would be like. When he first stepped into politics he'd chosen his own team, people he could trust. This time he didn't know any of the new aides, but accepted they had to have more experience and better skills than he himself could have mustered.

Harry pulled out the '*New Awakening*' political papers Christian had given him and scanned through them again. It was all so very thorough, all so written as if every step would fall automatically, sequentially into place. He pushed it back into his inside pocket.

Christian was a pill popper, he was sure he was behind the murders and he was pulling all the strings. It was time to head for home.

As Harry thought about locking up, getting on his way, he decided to take his gun from the safe with him. He couldn't put his finger on exactly why he needed it, but he felt he was on some kind of knife edge, a place where the stakes were very high, so high in fact, he might need to use levels of force he'd never even had to contemplate whilst he was a simple football supporter.

44

Cherry called Harry at 7-o 'clock in the morning. He was deeply asleep and struggled to come round. It had taken a long time to get off with the result that when sleep eventually came it was at a different level.

'Harry, you heard the news?' she asked cheerily.

'Nope, but I guess you're about to tell me,' Harry opined trying hard to rouse himself.

'Have you checked your email box today yet? I guess not… You see according to a couple of sentences released in a Reuters report late last night, I see the PM has overruled the House Public Accounts Committee.'

'I don't follow…'

'Apparently you were treated unfairly. Harry, you've been reprieved! They are now saying, after an age of deliberation, that as a new MP you should have been given adequate advice and support in making your first parliamentary expense claims. Upon investigation they find this wasn't done, so they're reinstating you in the House as from next Monday. Congratulations! Your parliamentary suspension is over! Expect the press to come calling sometime soon. You must have friends working for you somewhere Harry, things like this don't normally happen. As your closest, very closest, press contact, would you mind ever so if I had the first interview with you?'

'Sure, of course… What do you suggest? Bloody hell do you realise how early it is?'

'I'm so pleased for you Harry. Our baby's Dad, an MP, imagine…'

'I've got to go into work in an hour, but how about I meet you for coffee, Boston Tea Party, Vauxhall St. Shall we say 11-o 'clock?' Harry replied, tried to deflect Cherry's thoughts on to a different track.

'Make it 10.30 Harry, I'll bring Andy Stone down with me, we need a good picture…'

'See you down there, Cherry, 10.30 it is.'

So The Circle were delivering on their side of the deal, he thought. Not bad for a first instalment of all the other goodies sure to follow. He hurried to rouse himself, showered and got dressed. Thank God Sheena had left a supply of freshly ironed shirts on the side. He reached in his wardrobe for a smart suit, seeing he needed to look the part.

Then he saw his gun on the bed. Possessing such an item troubled him, it was a challenge, like having a secret pet that you couldn't let anyone discover at all costs. A waistcoat offered the best cover for a gun tucked in the belt, he filled the two side pockets with ammunition before checking over his appearance in the long mirror. He would pass muster. The slight bulge, well, it could be a mobile phone to the casual observer.

Today he took the red Audi to work. His reasoning was that it had been little used and he wanted to give it a run. Also, if he was re-entering the political limelight he would certainly use the elegant BMW and who knows when he might get the chance to give his favourite friend another outing? He put it through its paces and enjoyed the earthy, lively responsiveness of the accelerator, the firm ride from the lowered suspension and the grip the slick tyres gave him on the road.

Dan was there on the gate. He grinned in recognition of the sporty car with the fun loving Harry he imagined he knew sitting squat in the racing seat behind the wheel. Harry greeted him, pausing at the gate to see if anything had triggered Dan's sensitive security antenna. All was quiet and there was nothing to report. Perfect. He pulled up by the offices and climbed out, adjusting the gun in his belt for comfort.

He went up to his office, made a coffee and sat silently at his desk. It was then he decided it was time to do what Cherry had suggested, check his emails. Sure enough there was a message in his inbox from the PM's office. It was disappointing that it wasn't personally signed, but it was a great read. There it was, he was an innocent man, a pardon granted, the record expunged – whatever that meant, and his reinstatement as an MP was with immediate effect. He printed off a copy and laid it on his desk.

Plans to hold a by-election had never been introduced, pending the results of the on-going enquiry and now there it was, evidence there'd be no need for a fresh by-election. The other political parties could crawl back under their stones.

Amongst his other emails were various administrative instructions as to whom he should report, the new location of his parliamentary office and what should happen regarding his place on the Naval Panel he'd been required to resign from, etc. A mass of papers had been attached for him to catch up on. There it all was, he was back as an MP, on the cusp of greatness.

Christian stepped into Harry's office, rather startling him as he'd been so engrossed in his emails he'd not heard him arrive.

'Good morning, Harry. The Circle have delivered on their first instalment I see, judging by the look on your face. I understand from my friends in London that two civil servants were easily persuaded that when it came to a choice between personal harm to their families and conveniently explaining an administrative error on an MP's expenses they naturally chose the latter. A no brainer, eh?' he said, smiling smugly.

'I don't think I want to know,' said Harry, 'But since you ask, I had a letter from the PM's office granting me a pardon and telling me to report back to the House on Monday. It looks like my return has been given a huge leg up. Coffee?'

'Better not. The guys will be here very shortly and I want to get them started. How about a stirring speech from you this morning, you look the part in your waistcoat, you need to give them a morale boosting final hurrah, yes?'

'OK, I'll be down shortly. You get them organised. I've got my first press meeting at 10.30 in town, so I need to be up to speed for that too.'

'Oh!' said Christian almost as an afterthought, 'I nearly forgot, here's a list of names, it's your new party worker team. As I said, they'll be with you this afternoon, reporting here to you at the factory. Then they're in your hands. Don't worry about paying them, there'll be new party donations coming in to support you. The Circle have stepped up a gear. This time the world will change, mark my words.'

He placed the list on Harry's desk, turned and went downstairs. Harry noticed Christian was developing a slight facial tick, the corner of his mouth lifting slightly, it made him look as if his expression were half way between a smile and a sneer.

Harry was left on his own. Events seemed to be moving too fast and he knew that over the coming days the momentum would continue to build. He opened a new file on his laptop and put together a few headline reminder notes for his final speech for the guys; he recalled a football joke about losers, noting the punch line *take over bid* and thought it would go down well.

It was time. He went downstairs. Christian had the teams lined up in four rows of eight, their four leaders at the end of the rows. It reminded Harry of his visits to naval bases whilst in Parliament. These were serving soldiers now, ready for action, about to receive their commission. Standing at ease they all had eyes straight ahead. He realised Christian had organised this passing out parade. Harry strode to the front, cast in role as royalty to inspect the troops.

'At ease, please,' he said watching the men shuffle and adopt a more relaxed style. 'I expect some of you will have heard, I am re-entering parliament imminently as MP for this area.'

'Well done, Sir,' said Toby, 'good to have our MP back representing us.'

'Thank you, Toby.'

'There are one or two things I need to say,' continued Harry. 'First, You guys are 100% important to the cause, we need our military wing ready to help as directed. Secondly, over the coming weeks and months as I seek to build a populist government with partners in the House who will rally to the cause, then I will see to it that you and yours are properly rewarded for your patriotism. We will need to have new private security guards, let's call you, ready to protect and progress our cause.'

'Many of you will know I have a life time commitment to good football and hope that I will soon be invited to join the board at Plymouth Rovers. You know that the team are struggling this season and at our last home match someone threw a one pound coin on to the pitch. The board are still trying to work out whether it was a missile or a take over bid.'

There was some smiling and grinning. Then Harry handed over to Christian who began dismissing them with final orders, letting them go in in stages, Toby and the Plymouth guys leaving on foot after the three vans had gone.

Christian returned to Harry's office, his limping steps announcing his arrival before his head poked round the door.

'So it's farewell Harry. Keep using only the pay as you go mobile numbers, no slips ups, be ever vigilant. I'll touch base with you in London next week. The Devon lads know what to do without me being around. Might be as well you're off site in London by then, takes you out of the scene. Need to see our new MP safely installed in the House.'

'I'll head up there Sunday, stay in a hotel for a few days until I can get a flat sorted.'

'We'll sort something, a flat I mean… I've got somewhere temporary you could use in north London… until you get sorted,' offered Christian.

'OK. I need to go Christian, the press are calling…'

Harry watched Christian leave from his office window. He paused at the gate to say something to Dan, then stepped out into the street and disappeared from sight.

Harry glanced at the time, checked that his mobile held the note he'd been working on earlier and locked up his office; he dashed down to the Audi and headed into town.

Cherry and Andy Stone were already at the Boston Tea Party, conferring with one another in earnest conversation. When they saw him, he noticed their change in demeanour. He was now their MP again, not just Harry. A slight deference was detectable, in that he was asked how he wanted to play this.

'Let's start with some coffee, what are you both having. It's on me,' he added.

The three found a relatively private table near the door and awaited the arrival of their drinks. The barista looked bored and his manner careless as drinks slopped into their saucers.

'Do it again mate… properly,' said Harry menacingly, 'or I'll see you're out of a job.'

That changed things. The guy paid attention and returned five minutes later with fresh drinks, dry saucers and a grovelling apology, which Harry duly ignored.

The three rehearsed the new political scenario that had been a personal overnight surprise for Harry. Other pundits like the local Newsfeeds were beginning to click on to the change with the result Harry's phone was now hot with incoming calls. All at once he was a number one political sensation again. Apart from agreeing to a prime time lunchtime news channel piece he ignored all the others. When he had first been elected he'd enjoyed all the attention and the power of being master of his own destiny that came with it. Now he was once more beginning to relish the familiar vibes and so glad he had dressed up for the occasion.

'Any chance of a picture,' asked Andy, 'then I can leave you to chat with Cherry. I need to get on, OK?'

'Sure.' Harry followed Andy just outside, onto the street. He liked the idea of an urban backdrop, being seen as a man in the centre of the city he represented, a man connected... Eventually Andy was happy with what he'd got and put his camera in his bag and waved his farewell.

The day was sultry and humid once again, the air hanging hot and still in the bright morning light Harry felt overdressed with his waist coat on but didn't dare shed clothing with a gun in his belt. How he wished he'd left it in the safe. He re-entered the cafe.

'Harry, it's my turn for some attention,' chided Cherry pouting at him, as he came back inside. Harry was still confused how to respond to Cherry. He liked her, felt a duty to the kid she was carrying, his kid by God! He liked her flirting with him, but hadn't yet come to a conclusion in his heart, if he had one, as to whether he really wanted to stand by her or not.

He knew the party line was that marriage and family were important and he'd end up following protocols, but he wasn't ready to do this. She was suffocating him. He needed to do the interview and get out, back to work where he could focus on what he needed to do. She was a distraction. He picked up his coffee. Only tepid, he sipped it nevertheless.

'Fire away,' he said, 'it's your scoop!'

That seemed to settle things into work mode and she did her journalist thing firing questions at him, a little hand held recorder taking it all in. Harry was in his element, sensing the public mood, conveying a personal message of optimism like a golden aura. Soon she had done and he stood up ready to leave feeling pleased with how it had gone. That was when his heart sank.

His Mum, accompanied by his Aunt Zoe were about to enter. There was no way out before she spotted him and locked on. Cherry had switched off her recording and was filling her bag. She too then noticed it was Harry's Mum and stepped forward in front of Harry to greet her.

'Hello, Mrs McNamara, so nice… Has Harry told you? He's two pieces of exciting news. Harry…' she turned to him.

'Ah yes, Mum, I'm back in politics. Off to London on Sunday.'

'And he's going to be a Dad!' added Cherry.

'I've got some further news for you, Harry. So glad I've found you here so I can deliver it in person!'

'And what might that be?' asked Harry puzzled.

'You're about to get the police calling to see you again. I thought about what you said to me last time we talked. I told you I knew you were up to no good and I decided to find out what was going on.'

'What have you gone and done now Mum?' said Harry.

'Yesterday evening I went to your best friend's house and had tea with him and his Mum.'

'Stu?'

'Exactly. I've known him since he was in nappies and last night it took only minutes to get it out of him.'

'What precisely?'

'That you were running a political campaign from your offices.'

'Nothing unusual about that.'

'Well, I've just been to Plymouth Police Station before coming for my coffee and they're very interested in the story I had to tell, so as I say, expect a call from the police.'

'You really do know how to poke your nose in where it isn't warranted, you stupid cow. I'm so very busy, I could do without your time wasting interference. Stick to what you know! I've got important TV and media appearances to fit into my busy schedule, and I definitely haven't got time for your meddling. I think you need to call them and tell them you apologise for wasting police time. Now, if you'll excuse me, some of us have work to do.'

Harry walked out. If he'd have looked back and listened, he would have heard Cherry say, 'Did he tell you about our baby?'

45

Harry was in the Audi starting up when his mobile rang.

'It's Dan, we've a large police presence outside the yard gate. They're armed police. I think you need to get back. I've stood outside my box looking obvious. I don't know what to do...'

'Just be helpful, polite, hold them until I arrive. I'm a few minutes away. Let the IT team know, get them to close down, do it quick.'

'OK Harry.'

Harry put his foot down and felt power surge through the wheels as he moved off. He entered Shapters Way and the road was cordoned off. He pulled up, slipped his gun and ammunition into his glove compartment and walked down the street with a swagger of confidence. He was the MP, it was his factory, they had nothing, absolutely nothing on him.

'Good morning officers. What's happening here?'

'And who are you, Sir?'

'You're talking to your MP, Harry McNamara and this is my business you're standing outside, McNamara Metals. Has there been an armed robbery or something whilst I've been out?'

The officer was wrong footed and stepped away to speak into his radio. An officer nearer Dan turned and beckoned Harry forward.

'Harry, they say they've got a warrant to search the place. I said they needed to speak with you.'

The officer who had beckoned Harry forward waved a piece of paper. 'We're making a search of the premises Mr. McNamara. You'll have to wait here.'

'One moment. The business is closed this week for the summer holiday, but there is a small IT team in updating systems. Do you mind if I come along with you. They'll be freaked out at the sight of you guys.'

Harry didn't wait for an answer but confidently began striding toward the office block across the yard, wondering what on earth he could do about the shipping containers full of munitions at the far end of the site. He heard footsteps pacing fast to join him.

'Mr McNamara, please. This is our operation I need your cooperation.'

'You have it! Come with me, I'll let you in and we can talk to the staff together and then your boys in blue can play hide and seek amongst all the scrap cars, whatever it is they want to do...' Harry opened the office door keying in the code.

'Out of interest what is it you're looking for, can I help? We have a strict no deal policy when it comes to offers of stolen lead from church roofs. Scrap yards don't have the best of reputations, but I assure you we are a longstanding and very reputable family business.'

By the time Harry had finished talking he had walked the two officers into the Conference Room. He pushed open the IT room door and called out to the three people crouched over their workstations, 'Stu, Keri, Nicki, we've some visitors… Would one of you mind organising some teas and coffees, I'm sure we could rise to that. What would you two gentlemen like?'

The two officers separated. The one went back out into the corridor and began issuing instructions to the men waiting at the gate, the other looked at the three IT staff, mentally assessing them as geeks of little consequence, before turning to Harry and said, 'Mind if we have a word somewhere? Your office?'

'Follow me,' said Harry not following up on the earlier offer of refreshments. Once in his office, Harry nonchalantly took off his jacket, throwing it over the back of his chair and sat himself down. 'How can I help? I'm a very busy man, so how long do you think this might take?'

The officer remained standing. He put one hand to the back of his head as if in puzzlement.

'On the basis of information received we have reports that this site is being used as a training camp by extreme right wing militia.'

'My God, I need to speak with Dan on the gate, see if he has noticed anything. Personally, I've not seen anything untoward. I'm here most days, but not all the time. As I said, we've only a small IT team here currently, making the most of the chance to update software systems whilst everyone's off this week. I do of course have left wing political opponents who might try and discredit me. I'd urge you to

check out very carefully your sources officer.' The officer
went quiet.

'Would it help if I showed you round? It'll put your mind at
rest?'

'OK. Talk me through this building first, then we'll look
round outside. What have we got here?'

Harry give him the works including the full low down on
who was in the family photographs hanging on the wall
behind him. He was trying to build a picture of a successful
and caring small family firm that had served the city for
generations and earned its place as a reputable local
business. He went round the office block thoroughly before
taking the officer outside, every now and then asking the
officer what exactly he hoped to find.

As they went outside Harry cast a glance at what was
happening. The police were standing together in small
relaxed groups apparently having satisfied themselves they
hadn't stumbled upon a terrorist nest. They didn't seem
unduly unconcerned, their SA80 weapons now hanging
loosely at their sides. Mutually reassuring nods were
exchanged between police. Much to Harry's relief they
seemed satisfied. He thought they'd be going soon, but not
so.

'You were going to show me round,' reminded the officer
accompanying him.

'Sure, follow me. Most people like to start with the car
crusher. First we strip all vehicles of their useful parts and
valuable bits. This is a stationary machine, but you can get
portable ones. Using our hydraulic system, we can deliver a

force of 2,000 psi and impart a pressure upwards of 15 tons between the plates. What comes out is a metal box, like so. We use forklifts to place them in the storage area. The blocks are loaded into containers and then shipped to China for recycling. A lot of people wonder, in this environmentally conscious age, what happens to the oils and brake fluids that drain out. Well, we've thought of that. They are all collected down there, barrelled up and sent for processing. Nothing gets wasted here officer.'

Where do your work force operate from? Presumably they don't use your offices?'

Harry realised he'd never actually been in the workforce block, the low Victorian looking buildings against the boundary wall. 'Over there,' he pointed.

'Let's take a look,' the officer said, striding out front.

It wasn't locked. They walked in, the smell of blue overalls, oil and metal assailed the nostrils. A kettle, dirty mugs in a grimy aluminium sink completed a picture of run down facilities.

'Scheduled for some improvement soon, once we get the IT upgraded,' bluffed Harry.

The officer led them back outside and waved his arm expansively around the site. 'Tell me what I'm looking at,' he asked.

Over there are the rows of cars and vans awaiting scrapping. They come from all over the country, but mainly the South West. We even get some from you guys! The cars are stored up to several vehicles high, so your officers need to take care wandering round, its hard hats and health and safety on our site and with good reason. I'd advise against clambering around the working areas, too risky. Even I don't do it.' He seemed to be getting through as the officer's face betrayed some doubt about doing more for the first time. Harry pressed on.

'There's also some oxyacetylene equipment and air compressors, so everyone here needs to take care including your guys. Over there are the containers for China. Most of our business is with China. Empty containers come in and full ones go out on the back of the artics who travel between here and the docks. We ship up to 10,000 cubes of metal at a time. Those forklifts do all the carrying. That's about it. We've around thirty employees, probably just over, all of them good loyal workers.'

'Thank you Mr McNamara. Sorry to have troubled you. Your cooperation is much appreciated.' He called over to a colleague and waved toward the gate. It was the signal to leave. Men started back for the gate in ones and twos, no one too rushed.

At the gate, the officer with Harry swung round as if he'd forgotten something. He looked over Harry's shoulder. You say all these containers are for shipping to China. But those three have different logos on the side and are set apart from the others. Why's that?'

'I can see why you're a policeman!' Harry offered, thinking hard. 'The answer's simple. Those are destined for a different port and contractor. Our main Chinese scrap metal refinery is in Shanghai where most of our containers go. Those.' He pointed left.

'Those others are for our newest contractor, a dealer in Shenzhen in the south of China. We'll need to see how that goes to see if it's profitable. They don't seem to spend as much on painting containers, do they?'

The officer seemed satisfied and left Harry with Dan at the gate. They watched them depart together. Soon the street was quiet again.

'Thank you Dan,' said Harry.

'Do they suspect something, Harry? They'd had some tip off hadn't they?'

'I don't know Dan. But let me know if anything comes up. We all need to be on our toes. And well done. Here, take this for a drink later. Harry drew out a twenty pound note and pushed it into Dan's hand.

Harry returned to his office. In Elsa's absence all calls on the land line had been routed directly to his own desk and his phone was ringing away as he returned to his office. He reached over and picked it up.

'James Lea, Thomson and Thomson, here. I need to speak to Glenda Hill.'

'Who? Glenda's off this week I'm afraid. James? Who am I speaking to?'

After a few moments Harry knew exactly who he was talking to. It was the firm who served as accountants for McNamara Metals and he was calling after a conversation with the firm's bank who were being chased by creditors.

'Harry, where's the Chinese payments? Where's the money?'

'I don't know. I think it was late, it's being chased… Was it important?'

'Unless the money you're owed arrives from China today I think your bank won't allow you to continue trading. It looks like you'll need to go into immediate Administration, he said calmly.

'Come back to us if you want us to handle that for you. Maybe we can find a buyer, but in today's economic climate that isn't looking too promising. Harry, sorry to tell you, but your business has failed. Come back to me later today with your decision, the bank won't wait!'

46

Harry had a lot to think about. He hadn't reckoned on the business failing. It was all rather depressing. He was beginning to enjoy being a successful businessman. His first thought was to see if The Circle would help him out with a loan or something, but a quick call to Christian ruled that one out, Christian adding he didn't see that Harry needed the business anymore, now he was being paid as an MP.

Harry told Christian of the armed police raid just after the guys had left. He was more interested in that and kept asking probing questions before he was finally reassured, concluding that they had nothing of substance to go on. Harry decided against grassing on his own Mum. He'd deal with her himself.

Then he called Glenda from accounts at her home who answered by asking him if he'd read the file of papers she'd left him, they made the situation crystal clear. After a pause, Harry had to admit, though he'd looked at them, he hadn't sufficiently appreciated the gravity of the situation.

'This is an emergency, the future of the business depends on you taking immediate action. I need you in my office this afternoon to work out a rescue package.'

'Do you realise what the time is? He looked at his watch, it said nearly 5-o 'clock. 'I'll be in first thing, tomorrow,' she offered. Harry shrugged, thought twice, felt it too risky to have her around this week, relented and said, 'Monday will be fine, Glenda. But if you can give the matter your thought in the meantime, that would help greatly.'

Things were going downhill, an avalanche gathering momentum, something so big and disastrous he couldn't stop it on his own. He looked at Glenda's file again and saw nothing he could address. Looking up he saw the IT team were leaving for the day and he decided to follow suit.

Once in his Audi he felt more comfortable. He'd grown up with the car. It was like an old friend. Feeling jumpy, he checked to see if the gun was still there and it was, all black and sharp in the glove compartment. He left it there and drove straight home.

Once indoors he felt very alone. Sheena had been in and tidied up. She'd been very liberal with the air freshener and it made him sneeze. He flicked the TV on. Live news was coming in from Devon as police were conducting a series of anti-terrorist raids in various towns and cities. Harry couldn't sit down, his place featured and as he looked on he paced up and down watching, his gaze fixated.

The live TV showed what was happening in Yonder Street, Ottery St Mary. It had Charlie Evans's home firmly in the camera's sights recognisable even though spectators were being kept well back. Millie looked as though she were screaming as a burly officer in black restrained her. He watched as Charlie was taken, head forced down into a waiting police vehicle.

Harry's head was in a turmoil. He grabbed a beer, threw off his jacket and sat in his waistcoat having put the volume on mute. He needed to think. It could be that Charlie was being chased down for the stranglings of Barry Thornton and Nick Grayson. That would be it. Then there was Marcus Harrison… But no, it wasn't a murder investigation, but an anti-terrorism raid he was seeing on the TV. Intelligence led, had to be. A leak somewhere. Only a matter of time before they got to him.

He called Christian, but his mobile rang out.

Dan called him, 'Harry, they're back. Same lot, pulling up and getting out of vehicles now. Tooled up as before and moving like they're looking for and expecting trouble this time. I'll have to go…'

They were going into McNamara Metals again, no doubt they'd find what was kept in the shipping containers. They'd throw a big party, he would if he was them – it would be like finding the bloody crown jewels!

Then his Mum phoned. He didn't want to but took the call anyway. The betrayer. She'd been to see Stu and got stuck in. It was his own Mum who had shopped them all. Hadn't she told him as much back at Boston Tea Party.

'Hello, Mum. What happened to family loyalty?' he asked.

'Don't, Harry. I just wanted to speak to you before they come for you. They will you know.'

Harry picked up his jacket, phone held to his ear by his shoulder and walked over to the front window. The coast was still clear. He went to the front door and out to his car.

'Mum, I'm about to drive, haven't got hands free,' he lied. 'Must go. Call you later. Bye…'

Harry reversed slowly out of his drive in his Audi just as he spied in his rear view mirror a police car pulling up. It didn't announce itself but a dark blue BMW with four men inside bulked out in their anti-terrorism outfits. They needed no introduction. He drove forward slowly only to see the hidden blues and twos lights come on, but he was near the corner and knew the streets and knew his car. This was a critical moment. He switched to survival instinct mode and floored the accelerator pedal to the point where he knew he could just hold the camber of the road. Almost simultaneously he heard the car behind him roar into life to chase him down.

But Harry had taken the initiative on the corner and was round the next and the next and then they couldn't see him and would have to slow. He had spent a life time driving out of his neighbourhood and three streets on, he pulled up in a garage access road and jumped out, his gun now in his belt and ammo in his pockets. He walked briskly knowing exactly where he was headed.

To his delight it was Cherry herself who opened her door.

'Fancy an early evening sail?' he offered with measure calm.

'This is unexpected, Harry, but give a girl a minute.'

'You've got five, otherwise it won't be worth it,' he added, stepping inside her front door. 'Mind if we take your car? Left mine near home,' he lied.

She ran off upstairs and came down pulling a warm bright orange top on as she stepped into the hall way.

'Here, you drive,' she said, tossing him the car keys. 'Look what I've got,' she added, pulling a bottle of wine from the fridge and putting it into a plastic bag.

'C'mon, let's go,' said Harry, hardly giving the bottle a glance, his hand on the front door to close it, urging her to get a move on.

Harry drove more slowly than usual, so much so that Cherry commented. 'Just because I'm expecting our kid, you don't need to be so overprotective. Let's get down to the marina. I remember our last sail to Newton Ferrers, can't wait to go out on the water again. Where are you taking me this time?' she asked with a twinkle in her eye.

Harry sped up, eyes sharp, realising they were alone and had lost the police. In the early summer evening's light traffic he felt more relaxed and his breathing slowed. A window of opportunity, a vital space, had been gained, they'd lost him.

Pulling up at the marina, he parked some yards away from "Scrapfish", passed Cherry the yacht keys and told her to go and open up whilst he made a quick phone call. She climbed out adding, 'I know where you keep the wine glasses. Don't be long.'

Harry watched her go, then he called Dan.

'How's it going Dan?'

'They've been over the whole site and their asking me if I have keys to open the remaining shipping containers at the end of the yard. I've told them I'll bring the oxyacetylene over and it would open in a jiffy. Presently they're checking over the others. I haven't had any choice, Harry.'

'Well listen carefully. I want you to use your cutters to start a diversionary fire by the container and then make sure you get yourself well clear. Got it?'

'Yes, Harry, will do. Use oxyacetylene and make sure I start a fire, then get clear.'

Harry cut the call and headed to the yacht. He was just about to get on board when the phone rang again. 'James Lea again. Sorry Harry, not been able to hold the bank off, the business is going down. I'll be over first thing in the morning to sort it.'

'You do that,' said Harry and cut the call, adding as he did so, 'you blood sucking bastards.'

As he stepped on board Cherry handed him a drink.

'Everything all right, Harry. You look like you could do with some relaxation.'

Harry took a large swig and passed back the glass.

'Let's get under way, sailor, that's exactly what I need,' he said, reaching across to start up the engine before climbing out to untie the ropes to the quay.

47

Harry took the glass of wine and grabbed a sea captain's hat and beamed at Cherry.

'Cheers!' he said, before taking a large gulp and passing her back his glass. He quickly turned the boat away from the quay, increased the throb of the diesel engine to maximum and immediately began putting water between themselves and the quayside.

As they moved down Cutdown Creek and headed south toward open water, he looked up left at the historic landmark Mountbatten site with its military history. As a former RAF base, it had, until its closure, been the local centre for Air-Sea Rescue flights. This evening it looked empty and forbidding.

'Take the wheel for a minute, Cherry whilst I prepare the sails. You remember the drill.'

Unlike himself, he noticed she had had but the tiniest sip from her own wine and left the glass in the holder to stop it from spilling. Maybe she wasn't going to drink more, he wondered, thinking of the baby she was carrying.

It was tricky getting the sails ready, a steady breeze from the west creating a bit of a swell. He flaked the mainsail and this time used the sail ties to hold it in place, then hoisted the foresail before he clambered crab like moving from hand to hand making his way back to the wheel.

When they were sufficiently clear and well out in the estuary he cut the engine and instructed Cherry to hold to the course he gave her as he went to hoist the main sail. As he did so the yacht immediately sprang to life, catching the strength of the wind and began powering ahead gathering speed. Harry hurriedly took the wheel from Cherry who was looking a little pale.

Harry was gazing across the water past Plymouth Hoe, wondering whether he might get a distant glimpse of McNamara Metals when there was a sudden flash and a dull deep roar, a ball of orange rolling and rising into the sky and then dark grey cloud climbing above the orange, all followed by the unmistakable rumbling sound of a distant explosion and the sounds of ammunition popping off.

'What's that, Harry? Look over there. A fire?'

'Could be, or a fire works competition rehearsal,' offered Harry smiling, knowing that Dan had done his job. Cherry's attention soon returned to the sea.

'Harry, this isn't like last time. The sea is much bigger and the waves so rough,' she said apprehensively.

'Hold tight, you'll soon get your sea legs,' he ordered, thinking that she hadn't seen anything yet. He had in mind taking a course west once they were clear of Plymouth Sound. They wouldn't have too long before dusk so they'd need to moor up somewhere. His ability to find a quick plan seemed to have become stuck in pause mode and he found himself starting to wonder if the sail he intended was possible.

The nearest place of any size to the west was Looe and the wind state and sea conditions were working against him. A lot of tacking back and forth awaited him if he pressed on. He thought they'd still give it a go. 'I'm the captain,' he told her.

'I think I'll go and lie down inside,' said Cherry looking grey and unsteady.

'That's fine, I'll take her out and then look for some more sheltered water,' he lied.

Once he got beyond the shelter of the main harbour breakwater he had an evening ferry to avoid and once round it and in open water the sea was getting decidedly rough. He felt the roll of the dark wave shitting the prow of the vessel with increasing force and watched the sky darken.

They had been sailing for the best part of two hours and he still wasn't really out of the Sound, sitting just off Penlee Point and he realised after checking his watch they were making little to no progress in heading west. The conditions were now so rough he couldn't really take his hands off the wheel to see how Cherry was. Heading away seeking a safe haven west seemed good when they set out, but their progress was coming to a halt and what other option did he have but try and press on?

For some time he'd not heard a sound from Cherry in the cabin, so after another ten minutes he finally flipped the boat round to let the wind out of the sails and ducked down below for a quick check. There she was, all curled up in a ball under a blanket, with a bowl beside her, white as a sheet, having been very sick.

'Harry, I want to go back,' she pleaded, raising her head a little.

'OK, we'll do that, I've another plan,' he lied.

48

There was a reckless, wild freedom in the wild sea, the curling, foaming white horses catching what light there still was. When Harry swung "Scrapfish" to turn east it was as if he'd unleashed an arrow. With a sudden lurch the yacht shot forward at breakneck speed, the wind filling her sails, Harry forgetting himself was enjoying the challenge of guiding her, riding the wave tops like a champion steeplechase jockey at the National. He was in charge and for a while he thought, to hell with the world.

The distraction of it, the adrenaline rush, like being on the 'Over the Falls' at Ottery's bonfire night fair, but much more so. He was loving it. With the sinking sun dropping behind him, he continued racing east, keeping well clear of other vessels out in the bay, his target, no longer Looe far to the west or the quayside at nearby Mountbatten Marina, but Newton Ferrers and, why not, some drinks with Cherry at The Ship Inn before crashing out on "Scrapfish". Tomorrow was another day and he couldn't yet see that far ahead.

It had all seemed so possible, but with every crash down into the swell he felt his dreams simultaneously being hammered and undermined. He had a deep sinking feeling as if his entire world were about to collapse around him.

He glanced inside the cabin again to see Cherry curled up motionless, hanging on, feeling so awful she couldn't speak. Seeing her phone next to her, he reached in, grabbed it and with one flying arm threw it overboard. She never noticed.

Back at the wheel he looked ahead and saw that the swell was less the nearer to the land he sailed and so he guided the boat accordingly.

His mind began calculating. The family business had to all intents and purposes gone. It was all so much worthless scrap. Maybe the land would sell and pay off the creditors. He shrugged as he knew he didn't care a damn. As he looked across in the direction of the Citadel he could see clouds of black smoke still billowing up into the sky from the factory site, a reminder that everything eventually turned to dust.

Then he thought of his Mum, the only bit of family connection he had. She'd betrayed him, shopped him, grassed him up, the bitch. If she hadn't gone round to Stu and pumped him like only she could when she wanted to, then they'd never have had the police raids, the campaign would have been launched and he'd be back in parliament making things happen for the people. She'd been pressurising him, questioning his judgement, telling him unkind things when she should have backed him. That's what good Mum's do, back their sons all the way, no ifs no buts. It was all her fault…

As he saw it, England was against him, not yet ready for a man like him. They'd lost their chance. He could imagine all the foot soldiers Christian had trained being rounded up by counter-intelligence and questioned endlessly until they told everything. His part was no secret any more. They'd almost caught him at his house, but he'd outwitted them again, just.

Now it was a matter of time before they took him down with the others. Then what awaited him, a trial followed by humiliation and a long prison sentence? That wasn't going to happen. He'd find The Circle, they'd look after their own, they'd know the value he held for them.

Then he thought of Cherry. Stupid cow, getting herself pregnant. She'd made things complicated. Maybe she would lose it, being so early on. What was she going to do when she realised the truth of the situation? He knew now that it was her problem, her life, her mess and she'd have to get on with it without him.

For a news reporter she'd been stupidly distracted from the big story in her own life. It could have all been so different. She could have been his loyal wife, supporting him in parliament. It would have looked so good. A pretty, bright career woman on his arm…

Something caught Harry's eye. The water up ahead was choppy, the regular swell of the waves giving way to broken water of a different kind. He leaned out to get a better look. In his reverie he'd drifted inshore a lot further than he'd intended and it was time to make a correction. He swung her hard to port, but the strong westerly, now veering to the south was driving him where he didn't want to go.

'Cherry,' he yelled, 'get yourself out here quick, come and make yourself useful,' he yelled.

Harry changed the sails and flicked the ignition on the diesel engine to bring it to life. Turning the boat straight into the wind as fast as he could, he pushed the throttle to full ahead and the yacht began to nose into the incoming waves with huge crashes, so different to going with the wind moments earlier.

'Harry, I'm frightened,' Cherry called plaintively, gripping the sides of the cabin well.

'Put that life vest on then, just to be on the safe side,' he ordered. 'Then come and take the wheel whilst I see to the sails.'

Cherry did as she was told. Having something to occupy her taking her mind off her debilitating sea sickness, seemed to be helping her in what she saw as a crisis.

Harry saw to the mainsail first, lashing it down securely on to the boom, his arms clutching tight around it as he worked its length. Then he stood up to move to the fore sail, but he wasn't concentrating. He was looking to port to see if he could still see the smoke rising from McNamara Metals, but the land was hiding his view. He thought he could see its greyness rising above the land, but couldn't be certain. He was thinking that if he could ditch Cherry at Newton Ferrers, perhaps he could sail away, escape. So he was concentrating, but on the wrong things.

That was when a strong gust of wind took the boom and swung it hard catching Harry with a painful blow to the back of the knee and felling him to the starboard deck in a single blow. Before he could grab the guard rail he'd rolled onto his back, a wave doing the rest, effortlessly taking him from the deck and depositing him into the sea and into the heaving swell.

He half caught his breath before his head went under, thinking he should have put his life jacket on as he'd been taught. All too slowly up he bobbed and he snatched a quick breath, choking salt water with it, vainly looking for the boat which frighteningly, had in seconds, moved a great distance away from him. One moment he glimpsed it, the next he didn't, the swell hiding all but the tip of its mast from view.

Christ, why didn't she turn round and pick him up he raged – idiot! He tried to shout but trying to shout, his open mouth filled with bitter salt water, he couldn't get his breath, he sucked in, but cold bitter water made his inside wretch and fear gripped him as his desperation increased and panic seized him. The dark waves were rolling him along as if in a barrel.

Harry couldn't see Cherry's anguish as she saw Harry fall. She tried to turn the yacht in the swell but lost sight of Harry and panicked. She let go of the wheel and stood up glancing this way and that. She couldn't see him, he'd gone.

Desperately she found a rail to cling on as the boat flipped this way and that. Feeling for her phone to call for help, she found it wasn't there. Looking at the yacht's radio she was confused by it. Grabbing the wheel she found she was turning the yacht in circles. Seeing the choppy water of the approaching coast she became even more frightened and with an effort headed out to sea.

Harry was still alive. Finding it hard to stay afloat, the wind, waves and current taking him toward what he could hear were the rocks ahead, Black Rock near Wembury. He tried to think, but couldn't. His gun, heavy in his belt, was dragging him down and sharply poking into his stomach. He struggled, pulled it out and let it fall into the deep. Trying to steal glances ahead one minute at the rocks and back in the direction of the ever disappearing "Scrapfish" the next, he felt his grip on life being torn from him.

Harry may have drawn one final breath before his body crashed onto Black Rock.

As for Cherry, it was a further hour before an armed naval vessel pulled up alongside "Scrapfish". Clutching her belly with a self-comforting hand, she pointed to the dark water to tearfully tell them, 'Harry's gone!'

Afterword

When an author is asked, 'Well, what happened to Harry?' a gauntlet has been thrown down and what can one do but pick it up?

Harry McNamara first emerged in my second novel, **IStanbul**. Harry travelled to that city to support the England football team in a friendly match. It was an unforgettable trip for him because he found himself caught up in a terrorist incident at the Galatasaray stadium becoming an unlikely hero when he thwarted their plot. As a result he became a celebrity and returned to England as no lover of Muslims or for that matter anyone who didn't see the world through his right wing and hooligan lenses.

In my third novel, **Harry's England**, Harry is in central place as he stands as a parliamentary candidate in an unexpected Plymouth by-election. Much to everyone's surprise and with more than a little help from a shadowy extreme right wing international group called, The Circle, his Britain First Democratic Party gains momentum and he becomes a Member of Parliament. I found historian Todd Gray's well researched book, 'Blackshirts in Devon', looking at local right wing extremism in the 1930s fascinating and it inspired me to ask the question, could it happen today? Indeed what would happen if the populace became fearful through terrorist activity and someone like Harry stood for election?

Harry's Awakening picks up the story a couple of years on in an age increasingly wedded to populist politics. It is entirely set within the South West of England. Many people have assisted in the research for this book, including Howard and Susan Clayton in their knowledge of yachting and the waters off the south west coast. Philip Whitlock assisted in advising on the IT and social media aspects of the story; several others in telling me their stories about, for example, the Ottery Tar Barrels. Many shared personal stories behind this popular social fun event. I believe these have enriched the authentic feel of the novel. Others in the police, health and academic fields as well as Ottery Writers, Exeter Authors Association and book club friends have advised, often without knowing.

Writing novels began for me in 2015 with the stories of Adam, Ali and Kaylah. Here the reader is first introduced in **Flashbacks** to what has sadly become a reality – terror on the streets. The book's climax is set in the centre of London on Armistice Day. Aspects of the storyline have been disturbingly prophetic. For those who follow Adam and Kaylah stories, sadly neither make an appearance in the latest novel.

Flashbacks was followed by **IStanbul**. It was a privilege for me to spend time in the beautiful historic city of Istanbul in the spring of 2016. Turkey is a country to watch. It lies in the borderlands of east and west and has seen recent political upheaval and religious revival replacing Ataturk's secular republic. The novel **IStanbul** imagines a possible future scenario in which an attempt is made to destabilised that country.

Early in 2018 I was fortunate to make a visit to Oman, the location for my fourth sequel **Domain**. My reason for going there was to respond to an invitation offered me to visit when I helped host an Omani group in Leicester a few years ago. I had been impressed by what I heard from them about the Omani tradition of 'tolerance' and the Ibadi Muslim culture in that country. So I wanted to see the place for myself. I arrived to discover an amazingly dramatic and challenging land and a welcoming people. When I learned of the political situation in the country and added a little imagination of my own to the situation, I found Oman promised to be a fabulous setting for **Domain**. Since the writing of the novel Sultan Qaboos, who provided amazing leadership in the country has sadly died.

In many ways **Truth** is a very different novel. It imagines the story of the Revd. Ruth Churchill who was introduced to the reader in **Flashbacks**. It tells the story of an eight day period of intense pressure in her north London parish the a corner shop knife crime turns out to be rather more than it appears. Once again the reader is taken on a journey, this time to visit an historic conflict between Hindus and Muslims in India, and as recent events on the streets of Delhi and elsewhere in 2020 indicate the legacy of rioting and murderous behaviour is still felt to day

I am indebted to various editors, amongst whom are Jeni Braund, Steve Chapman, Ruth Ward and Margaret Whitlock, all kindly advised on the text – the remaining errors are mine! Many other people answered my obscure questions, friends and former colleagues in the inter-faith and Prevent worlds offered their insights – you know who you are and thank you once again!

Finally, I must underline that although there appears to be a very thin veil between my writing and what actually happens in the world, all my novels and characters are fiction. There is no attempt to demonise anyone or besmirch reputations of countries or cities or religions. Sadly though, the subject of extremism and terrorism means these stories deal with challenges that are deeply felt and all too many people's lives are damaged by such events. My hope is that stories provide ways to talk about different and opportunities to gain insights and understandings of others as well as see the dangers that extremist views present.

I am always willing to hear from readers and reply to any questions. Please contact me through my website:

http://jehallauthor.com

Suggested
Book Group Questions

1.   The story picks up Harry's life from the end of 'Harry's England'. Did the opening chapter enable you to reconnect with Harry?

2.   Harry is a character who has strengths and weaknesses. What would you say these were?

3.   The novel is entirely set within the South West of England. Did this work for you?

4.   Harry's family, his grandfather Michael, father Patrick and mother Bev all play a part in shaping Harry's life. What are their respective contributions?

5.   Harry and Cherry have a relationship What kind of relationship is it? What other key relationships are there in this novel?

6.   The political background to the story is one where populist right wing views gain ground. Opportunities to promote such views exist through on line activism? Is this a contemporary concern?

7.   McNamara Metals becomes the base for Harry and the plot. Did you feel you knew what kind of place this was?

8.   How did you feel the story line developed, and did the ending satisfy you?

9.   What does the reader take away from this book?

Flashbacks

J E Hall

This, the author's first novel, introduces the characters featured in subsequent books.

In Flashbacks, Adam Taylor from Muswell Hill, north London, goes on an adventurous solo cycle ride across Europe to the Middle East before going to University. It ends unexpectedly. Is his life over?

Ali Muhammed is haunted by flashbacks since seeing his father shot before his eyes. He is subsequently trained by IS and is sent to London as a jihadist.

Kaylah Kone has Afro-Caribbean cultural roots. A business studies student in London, she finds her life becomes tangled up with Ali.

All three characters and those around them are drawn into a terrorist plot to attack an Armistice Day parade outside Parliament. Can Ali be stopped and tragedy averted?

'Controversially current, intense and compelling debut thriller, grappling with themes and issues pertinent for contemporary societies'

Dr Irene Pérez-Fernández
University of Oviedo
Spain

IStanbul

J E Hall

This novel is a sequel to Flashbacks.

Ali Muhammed's lone-wolf attack in London on Armistice Day is followed by plans for a new and ambitious terrorist initiative in Turkey. Forces are mobilised. Ali travels from Mosul to Istanbul, and with local help, he hopes IS can destabilise the country.

Adam Taylor, traumatised by the events of the previous year, begins a new life as a student. He is determined to understand Islam better. At the end of his first year he goes to Istanbul with three other students to explore and learn from this great city.

Kaylah Kone, in new circumstances agrees to help the security services.

Unimaginable tension and life-changing events in Istanbul take the reader on a compelling adventure.

'In the context of our multi-faith world and with a mix of the familiar and unfamiliar this drama succeeds in both entertaining and challenging the reader.'

Rt Rev Dame Sarah Mullally
Bishop of London

Harry's England

J E Hall

Harry McNamara is from Plymouth in the South West of England. A young man with ideals, not ones you'd probably agree with, but he can be very persuasive.

When he declares his intention to stand as an extreme right wing candidate for his parliamentary seat, after a slow start, his campaign suddenly gains momentum.

There are unknown sinister forces at work behind the scenes and Harry is suddenly on a roll.

Terrorist attacks in Exeter and Plymouth unsettle the population. Might these turn things Harry's way?

Adam Taylor, Raqiyah Nahari and Clive Kone don't like Harry one bit, but what can they do?

In the background the police and security services have a job on their hands.

Will Harry get elected?

'A novel of our times with all the twists of an accomplished thriller'

Ann Widdecombe

Domain

J E Hall

When Raqiyah Nahari finishes her degree course at Exeter
University she returns with Adam Taylor to her home in
Muscat, Oman. As the plane lands, they learn of the Sultan's
death.

This novel, set entirely within Oman, lands the couple in
time of national crisis. Her father is in trouble. What is his
story?

The couple flee to the interior. Conservative forces are at
work. Can Raqiyah's brother passim help them escape or
will it be the end of them both?

'John Hall has a deep knowledge and understanding
of people of different cultures and faiths –
those things which should bond us together…
but sadly also those that divide us'

John Geater

Truth

J E Hall

Set in north London, but reaching far beyond, this story focusses on the world of the Revd Ruth Churchill.

She finishes in church for the day, is just locking up, when she becomes caught up in a knife crime.

All is not what it seems and in a hell of a week, pressures on her mounting in all directions she finds her family and herself caught up in events she could not imagine, a time the family will never forget.

'I have made friends with Ruth!
She is a really compelling character,
nicely drawn – someone whose life and dilemmas resonate clearly
and with compassion.
Ruth's story speaks to so many complex issues of our time.
Written with a real pace and excitement… in a word, our world
spinning in ever tighter circles.'

Chris King

What's Next?

J E Hall is currently working on his next novel.

It returns the action to north London and is due to be published in late 2020.

See the author's website for further details, for reviews and anticipated date of publication:

http://jehallauthor.com